STEEL ASHES

KAREN ROSE CERCONE

BERKLEY PRIME CRIME, NEW YORK

STEEL ASHES

A Berkley Prime Crime Book / published by arrangement with the author

PRINTING HISTORY
Berkley Prime Crime edition / June 1997

All rights reserved.
Copyright © 1997 by Karen Rose Cercone.
Book design by Casey Hampton.
This book may not be reproduced in whole or in part,
by mimeograph or any other means, without permission.
For information address: The Berkley Publishing Group,
200 Madison Avenue, New York, NY 10016.

The Putnam Berkley World Wide Web site address is
http://www.berkley.com

ISBN: 0-425-15856-X

Berkley Prime Crime Books are published
by The Berkley Publishing Group,
200 Madison Avenue, New York, NY 10016.
The name BERKLEY PRIME CRIME and the BERKLEY PRIME CRIME
design are trademarks belonging to Berkley Publishing Corporation.

PRINTED IN THE UNITED STATES OF AMERICA

10 9 8 7 6 5 4 3 2 1

It is a part of our history few wish to remember.

A time when our cities were filled with immigrants invited to enjoy the freedom and opportunity our nation offered—only to be forgotten once they arrived. Strangers in a land so far and foreign from their own, they had no one to turn to in their hour of need—except the few honest citizens who were determined to help everyone in this country find justice.

This is the story of two such people…

STEEL ASHES

"Is Detective Kachigan down there?"

Intent on noting the exact position of the murder weapon in his notebook, it took Kachigan a minute to realize why that simple question made the circle of firemen around him turn and stare. Despite its calm, the inquiring voice had been female.

The rain had slowed to a drizzle, allowing Pittsburgh's morning sky to take on its usual sulfur yellow. Without her umbrella, the dark-haired social worker looked even more bedraggled than before, but her impatience has faded into something much more grave. She had come to the very edge of the cellar despite Ramey's restraining arm in her elbow.

The social worker glanced toward the soft clink and thud of the bodies rolled into blankets. "This was definitely arson, then?"

"I don't know whether or not it was arson," Kachigan said.

"But it was definitely murder."

MORE MYSTERIES FROM THE BERKLEY PUBLISHING GROUP...

SISTER FREVISSE MYSTERIES: Medieval mystery in the tradition of Ellis Peters...

by Margaret Frazer

THE NOVICE'S TALE	THE BISHOP'S TALE
THE OUTLAW'S TALE	THE BOY'S TALE
THE SERVANT'S TALE	THE MURDERER'S TALE

PENNYFOOT HOTEL MYSTERIES: In Edwardian England, death takes a seaside holiday...

by Kate Kingsbury

ROOM WITH A CLUE	GROUNDS FOR MURDER
SERVICE FOR TWO	PAY THE PIPER
CHECK-OUT TIME	CHIVALRY IS DEAD
DO NOT DISTURB	RING FOR TOMB SERVICE
EAT, DRINK, AND BE BURIED	

GLYNIS TRYON MYSTERIES: The highly acclaimed series set in the early days of the women's rights movement..."Historically accurate and telling." —Sara Paretsky

by Miriam Grace Monfredo

SENECA FALLS INHERITANCE	NORTH STAR CONSPIRACY
BLACKWATER SPIRITS	THROUGH A GOLD EAGLE

MARK TWAIN MYSTERIES: "Adventurous . . . Replete with genuine tall tales from the great man himself." —*Mostly Murder*

by Peter J. Heck

DEATH ON THE MISSISSIPPI	A CONNECTICUT YANKEE IN CRIMINAL COURT

In memory of

ANTONIO CERCONE, MARIA SILVESTRI,

GUISEPPE AMANTEA *and* FILOMENA VECCHIO

*Their courage and determination to come to America
made this book—and its author—possible.*

1

THE REEK OF BURNT TIMBER AND CHARRED SHIN-
gles met Milo Kachigan a block away from Breed
Street. He lifted his chin from his rain-damp collar, hoping to glimpse the fire he'd come to investigate. Even though he could hear the shouts
of firemen and the restless jingle of their horses' bells, all he
could see was a dim red glow through the haze of smoke
from the mills along the river. In a booming year like 1905,
even a night of autumn rain couldn't wash the grit and ash
from Pittsburgh's murky sky.

The sulfur-smelling rain stung Kachigan's eyes, deepening
the headache that had started with the predawn ring of his
telephone. He scrubbed at the familiar throbbing pain under
his cheekbone but didn't bother to duck his chin into his
collar again. A train whistled ahead of him, echoing off the
steep hillside where the South Side's strip of Monongahela
floodplain ended. The sound told him he couldn't be far from
the straggle of tenement houses jammed in between the
tracks and Breed Street.

He found the fire as soon as he turned the corner of South
Fourteenth—sullen flames licking up along charred beams
and adding heat-shimmers to the already smoky night. Kachigan's memories of patrolling this beat said that the skel-
eton of glowing timbers had once been row houses, but he
couldn't remember if there had been two or three squeezed
onto the single lot. Behind it, the dark bulk of St. Witold's

Polish Catholic church reflected the firelight from wet brick walls, hosed down by the firemen to keep the flames from spreading.

A blue-coated police patrolman loitered at the west end of Breed Street, watching the fire. His blunt face split with a grin when he saw Kachigan. "Fancy seeing you here, Milo my boy," he said, then slapped at his rain-soaked cap in exaggerated dismay. "Sorry, I meant to say, 'Detective Kachigan.' "

"Cut it out, Ramey." It wasn't easy being promoted from patrolman to detective in Pittsburgh, especially when you weren't born and bred to the neighborhood where you worked. It would have been even harder, Kachigan knew, if the patrolmen of Station Seven had known the kind of neighborhood he *was* born and bred to. In light of that saving grace, the ribbing he took from Frank Ramey was a minor annoyance. "Did you call the fire in?"

The patrolman shook his head. "I don't think Pedone did either, assuming the *paisan* even knows how to use a telephone."

Kachigan reached into the pocket of his overcoat, pulling out a stub of pencil and his battered evidence book. "What time did you hear the fire whistles go off?"

"Three-thirty-five this morning. I checked my watch." Ramey lifted his eyebrows in mock surprise. "Now, don't be telling me Captain Halloran assigned you to this fire, *Detective* Kachigan?" He laughed at Kachigan's grunt. "Old man Mallone didn't feel like getting out of bed so early, huh? I told you that's why Halloran wanted another detective at the station."

Kachigan didn't bother to deny that, since he knew it was the truth. A crash from the burning row houses yanked his attention back to the fire in time to see one of the upstairs beams fall through the lower stories. Bright embers burst out from the charred wood as it splintered.

"Anyone get hurt here, Ramey?"

The patrolman shrugged. "There's a couple of hunkies missing. Nobody knows if they got scared and took off, or got burned up inside." Ramey raised his voice to be heard over the crash of falling timbers. "If they did, it's going to be a murder case, my boy. You think you're ready for that?''

"Two people dead in a house fire isn't murder."

"It is, if the fire was arson." With a groan of yielding timber and a scatter of warning shouts, the last beam collapsed. Like an old woman sitting down for the last time, the skeletal outline of the row house folded down into the ash-covered pool of water that its cellar had become. The roof came after it in flaming rafts, curling in on itself and sizzling as it hit.

"Who says the fire was arson?" Kachigan demanded, coughing from the wave of ash that rolled out from the collapse.

"Tenants." Ramey pointed to the far end of the block, where a line of sawhorses blocked access from busy Fifteenth Street. "I sent Pedone over to make sure they didn't scamper. A lady from the settlement house came to help them, and she didn't seem too happy about waiting for a police detective to show up."

Through the milling ash and windblown spray from the firemen's hose, Kachigan caught sight of three people huddled under a gas lamp, watching the row house sink into diminishing flames. A wiry young man in police blue stood behind them, swinging his nightstick restlessly in one hand.

"I'd better get their statements and let them go." Kachigan tucked away his notebook. "Watch the fire chief for me, Ramey. I want to talk to him before he leaves."

The patrolman made a rude noise. "Oh, they'll be having fun for hours yet, smashing everything to bits with their big shiny axes. You'll have plenty of time to write things down in your little book."

Kachigan grinned, unoffended by this last sally. His slow writing had been a target of patrol station humor long before he'd been jumped up in rank, and he'd learned not to let it bother him. He wondered if he'd eventually be able to tolerate the jokes about his promotion, too, or if that spot would stay raw until someone else got promoted after him.

"At least I can write," he retorted. "Unlike a certain desk sergeant, who just *thinks* he can."

The sound of Ramey's laughter followed Kachigan into the plume of smoke drifting from the burnt row house. Inside, the dying gusts from the fire were hotter than he'd expected, slapping his breath back into his throat and drawing a deeper stab of pain from his damaged cheekbone. Kachigan rubbed at it again, resigning himself to an all-day headache. The sliver of metal embedded in his face always seemed to choose the worst times to remind him of its presence.

The echo of his footsteps on the brick street must have been brisk enough to sound official. By the time he emerged from the fire's dying plume of soot and ash, Kachigan found four faces turned toward him in the smoke-hazed gaslight. The only one that held anything close to a welcoming expression was the thin dark face under the blue police cap. As the youngest member of Kachigan's former patrol squad, Silvio Pedone still liked to hand his problems over to the authority he trusted most.

"Here is the detective in charge now," he said politely enough, but from behind the group, he made an expression of Italian exasperation for Kachigan's benefit. "I tell you he comes to see you as soon as he gets the call."

"I still don't see why we couldn't have called him ourselves." The owner of that impatient voice was a woman in a russet wool coat, soaked dark with rainwater across the shoulders and down the back. She possessed an umbrella, but she was holding it over a younger woman whose only protection against the weather was a thick, faded quilt. "We've been standing out in the rain for an hour!"

"I'm sorry for that." Kachigan's glance went from the armful of possessions the younger woman held huddled under her quilt to the smudged face and tangled hair of the young man beside her, bare-chested under a borrowed fireman's oilcloth coat. These two were clearly the tenants. Their companion must be the woman from the settlement house. "Fire chiefs don't like us investigating a house fire before it's even done burning."

The social worker gave him an unsympathetic look. "They could have a little consideration for people who've lost everything they owned."

"They did." Kachigan jerked his chin at Pedone and got a thankful look in return, as the patrolman went back to directing foot traffic around Breed Street. "Usually, they don't let us in until the ashes are cold."

"Yes, that's what they said." Her dark eyebrows rumpled with her frown. "But I told them we weren't going to wait that long."

So he had her to thank for the telephone call that woke him up two hours before dawn. Kachigan stifled a sigh and turned toward the young tenants, pushing back his bowler hat until he felt rain cascade onto his shoulders.

"I'm Detective Milo Kachigan from Patrol Station Seven," he said, addressing himself to the young woman first, in the American manner. "Do you speak English?"

"Quite well." She had an unexpectedly cultured voice, with a German tinge to it. "My name is Irene Prandtl."

Kachigan pulled out his evidence book and wrote it down. "And you speak English too, Mr. Prandtl?"

Cold blue eyes met his, narrow in a freckled face. The pucker of a burn slashed red across one cheekbone, too faded to have come from the fire tonight. A steelworker, Kachigan guessed, since he wasn't old enough to be an iron puddler.

"English or Gaelic, whichever you'd prefer," he said pointedly. "My name's Mahaffey."

Kachigan lifted one eyebrow, glancing from the young man's clenched fists to Irene Prandtl's fine-boned hands. Neither wore a wedding ring. In this day and age that wasn't so unusual, but Kachigan knew better than to comment on it. He'd seen the aftermath of enough house fires to know how men tended to react when they lost all their hard-earned possessions. Judging by the anger that already simmered in Mahaffey's voice, it wouldn't take much to push him into frustrated rage.

"English will do," he said calmly. "Your first name, sir?"

"Daniel." Irene Prandtl answered for her companion, easing the tension with her pragmatic voice. "And our address is—was—fourteen-oh-seven Breed Street. We've lived there for a year."

Obviously, she knew the way police investigators worked. In the minute it took him to write the information down, Kachigan wondered how she'd come by that knowledge.

"One of my patrolmen told me you thought someone set this fire," he said when he'd finished writing. "Why is that?"

Prandtl and Mahaffey exchanged consulting glances. She was the one who finally spoke. "The fire started with a loud bang, Mr. Kachigan. By the time we got out of bed and ran to the window, the other half of the house was already burning. We barely made it downstairs before our side caught fire, too."

"Could it have been a natural-gas explosion?"

Irene Prandtl shook her head. "We're not rich enough to rent a house with gas. And we hadn't bought any coal for the winter yet—we were burning gathered wood. So were the Janczeks."

"Those were the people who lived on the other side?"

"Yes." Her gaze went past him to what was left of the row house, a sunken pile of rubble. The firemen had shut off their hoses and were reeling them back onto their wagon. With the water turned off, ghost-thin wisps of steam began to rise from the warm timbers. "Yes, they were."

Kachigan followed her gaze. "You don't think they made it out?"

Prandtl shook her head again, while Mahaffey cursed beneath his breath. "There wasn't time," she said simply.

The woman from the settlement house swung around, scowling at the ruins of the fire. Her strong-boned profile looked oddly familiar to Kachigan, although neither her voice nor her sober face had rung a bell.

"I knew Lide Janczek," the social worker said. "She would have come and waited with us here, if she'd gotten out."

Kachigan scrubbed a hand across his face, wiping off the gathered drops of rain. "Who else lived on the other side, besides this Lide Janczek?"

"Her husband," Prandtl said. "His name is—was—Josef. There were no children."

She looked up at her companion, silently prompting him. Mahaffey grunted. "Janczek worked with me at Black Point Steel, before I got laid off. At the Taylor Mill works," he added, before Kachigan could ask.

"Where do you work now, Mr. Mahaffey?"

"Nowhere."

Kachigan wrote it down, carefully keeping his face neutral. "And Lide Janczek? Did she work anywhere?"

"She had started to work part-time at Carey Settlement House," the social worker said. "Irene told her we needed someone who could speak Polish. Lide could speak it and read English too. She helped people with their immigration papers."

Kachigan frowned, watching the firemen kick apart the charred wet rubble in the row house basement. The rain hadn't stopped, but the world seemed to be turning brighter. After a moment, he realized that dawn had lit a dull silver glow in the east, pouring what light it could through the thick smoke of the mills. He looked back at Irene Prandtl and Daniel Mahaffey.

"You say the fire was started by an explosion, and that the Janczeks' side of the house burned first. If this was arson, then it must have been meant for them." He saw the couple exchange an uneasy look, as if this thought hadn't occurred to them. "Do you know if either of your neighbors had enemies?"

The silence that followed was long and uncomfortable, but Kachigan let it stretch. Eventually, with the first hesitancy he had seen in her, Irene Prandtl spoke. "Maybe the landlord—" she began, but a scowl from Mahaffey cut the suggestion off. "I heard men arguing over there last night," she added hastily. "But I didn't recognize their voices."

Kachigan refused to be distracted. "Who is your landlord?"

Neither answered, although Prandtl's fingers tightened in the folds of her quilt. Kachigan made his voice gentle, so his next words would be taken not as a threat but simply as information. "If you don't tell me, I can find out from the city tax rolls."

Surprisingly, it was Mahaffey who gave in. "We don't know who it is for sure," he said sullenly. "Some millionaire out on the East End, who don't want anyone to know he invests his money in hunky tenements like this. He comes slumming down to the A.O.H. once a month, and we pay the rent there."

Years of patrolling the South Side had left Kachigan familiar with every ethnic association that held a liquor license. "The Irish social club on Sarah Street?"

Mahaffey nodded. The social worker opened her mouth to add something, but a flurry of shouts from the rubble interrupted her. A moment later, Kachigan heard Ramey yell his name.

"Excuse me," he said to Prandtl and Mahaffey, then strode back toward the burnt row house before the woman from the settlement house could protest. On the other side of the block, a fireman was fetching blankets from their wagon, while the rest gathered in one corner of the rubble-filled foundation. Ramey squatted on the ground beside the men, as close as he could get without intruding on their professional territory. He looked up when Kachigan reached him, his blunt face serious for once beneath a dusting of soot.

"They found them."

Kachigan nodded, teeth clenched against the lurch of sickness in his throat. He'd already guessed as much from the bitter smell of burnt flesh and hair that had floated out to meet him three paces from the edge of the cellar. "Two bodies?"

One of the firemen heard him, tipping a dour, sweat-streaked face up to answer. "Looks like two. So far at least."

Kachigan grimaced, craning to try and see past the circle of bowed heads. "Looks like?"

"They're a bit—scattered. We're trying to fit them back together."

Ramey cursed and turned away, ostensibly to help unfold the blankets. Kachigan swallowed down a protest from his stomach and forced himself to ask, "Can I come down?"

Several faces turned up at that request. "You the new detective from Station Seven?" demanded a burly man with a fire-reddened face. He wore nothing that identified him as the chief, but the silence that fell across the other men as he spoke was identification enough.

"Yes." Kachigan showed him his evidence book. "I'd

like to record where you found them, before you take them
up. I may need to testify about it later.''

The chief threw a considering look at the water-soaked
rubble that now filled the cellar, then nodded. ''Come down
through there,'' he said, pointing at what remained of a
sunken cellar door. ''And watch where you step once you're
down here.'' From the grim tone of his voice, Kachigan suspected that warning hadn't been issued to keep him from
spraining an ankle.

Inside the close, dripping confines of the cellar, the choking odor of burnt bodies overwhelmed the other smells of
the fire. Kachigan paused at the bottom of the steps, shaken
by an unwelcome gust of memory. The first time he'd
smelled that smell, he'd been a fifteen-year-old laborer in a
Monessen steel mill where an overhead ladle had broken and
spilled liquid iron over a coworker twenty feet away. The
man's explosion of screaming had shaken Kachigan so much,
he hadn't even felt the impact or noticed the blood trickling
down his cheek, where a shard from the ladle's flying bolt
had embedded itself.

''You going to be all right, buddy?''

''I think so.'' Kachigan had the stomach of a seasoned
police patrolman, but he knew his limits. He dug his woolen
scarf out and wrapped it over his nose and mouth.

''Never smelled burned bodies before, eh?'' asked a fireman.

''Uh—no.'' Kachigan hoped that sounded embarrassed
rather than untruthful. It grated to deny his own past, but
with Ramey watching from the street above, he had no
choice. That stint in a Monessen steel mill belonged to the
son of an immigrant Armenian steelworker. It didn't belong
to a newly promoted police detective whose name and col-
oring could pass for Irish. ''Don't worry, I won't get sick.''

The chief grunted. ''All right, let him in.''

The circle of sooty backs opened reluctantly, as if the firemen didn't like exposing the remnants of Josef and Lide
Janczek to outside view. A glance at the gaunt shapes of
flaking charcoal and lime-white bones showed Kachigan
why. There would be no point in bringing Daniel Mahaffey
over to identify these corpses, much less either of the women.

The only clue to their identity was size—one of the two bodies, presumably Josef's, was much larger than the other. Kachigan frowned, noting that the man's body was far more disrupted than his wife's.

"Did one of the beams fall on top of him?" he asked the fire chief, indicating the gap between Janczek's torso and legs.

The burly man shrugged. "Could be. They probably fell from one of the upper stories. Can we take them up now?"

"Yes." Kachigan filled a page of his evidence book with a sketch of how the bodies lay, while Ramey began handing down blankets. The fire chief crouched to begin shifting the remains of the dead man onto one of them.

"That's odd," he said gruffly.

"What is?"

"The way his spine is broke through so straight—"

The puzzled voice sliced off, and silence fell with it. Kachigan looked up from his book to ask what was wrong, then saw the way that Josef Janczek's torso had rolled onto the coarse wool blanket. He shut his mouth again.

A blackened lump stuck out from between the dead man's vertebrae. No gleams betrayed the metal beneath the fire's dark tarnish, but a shower of disintegrating ash floated out of the round hole at one end. A mutter of recognition went through the ring of firemen. It was, after all, a tool they used every day.

"Poor bastard." The fire chief's voice grated between disbelief and sympathy. "Someone butchered him with an axe."

Kachigan whistled silently under his scarf. It was just luck that axe-head had stayed buried in the dead man's bones—the collapse of the house beams could have easily broken it free and flung it so wide they'd never have found it. Perhaps that was what the killer had counted on. "And then burned the house down to hide the murder?"

The chief shrugged. "Maybe, but you couldn't prove it by me. No scorched patches on the walls, or any smell of kerosene or lamp oil that I've noticed down here."

Kachigan didn't ask him how he could smell anything past the burnt bodies. He jotted the information down along the margins of his sketch, wishing he could print as fast as he could draw. The stench in the basement was slowly penetrating the rain-damp wool smell of his scarf, making his stomach lurch again.

"Is Detective Kachigan down there?"

Intent on recording the exact position of the murder weapon in his notebook, it took Kachigan a minute to realize why that simple question made the circle of firemen around him turn and stare. Despite its calm, the inquiring voice had been female. He frowned and shouldered his way out of the circle, careful not to leave a clear view of the bodies behind him.

The rain had slowed to a drizzle, allowing Pittsburgh's morning sky to take on its usual sulfur-yellow hue. Without her umbrella, the dark-haired social worker looked even more rain-soaked and bedraggled than before, but her impatience had faded into something much more grave. She had come to the very edge of the cellar despite Ramey's restraining arm on her elbow.

"Have you found them?" she asked. "Lide and Josef?"

"Yes."

"Then there's no point waiting anymore. I'm going to take Irene and Daniel back to Carey House."

Kachigan frowned and slid his rain-softened evidence book into his coat pocket before he started up to meet her. His shoes sloshed uncomfortably, and he realized he'd been standing in ankle-deep water without knowing it. "Hold on. I need to talk to them again."

"Smelling like that?" the social worker demanded.

Kachigan stopped halfway up the steps to give her a wary look. Her voice had been loud enough to ring echoes off the church behind them, but he was relieved to see irritation rather than hysteria glinting in her eyes.

"That bad?" he asked.

She snorted. "Yes, Detective. Irene's already had enough shocks tonight, and she doesn't need one more. Besides, she's going to take a chill if we stand out in the rain much longer. If you want to ask her more questions, why don't you come down to the settlement house later this morning to do it?"

"All right." Kachigan ran a hand across his grimy face, scrubbing off rain and soot but not the frown that felt embedded there. His headache throbbed implacably beneath it. "But I'll have to take the Janczeks to the undertaker first. Will you make sure your friends don't leave before I get back?"

The social worker glanced toward the soft clink and thud of the bodies being rolled into blankets. "This was definitely arson, then?"

"I don't know whether or not it was arson," Kachigan said. "But it was definitely murder."

2

THE DOORBELL RANG RIGHT IN THE MIDDLE OF
"The Benefits of Socialized Pension Systems for
the Laboring Man." Helen Sorby lifted her pen
so it wouldn't bleed onto the final draft of her
manuscript, and glanced across the wide oak table
at her brother. He hunched over a canvas map sheet covered
with city blocks, sighting so intently along his ruler that it
looked as if he were holding it down with his nose.

"Thomas, the door." That earned her only a preoccupied
grunt of reply. "It's your turn to answer it."

"Is not."

Helen dipped her pen back into the inkwell and rubbed
her tired eyes. Lack of sleep and the grim events of the morning made her disinclined to play games with her fractious
twin. She tapped her pen on a blotter, hoping their unwanted
visitor would just go away. Thunder grumbled outside, but
it couldn't quite drown out the second ring of the bell.

"Thomas, it really is your turn to go. I answered the door
for the iceman, right after I came back from Carey House."

"And I got the morning mail. Including all your socialist
newspapers."

"That doesn't count."

"No?" Thomas looked up from the map at last, brown
eyes wide with pretended innocence. "That's funny. It
counted yesterday, when *you* did it."

The bell rang a third time, buzzing impatient echoes

through the dripping of autumn rain. "Oh, all right, I'll get it." Helen gathered up her sensible serge skirts, then paused to file one last grievance from the drawing room doorway. "Thomas, not *all* my newspapers are socialist."

All that got her was another preoccupied grunt. With a sigh, Helen left him drawing the spaghetti tangle of a railroad yard and went to answer the door.

The stained-glass transom over the front door was dim with rain-blown soot, its crimson flowers darkened to garnet. As usual, Helen lifted her skirts and took an undignified step up onto the seat of their telephone stand, so she could peer down through a clear glass panel and see who was calling. Her curious gaze encountered only the back of a dark blue overcoat and an uninformative bowler hat. Oh, well. At least it wasn't Aunt Pittypat come to drag her off to some ladies temperance tea.

She swung open the door, catching ___ ᵏ the loose strands of dark hair that insisted on plastering themₗ. ᵛes across her face. "Can I help you?"

The visitor turned around, and Helen's gaze was met and captured by a familiar glint of dark blue eyes. Her mouth fell open in astonishment.

"Detective Kachigan?"

There was no doubt that it was him. Even seen in early morning smoke and darkness, the honed intelligence of his face had been distinctive enough to remember. But how on earth had he managed to track her down, barely four hours after she'd taken Irene Prandtl and Daniel Mahaffey away from the fire on Breed Street? She hadn't even given him her name!

"Miss Helen Sorby." The policeman didn't make it a question and Helen didn't bother to deny it. "They said at the settlement house that I would find you here. May I come in? I'd like to ask you a few questions."

Helen eyed him warily. "Questions about what?"

"About the murders of your friends last night." A gust of sooty rain spattered across his hair, darkening its dusty brown to sable. "If you don't mind, I'd like to talk to you without getting any wetter than I already am."

Helen took a reluctant step back from the ivy-carved front

door, becoming aware that soot now dusted the front hall as far back as the mahogany receiving table. Nothing stayed clean on Pittsburgh's South Side for long, not when the steel mills were running at full capacity.

"What do you want to know, Mr. Kachigan?"

Muscles clenched along the detective's jaw, tightening his face into a frown. "What I want to know, Miss Sorby, is where you've hidden Irene Prandtl and Daniel Mahaffey."

"Where I've *hidden* them?" Helen glared at Kachigan. "I haven't *hidden* them anywhere. I took them where I said I would, to the Martha Carey Settlement House."

"Well, they're not there anymore. Are they here?"

"Of course not!" Helen read the doubt in his narrowed eyes. "You can search the house if you don't believe me, Detective. Or just ask my brother. The *last* people he'd let me bring home are Irene Prandtl and Daniel Mahaffey."

Her exasperation with Thomas's unenlightened politics must have shown in her voice. The tightness in the detective's face eased a little. "Your brother doesn't approve of your social work with the local immigrants?"

Helen bit her lip, aware that they'd veered onto dangerous ground. Her instincts told her that the less this policeman knew about the radical socialist ties that bound her to Irene Prandtl and Lido Janczek, the better off they'd all be. "That's not what you came here to ask me, is it?" she countered.

"No." Kachigan stripped off his gloves and tucked them into his damp hat. "If you'll set these somewhere for me, Miss Sorby, I'll get out the list of questions I do want to ask you."

She did so, belatedly aware of her lack of manners. "Can I take your coat too, Mr. Kachigan?"

The policeman shook his head. "Better let me hang it up myself. It smells too much like—" He left the sentence hanging, but the faint sweetish odor that clung to the overcoat finished it for him. Helen pointed him toward their wall rack and he hung his coat on the farthest peg, fishing a small black notebook out of one pocket and a pencil out of the other. Then he paused for a moment, eying Thomas's battered surveyor's vest with its measuring tapes and clipboard.

"This brother of yours—is he the Thomas Sorby who

makes maps for that fire insurance company?''

"Yes. You know him?''

"He's been pointed out to me.'' Kachigan turned to face her and Helen blinked in surprise. Without his bulky over-coat, the detective was thinner and more athletic than she would have expected a desk-bound police officer to be. His suit rubbed a little too tightly across his shoulders and hung awkwardly elsewhere, as if it had been bought unfitted off the shelf of a dry-goods store. "The police like to keep track of men who climb up onto other people's roofs for a living. Does your brother know where you were at five o'clock this morning, Miss Sorby?''

Helen blinked at him, a little surprised by the abrupt change in subject. Then she realized the question had been meant to catch her unprepared and embarrass her. "Of course he does. I told him about it over breakfast.''

"He knows his sister went to Breed Street in the middle of the night, and he doesn't care?''

Helen glared at him, incensed by his nineteenth-century assumptions. "Social work doesn't happen at convenient times and places, Mr. Kachigan. Does your sister know you went to Breed Street in the middle of the night?''

Kachigan opened his mouth, then blew out an aggravated breath and closed it again. "You're much too easy to argue with, Miss Sorby,'' he said. "Could you try to just answer my questions as simply as you can?''

She scowled, but nodded wordless agreement. Let him see how much he liked simple answers. Kachigan licked his pen-cil and started to write in his book again, slowly and care-fully.

"After you left Breed Street this morning, did you take your friends directly to Martha Carey Settlement House?''

"Yes.''

"You didn't stop to let them use a public telephone any-where? Or stop to talk to any friends?''

"No.''

"And you have no idea where they might be now?''

"No.''

"They didn't tell you *any* of their plans for the future?''

"Of course they did,'' Helen said sweetly. "But I think

that would be too complex an answer for you, Mr. Kachigan. You might not have time to write it all down.''

He gave her a sharp look. ''Let me worry about that. What did they tell you, Miss Sorby?''

''They told me they were going to stay at Carey House until they could find another house they could afford to rent.'' Helen gave him a challenging look. ''Are you sure they're not still there? They might have been sleeping.''

Kachigan took a long moment to finish writing before he responded. ''When I stopped at the settlement house to see them, the director told me that they drove off in a hired cab an hour after they arrived. Would she have any reason to lie about it?''

''Julia Regitz Brown? No.'' Helen frowned, thinking about it. ''But if she said they left an hour after I dropped them off, why did you assume that *I* was the one who had hidden them?''

''You might have come back after arranging a safer place for them to stay,'' Kachigan said neutrally. ''After all, you knew the police would come looking for them at Carey House.''

Helen glared at him again. ''So you're already assuming that Irene and Daniel are criminals, and I'm in cahoots with them? Why? Just because they're poor and aren't married''

''No, Miss Sorby.'' The muscles along Kachigan's jaw tightened. ''I'm assuming it because they disappeared before I could question them about the murders this morning.''

''A lot of innocent people get scared when the police want to talk to them! If you people didn't solve so many crimes by railroading the nearest poor immigrant—''

Her indignant tirade was interrupted by the appearance of her brother in the drawing room doorway. Thomas glanced at the police detective in his nondescript blue suit, then back at Helen. His eyes gleamed with amusement.

''Having trouble getting rid of a salesman?'' he asked innocently.

Helen shook her head, taking a deep breath to drag her temper under control. Her voice had a tendency to rise to a shout without her knowing it, especially when she was annoyed about something. She took refuge in introductions.

"Thomas, this is Detective Kachigan from the police—"

"Pittsburgh police," Kachigan interjected. "Not mill police." The men shook hands with polite reserve. "Assigned to Patrol Station Seven, just down the street. I stopped by to ask Miss Sorby a few questions about the fire last night."

Thomas gave his twin a reproving look. "Well, there's no need to stand out here in the cold draft to do that. Why didn't you invite the detective in, Helen?"

"I didn't want to disturb you."

Thomas snorted. "In that case, maybe you shouldn't have shouted at him. Come in and sit down, Mr. Kachigan."

Helen followed her overly sociable twin back into the drawing room, glowering at the back of his oblivious head. Thomas paid her no attention, shoving a stack of her newspaper clippings from one of the spare chairs and offering it to Kachigan. Helen frowned when the police detective remained standing, until his lifted brow reminded her to resume her own seat first. Living alone with one graceless brother tended to make a woman forget the niceties of social etiquette. She took a deep breath, and tried to sound polite.

"What else did you want to ask me, Detective?"

"The same question I asked you a minute ago," he replied, with what sounded to Helen like equally false politeness. "Can you think of any place that Irene Prandtl and Daniel Mahaffey may have gone after leaving the settlement house?" He held up a hand before she could deny it. "Don't answer right away. I have a question or two for your brother, now that I've met him. You can use the time to collect your thoughts."

"That will be a new experience for her," Thomas remarked, avoiding Helen's glare by dint of long practice. "What can I help you with, Mr. Kachigan?"

Kachigan tapped at the half-drawn map on Thomas's drawing table. "If I understand it correctly, Mr. Sorby, your job is to map all the buildings in the city, gathering information for fire insurance agents to use in setting their rates. Is that right?"

"Yes. The Sanborn Map Company just started a new six-volume map atlas of Pittsburgh last year."

"Have you mapped much of the South Side yet?"

"No, none of it. I've made some corrections to the 1893 map sheet, but that's all."

The detective tapped his pencil against the spine of his book, looking quietly frustrated. "So you can't tell me if there was a natural gas line into the house at fourteen-oh-seven Breed Street?"

Thomas shook his head regretfully. "I couldn't do that even if I *had* mapped that block. Sanborn only records utilities for the major buildings." He pointed at some of them on his half-drawn map. "Churches, stores, factories. Structures that might take other buildings with them if they burned."

Kachigan looked down at the map again. "So the only information you record for private houses is the size and type of construction?"

Thomas nodded. "And proximity to the local fire station, or to fire hazards like paint stores or oil refineries. It saves insurance agents from making a hundred inspection trips a year."

"I see." The detective tapped the end of his pencil on one of the skeletal houses sketched across Thomas's half-finished map. "Even an outline map like this would be of some use to me in trying to reconstruct how this fire was set. You mentioned having an 1893 map sheet of the South Side. Would this set of row houses have been mapped back then?"

"Should have been," Thomas said. "Everything built on Breed Street looks at least twenty years old to me. Would you like me to check for you?"

"If you'd be so kind."

"It's no problem." Thomas unfolded himself from his chair. "My files are upstairs in the attic. You don't mind waiting while I dig through them?"

"Not at all." Kachigan smiled faintly. It was the first sign of amusement Helen could remember seeing on his thin, intense face. "I'm sure Miss Sorby can fill the time by yelling at me about something."

Thomas snorted his appreciation of that and ducked through the side door to the dining room. Helen forced herself to sit quietly after he was gone, although it didn't im-

prove her temper to suspect that had been the policeman's
intention all along.

"Well, Miss Sorby." Kachigan rubbed his thumb along
his left cheekbone as if it pained him. It was an absent-
minded, habitual gesture. "Have you managed to recollect
any of the places where your friends might be?"

Helen gave him a long, measuring look. "Let me ask you
a question first, Mr. Kachigan. Are you really going to use
Thomas's map to study that row house?"

His scowl radiated far too much irritation to be assumed
for her benefit. "Why would I waste his time and mine, if I
wasn't?" Kachigan demanded. "In a murder investigation,
you gather as much information as you can get. That way,
you can try not to railroad *anyone* for the crime."

"Does that mean you're not going to arrest Irene and Daniel for murder as soon as you find them?"

"No, Miss Sorby. Not unless I find evidence in the mean-
time that links them to the murders." Kachigan's gaze met
hers unwaveringly. "The fact that they're hiding makes me
suspect they're involved more deeply than they told us. And
if they're *not* the murderers, then they're probably in danger
because of that. Do you know any place at all where they
might have gone?"

Helen bit her lip, wondering how on earth she was going
to get out of this. The last thing she wanted to do was betray
Irene and Daniel to this too-sharp policeman, but refusing to
answer might make him even more suspicious. She picked
up her pen and threaded it through her ink-stained fingers,
trying to look thoughtful. "The only place I can think of
where they might be is with Irene's parents," she said at
last. "They own a cigar factory up in the Hill District—it
should be listed in the Polk address directory."

Kachigan lifted an eyebrow. "Then they're Jewish?"

"I believe so." Helen frowned, watching him write it
down. "Why is that important?"

"For one thing, it helps explain why Irene Prandtl's living
out of wedlock with an Irish Catholic boy."

Helen's temper got the better of her again. "Irene and
Daniel have what is known as a companionate marriage, Mr.
Kachigan. It has nothing to do with their religions."

"Doesn't it?" He gave her a speculative look, but didn't pursue it. "What about Lide and Josef Janczek, Miss Sorby? Was their marriage imaginary too?"

She scowled at him. "No, of course not. They had to be legally married to get their immigration papers."

"All right." He wrote that down in his book as well. "How well did you know the Janczeks, Miss Sorby?"

"I only knew Lide. Irene introduced me to her at a public meeting in the Carnegie Library." She saw his puzzled look. "The new branch library here on East Carson Street, not the big library in Oakland."

"What kind of public meeting?"

"The South Side Temperance League." The partial untruth made Helen uncomfortable and she turned to avoid his gaze, searching through the clutter on the sideboard behind her until she found one of Aunt Pittypat's ubiquitous pamphlets to give him. "It's a group of local women and clergymen that meets every Thursday evening. My Aunt McGregor is one of the founders. I serve as her secretary."

Kachigan continued to write for several minutes after Helen finished speaking. She resisted the urge to ask him what he was jotting down, folding her hands together in her lap and reminding herself that the less involved she became in this affair, the better off she would be. Unfortunately, minding her own business had never been one of Helen's talents.

"Is that all you wanted to ask me?" she inquired, when she was unable to bear the scritch of pencil on paper any longer.

"Yes." Kachigan looked up warily. "It sounds like you have something that you want to tell me."

"Yes." Helen glanced up, hearing the cascade of Thomas's footsteps down the stairs. Her twin came into the room with a bound sheaf of fire-insurance maps and the sweet, dusty smell of decade-old paper clinging to him. "But I can wait until you see the map."

"There's not much to see." Thomas thumped the map atlas open, making soft fingers of dust roll out from the wide pages. He turned pages, until he found one that was mostly railroad tracks, then ran a finger down Breed Street until he stopped at a narrow double outline. "There's your row house, Detective."

"Ah." Kachigan leaned over the map, turning it so it faced his and Helen's side of the table. Aside from the bare outline of the building, the only notation Helen could see on 1407 Breed Street was the cursive *F* that stood for "flats" and the 2*b* for "two stories with basement." "What does the yellow color mean?"

"All frame construction."

"Hmm." Kachigan ran his hand across the insurance map, up to the sewn binding that kept it neatly paged in place. "I don't suppose you can detach this and loan it to me?"

Thomas shook his head. "No, but I can sketch up a quick copy." He gave his sister a teasing glance. "Or Helen might do it, if you ask her nicely. She's as good a draftsman as I am."

Kachigan gave Helen a polite look of inquiry, as if they hadn't spent the last few minutes in tense verbal fencing. "Would you be so kind, Miss Sorby?"

"On one condition, Mr. Kachigan," Helen replied with what she hoped was equal coolness. "If you'll let my brother examine the ashes of this house fire for you."

"To see how it started, you mean?" Kachigan's sharp glance slid over to her brother. "Can you do that?"

Thomas shrugged. "I did surveys for a fire insurance investigator in New York City, before I hired on with Sanborn. There's a lot you can tell from the way a building burns, if you get to it right away." He looked questioningly at Helen. "But why do you want me to look at it?"

"Because the person who set that fire killed my friend Lide Janczek from Carey House." She gave her brother a meaningful look. "I want to make sure that the police find the real killer, not just a convenient immigrant to railroad."

Her blunt words made Thomas wince, but Kachigan merely shook his head. "At this point, I'll take all the assistance I can get, no matter what the motives behind it. I'll tell my patrolman to expect you later today, Mr. Sorby." He tucked his notebook away and stood up. "I can see myself out."

"No, I'll do it." Helen jumped up before Thomas could

volunteer. Kachigan gave her a speculative look, but followed her back to the front hall obediently enough.

"You had something else you wanted to talk to me about, Miss Sorby?" he asked, taking his smoke-stained coat from the rack.

"Yes." Helen lifted his damp hat and gloves from the receiving table and handed them to him. "If there's anything I've learned as a social worker, Mr. Kachigan, it's that the best way to stop someone from being framed for a crime is to expose the real criminal. I just wanted you to know that I'm going to make sure you do that."

"How?" The policeman sounded more curious than annoyed.

"With this." She showed him her ink-stained steel pen. "You see, I also write investigative articles for several of the major New York magazines, Mr. Kachigan. And I can write about any subject I want, including police investigations of immigrant murders."

"Is that a polite way of telling me you'll be watching to make sure I do my job, Miss Sorby?"

"No," Helen retorted. "It's a polite way of telling you that I'll be helping you do it."

"No, you won't." The steely emphasis the detective put into that sentence made Helen scowl. She opened her mouth to argue, but Kachigan's next words distracted her. "Do those New York magazines run your picture with your articles, Miss Sorby? The longer I'm around you, the more familiar you look."

"No." Helen swallowed to steady her voice, and swung the door open abruptly. "No, they don't. Good day, Mr. Kachigan."

He eyed her from the stoop, and Helen got the uncomfortable impression that he had filed away her curt response to think about later. All he said, however, was, "Well, they should. Good day, Miss Sorby."

Helen slammed the door, then fell into the telephone seat with a groan. She knew what the detective was remembering, even if he didn't. The city's newspapers had plastered her photograph everywhere during last November's scandal, usually adorned with a ribbon proclaiming her a "prominent young socialist.'' She only hoped Milo Kachigan hadn't read the headlines that went along with the picture. If he recalled them, Helen suspected that the Janczek murders would get filed under ''more socialist trouble,'' and forgotten about.

And one more criminal would have escaped justice because of her.

3

"WHAT DO YOU MEAN, THE BODIES ARE GONE?"
Milo Kachigan could hear the snap of frustration in his voice, but couldn't summon the will to stifle it. After a long afternoon spent finding no trace of the row-house landlord in the city tax rolls, the last thing he wanted to hear when he walked through his front door and picked up the telephone was that his murder victims had vanished. He sailed his hat toward the coat rack, not even caring when it landed on the floor in a shower of soot. "Don't tell me that livery-stable undertaker sent them out by mistake to get buried!"

"No, Detective." The desk sergeant's stiff voice emerged clearly from the bell of Kachigan's telephone, losing none of its bitterness to electricity. Sergeant Walter Todd had been next in line for the promotion that the precinct captain had given to Kachigan. Unlike Ramey, he never failed to give the new detective his proper rank, but that was the extent of his cooperation. "Some men from Janczek's old steel mill came to claim the bodies for burial. Nothing we could do about it."

And nothing you *wanted* to do about it either, Kachigan thought. "Did you at least ask who the men were?"

Silent irritation at this waste of important desk-sergeant time crackled down the phone line. "I didn't have to ask them. They had mill police uniforms and papers that said they could pick up the two burnt hunkies. I didn't argue with them."

"Papers?" Kachigan paused in the process of pulling his soot-stained collar free of his shirt, alerted by the creak of a floorboard from above. He craned his neck to glance up around the tight bend of his stairs. "What kind of papers?"

"The kind that have Captain Halloran's signature on them."

By long training, the curse that rose to Kachigan's lips remained unsaid. "Is the captain gone for the day?"

The reply was a painful thump from the receiver pressed to his ear. Hoping that meant the desk sergeant had slapped a palm over his speaking bell to shout a question upstairs, Kachigan yanked his collar off and took a step toward the stair.

"Pap, is that you?"

A familiar wordless grunt answered him from above. "Wait for me to help you down," Kachigan called up to his father fiercely. The receiver chattered in his hand, and he lifted it in time to hear Todd say, "—wants to see you now."

"All right." Kachigan would have to assume that "he" meant Captain Halloran. Not that it wasn't beyond old Mallone to pull rank on him, but he'd never known Mallone to stick around past the 4:30 whistle from the Jones & Laughlin plant. "I'll be there in ten minutes," he said and hung up before Todd could reply.

Another grunt, from a little farther down the stairs, told Kachigan that his father hadn't waited. Cursing aloud and in fluent Armenian, he took the steps two at a time to meet him.

"If you could just hold on a minute, Pap—"

Istvan Kachigan grunted again and edged his age-spotted hands farther down the stair rail, preparing to lower himself to the next step. His balding head reddened with the effort of swinging his legs forward from the hip. A collapsing steel-mill catwalk had left him with detached ligaments and knees so stiff they barely bent, but it had left intact all his Armenian pride.

"Got to learn to do this somctime," Istvan said between clenched teeth. His voice still lifted and fell with the rhythmic accent that Kachigan had worked so hard to lose. "If

I'm going to live here, I got to get to the kitchen and cook. Otherwise, I'll starve waiting for you to make supper.''

The glint in the old man's fire-blue eyes told Kachigan he was feeling good enough for the kind of verbal sparring that had enlivened all their family dinners back in Monessen. He grinned and retaliated. ''If you wanted your meals on time, Pap, you should have stayed with Sofia. She loves to cook for you.''

His father snorted. ''Your sister has too many babies. Somebody should do her a favor and kick that useless glass-worker she married between the legs.'' He slid his hands down the rail, preparing for another step. ''Move, please.''

Kachigan knew he could have lifted and carried his father—they had the same wiry bodies, almost to the inch, but Istvan weighed less now that his leg muscles had shriveled. But he forced himself to retreat a step at a time before the old man's painfully slow descent. His father was right. If he was going to stay here, he'd have to get around on his own.

''We need another handrail,'' Istvan said, rasping for breath at the bottom of the stairs. ''On the other side, like Sofia's.''

''What we need is to make the dining room into a bedroom and bathroom for you.'' Kachigan handed his father the downstairs walking sticks that leaned against the wall.

Istvan snorted. ''Who is this 'we'? None of those left-handed Irishmen you work with knows how to hammer nails.'' He poked one home-carved stick at his son. ''And even if they did, you couldn't let them come home and see the old man, eh?''

''No,'' Kachigan admitted grudgingly. He tried to remember if his pretense of being Irish had grated as much before as it did now that his father had moved in. He couldn't recall feeling more than the occasional twinge of guilt at dropping into Irish bars like the Ancient Order of Hibernians club on Sarah Street. But the old man had moved in at about the same time he'd been promoted to detective. Kachigan wasn't sure which change had created this gnawing irritation at pretending to be something he wasn't.

''Hey.'' The stick poked at him again, more gently this time. ''Milosh, you want supper? I'm going to make *kuftah*.''

"I can't stay, Pap. The precinct captain wants to see me."
Milo brushed soot off his collar and stuffed the stiff cotton
band back into the neck of his shirt. "I'm going to check on
the burnt house on my way back. I'll see you around ten."

His father blew out an aggravated breath through his
moustache. "I'm here two months and I still can't figure out
whether you work day-turn or night-turn. You're up at four
this morning, now you go out again at five—even steelworkers only work a twelve-hour shift." He squinted at his
son, eyes bright with amusement again. "You on the long
turn this week, huh?"

"Pap, when you're the one assigned to a murder case,
every turn is a long turn."

Istvan grunted and began shuffling toward the narrow back
kitchen. "Must be why they picked an Armenian boy to be
the new detective," he said over his shoulder. "Smart
enough to do the job, eh? But too stupid to know when to
stop."

Kachigan took the flight of stone steps up to Patrol Station
Seven's corbeled entrance at an impatient trot. The deliberate
exertion drained off some of the anger that had been building
in him since he'd left home, leaving just enough to burn
away the grogginess of his too-long day. The familiar smell
of cigar smoke and bitter coffee greeted him inside, along
with the tinny clatter of typewriter keys.

"Captain Halloran in his office?" Kachigan demanded,
barely pausing in front of the front desk. Sergeant Todd had
the receiver of their only telephone plastered to his ear again,
taking illiterate notes as some irate citizen bellowed at him
in what sounded like a mixture of English and Serbian.

"Yeah, but he's got a visitor." The sergeant slapped a
massive hand across the speaking bell. "And so do—"

"Thanks." Kachigan took the stairs to the second floor
too fast for the desk sergeant to yell after him, turning left
toward Captain Halloran's office. A rumble of voices seeped
under the glass-paned door, ominously loud. Kachigan rattled
his fist against the door, then went in without waiting for
permission.

"Kachigan." John Halloran looked up, a frown stiffening

his lean, dark-jawed face. He was a quiet, soft-spoken man—
a little too quiet, Kachigan often thought, for the com-
mander's post he held. "Where've you been?"

"Out looking for the man who killed my murder victims."
Although he kept his voice respectful, Kachigan never
minced words with his captain. He suspected it was one of
the reasons he'd gotten his early promotion. "Which won't
matter, if I can't *prove* they were murder victims. Why did
you give Black Point Steel permission to take their bodies?"

"Because I asked him to." It was the burly giant sprawled
in the visitor's chair beside Halloran's desk who replied. He
had a rumbling voice to match his barrel chest, but for all
his stolid size, Kachigan noted, he'd still managed to cut in
before Halloran had a chance to answer. "As a personal favor to me."

Kachigan scowled at him. "And who are you?" he demanded, overriding in turn whatever Halloran was trying to
say.

"Bernard K. Flinn."

Kachigan schooled his face to remain set in its frown, but
his breath hissed out in recognition. There were a hundred
private coal-mine and steel-mill police forces in Pittsburgh,
but in any given year only a few of them came into conflict
with the labor forces they were supposed to protect. Somehow, Bernard K. Flinn's name always seemed to appear in
conjunction with those battles. Like a modern-day mercenary
captain, he moved from one strike-locked company to another, earning a level of pay comparable to the steel barons
themselves. Now that Kachigan had met him, he could see
why. Flinn exuded strength and ruthlessness the way an
open-hearth furnace blasted heat.

With the shouting stopped for the moment, Halloran
cleared his throat. "Mr. Flinn has offered to pay for all the
Janczeks' funeral expenses. There's no reason why the city
should—"

Despite himself, Kachigan's eyebrows rose challengingly.
"Is that standard Black Point Steel policy?"

Bernard Flinn flicked one massive, scarred hand. "Out of
sympathy for their unexpected death, Black Point Steel man-

agement has decided to give the Janczek family special consideration.''

Kachigan repressed a disbelieving grunt. In a city of iron and steel concerns that routinely worked men twelve hours a day seven days a week, Black Point had a reputation as a brutal employer. Something had convinced them to confiscate the remains of their former employee and his wife, but he doubted it had anything to do with sympathy.

''Has Josef Janczek already been buried?''

Flinn shrugged, big shoulders rolling inside his tailored suit coat. ''You'd have to call our main office to find that out.'' He leaned farther back in his chair, eyes narrowed in a deceptively sleepy look. ''Why? You want him back?''

Kachigan gritted his teeth. ''We have compelling and sufficient reasons to believe that Josef Janczek was murdered before his house burned down. His remains are—were—being held in custody as evidence.''

'' 'Compelling and sufficient reasons'?'' Flinn threw a disgusted look at Halloran. ''You hiring lawyers now?''

''I'm hiring men who can do the job.'' Halloran's voice was as stiff and unrevealing as his face. ''Detective Kachigan has a valid concern. That's why I sent a photographer over to take a picture of the axe wounds in Janczek's back, right after you telephoned me this morning.'' He sent Kachigan a curt nod. ''The plates should be ready to send to the city coroner tomorrow.''

''Thank you, sir.'' Kachigan hoped the relief in his voice hid the tinge of surprise. He'd never seen Captain Halloran confronted with a challenge quite this grisly before, and hadn't been sure how he would react. Maybe there was more competence behind the older man's reserve than he'd realized.

Flinn sat up straighter in his chair, scowling at them both. ''Someone chopped Janczek apart with an *axe*?''

''That's right,'' Halloran answered. This time, Kachigan managed to hold his tongue until his superior officer got around to speaking. ''The fire was set in an attempt to hide the crime.''

''Sweet Christ.'' Flinn rubbed a palm across his mouth.

"Some hunky bastard straight off the boat got fleeced and didn't like it, eh?"

Kachigan frowned at him. "You're saying Janczek was some kind of confidence man?"

He must not have kept all the disbelief out of his voice, because the steel-police chief shot a glare back at him.

"I'm saying Janczek was a damned good gambler," Flinn said flatly. "My guards patrol all the bars in the Strip, to keep our mill workers out of trouble." And out of unions, Kachigan added silently. "They told me months ago that Josef Janczek was a cardsharp. Nobody who knew him would play with him there."

"If Janczek was killed by someone he cheated at cards, why did we find his wife's body in the ashes with him?"

"Maybe she was a witness. Or maybe she was asleep upstairs and didn't even know he was dead." There was no question the big man could think fast on his feet. The glitter of laughter in his pale gray eyes told Kachigan he was enjoying the verbal combat. "She could have still been alive when the fire started, even if her husband wasn't."

"But the fact is that her husband wasn't," Halloran said brusquely. "I gave you the Janczeks' bodies to bury, Mr. Flinn, but that's all you're getting. I'm not going to dismiss a murder case just because your company's name might appear in it."

Kachigan took a deep breath, realizing what this private conference had been about. Flinn swung around to aim a fierce scowl at Halloran, but the captain didn't flinch. He might be too slow-spoken to bandy words with Bernard Flinn, but once Halloran made his mind up, he was as stubborn as a stump.

"Why the hell can't you?" Flinn demanded. "I just told you what must have happened."

"No, you told us what you'd like us to think happened," Kachigan retorted, before he could stop himself.

Bernard Flinn stood up to face him, moving much faster than seemed reasonable given his size. The sense of danger in the room deepened. "You want compelling and sufficient reasons, Kachigan? I'm warning you, you kick too much dust on Black Point Steel with this damned investigation, my friends in City Hall will find compelling and sufficient reasons to fire you!''

A light scratch against the door, tentative as a cat's, stopped Kachigan before he could snap back. Halloran barked his usual acknowledgment, but the door didn't open. ''Go see who's there,'' he ordered Kachigan at last.

The detective rose, feeling the weight of Flinn's cold stare on his back, and went to open the door. The sober face that met his gaze on the other side was the last one he expected to see.

''I came to deliver the map you wanted.'' Helen Sorby held out a roll of heavy paper tied with baker's string. ''I was waiting in your office, but the desk sergeant told me you were here. Have I come at an inconvenient time?''

''Not at all,'' Kachigan assured her. He glanced over his shoulder at his captain. ''If you'll excuse me, sir—''

Halloran's mouth twisted with unusually acid humor. Kachigan would hear about this lucky escape later, he knew. ''Yes, by all means, go. We don't want to keep a lady waiting.''

Kachigan gave Flinn a curt nod, then closed the door behind him. Helen Sorby let him take her elbow in a polite grasp and steer her down the hall, but she cast a frowning glance over her shoulder at the captain's office.

''Was that Bernard K. Flinn in there?''

''That's right.'' Kachigan guided her into the cubicle he'd been given on promotion to detective, leaving the door wide open behind them so no comments could be made. Across the hall, the usual racket of jokes and curses from the coffee room softened respectfully. He tugged the map out of her fist, since she didn't seem inclined to offer it. ''You know him?''

''I know *of* him. He's the steel and coal companies' worst policeman.'' She paused. ''What was he bribing you to do?''

The anger Kachigan had been repressing exploded without warning. ''I wouldn't take money from Bernard Flinn if he was contributing to the policemen's widows and orphans fund!'' He gave Helen Sorby the glare he wished he could have given the Black Point police chief. To her credit, she only flinched a little. ''He may own the mayor and half of city council—and probably a few union bosses too—but he damn well does *not* own me! Have you got that straight, Miss Sorby?''

Quick color chased up her cheeks, but her gaze never wavered. ''Then what was he *trying* to bribe you to do?''

Kachigan stared at the social worker for a moment, but found he couldn't stay angry at her. Her question was too perceptive and too near the truth to sweep aside. ''He wanted us to drop the Janczek murder investigation.''

Helen Sorby's brows creased again, this time in confusion. ''But why should he care, unless—Flinn doesn't work for Black Point Steel now, does he? As their police captain?'' Kachigan nodded, impressed with her quick understanding. ''In that case, you really *are* going to need my help, Mr. Kachigan.''

''Excuse me?''

The social worker gave him an impatient look. ''The other steel and coal policemen have to stay within some bounds, or the muckrakers on the city newspapers would crucify them. Bernard Flinn doesn't have to worry about that.''

Kachigan looked up from unrolling the map she'd brought, his attention caught by the certainty in her voice. ''Why not?''

''Because his uncle William used to run the Allegheny County machine back in the nineties, along with Lyman Magee. And Magee's family still owns the *Pittsburgh Times*.'' She looked surprised. ''You didn't know that?''

''I didn't move to Pittsburgh until after my mother died in 1901. But why does it matter whether or not the Pittsburgh papers will write stories about Flinn? I'm investigating a murder, Miss Sorby, not political corruption.''

''What if it turns out Bernard Flinn is implicated?'' she demanded. ''No judge in the city is going to arraign him— not unless the papers have whipped up enough public indignation to force them to.''

''Then I'll just have to find an honest judge.''

''Or an honest journalist!''

He grunted, scanning the fire-insurance map. Helen Sorby had redrawn the entire block and even penciled in the colors marking the type of construction. "What does blue and red mean?"

"Concrete block with a brick wall." She sounded impatient. "You're not going to learn anything from that map, Mr. Kachigan. Let's go see what Thomas has found out about the fire."

Kachigan shook his head. "Miss Sorby, I don't think—"

"No one else will help you expose Bernard K. Flinn," she insisted. "I can guarantee the magazines that publish me will."

"We don't know for sure that Flinn's involved," Kachigan pointed out. "All he's done so far is try to hush up an ugly incident that could start rumors about Black Point Steel."

"Then he'll keep on trying to hush it up, no matter who the culprit is, won't he?" Helen Sorby tilted her head to one side, regarding Kachigan with the first smile he could remember seeing on her solemn face. It lit her dark eyes with unexpected amusement. "You might as well let me come with you, Mr. Kachigan. Thomas will tell me everything anyway, as soon as he comes home."

Kachigan didn't doubt that. He consulted his pocket watch, then sighed. "All right. I have to walk you home anyway, and it's only a block out of our way."

Helen watched him fold the map and tuck it away in one nearly empty desk drawer. "Why do you have to walk me home?"

"Because it's after six and starting to get dark." The coffee room had already emptied its second-shift patrolmen out onto their beats, and Sergeant Todd had been replaced by Silvio Pedone, taking his weekly turn on the night desk. The young Italian caught sight of Kachigan's companion and whistled, then grinned at his superior officer's reproving look. Kachigan resigned himself to being the butt of station gossip tomorrow.

"Why does it matter that it's getting dark?" Helen Sorby persisted.

"It's dangerous for women to walk alone after dark in this neighborhood." Kachigan held one of the outer doors open so the social worker could go through. She promptly opened

the other one for him. He gritted his teeth and caught her by
the elbow, sweeping her out into the smoky twilight with
more force than politeness. "You're old enough to know
that."

"Ah. No doubt you're worried that I might attack some
innocent young mill worker on his way home from work."

Kachigan stopped at the bottom of the stairs to give her
an exasperated look. "Miss Sorby, do you *like* arguing with
people?"

"Sometimes," she admitted candidly. "And sometimes
it's the only way to make them realize how old-fashioned
and pig-headed they're being. Do you want to go down Fourteenth or Thirteenth?"

"Fourteenth." That was the route with wider sidewalks
and more closely spaced gas lamps, and it led past his own
small red-brick home. The lights in the kitchen would tell
him if his father was still downstairs. If the old man had
been feeling good enough to wrangle with him, he'd probably still be puttering around in the kitchen, fixing his stuffed
meatballs. If Helen Sorby hadn't been with him, Kachigan
thought wryly, he could have stopped in and stolen one or
two to take along.

He glanced over at his companion, liking the easy way she
matched his pace, not gasping or toddling as so many fashionably dressed women did. Evidently, she didn't need to
strangle herself with a corset to create her waist, or the flow-
ing curves below it. The social worker looked up and caught
him watching her in the gaslight, but didn't seem concerned
by it.

"I rang up some of the insurance agents Thomas deals
with this afternoon," she informed him. "None of them held
an insurance policy on fourteen-oh-seven Breed Street, or
knew who might have owned it. Did you find it listed in the
city tax rolls?"

Kachigan frowned. "Miss Sorby, I seem to recall telling
you that I didn't need your help with this murder investigation."

"I know." Helen Sorby tucked her gloved hands into her
pockets. The long, dark shadow of St. Witold's church had
fallen over them, making the wind from the river feel much

colder. "But we have something in this country called the freedom of the press, Mr. Kachigan. It means you can't stop me from looking at the tax rolls myself, so you might as well tell me what you found there."

He sighed and gave in. "Nothing," he admitted. "They had records for the house at fourteen-oh-one Breed Street and for the one at fourteen-eleven, but fourteen-oh-seven wasn't listed. It was as if it didn't exist."

"Well, that tells us that the landlord is rich enough to bribe his way out of paying taxes."

Kachigan snorted. "Which narrows him down to one of about ten thousand men in Pittsburgh."

"True." They rounded the corner of St. Witold's in silence, then turned onto Breed Street. The charred remnants of the former row house made a gaping vacancy along a street crowded with semidetached houses and duplexes on one side and railroad tracks on the other. The South Side had few of the lawns and detached kitchens and backyard stables that marked richer Pittsburgh neighborhoods. Here, immigrant mill workers had lined every alley with narrow brick houses and wooden tenements, punctuated only by an occasional bakery or bar.

In the smoky twilight no one was visible on the sidewalk beside the burnt row houses, but occasional flurries of ashes rose out of the rubble below. Kachigan released Helen Sorby's arm and went to squat at the very edge of the foundation, peering down into the shadowy basement. Not much to his surprise, his companion tucked in her skirts and knelt beside him.

"Have you found anything yet, Thomas?" she inquired.

An ash-darkened face lifted. "Helen, I can't tell you that," her brother said, sounding aggravated. "What are you doing here, anyway?"

"Helping investigate this murder," she retorted. Thomas Sorby glanced up at Kachigan, one eyebrow raised in doubtful inquiry. The detective answered the unspoken question with a resigned nod.

"It's all right to talk, Mr. Sorby. I've agreed to let Miss Sorby follow my investigation for her magazine." Kachigan felt more than heard the triumphant breath she took beside him. "Have you found out how the fire started?"

"I think so." The surveyor's sooty face made his grin stand out like the Cheshire Cat's. He hefted something in his hand, then heaved it toward the sidewalk. Steel rang cold against the slate, then skittered toward Kachigan's feet. "What do you think of that?"

"It looks like part of a coal furnace." He ran his fingers across the heavy fire-blackened chunk of metal, feeling its chill even through his gloves. The edges were oddly scalloped. "Where did you find it?"

"In the southwest corner of the basement. There's a bunch of others down here just like it, all scattered around."

Helen Sorby frowned. "What does it mean?"

Her brother lifted two more chunks of metal from the ash near his feet, fitting them together so they could see the ragged scar between them. Viewed from the front, the curled-back edges made a pattern like a dark iron starburst.

"If you ask me," Thomas Sorby said, "I think it means the coal furnace exploded."

THE INQUISITION BEGAN AT SUPPER THE NEXT day.

Thomas had actually tried to start it the night before, right after they'd parted company with Detective Milo Kachigan at Fourteenth and Sarah Street. Helen had postponed her twin's questions by pleading tiredness, which she'd proved by going to bed before supper and not waking up again until after Thomas had left for the next day's mapping expedition. She'd tried the same excuse when he came home that evening, but her brother had merely snorted and put her to work stirring a pot of polenta. Sighing, Helen resigned herself to being quizzed about her latest crusade.

"So," said her brother unexpectedly, "how long have you known this policeman of yours?"

Helen glared at him across the heat-shimmer of their wood-fired stove. "He's not *mine*. I met him yesterday morning."

"Oh." Thomas sliced garlic into a black skillet sizzling with olive oil, filling the kitchen with its nut-sweet aroma. "Well, you seemed awfully chummy with him by last night. Is he married?"

"I don't know—I mean, it doesn't matter!" Helen took out her frustration on the polenta, beating it to get out the lumps. "I wish you and Aunt Pittypat would stop pushing me at every man I meet. Why are you in such a hurry to get me married again? Don't you remember what a mess I made of it the first time?''

"Yes, but you never make the same mistake twice.'' Her twin rolled open a can of anchovies and sent them splattering into his hot oil. ''And you know why I'm doing it—I want to move my map library into your room. If I had to guess, I'd say Aunt Pat just wants to give you a couple of cats as a wedding present.'' He glanced up as the bells of St. Casimir's rang from three doors down. ''And speaking of Aunt Pat, wasn't she supposed to pick you up at six for one of those temperance meetings of hers?''

"Oh, glory, she was. I forgot.'' Helen smacked the spoon into the polenta, then glanced down at her ink-stained skirt. ''And she'll never let me go in my work clothes. Here, stir this.''

"Why are you worried?'' her brother said. ''You know Pittypat will get here fifteen minutes late.''

"And it will take me that long just to lace my corset!''

She managed to squeeze herself into the corset in record time, thanks to a careful selection of which dress she wore. Even so, she could hear someone tapping at the door while she descended the stairs. Ignoring the tantalizing smell of cooked polenta that drifted out from the kitchen, Helen hurried down the last few steps and stepped up onto the telephone seat. Outside, a buxom, fur-bundled figure with an assortment of stuffed birds on her head hovered in front of a dilapidated horse-drawn carriage.

"Helen.'' Pat McGregor sighed in relief when the door opened. ''Where on earth have you been, child? I've been knocking for hours.''

"I'm sorry. I forgot about the meeting tonight.''

Pat McGregor snorted, a surprisingly earthy, Irish sound coming from such an amethyst-bedecked, lace-trimmed lady. ''Of all the times to be absent-minded! Dearest, have you forgotten entirely that we're taking Dennis McKenna with us tonight?''

"Dennis McKenna?'' Helen repeated blankly.

"Sounds like she forgot to me.'' Thomas came out from the kitchen, smelling of fish and garlic. ''I put the rest of the polenta in the icebox. Are you coming in, Aunt Pat, or would you rather yell at Helen out on the sidewalk where all the neighbors can hear?''

"I don't have time to come in," Aunt Pittypat declared. Her nephew shrugged and disappeared into the drawing room, leaving Helen to her fate. "Dearest, surely you remember that I telephoned you last night about Mr. McKenna's visit? Mr. Dennis McKenna—the famous temperance lecturer from Chicago!—is here right now in Pittsburgh." Her voice dropped to a conspiratorial whisper. "He's waiting for us in the cab."

Helen glanced at the grimy window of the carriage. It hardly seemed like a vehicle fit for a famous temperance lecturer, but then she had her doubts about just how famous Dennis McKenna really was. She tried to remember talking to her aunt the night before, but no memory came. "Aunt Pat, was it *me* you telephoned?"

"Oh, dear." Pat McGregor brushed back one stray silver curl from her forehead, looking bemused. "Perhaps it was Elsa Hanneman—but no matter, dearest. You do remember me telling you about Mr. McKenna, don't you?"

"Vaguely." Helen tugged her aunt inside. "You can at least come in while I put my coat on. That way you can tell me about Mr. McKenna again, so I don't embarrass myself in front of him."

"Oh, very well." Aunt Pittypat wedged herself and her furs into the telephone seat, watching Helen take her worn russet coat from the peg. "I wish you'd let me buy you a good winter coat, dearest. Sables would bring out the color of your hair—"

"And cost a fortune," Helen finished for her. "I've wasted enough of your money already, Aunt Pat."

"It's not as if I don't have a great deal more," her aunt pointed out, quite truthfully. Pat McGregor's second husband had been one of the fortunate few to lend money to a fellow Scot named Andrew Carnegie, back in the days when only a straggle of iron foundries lined the banks of Pittsburgh's rivers. Henry McGregor had kept his single share of stock tucked away for years in an old cigar box, while he supported his wife on the comfortable wages of a bank manager. When Andrew Carnegie had finally sold his steel empire to J.P.

Morgan in 1901, that single share brought Henry McGregor ninety thousand dollars and a luxurious, if short-lived, retirement.

"Mr. McKenna," Helen reminded her aunt, reaching for a plain wool scarf. "Tell me who he is again, please."

Pittypat's face brightened with enthusiasm. "Dearest, you remember the advertisement I placed in the *Ladies Temperance Monthly* for public lecturers who could make our Pittsburgh factory men take the pledge? Well, Mr. McKenna wrote in reply last month and I've been corresponding with him ever since. He's a former workingman himself, you see, so he knows just how to explain the evils of drinking to the men we need to reach. His orations in Chicago attracted thousands of men from the mills."

Helen frowned at her. "Who told you that, Aunt Pat?"

"He did, dear, of course. That's why I decided to sponsor a lecture for him when he came here on his speaking tour."

"Of course." Helen heaved a sigh, but made no attempt to convince her aunt that Dennis McKenna might not be the most reliable source of information on his own success. Pittypat adopted would-be temperance lecturers in the same warm-hearted and undiscriminating way she adopted cats. Helen helped her aunt to her feet, then ushered her out into the smoky glow of sunset. "Well, Aunt, I'm ready. Introduce me to the famous Mr. McKenna."

Pat McGregor tossed an uneasy look over her shoulder. "You will be nice to him, won't you, dear? He's a very earnest young man. In fact, I thought you might like to spend some time with him while he's here—"

"No," Helen said firmly, and swung open the cab door to keep her aunt from pursuing the suggestion any further.

A serious, spectacled face peered out of the dim interior. "Mrs. McGregor, do you require assistance getting in? I would come out but—" The temperance lecturer gestured helplessly at the untidy stack of printed papers balanced on his narrow lap. Some had already spilled down to join the sodden mat of newspapers and other, less identifiable debris on the cab's wet floor. Helen caught a glimpse of a badly reproduced photo and the words "Workingman's Temperance Lecture" beneath it.

"No, dear." Pat McGregor tapped her umbrella on the peeling leather roof. She always used the same cabdriver, chosen for the care he gave his aging horse rather than the care he gave his carriage. "Joe O'Grady never fails to open my door for me."

"When he's awake," Helen added.

Her aunt gave her a reproving look and rapped on the roof again. A grunt and creak from above, and O'Grady descended his side steps, rubbing at his wrinkled eyes and yawning.

"Ready to go, ma'am?"

"Yes, Joe. Take us down to the Carnegie Library please."

The old man grunted again and assisted her to her customary seat. Helen shook her head at his dirty mittened hand and clambered into the cab herself, picking her way carefully through the clutter inside. Her aunt's fashionably wide flounced skirts forced her to tuck herself in next to the famous Mr. McKenna. The temperance lecturer slid over politely, spilling more fliers onto the floor in the process.

"Helen," Aunt Pat said, as the cabman coaxed his old mare into a half-hearted trot. "I'd like to introduce you to Dennis McKenna, the temperance lecturer from Chicago. Mr. McKenna, this is my niece, Helen Sorby. Helen is a social worker and a journalist," she added, with the unstinting pride that made her niece and nephew love her despite her eccentricities.

"A pleasure, Miss Sorby." Dennis McKenna leaned over to give her hand a diffident shake. His accent was educated and his haircut a fashionable crop, but Helen was surprised to feel calluses on his ungloved palm. Perhaps this thin-boned, quiet young man wasn't entirely the trickster she'd taken him to be. "You write about the crusade for sobriety?"

"Among other things." Helen eyed his stack of fliers. "Are those for your temperance lecture in Pittsburgh, Mr. McKenna?"

"Yes, indeed." His clear gray eyes met hers a little too straightly, she thought. "I find I get the best turnout if the lecture has been advertised well in advance. I thought I might start posting them—"

Helen frowned at him. "I don't think so, Mr. McKenna.

At least, not until the South Side Temperance League decides whether or not to sponsor you, at the meeting tonight.''

The temperance lecturer glanced anxiously toward Pat McGregor, who gave Helen a reproving poke with her umbrella. ''I've told Mr. McKenna that our decision will undoubtedly be made in his favor, Helen.''

''But I'm by no means assuming it,'' McKenna added hurriedly. ''That's why I had these fliers made up without any date or place mentioned.'' He showed Helen the blank space between the lecture title and the smudged text that presumably listed his background and accomplishments. ''I carry them with me to every town, in order to save my sponsors the expense of having them printed.''

''Very thoughtful of you, Mr. McKenna,'' Aunt Pat approved. ''Now, all we have to do is fill in the time and place by hand.''

On two or three hundred fliers, Helen thought wryly, but she'd written too many social invitations for her aunt to imagine that minor consideration would stop her. Instead, she asked, ''Do you have a particular date and place in mind, Aunt Pat?''

''Yes, dearest.'' Pittypat looked quite pleased with herself. ''I've arranged with one of the city aldermen for the lecture to be held downtown, in the middle of Market Square, next Tuesday.''

''And how much money did that cost?''

Her aunt's face took on the defensive look that meant she'd paid more than she should. ''It was only a small donation, and they promised me it would all go to the city orphans' fund.''

Helen shook her head, but knew better than to object. Once Pat McGregor had decided to give money to a charitable cause, no matter how questionable, there was no swaying her. The squeak and sizzle of an electric trolley hurtled past in the twilight, its outside platform thick with clerks and office workers going home. The flying sparks overhead appeared to remind Aunt Pat of something—she lost her defensive look and peered at Helen worriedly. ''Dearest, did you read in the papers yesterday, about what happened to poor Lide Janczek?''

"Yes." Helen was careful not to tell her easily scandalized aunt just how firsthand her knowledge was. "The police have asked Thomas to help them investigate the fire."

"Have they?" Pittypat noticed Dennis McKenna's bewildered look, and explained, "One of our young temperance league members lost her life in a tenement fire yesterday. And her husband too, I believe the papers said." She glanced back at Helen. "Didn't your friend Irene Prandtl live near the Janczeks, dear?"

Helen nodded. "In the same set of row houses. She and her companion survived, but they lost everything they owned."

"Then we'll have a collection for them tonight," Pat decided spontaneously. There was nothing she liked as much as helping out unfortunate victims, no matter what they were victims of. Small wonder that under her erratic guiding hand the South Side Temperance League had evolved into a haven for local socialists. "There are several of our members who knew them—those dear Ukrainian girls from Breed Street, I think, and that young priest from St. Witold's, too. What is his name, Helen?"

"Father Zawisza," Helen said drily. "But I wouldn't expect a donation from him, Aunt Pat. Irene is Jewish, remember?"

"All the more reason for him to stretch out his hand to her," Pat McGregor declared. "Don't you agree, Mr. McKenna?"

The temperance lecturer blinked behind his spectacles, looking taken aback. "Why, yes. Yes, of course." The carriage rolled to a slow stop beside the skeletal iron work of the Brady Street Bridge. "Um—have we arrived?"

"Indeed we have." Aunt Pat gathered up her wide skirts while Joe O'Grady made his creaking way down the side steps of the cab to open the door for her. Ensconced on the corner lot beside the bridge, the new brick library building gleamed in the last glow of sunset like a dark rose among the weedy storefronts of East Carson Street. Even the evening haze of mill smoke couldn't dim the glitter of its large windows and expensive brass door. "Don't forget to bring your fliers, dear."

McKenna scrambled out after her, papers clutched to his thin chest. Helen stepped out last, not quite sure if she should be pleased or insulted that the temperance lecturer hadn't bothered to offer her a hand. The dark gleam of the Monongahela River reflected the sunset, a long blood-red ribbon stretching to the triangle of smoke-wreathed buildings that was Pittsburgh. The river was encrusted with a massive fleet of coal barges along both sides, waiting for winter storms to swell the city's two other rivers and set them free.

Aunt Pittypat might have looked plump and delicate, but she could stride as briskly as any Irish housewife when she wanted to. The temperance lecturer had to hurry to catch up with her. "Mrs. McGregor, I've been thinking that it might be best, in view of what Miss Sorby said about making your decision tonight, if I absented myself from your meeting."

"My dear Mr. McKenna, don't be silly." Pat tucked his hand through hers and swept him toward the handsome brick stairs that flanked the library entrance. "I can't wait to introduce you."

Helen followed them inside, greeting the coatroom attendant in fluent Italian as she handed over her coat. As usual on a Thursday evening, only a scatter of school-age children were in the mahogany-appointed reading room, immersed in newspaper comics and picture books. The lack of adults made Helen shake her head in disgust. The mill workers who'd made Andrew Carnegie's fortune for him were far too tired after their twelve-hour shifts to use the library he'd supposedly built for them.

"Indeed, Mrs. McGregor, I must insist." McKenna drew himself up at the threshold of the mahogany stairs, his narrow face firming with decision. "It is most difficult for a group of sponsors to reach a true decision when the lecturer is standing in the room. Especially a group composed of warm-hearted, caring individuals such as yourself." He glanced at Helen, a hint of challenge in his eyes. "Don't you agree, Miss Sorby?"

"Yes," said Helen frankly. "I do."

"But I don't think—" Pat looked from one to the other, then sighed and gave in. "Oh, very well. But, Mr. McKenna, please *do* wait up here for our decision."

The temperance lecturer bowed gracefully, a gesture that went better with his educated accent than with his cheap tweed suit. "My pleasure, Mrs. McGregor. Don't rush your meeting on my account. I'll work on my lecture notes while you decide."

A floor below, in the chilly public meeting room, the crowd was older but not much thicker. Helen scanned the assembled matrons and clergymen, then went to say hello to the two young Ukrainian sisters from Breed Street who faithfully attended every meeting. The Petrenkos had shyly admitted to her that they came to practice their English rather than promote socialism, but Helen still considered that their diligent attention to each week's meeting should be properly acknowledged. Once their English had improved a bit more, she hoped to enlist them in teaching other Ukrainian immigrants down at the settlement house.

"Marina and Oksana, it's nice to see you." She waited through their carefully practiced responses. "I wasn't sure you would come out on such a cold night."

They glanced at each other, trading soft words in Ukrainian while they deciphered Helen's comment. "The wind is very cold," Marina Petrenko agreed at last. "But we do not come so far."

Her older sister smiled and nodded agreement. Helen searched for another innocuous and easily translatable remark. "Did you see the fire the other night?"

This time there was no hesitation. "Bad fire!" Marina said. "Close to our house, so close we feel heat. We are scared!"

The genuine emotion in her voice overwhelmed the polite murmur of chitchat. In the hush that followed, the normally silent Oksana added, "Two neighbors die in fire. Very bad."

"Yes, dears, it is." Pat McGregor nodded at the young women from across the room. They darkened with startled color when they realized they were the center of attention, and slid closer to Helen as if she could protect them from any more conversation.

Aunt Pat never noticed, taking off her lace-trimmed gloves and turning to address the room at large. "You've all probably heard about the unfortunate fire that claimed the lives of our dear friend Lide Janczek and her husband. But you may not know that our other friends, Irene Prandtl and her— er—her—'' As usual, Pittypat couldn't decide how to refer to a relationship she didn't approve of. Helen sighed and came to her rescue.

"His name is Daniel Mahaffey," she told her aunt.

"Yes, of course. And both he and Irene have lost all of their possessions. So I thought, before we started our regular meeting, that we might take up a collection for them." Aunt Pat removed her high-crowned hat and turned it upside-down on a table, unceremoniously flattening several silk flowers and one small stuffed bird. "To help them start again," she said.

Several older matrons in the group promptly opened their silk handbags to contribute, and even a few of the clergy fished into their pockets. By the time Aunt Pat had finished passing her hat around, her face was flushed with pleasure.

"I know our comrades Irene and Daniel will appreciate every cent of this," she declared, hoisting the hat in both hands. "We'll deliver it to them immediately, won't we, Helen?"

If we ever manage to find them again, Helen thought. Aloud, all she said was, "Of course, Aunt Pat."

Pat McGregor gave the coin-filled hat a considering look. "Perhaps we should also commission a memorial service for the Janczeks—" She broke off, tugging at one amethyst earring in dismay. "Oh, dear. Lide was an atheist as well as a socialist, wasn't she? I don't suppose a Mass will—"

"—do her any good at all," finished a sour male voice.

Helen turned, although she'd already guessed which clergyman had spoken. Father Karl Zawisza of St. Witold's church had a distinctive voice, as German-tinged as his white-blond hair and far more grating than most of the Polish accents Helen heard down at the settlement house. Unfortunately, it was a voice they often heard at these meetings, since Father Zawisza was one of the most dedicated socialists in Aunt Pat's "temperance" group.

"I don't suppose Lide would have wanted such a service, in any case," Helen said, to fill the awkward pause that followed.

"But perhaps we could remember her with some brief remarks at the meeting today," Aunt Pat suggested hopefully. "Lide was a very faithful member of our society." She slanted an uncertain look at Father Zawisza. "I believe she said you encouraged her to join us last June, did she not?"

His cold blue eyes narrowed. "Certainly not. I spent June at the Industrial Workers of the World meeting in Chicago."

"But I'm sure she said—" Aunt Pat floundered to a stop, paralyzed by the glacial look Zawisza gave her. "I suppose I must have misunderstood."

"Undoubtedly."

Helen's previous dislike of the young priest flared into anger at that brusque dismissal. "No, you did *not* misunderstand, Aunt Pat. Lide told me that she'd learned about our meetings from Father Zawisza, too. So if anyone is mistaken, it's him."

Pale streaks of red crawled up the skin that stretched tightly over Zawisza's high-boned cheeks. "Miss Sorby, I assure you that I wouldn't have spoken to Lide Janczek if she'd accosted me on the street. If she told you otherwise, she lied."

"But why would she do that?" Helen demanded.

"To entangle us all in *her* politics!" The priest's voice rose with fierce conviction. "Lide Janczek wasn't just an atheist, Mrs. McGregor. She was an anarchist! And I can tell you that there's been a campaign by anarchists to discredit the entire IWW movement this year. Just when the Socialist Labor Party has endorsed the IWW's charter and we have a chance to work out a reasonable strategy for next year's elections—"

One of the other South Side clergy, an older man from the Welsh Congregational Church, cleared his throat. "I hear that Daniel DeLeon of the Socialist Labor Party has been traveling the country all this autumn, calling for general strikes. Do you call that a reasonable strategy?"

"If you ask me, *that's* anarchy," another minister said.

That lit the powder keg, igniting a long and furious group discussion over whether the Industrial Workers of the World should have accepted the endorsement of the more radical

Socialist Labor Party and how much chance either of them
had to win the 1906 election. Aunt Pat made a few vain
attempts to steer the conversation back to the issue of spon-
soring her workingman's temperance lecture, then gave up
and let the argument grind itself to a frustrated and indecisive
stop.

"Because there's no use trying to keep men from yelling
at each other, whether they're priests or not," she explained
to Helen, while the meeting broke up in noisy disarray. "You
simply *cannot* convince them that they can't resolve national
issues in groups of twos and threes." Pat McGregor cast a
dark look at Father Zawisza, still arguing with the Welsh
minister as they climbed the stairs. "I *do* wish that young
man hadn't brought up the Wobblies! We never even got to
decide what to do about poor Mr. McKenna."

"I know," Helen agreed, although what she really regret-
ted was the lost opportunity to find out why Father Zawisza
thought Lide Janczek was an anarchist. As Helen recalled,
Lide's political convictions had been socialist in both theory
and practice. Maybe the priest was confusing her with Irene
Prandtl. "What will you do?"

Aunt Pittypat sighed. "I suppose I'll have to call up Elsa
Hanneman and a few of our other wealthier members, and
ask them to support the lecture privately. Or I could just
sponsor it myself. Mr. McKenna's speaking fee is really very
modest."

So much for hoping that tonight's long argument had de-
flected Pittypat from throwing her money at the hopeful
young man upstairs. "How modest?" Helen demanded.

"No more than I spend each month on the butcher's bill
for my cats." Pat pulled on her gloves and tucked her coin-
stuffed hat under one arm. "In fact, not even half that
much."

Helen did a quick calculation while they climbed the stairs.
"I suppose that's reasonable," she said grudgingly. "He
hasn't asked you for anything else? A train ticket, or more
fliers?"

"No." Her aunt gave her a compassionate look. "Dearest,
not every man you meet is a swindler."

Helen felt her face grow hot. "No, but a lot of people who

call themselves temperance lecturers are!'' Her voice rang loudly in the emptying hush of the library, making Pittypat wince and squeeze her arm. Across the room, light flashed off spectacle lenses as Dennis McKenna looked up from his papers.

''Ah, Mr. McKenna.'' Aunt Pat went forward to meet him, smiling. ''I hope we didn't keep you waiting too long.''

''Not at all.'' The temperance lecturer scooped up his notes, scribbled on the backs of some of his fliers and added them to the rest of the stack. Helen wondered if he'd remember to take the writing off before the fliers got posted around town. ''What was the outcome of your meeting?''

Pat McGregor beamed at him. ''Good news, dear man. We have definitely decided to sponsor your temperance lecture. So, shall we plan it for next Tuesday night in Market Square?''

Dennis McKenna bowed his head solemnly. ''Whatever location and time you think best, ma'am. You know this city better than I do.'' He paused, glancing sidelong at Helen. ''Will that give us enough time to address all the fliers?''

Knowing that McKenna was perceptive enough to guess who did the addressing didn't make Helen feel any easier about her aunt's decision to sponsor him. Something about his earnest gaze reminded her too much of her former husband. ''I can find the time to write them out, Mr. McKenna. Don't worry.''

''But, Helen, if he wants to help, I think you should—'' The main door of the library slammed shut in a gust of wind and Pat McGregor broke off, blinking at Helen in surprise. ''Why on earth did you jump like that, dearest?''

Helen took a deep breath, watching a familiar blue-coated figure enter the reading room. ''The man who just walked in, Aunt Pat—he's the detective investigating the Janczeks' murder.''

''He is?'' Pittypat scrutinized Detective Milo Kachigan without much favor. Her first and distinctly unlamented husband had been an Irish police patrolman. Helen often suspected he was the cause of her antidrinking fervor. ''How odd to find a man like that in a library. Don't you think so, Mr. McKenna?''

"Perhaps he's doing research on one of his cases."

"Perhaps," Helen agreed, but the flutter in her stomach insisted otherwise. And when the police detective caught sight of them and altered his course through the reading room, the glitter of suspicion in his eyes confirmed her intuition.

At least some of the lies she'd told Milo Kachigan yesterday were coming back to haunt her.

KACHIGAN HAD SEEN STRIKERS GO OVER POLICE
barricades with the same look on their faces that
Helen Sorby wore now: brows tense, mouth tightened into a resolute line. He felt his own frown
deepen. There had always been a chance that the
social worker had answered his questions honestly yesterday,
although even then he'd wondered why her steady gaze had
faltered occasionally. But today's militant expression confirmed what he'd already surmised: she was withholding information.

"Good evening, Miss Sorby." He made sure none of his
seething impatience spilled into his voice. The soft-cheeked
matron leaning on Helen Sorby's arm was already eyeing
him in dismay, and there was no sense making her even more
upset. Although her round face and Irish freckles bore little
resemblance to the social worker's olive skin and angular
bones, there was a hint of the same stubborn loyalty around
their eyes. "You must be Helen's Aunt McGregor. I'm Detective Milo Kachigan of the Pittsburgh police."

"Detective Kachigan." It sounded as if she were memo-
rizing it for a future complaint. "How odd to meet you
here."

Kachigan's mouth twitched. At least someone in this family could be honest. "Your niece mentioned your weekly
meeting to me yesterday, ma'am. I took the liberty of drop-

ping by to ask her a few questions. I hope the temperance
work went well tonight.''

The quiet emphasis he'd put on the word "temperance"
got the him the glare he'd expected from Helen Sorby. "It
went extremely well. In fact, we were just discussing its outcome.'' She gestured at the weedy young man on her right,
who was regarding Kachigan with a bemused look from behind his spectacles. "This is Mr. Dennis McKenna, a traveling temperance speaker from Chicago. The league has
agreed to sponsor a workingman's lecture by him next week,
in downtown Pittsburgh.''

"Is that right?" Kachigan's doubt must have shown on
his face—the social worker scowled and swept up a smudged
flier from the library table to shove at him. Kachigan glanced
at the barely legible text in surprise. Apparently, at least
some of what the South Side Temperance League did was
actually temperance work. "Don't let me interrupt your planning, then. I can wait until you're done to ask my questions.''

"We weren't really planning anything." McKenna's diffident gaze wavered back and forth between the women.
"Um—were we?''

Helen Sorby's aunt came to his rescue. "We do need to
talk about your lecture, Mr. McKenna, but we can't do it
here, because the library closes soon. Let's just fetch our
coats and we can be off. I'd offer you a seat in the cab with
us, Detective,'' she added with false politeness, "but I'm
afraid it's far too small.''

"That's quite all right," Kachigan said. "I'm sure Miss
Sorby won't mind walking home.''

Mrs. McGregor sent him a severe look. "I always take
Helen home in my cab after our meetings, Mr. Kachigan.
The South Side is much too dangerous for a young woman
to walk alone at night.''

Kachigan looked quizzically at Helen Sorby, whose face
had stiffened with embarrassment. "Very true, ma'am, but I
think your niece will be safe enough under police escort. And
that will free you up to consult with Mr. McKenna about his
temperance lecture.'' With the older woman safely netted in
her own polite social fiction, he turned his attention back to
Helen Sorby. "It will also allow your niece to consult with

me. I find that I need some immediate assistance with *our* murder investigation, Miss Sorby. Or have you already forgotten that you wanted to help me find out who killed your friend Lide Janczek?''

He made his voice just doubtful enough to provoke Helen Sorby into lifting her chin, eyes dark with anger. "I haven't forgotten," she said hotly. "You'll excuse me, Aunt Pat."

It wasn't a question, but Mrs. McGregor answered it anyway, with a wail of distress. "But, Helen dearest, I really *do* need to talk over the lecture arrangements with you! I had some improvements I wanted to make in Mr. McKenna's flier—"

"Ring me up about it later. And this time, *don't* call Elsa Hanneman instead." Helen Sorby reached out to scoop up the untidy mass of papers from the table. "I'll have these addressed for you by Saturday, Mr. McKenna. Good day."

She swept past her two companions before either of them could utter another protest, ducking into the coat room just long enough to snag her coat from its hook without waiting for the attendant. Once Helen Sorby's mind was set to something, Kachigan noted, there didn't seem to be much chance of stopping her. He frowned, watching her juggle the stack of posters she held so she could pull on her coat with one hand.

"Can I carry those for you?"

"No."

She did let him hold the brass door open for her, though, walking without objection into the chilly, smoke-dusted November night. The traffic along East Carson Street had dwindled from its evening rush, but it was still noisy enough with horns and horses that Kachigan led them around the corner of the library to the quieter streets near the river. It was a cold and windy route, but Helen Sorby did not complain.

"Well?" she demanded. "What do you want to ask me?"

Kachigan gauged the hostility in her voice and decided his best strategy was attack. "Miss Sorby, does the Carnegie Library know that they're hosting a weekly meeting of socialists?"

Her brisk strides faltered, but only for a moment. "Of course they don't," she said in a caustic voice. "Do you think Andrew Carnegie would let any building erected with his money actually be used for the improvement of his workers' lives?''

''Is that what you use it for?''

''Among other things.'' The wind whipped a strand of her hair out of its pins and across her face, forcing her to juggle the fliers while she reached for a scarf stuffed in her pocket. Unable to stand it anymore, Kachigan hauled the stack of papers out of her hands, so she could knot the scarf under her chin.

''Thank you,'' Helen said grudgingly. She slid her fingers into her coat pockets when she was done, fast enough to make Kachigan suspect they were freezing. ''How did you guess?''

''That your temperance league was actually a socialist group?'' Kachigan shrugged. ''It was obvious from the way you described it yesterday that you were lying about something. And once I'd seen the kind of newspapers you read, I suspected what it was you had to hide.''

''But if you guessed that yesterday—'' Helen Sorby's voice lifted, its hostility washed away by surprise. ''Why didn't you say anything when I came to give you the map?''

''Because your politics aren't any of my business.''

Her frown crept back, creasing her forehead. ''But you must have known that if I met Lide Janczck at this meeting, she was probably a socialist too. And you still acted as if—'' Helen broke off so abruptly, Kachigan could guess how the sentence had been going to end.

''—as if I still wanted to solve her murder? I do. Murder is against the law, Miss Sorby, no matter what the victim's politics are.''

Helen Sorby took a deep breath, then slowly blew it out again. When the wind swept the mist away from her face, the expression behind it was thoughtful rather than combative.

''I suppose you want to know everything about our meetings.''

Kachigan nodded. ''Names, dates, activities.''

''And you expect me to tell you all of that?''

''It seems only fair,'' he pointed out. ''You want me to

tell you everything I know about this crime, don't you?''

"I'm not planning to put everything you tell me in a police file that anyone in city government could read!''

"Neither am I.'' Kachigan raised his voice to be heard over the hoot of a passing coal barge on the river. "Do you see me taking notes on this conversation, Miss Sorby?''

"That doesn't mean anything.''

"Yes it does.''

A trolley clattered past them on Twenty-fourth Street, its connecting rods sparking at the line junction and throwing electric shadows up against the surrounding houses. Helen gave Kachigan a searching, upward look in the brief light. The detective wasn't sure what she could read in his face, but it must have convinced her that he meant what he said.

"My aunt McGregor started the South Side Temperance League back in 1902,'' she told him abruptly. "But it was only an anti-drinking group until the mine strikes in 1904. That was when I joined. It's been primarily a socialists' group since then.''

Kachigan refrained from drawing the obvious conclusion. "What kinds of things do you do?''

"Argue about politics, mostly,'' Helen admitted. "But we've sponsored some lectures for workingmen and university students, and last summer we sent a delegate to the IWW conference in Chicago.'' She must have seen the puzzled look he gave her. "The Industrial Workers of the World, Mr. Kachigan. It's the union Bill Haywood and Eugene Debs founded as an alternative to the American Federation of Labor.''

"Oh, the Wobblies.'' He raised an eyebrow at her. "And that's it? You haven't threatened to disrupt any elections? Exposed any factories using child labor? Organized mass demonstrations at the mills?''

"We're not that well organized, Mr. Kachigan,'' Helen Sorby said between her teeth. "Not yet.''

He grunted, guiding her around a corner onto Twentieth Street and away from the river. Stymied by the closed ranks of houses on either side, the cold wind died to a whiffle. "When did the Janczeks join your group?''

"*They* didn't,'' Helen said. "Lide joined last June.''

He frowned. "Josef wasn't a socialist?"

"Not as far as I know."

"But Lide was?"

"Oh, yes. The first night she came, she brought along a German-language edition of Karl Marx and discussed it in Polish and German with some of the priests." Her voice turned thoughtful. "I think she must have come from an intellectual family back in Krakow. She owned a lot of books."

"And she was happy married to an immigrant steel-worker?"

Helen gave him an irate look. "You don't know what Josef Janczek might have been before he came here! Steel work is usually the only job an immigrant can get in this city. That doesn't mean he was stupid. He just wasn't a so-cialist."

Kachigan mulled that over for a moment. "What about Daniel Mahaffey and Irene Prandtl? Were they both social-ists?"

"Yes." Helen's voice turned distinctly cautious. "They used to belong to our group, but they quit about a month ago."

"Why?"

A renewed blast of wind tugged at them while they crossed East Carson Street and Helen thrust her hands deeper into her coat pockets. "Daniel had gotten laid off from his job at the mill, and he had to take a night job to pay the rent." She paused, obviously searching for nonjudgmental words. "And Irene—I think Irene got impatient with us. She's in favor of more—um—militant worker actions than most of our group."

"So she's an anarchist?"

Helen glared up at him. "Why should her politics mat-ter?" she demanded, without really answering. "You can't possibly suspect her of blowing up her own house!"

"No, but someone might have blown it up because of her. We don't know that the Janczeks were the intended victims of this crime, Miss Sorby."

"But Josef was murdered before the fire—"

"Maybe because he caught someone trying to set it. Has

it occurred to you that there may be a very good reason why your friend Irene and her lover slipped away from the settlement house, without telling you or anyone where they were going?''

"You think they know someone is after them?''

"I think they know *something*," Kachigan said definitely. "And I think we'd be a lot closer to solving this murder if we could find out what it is they know."

"You didn't find them at her parents' place this morning?"

"No, I did not." Kachigan's exasperation came flooding back full force. "As far as I can tell, Miss Sorby, Irene Prandtl's parents would be happier if they never heard their daughter's name spoken again. And you knew that when you sent me there!"

"I suspected it," she admitted, glancing away from him. The flashing electric bar-sign from the A.O.H. at the far end of the block threw oddly colored reflections across the sidewalk, although Kachigan doubted Helen was actually looking at them. "But I still thought it might be worth checking."

"You're a terrible liar," he said frankly. "Why don't you just say that you wanted to divert me from your friends' trail?"

Her startled gaze swung back to him. After a moment, a flash of amber electric light showed him the unexpected smile that curved her lips. "All right, I did want to divert you from their trail. Daniel and Irene have a lot of friends— other anarchists—whose names she wouldn't tell me. I didn't think Irene would want me sending you after them. She always said it would be better if I didn't know what they did for a living."

Kachigan didn't doubt that, since Helen Sorby's eyes hadn't wavered from his while she said it. "Probably hoodlums, then. And I bet Mahaffey's 'night job' was helping them out."

"You don't even know him! How can you say that?"

"Because when I asked him where he worked yesterday, he said nowhere. Why would he do that if he had a legitimate job?"

That silenced her, at least for the moment. They turned

west onto Sarah Street, shadowed on this block by the blunt square bulk of St. Casimir's Catholic church. Its bell was chiming the half hour.

"We're nearly home, Mr. Kachigan. Are there any other questions you want to ask me?"

He paused, trying to decide if he should risk it. "Just one. Did you ever find out what happened to your husband?"

They were close enough by then that he could hear the social worker's swift intake of breath. Along with the averted turn of her head, it made him feel as if he'd slapped her. A long silence stretched between them, cold as the wind off the river.

"In profile, you always looked familiar to me," Kachigan said at last, to break the chill silence. "This morning, I finally remembered where I had seen you before. It was a photograph in the *Pittsburgh Times*."

"From last November," Helen Sorby said flatly.

"Yes. I remembered enough of the story that went with it to look it up in our files this morning." Kachigan gave her a searching glance. "The paper said a traveling union organizer named James Foster Barton had disappeared during the pressed-car strike in McKees Rocks. You were mentioned in the photograph caption as his wife, and the last one to see him alive."

"Yes." All of the passionate intensity in Helen Sorby's voice had leached away, leaving it toneless. "As far as I know, Detective Kachigan, he's still alive."

Kachigan waited, but no further explanation came. He decided to risk another probe. "Have I been incorrect?" he asked. "In calling you Miss Sorby, I mean."

"No!" They reached her ivy-carved front door and she turned, yanking the stack of fliers out from under Kachigan's arm with a violence that took him by surprise. "I may have lied to you about Irene's parents, but I didn't lie about my own name!"

"All right." With the hard-earned patience that five years of walking a beat had given him, Kachigan put his clamoring questions aside and waited in silence while she fumbled for the key. The latch turned before she could insert it, and Thomas Sorby swung the door wide. He looked satisfied rather than surprised to find Kachigan on his doorstep.

"Aunt Pat rang up to tell me you'd be bringing Helen home," he said. "I just finished mapping your burnt row house. Can you come in for a moment and see what I found out?"

Kachigan paused on the doorstep, looking questioningly at Helen Sorby. The gaslight in the hall showed him an unemotional face. "You may as well come in," she said. "You have no idea how annoying Thomas will be if he doesn't get to spill out his news to you right away."

Her brother grinned, hanging her coat on the rack for her. He turned to do the same for Kachigan. "What Helen means is that she wants to hear all the gory details, and she knows she can't if I have to tell you down at the patrol station tomorrow."

"No, I do not." Helen's voice sounded unusually sharp to Kachigan, and perhaps to her as well. She took a deep breath, and resumed more quietly. "The meeting tonight was nothing but arguments, and it's given me a headache. I'll leave you two to your 'gory details.' "

She nodded politely at Kachigan, then started up the carved oak staircase that graced the front hall. Thomas reached up and caught her before she'd taken two steps, detaining her long enough to drop an affectionate kiss on her cheek.

"Don't worry," he assured her. "I'll give you the details at breakfast tomorrow, if you want them."

A glimmer of amusement lit Helen Sorby's serious face. "You'd better," she said and pinched her brother's chin through his beard before running up the rest of the steps.

Kachigan made sure his gaze was leveled at Thomas Sorby by the time the young man turned back to face him. "You didn't have to take the time to map those houses, Mr. Sorby. Your evidence yesterday was more than sufficient for my purposes."

"I know, but it gave me a good excuse to miss the temperance meeting tonight." The surveyor led Kachigan back into the drawing room, which seemed to be the heart of the Sorby household. "Not that I really need an excuse for Helen, but Aunt Pittypat's always after me to come and take the pledge. To set a good example for everyone else's male relatives, I suppose." He motioned Kachigan to the seat that Helen usually occupied at the drafting table. The detective carefully pushed aside the litter of books and manuscript pages and eyed the ink-blotched map Thomas was unrolling. It looked nothing like the neat street map he'd been working on earlier that morning.

"What's this?"

"Your fire site, Detective, or at least as much of it as I could reconstruct."

Kachigan scanned the sketch, finding scattered labels that marked foundation blocks, water lines and furnace piping. The utility he was looking for didn't appear. "They definitely had no gas line, then?"

"None that I could find." Thomas leaned one forearm on the table and tapped at the two dark circles he'd drawn against the east wall of the row houses. "Both houses had their own furnaces in the basement, linked to upstairs radiators." Sorby traced an arc around the right-hand coal furnace. "You see this stippling I've drawn here?"

"Yes." It was the splatter of dark ink that had first caught Kachigan's attention. Some of the marks were larger than others, but all of them lay within the west side of the basement. Taken together, they made a pattern like an irregular starburst. "Are those the broken pieces of the furnace?"

"Mmm-hmm." The surveyor traced the blue pencil lines that crisscrossed the map. "These are where the house beams fell. You can see that both furnaces got crushed when the timbers collapsed on them, but only this one spread out in so many pieces."

"So you were right last night about the furnace exploding and causing the fire." Kachigan pulled out his evidence book and pencil, and jotted that down. "All we have to figure out is how someone made it do that."

Sorby looked dubious. "Usually when a furnace explodes, it's because of accidental overheating. Someone closes the relief valve to save water in the summer and forgets to turn it back on in the fall. When all the water in the boiler-jacket turns to steam, the pressure rises and the whole thing blows apart."

Kachigan nodded. "I've seen that happen, back when I was a kid in Monessen. But the people in that case weren't hacked apart with an axe beforehand."

"True," Thomas admitted. "The problem is that I found no smell of dynamite or blasting powder anywhere in that basement. And some always stays behind after an explosive's been set off."

They fell silent for a while, contemplating the sketch on the table between them. "You could overheat a coal furnace on purpose, couldn't you?" Kachigan asked. "Using only coal?"

"It wouldn't be easy." Sorby scrubbed his fingers through his short beard. "You couldn't just drain out some water and walk away. You'd need to stay for a while, stoking the firebox with coal to get it good and hot. Leave too soon, and the thing might cool off without exploding. Leave too late, and you'd become part of the explosion."

Kachigan grunted. "But a man with some iron and steel experience might have a little more luck timing it right than you or I would. After all, they see metal heated to its limit every day in those old Bessemer converters."

Sorby gave him a speculative look. "You have a suspect in mind?"

"No one particular yet." Kachigan picked up the map, folding it into careful thirds before he tucked it away. "But one of the possibilities I'm looking into is that Josef Janczek's murder was related to his work at Black Point Steel."

Sorby whistled softly. "You have evidence of that?"

Kachigan's mouth twisted in what was not quite a smile. "Not exactly. Mostly I suspect it because the Black Point police chief tried to convince me that it wasn't true." He gave the younger man a sharp glance. "I trust you'll not let that information go any further than your sister, Mr. Sorby."

"And get my door knocked on in the middle of the night by the steel-mill police?" Thomas Sorby shook his head vehemently, before he led the way back to the door. "No thank you."

They emerged with soft steps into the front hall. The staircase that had been dark before now glowed with muted gaslight from the floor above, casting slanted shadows down through the banisters. The additional light opened up the upper reaches of the narrow hall, revealing a mahogany-framed oil painting that Kachigan hadn't noticed on his previous visit. He stopped with his coat half on, arrested by the picture of Helen Sorby with her hair dressed in an old-fashioned coronet, seated on a chair with two plump children on her knees. A man with mutton chop whiskers, dressed in a frock coat, stood behind her.

"Your parents?" he asked after a minute.

"Mmm-hmm. Mum looks just like Helen does now, doesn't she?"

"Yes." The unsmiling young woman in the picture had the same strong bones her daughter owned, perhaps a little more hollowed around the cheeks and a little more pronounced at the jaw. The children on her lap stared wide-eyed out from the frame, small replicas of their parents. "It's a good portrait."

Thomas Sorby grinned. "You should be telling Helen that, not me."

Kachigan paused with his hand halfway to the door latch. "Your sister painted that picture?"

"From an old photograph." Sorby shook his head in brotherly criticism. "She wouldn't let me do a mechanical enlargement for her—insisted on doing it all herself. You may not have noticed yet, Detective, but Helen can be awfully stubborn."

"I've noticed." Kachigan rummaged for his notebook, a new set of plans unfolding in his mind. He tore a leaf out of the book and slowly inscribed a note on it, then he folded the paper and marked the outside with Helen Sorby's initials. "Do me a favor, Sorby. Give this to your sister at breakfast tomorrow."

"A compliment on the picture?"

"Not exactly. A favor I'm asking from her."

Thomas eyed him quizzically. "You could just stop by in the morning and ask her yourself, you know."

Kachigan shook his head. "I think I'd better wait until Miss Sorby invites me back. I asked her some questions tonight that she didn't particularly want to answer. I'm afraid she may still be a little angry about it."

"Did she answer your questions?"

"More or less."

"Was she shouting at the time?"

Kachigan frowned. "Her voice wasn't soft, but I wouldn't say she was shouting."

"Then she wasn't angry," Thomas said with conviction. "Annoyed, maybe, but definitely not angry." He rubbed one ear, with a reminiscent wince. "Trust me, Detective Kachigan. When Helen gets angry at you, you'll know."

6 THE OUTSIDE OF THE FOLDED PAPER READ SIMply, "H.S."

"Thomas, who did you say this was from?" Helen frowned at the note she'd picked up from the telephone table. The paper was ragged along one edge, as if it had been torn from a book, and the handwriting was unfamiliar.

"Milo Kachigan." Her brother waited for her to swing open the kitchen door for him since his arms were full of packages. The smell of coffee greeted them on the other side, puffing out of the percolator on the stove. "He left it for you last night, but you were asleep by the time he was gone."

Helen winced. Actually, she'd stayed awake long into the night, sitting in the darkness so her brother wouldn't know. Even though some part of her had always expected that Kachigan would ask her about James Foster Barton, the question had come so unexpectedly and so soon that she'd been thrown completely off-guard. She couldn't decide if she'd said too little in answer to the detective's final question, or if she'd said far too much.

"Aren't you going to open it?" Her brother lined their morning purchases up along the counter. Bread, butter and coffee was their standard breakfast fare, with jam or honey added only if Helen had recently sold a magazine article and could afford it. Since Thomas never had time to bake bread, and Helen always burned it, they'd fallen into the habit of walking down to East Carson Street every morning to fetch a fresh loaf, plus whatever other groceries they needed for the day.

"I suppose." Helen unfolded the note with a quick decisive snap. Better to know the worst right away.

I would appreciate it if you could sketch me a picture of your friend Lide Janczek. I have no other way to trace her movements on the day of the fire. MK.

Helen blinked, taken aback. "He says he wants me to draw a picture of Lide. Where on earth did he get that idea?"

"Don't look at me." Thomas shook their Italian loaf free of its waxed paper wrappings. "I never suggested it."

Helen frowned. "Then how did he find out I could draw likenesses?"

"Oh, well." Thomas cleared his throat. "He did happen to see the picture of Mum and Da' out in the hall, before he left."

"And I suppose you just happened to tell him that I did it."

"Yes." Still standing, her twin tore off one end of the bread and dipped it into the butter dish. Helen gave him a speaking look while she went to fetch the furiously boiling percolator, and he rounded the dining room table to drop into his seat, shaking out his napkin with ostentatious formality. The effect was somewhat spoiled by the bread clamped between his teeth. "You're not yelling at me," he said, when he took it out. "Does that mean you're not offended?"

"Offended?" Helen poured out thick black coffee into their cups. "No, I'm not offended." The last thing she'd expected, after the icy way she'd left Kachigan last night, was that he would ask her to do him a favor this morning. "Just surprised."

"Did he say why he needs a picture of Lide Janczek?"

"He wants to track her movements on the day of the fire." Helen sat down and pulled off a chunk of bread, not bothering with the bread knife since her brother had already mangled the loaf. "He must not have found a photo of her."

"Not surprising, since everything the Janczeks owned is burnt to a crisp now."

"True." Helen added a dollop of honey to the butter on

her bread, then smeared them together in a vain attempt to keep the honey from dripping.

"So, are you going to draw Mr. Kachigan his picture?"

"I'm not sure." Helen glanced down at her coffee cup, seeing the sparkle of tiny butter drops on the dark surface. "That I can, I mean. I'm a draftsman like you, Thomas, not a real artist. I need a photograph to help me draw."

"Then get someone to help you with Lide's picture." Thomas patted at the canvas waistcoat he wore for mapping, making sure his pencils, notebooks and surveying tapes were in all the right pockets. "Aunt Pittypat knew this Janczek girl, too, didn't she? Get her to check your drawing."

Helen opened her mouth to object that their aunt never rose before noon, then had an even better idea. "Thank you, Thomas. I believe I will do something like that."

Her brother grunted and disappeared through the passageway door. A moment later he stuck his head back around it, looking suspicious. "Something like *what*?" he demanded.

"Like getting someone to check the drawing." Helen busied herself spreading butter and honey on another chunk of bread to avoid meeting Thomas's eyes. "I've thought of some people I can talk to before Aunt Pittypat gets up." People who could also give her information about the Janczeks' murder, but Helen thought it better not to mention that. Even a man as easygoing as her twin would likely balk at the thought of his sister going door to door among the immigrant households of Breed Street.

"What's the hurry? You can visit Aunt Pat this afternoon."

"Yes, but I want to get it done before that. I have classes to teach at the settlement house today, remember? And I'm sure Mr. Kachigan would like to have his drawing as soon as possible."

Thomas grunted. "I told him you weren't angry last night," he remarked. "You might say so when you give him your picture. He doesn't think he should come here anymore."

And with those unexpected words, Thomas withdrew and left Helen sitting speechless at the kitchen table, butter and honey slowly dripping onto her serge skirt.

• • •

Helen's doubts about her ability to draw a recognizable likeness of Lide Janczek receded while she was absorbed in the actual process of sketching. The young woman's face took shape swiftly under her pencil: broad Slavic forehead, thin pale hair, jutting cheekbones, pointed chin. The addition of a loose Russian-style blouse and an unfashionably small hat gave the sketch a passing resemblance to the dead girl, at least in Helen's critical opinion. Satisfied, she tucked the sketch and her pencil case into her moth-eaten rabbit muff and set out for Breed Street.

By the time she'd covered half the block on which the Janczeks had lived, Helen's confidence had turned to creeping doubt. Of the seven houses on whose doors she had so far knocked, most were either unoccupied or answered by young matrons who spoke only Polish or Lithuanian. The few older ladies she'd found who seemed to understand English politely looked at her sketch and then shook their curl-papered heads.

Helen might have blamed the problem on bad communication, except for the single misplaced Italian housewife who lived at the end of the street. Mrs. Follador had been so delighted to hear Helen respond to her Italian greeting in the same language that she drew her inside and fed her hot chocolate and biscotti, gossiping all the while. However, when Helen showed her the sketch of Lide Janczek, Mrs. Follador looked just as blank as her Eastern European neighbors.

"Those people in the rented houses, they never stay long," she explained, her voice crisp with the accent of central Italy. "In one month, out the next—I hear the landlord is very, very cheap." She shook her head in disapproval. "What a *minchióne!* He lets those row houses get so rundown they burn, when he could have sold them to the church next door, long time ago."

"Do you know who the landlord is?" Helen asked, in the softer, southern Italian she'd learned from her mother. She hoped her phrasing meant the same thing to her hostess as it did to her. Italians had as many kinds of dialects as they had pasta.

Mrs. Follador disappointed her with a massive shrug.

"Some rich man from Shadyside, I think, or maybe from Point Breeze. One of those places where all the houses are mansions." Her eyes twinkled over the rim of her coffee cup. "He takes the money out of these ugly tenements and makes his own house nice, eh?"

"No doubt," Helen agreed. Her opinion of absentee landlords wasn't much higher than her opinion of Republicans. "So you never talked to any of the people who lived in the row houses?"

"No. They were all young couples who lived there." Mrs. Follador's brow wrinkled in majestic disapproval. "At night they drank, played music, talked in the street. I saw the Polish priest go from his house to talk to them, but not once did I ever see them go to church. What would I have to say to them?"

Helen sighed in defeat. "Thank you," she said, and handed the woman a temperance flier, brought along mostly as an excuse in case she ran into Thomas. "Your husband might be interested in this."

"And who is it, eh?" Mrs. Follador squinted down at the smudged photograph. "Some criminal wanted by the police?"

Helen's mouth quivered with restrained laughter. "No, it's a man who's going to give a temperance lecture in Pittsburgh next week." She saw the baffled look Mrs. Follador cast at the text. "It's a speech for workingmen, to convince them not to drink."

That gained her a gust of frank Italian laughter. "Ah, good luck to him! I should live to see the day someone convinces August Follador to give up wine." She wagged the flier under Helen's nose. "Even if he *could* read this, which he can't."

And that, thought Helen wryly, was probably the major reason that Aunt Pittypat's campaign for workingmen's temperance had failed to gain many converts so far. She thanked Mrs. Follador anyway and said an extended goodbye, managing to escape at last with only a handful of biscotti sent along with her "for luck."

Outside on the windswept sidewalk, Helen paused to tie the strings that anchored her modestly feathered cap to her tousled hair. She folded the sketch of Lide Janczek and tucked it inside her muff along with the Italian cookies. Perhaps she should walk over to Patrol Station Seven now and give the sketch to Milo Kachigan—but something in Helen knew the drawing wasn't quite right. She'd drawn Lide's bone structure and hair, but some vital element in the woman's expression was missing.

"Meess Sorby?"

Helen blinked and swung around, recognizing the hesitant voice as soon as she saw the apple-cheeked Ukrainian faces behind her. "Marina! And Oksana—how nice to see you!" She didn't have to manufacture the warmth in her voice; She'd been hoping all morning that she would find the Petrenko sisters behind one of the doors of Breed Street. "You know you're supposed to call me 'Helen'!"

The sisters exchanged a translating murmur of Ukrainian, dark eyes never leaving Helen's face. "We are not sure it was you," Marina admitted, smiling up at her. "Here on Breed Street, we live but you don't, mmm?"

Helen returned the smile. "I'm trying to find people to tell me what Lide Janczek looked like," she said, using the clearest words she could find. "The police want me to make a drawing of her." That produced only blank looks, until she pulled out her sketch and unfolded it for them. "A drawing."

"Ah. Drawing," said Marina, but it was Oksana who took the sketch in careful fingers and examined it. She said something definitive in Ukrainian, and Helen looked expectantly at Marina.

"Oksana says you must come to the house with us," Marina explained after a moment of thought. "We show you our picturegraph."

"Your picturegraph?' Helen's breath caught. "You have a photograph of Lide?"

In answer, Marina tugged at her hand, leading her down to the smallest, most freshly painted house on the block. A faint shadow of soot clung to one side of its bright yellow clapboards and white trim, where it faced the gaping ruin next door. Marina hadn't been exaggerating, Helen realized, when she'd spoken about feeling the heat of last night's fire.

Inside the Petrenko house, the air smelled of fresh laundry

and cooked cabbage. A trio of wide-eyed children too young
for school came spilling down into the front hall to stare at
Helen. They were promptly chased upstairs again by an older
sister who should have been in school, but wasn't. She
showed Oksana a half-sewn shirtwaist, made of cotton lawn
so fine it shimmered in the light, and got an approving pat
on the head. With a shy bob toward Helen, she scurried back
into a room off the hall. A moment later, the foot-pedaled
thump of a sewing machine began inside.

"Our little sister helps us now with sewing," Marina explained. Oksana had vanished in the direction of the kitchen.
"We get many orders for Russian blouse with silk embroidery, more than we two can do alone. Even Mama helps
after work."

"But shouldn't your sister be in school?"

Marina shook her head, taking Helen's coat and ushering
her into a tiny, slip-covered drawing room. "Sasha grows up
in Ukraine, like us. She has no English." She made shooing
motions out at the hall, where a row of interested faces
peered down through the banister. "The little ones, they will
go to school. They are born after we come to meet our *dya-
dya* in America. Already they learn English playing in the
street."

Oksana reappeared with an enormous brass urn of tea and
a tray of cookies, while Marina went to fetch something from
the mantelpiece. Helen glanced around, searching for a surface on which she could draw. The small tables in the room
were all crowded with enameled dishes and ornate brass can-
dlesticks.

"*Ruiskatut*." Oksana handed her a delicate glass plate,
then gestured at the dark flat cookies in wordless invitation.

Helen eyed the size of her plate and the number of cookies
on the tray measuringly. "If you don't mind, I'd like to put
them all on my plate. So I can use the tray to draw on."

Oksana may not have been able to speak much English,
but she certainly understood it. She piled the *ruiskatut* into
an unsteady pyramid on Helen's plate and offered her the
empty tray. Helen set it on her lap and unfolded her drawing
across it.

"Here is photograph, Helen." Marina perched on the sofa

beside her, an old cigar box tucked under one arm. She lifted the smoke-wreathed picture of Prince Albert to reveal a stack of faded newspaper clippings below. Helen's eyebrows lifted when she saw the thick dark imprint of Cyrillic lettering.

"Are these newspapers from Russia?" she asked, startled. Although she couldn't recognize the names of the days or months, she could clearly see that the year was 1905. What on earth was Lide Janczek's photograph doing in a recent overseas newspaper?

"From Chicago," Marina said, lifting one clipping to show her Teddy Roosevelt's toothy grin. "Our uncle Pavel sends us, so we can read American news."

While Marina combed through the clippings, Oksana handed Helen a fragile bone-china cup steaming with pale but fragrant tea. Along with it, she offered a glass dish of tiny, preserved berries. "To sweeten," she explained.

"Oh." Helen stirred an experimental teaspoonful into her cup and rescued a *ruiskatut* about to fall from the teetering pile on her plate. It tasted strongly of brown sugar and rye flour. Marina muttered to herself in Ukrainian, then made a triumphant noise and tugged out the clipping she wanted. She unfolded it for Helen, smoothing the paper with careful fingers.

"Lide." She pointed at the large photograph at the top.

Expecting a picture of Lide Janczek alone, Helen was surprised by the crowd of young faces that gazed back at her from the page. They carried a banner, its lettering obscured by the angle of the photo, and some had their fists raised militantly over their heads. Helen thought she knew where the photograph had been taken, but she turned to Marina for confirmation.

"Can you tell me what the newspaper article says?"

Glowing with pleasure at being the one who could enlighten, Marina bent over the clipping. She pointed at the headline first. "Industrial Workers of World—mmm—make meeting?"

"Convene?" Helen suggested. She saw Oksana spread berry jam on her own *ruiskatut*, and reached for another cookie to try it.

"Convene, yes. Convene to decide on—plan of action?"

"Strategy," Helen said around a mouthful of cookie and fragrant jam. It was easy to guess what words Marina was searching for, since similar headlines—and similar photographs—had appeared in the Pittsburgh papers this past June. The founding of the Industrial Workers of the World in Chicago, by such infamous radicals as Big Bill Haywood and Daniel DeLeon, had sparked irate editorials in all the major industrial cities, including Pittsburgh. It had also spurred the rival American Federation of Labor to publicly denounce them.

Helen leaned over the photograph, searching the sea of solemn black and white faces. "Which one is Lide?"

Oksana pointed to a woman's head near the edge of the photo. Lide Janczek had been caught in three-quarters profile, her face lifted but partially shadowed by the tall man next to her. Helen took the clipping from Oksana's lap and set it next to her sketch, comparing the two images critically. She'd caught the shape of the young woman's face fairly well, she thought, although she'd made the chin a bit too short. What she'd drawn wrong were the eyes and the mouth. Lide's eyes were large and pale, as Helen had tried to show them, but her eyebrows and lashes were so white a blond that they barely showed in the photo. Helen scrubbed her gum eraser over the clearly defined brows and lashes she'd put on her sketch, and sighed. *That* was better. As for the mouth—Helen tapped one finger on her drawing, trying to decide what she had missed.

Marina pointed at the clipping helpfully. "Lide smiles, always. Like she knows something."

It was true, Helen recalled. Lide Janczek had always come to their meetings with a secretive smile tilting the corners of her lips. She erased the neutral expression she'd used for Lide's mouth and replaced it with a cryptic upward curl.

"There," she said. "Does that look more like her?"

"Much better," Marina approved, while Oksana smiled and nodded too. "Have more *ruiskatut*, Helen."

"Thank you, no. I'm full." She added another teaspoonful of sweet preserves to her tea, though, then bent over the photo again. Closer inspection confirmed what she thought she'd seen earlier: the shadow across Lide Janczek's face came from the encircling arm of the tall man beside her. She studied his face, seeing strong Roman bones beneath center-parted dark hair. He looked more Italian than Polish, she thought.

"Is that Lide's husband next to her, Marina?"

Marina glanced at the photo and shook her head doubtfully. "No, can't be. Josef Janczek was not so tall."

Oksana made a sharp comment in Ukrainian. Helen looked inquiringly at Marina, and found her wide-eyed with fascination.

"Oksana says Lide has other men besides husband," Marina reported. She asked her sister something and got a lengthy reply. "Oksana says she sees men leave, when she gets up early to start bread. Sometimes same men, sometimes different."

Helen frowned, not sure that Oksana's interpretation was necessarily the correct one. "But if they're visiting at night," she asked slowly, "wouldn't Lide's husband be home?"

The Petrenkos looked at each other. "Maybe they come when he works night turn at mills?" Marina suggested, but Oksana shook her head. They conferred again in Ukrainian; then Marina looked up at Helen and shrugged.

"Oksana thinks he is home," she said, clearly puzzled. "She thinks he knows about these men."

Helen thought so too, although she doubted it had anything at all to do with Lide Janczek. It was far more probable that those men were coming surreptitiously to meet Josef Janczek than his wife, and given Bernard K. Flinn's interest in this case, she thought she knew why. Seeing how intrigued Marina was by Oksana's interpretation, however, she didn't try to convince the Petrenkos that her unionizing version was far more likely.

"May I borrow your newspaper story?" she asked instead. "I'd like to show it to the policeman working on this case."

Their quick nods made her wonder if they really understood her request, but Oksana answered that by folding the clipping and handing it to her. "Police keep," she said, speaking in English for the first time. "Use to catch killer."

Helen blinked, then realized gossip about the Janczeks' death must have already spread through Breed Street.

"Thank you," she said, and rose. "And thank you for the tea," she added sincerely. "I like the way you sweeten it."

That provoked a flurry of happy activity, and by the time Helen made it out the Petrenkos' door, she was carrying not only her sketch and the newspaper clipping, but also a cloth bag of Ukrainian tea, a paper doily folded around several more *ruiskatut* and a small glass jar of berry preserves. A good thing she'd already had Mrs. Follador's biscotti to carry, Helen thought, or she might have had the tea urn foisted on her as well.

Outside, Pittsburgh's morning chill had brightened into fitful autumn sunlight, occasionally shadowed by towering black smoke from the mills. Helen juggled her awkward packages, then began packing them into her muff until it bulged like a squirrel's cheek. When Aunt Pittypat's fliers refused to fit, she frowned and scanned the line of telephone poles along Breed Street, looking for ones with tacks from previous postings.

Something fell in the adjacent Janczek basement, kicking up a feathery plume of ash for the wind to tear apart. Helen couldn't see anything moving, but she heard crunching footsteps in the rubble. She tucked her fliers under one arm and walked down the crooked slate sidewalk, fairly sure she would find Thomas.

"What are you doing down there?" she demanded, catching sight of the ash-covered figure crouched in a corner of the basement. "You're supposed to be working today."

A familiar face turned up toward her, but it didn't belong to her brother. "I *am* working today, Miss Sorby," Kachigan said. "This happens to be my job." He lifted his sooty eyebrows inquiringly. "What's your excuse for being here?"

Helen bit her lip. "I'm posting fliers for the temperance lecture," she said stiffly. When she saw the way that chastened caution replaced the friendly greeting in his eyes, she took pity on him and added, "I'm also drawing the picture of Lide Janczek you wanted, Mr Kachigan. I've found a photograph of her, too."

"You have?" He whistled softly. "Miss Sorby, I'm starting to be glad that you insisted on investigating this case with me."

"You may finish being glad just as fast," she warned. "I think I've also found out who killed Lide and her husband."

His eyebrows shot up. "Who?"

"Bernard K. Flinn."

7

"BERNARD FLINN?"

Somewhere in the past two days, Kachigan had passed the point of trying to keep his voice carefully measured around Helen Sorby. The outright skepticism in it now made her glare at him, but didn't drive her away. If his rude questions last night hadn't done that, Kachigan thought wryly, nothing could.

"Well, why not?" she demanded. "You were the one who told me Bernard Flinn was trying to cover something up."

"He is. But this"—Kachigan gestured at the wrecked basement, with its charred beams and gray drifts of ash—"isn't how the coal and steel police usually dispose of troublemakers. You said it yourself yesterday, Miss Sorby. Murder isn't a crime for them. Why go to all this trouble to hide it?"

Helen Sorby frowned at him, but by now Kachigan was starting to know her expressions. This one looked more thoughtful than annoyed. "Maybe they didn't want their other workers to know who killed Josef," she suggested. "If there's trouble brewing at one of the mills, an outright murder could ignite it."

Kachigan was momentarily startled. He had to keep reminding himself that this ordinary-looking young woman was not just a local social worker, but an investigative journalist who worked for the top magazines in the country. "That might be true," he said. "But I assume your brother told you this morning how our fire was set? Can you really see Bernard K. Flinn's policemen risking their lives to stoke a coal furnace to overheating when they could have just thrown a stick of dynamite in it?"

Helen Sorby surprised him with a disgusted look, until he saw the mockery behind it. "How dare you ruin a perfectly good theory with common sense?"

Kachigan's mouth twitched. "It's not common sense, it's envy. There you stand, clean as a new penny and full of information, while I've spent all morning in this mess just to discover that the Janczeks owned two alarm clocks and no bathtub."

She bit her lip, then blossomed suddenly into laughter. Kachigan watched with unexpected appreciation. Helen Sorby might wear a sober frown most of the time, but when she laughed it was with full-throated amusement that lit her face like sunlight.

"Poor Mr. Kachigan," she said at last, gently mocking. "All that hard work for nothing."

"Not exactly nothing. I know the Janczeks must have taken their baths in a washbucket."

"Well, I could have told you that. Lide always complained about having to carry water to fill it." Helen tucked up her skirts to kneel at the edge of the basement. "Is that all you found?"

He nodded. "Although maybe what I *didn't* find is more important." He ticked each item off on charcoal-stained fingers. "No safes or lock-boxes, even though they should have survived the fire. No metal gun barrels. No metal shell casings for bullets or bombs." Kachigan started across the narrow basement toward the cellar steps, kicking up ash with each step. "For anarchists, they were either very neat or very poor."

"Of course they were poor." Helen's scowl furrowed her forehead again. "Why else would they have been living in a tenement like this, without gas or running water?"

He paused at the bottom of the steps, brushing off the charcoal and ash that clung to his coat. Unfortunately, there was nothing he could do about the smell. "Then why were the Janczeks able to afford a bicycle?"

"You found one in their basement?" The social worker's eyes widened when he lifted the unmistakable spoked wheel encircled with charred rubber. "Lide never mentioned that to me. Maybe Josef won it in a card game."

"Or just won money enough to buy it."

"Yes." Helen came to meet Kachigan when he climbed out of the rubble. If the odor of charred, wet timber bothered her, her intent expression didn't show it. "I suppose they must have had some way to get extra money, if Lide could afford to travel to Chicago last summer."

Kachigan's eyes lit with interest. "She went to Chicago? How did you find that out?"

"By talking to her neighbors." Helen reached into her rather lumpy muff and took out a folded square of paper. "There, that's the sketch I managed to draw for you."

He unfolded it and studied the surprisingly lifelike portrait rendered in a few pencil strokes. Lide Janczek's pale eyelashes and brows should have made her look childlike and vulnerable, but something about the dead woman's self-possessed smile gave Kachigan the opposite impression.

"This is very good," he said, without thinking.

Helen gave him a skeptical look. "You'd better wait until you see the photograph I found before you pass judgment." She dug into her muff again. This time, Kachigan watched her excavate a jar of ruby-colored jam and a paper bag that smelled of anise and vanilla before she found what she was searching for. She shook out the flimsy piece of newsprint with care.

Kachigan's eyebrows flew upward when he recognized the Cyrillic typeface. "Where on earth did *this* come from?"

"From my friends Marina and Oksana Petrenko. Their uncle sent it to them from Chicago." Helen came to stand beside him. "Do you recognize Lide Janczek?"

Kachigan scanned the sea of young faces, looking for pale eyes and tight-drawn hair. He spotted her at once. Even in this militant scene, Lide Janczek had a secretive smile on her lips.

"That woman there, on the right?"

"Yes."

"So she went to Chicago to attend the Wobbly convention.'' He whistled, then saw the way Helen Sorby was staring at him. "What's the matter now?"

"You can read that?"

Kachigan clenched his teeth, hoping the jerk of dismay that went through him hadn't shown on his face. He'd trained himself while he was a patrolman not to speak or read the language of his childhood—easy enough to do on the South Side, with its lack of Armenian neighborhoods. But he'd forgotten that no Irish boy would have grown up knowing enough Russian words to read a headline. He kept his eyes trained on the photo, as if he'd only half-heard Helen's question, while he considered what to do.

"Miss Sorby, I grew up in a town where the only candy store was owned by Russians," he said at last. "I can't speak the language, but I learned all the letters." He pointed at the headline below the photo. "Look, *veh* is their 'w,' *oh* is 'o,' *beh* is 'b.' It's a transliteration of the word 'Wobbly.' ''

"Oh." She eyed him oddly for a moment, then appeared to accept the explanation. "Can you tell if it says anything about Lide in there? My friends only translated the headline for me."

Kachigan scanned the rest of the article, then shook his head. "I don't see her name spelled anywhere. I think it's just a description of the IWW congress and manifesto." He eyed the photograph again. "Is that Josef Janczek beside Lide?"

Helen cleared her throat. "Um—apparently not. Oksana Petrenko says Josef wasn't so tall."

"Is that right?" Kachigan glanced up and saw a coppery hint of color beneath the social worker's olive skin. His scrutiny seemed to deepen it, so he looked at the clipping again. "Did the Janczeks believe in free love as well as socialist government?"

"Oksana thinks so." Helen described the early morning departure of visitors that the Ukrainian girl had witnessed. "But I think those were more likely to be fellow steel workers coming to see Josef than—than visitors of Lide's. Don't you?"

"Much more likely," Kachigan agreed. "With the steel company police patrolling all the bars and social clubs, any men who want to unionize would have to meet at home. If the neighbors think they're coming over to sleep with each other's wives, that makes them all the safer."

He became aware the moment after he said it that he'd spoken far too frankly, but Helen didn't look disturbed. "I told you it implicated Bernard K. Flinn," she said triumphantly.

"Yes."

Silence fell between them, thoughtful and easy. The distant whistle of a coal barge drifted through it, blown by the wind up from the Monongahela River.

"We can't assume Flinn was the only one who might have wanted to kill the Janczeks," Kachigan said, after a moment. "We haven't ruled out the landlord, either. Your friend Irene thought she heard him arguing with Josef that night."

"But why would he have wanted to burn his own property?"

"I've had three land agents come by and offer to buy the property from me just this morning. I had to show one of them my badge to convince him I really wasn't the owner. Demand for tenement housing is so high that the land is worth more now than it was with the old row houses on it."

"Hmm." Helen eyed the dark brick spires of St. Witold's Church, looming behind them. "One of the women I talked to this morning told me that the church wanted to buy the land, too."

Kachigan turned to eye the small rectory on the far side of the sunken basement. Like the adjacent houses, its bricks were blackened on one side from proximity to the fire, marring its tidy appearance. "It does look like they could use a bigger priests' house. But I doubt they would resort to arson to get it."

"My cousin Gillan would have, if he was the priest here," Helen said candidly. "Although only if the building was vacant, and he couldn't get the owner drunk enough to donate it to him. But he served down at St. Peter's, and anyway he's retired now. Do you think we should talk to the priests at St. Witold's?"

He had no difficulty following her logic, since it was much the same as his own. "To see if they ever tried to buy this place from the landlord? It's worth a try. They might at least know his name.''

''Yes, that's what I thought.'' Helen drummed her fingers on her muff while she waited for Kachigan to finish folding her sketch and the news clipping. He tucked both papers into his waistcoat pocket, then looked questioningly at her.

''Surely you're not waiting for me to walk you home?''

She made an impatient noise. ''No, of course not. I'm waiting for you to walk me to St. Witold's, so I can help interview the priest. The morning Masses should be over by now.''

''I don't think—''

''If you don't let me come with you now, I'll just have to come back later without you.''

Kachigan studied her determined scowl. ''You would, wouldn't you?''

''After dark, too,'' she added tartly.

''In that case—'' He held out his arm to her. Helen brushed a bit of charcoal from his sleeve before taking it, then glanced up at him inquiringly.

''Have you had breakfast, Mr. Kachigan?''

The unexpected question made him blink. ''Yes, of course.''

''How long ago was that?''

''About six o'clock this morning. Why?''

She used her free hand to pull the brown paper bag out of her muff again, then shook it open to show him the cookies inside. ''Your stomach's growling. Eat some biscotti.''

Kachigan laughed and reached for one of the small biscuits. They rounded the corner of Fifteenth Street and began walking toward the main entrance of St. Witold's. ''Do you always carry rations for starving detectives, ma'am?''

''No, but I seem to get cookies forced on me wherever I go. I have some *ruiskatut*, too, not to mention jam and tea.''

''*Semper paratus*?''

She threw him a skeptical look. ''I find it hard to believe you were ever a Boy Scout, Mr. Kachigan.''

''No,'' he admitted. ''By the time they started a troop in Monessen, I was already—'' With an effort, Kachigan caught himself from saying ''working in the mills.'' After the mistake he'd already made with the Russian headline, that was all he'd need to make Helen Sorby suspicious. Poor boys from mill families rarely became policemen. "Too old," he finished, taking another biscuit to cover his hesitation. "Was Thomas?"

"A Boy Scout, you mean? Of course. Where do you think he learned to make his first maps?" Helen eyed the detective curiously while they started up the wide stone stairs to St. Witold's doors. "You'd better swallow that cookie fast, Mr. Kachigan. You know the only thing you're allowed to eat in church is the Communion wafer, and that's only because it tastes like wet newspaper."

He turned his startled cough into a half-genuine snort of laughter. "You're going to have to do penance for that, Miss Sorby," he retorted. Fortunately, his Armenian Orthodox rituals were close enough to Roman Catholic to guide him. "Two 'Our Fathers' and two 'Hail Marys.' " Kachigan swung open the brass-handled front door. "After you, ma'am."

Helen frowned at him, but since there was only one door and he was already holding it open, she had no choice but to go through. He followed her inside, scrubbing cookie crumbs off his chin with the back of one hand.

St. Witold's was a surprisingly large and modern church, given the small working-class Polish neighborhood it served. It shared the Monongahela floodplain with the other Polish parishes of St. Casimir's and St. Adelbert's, and also with St. Peter's, the Irish patriarch of the South Side's Catholic churches. St. Witold's stained glass windows were plain but clean of soot, and if its pews lacked the velvet kneelers of richer parishes, they were still polished to a high gloss.

Helen dipped two fingers in the holy water font beside the door and crossed herself, and Kachigan carefully followed her example. A few older women in babushkas were reciting a rosary near the altar, while a white-haired janitor cleaned the votive candle stands in the side alcove. There was no sign of a priest.

"There should be an office somewhere around here," Helen said to Kachigan. "To take care of parish business."

He'd already spotted the hall that led past the altar at the far end of the church. It was shadowed with bluish electric light, not the warm glow of gas that illuminated the sanctuary itself. Helen nodded when he pointed the hall out to her, and led him briskly toward it. Small bronze Stations of the Cross gleamed down at them from the roughly plastered wall, reminding Kachigan a little of the icons he'd grown up with.

A low-pitched muttering met them at the entrance to the hall, resolving into two Polish-speaking voices as they approached the open door at the far end. One of the priests had a more guttural accent than the other, Kachigan noticed. Helen wrinkled her nose in distaste when she heard it, as if she recognized the voice, then reached out to knock at the office door.

Inside, two black-robed men looked up from the ledger they were discussing, and two sets of blue eyes narrowed. But while the older priest's face had crinkled with a smile of welcome, it was impatience and hostility that slitted the younger man's gaze.

"Father, if we could interrupt you for a few minutes," Kachigan said, addressing himself respectfully to the older priest. "I'm Detective Milo Kachigan, from the Pittsburgh police. I'd like to ask you a few questions."

The older man's smile faded, and he glanced up at his colleague, saying something in soft, worried Polish. The younger priest shook his head, his reply both curt and guttural.

"Father Taddeusz doesn't speak English," he said to them in that language, when he was finished answering the older priest. "I can translate for you, if it's really necessary."

The critical note in his voice said he didn't think it was. Kachigan swallowed the edged reply he wanted to make.

"You can probably answer my questions just as well, Father," he said instead. It was hard to use the polite term to a man so much younger than he was, and so arrogant with youthful certainty. "If you don't mind."

The priest made an impatient noise. "What I mind is being interrupted in the middle of parish work," he said shortly. "The sooner you ask your questions, the sooner you can be gone."

Kachigan's arm must have stiffened with the force of his

restraint. He felt Helen's gloved fingers tighten on it warn-ingly, and gave her a brief, reassuring glance. She released him readily enough when he reached for the notebook in his waistcoat pocket, but her face wore a graver look than usual.

"If I could get your name for my report—"

"Father Karl Zawisza."

"Thank you." He wrote it down. "I'm investigating the fire at fourteen-oh-seven Breed Street. Has your church had any dealings with the owner of that property?"

Zawisza's pale eyebrows rose in a look more arrogant than surprised. "Why should we? He's not a member of our par-ish."

"You never looked into buying the property from him?"

Genuine indignation glittered in the priest's ice-blue eyes. "We're in the business of saving souls, Mr. Kachigan, not gouging laborers for run-down housing!"

Kachigan gave him a sharp look. "I thought you might want the land so you could expand your own rectory."

"Not as long as I'm assigned here." Zawisza thumped one hand on the ledger in front of him. "We barely have enough money to pay our own coal and gas bills, much less aid parishioners who need our help during strikes and layoffs at the mills. The last thing we're going to waste money on is our own comfort!"

Kachigan didn't doubt that. Metal-hard conviction grated in Karl Zawisza's voice, the kind of conviction that turned men into saints or political exiles. If this had been a medieval monastery instead of a twentieth-century parish, the young priest would be wearing a hair shirt and sleeping in a bare-rock cell.

Helen cleared her throat to break the silence. "Perhaps Father Taddeusz knows the name of the man who owns those row houses. He's been here longer than you have, I believe."

The young priest gave her an unfriendly look, but trans-lated the question for the older man without comment. Father Taddeusz shook his head, then added a long, explanatory murmur of Polish. Kachigan waited for Zawisza to translate it.

"Father Taddeusz says the building originally belonged to a brewery owner in Allegheny, but it's passed hands several times since then. He doesn't know who owns it now."

Kachigan nodded politely at the older man. "Thank him for us," he told Zawisza, putting his notebook and pencil away. "If he remembers anything about the landlord, I'd appreciate it if you'd let me know."

Zawisza frowned at him. "I hope at some point you'll get that rubble cleaned up. It's a hazard to the children who come to our catechism classes here."

"Precisely why we'd like to find the landlord, Father," Kachigan said drily.

He didn't wait for the priest's response, turning to offer his arm to Helen instead. She took it with such alacrity that he guessed she was as irritated by Zawisza as he was. Her long, frustrated strides through the church proved it.

"That man *annoys* me," she informed Kachigan, before the door of St. Witold's had even swung shut behind them. "He thinks his priorities are the only ones the world should care about! I have *no* idea why he ever became a priest."

Kachigan lifted an eyebrow at this vehemence. "You know him? Let me guess, he's a member of your temperance league."

"Yes." She eyed him warily. "And now I suppose you want me to tell you everything I know about him."

"I let you come along while I interviewed him."

"True." She glanced down at the watch pinned to the lapel of her coat, frowning. "Can you walk me down to Sidney Street while I do it? I have a class to teach at the settlement house."

"Gladly." Kachigan swung north on Fifteenth with her, heading downhill toward the river. Ahead of them, the lunchtime squeals and shrieks of the children playing at the Birmingham Public School rang halfway down the block. "A civics class to help immigrants pass their citizenship tests?"

"No, a gymnasium class for women who work in department stores and candy factories. They take it on their lunch hour." Helen pushed up her loose coat sleeve and tightened her fist, showing him the respectable clench of muscle under her plain muslin sleeve. "We swing wands and lift dumbbells, then do running and dance steps to loosen the cramps in their muscles."

"And after all that, they go back to work?"

"Of course. It's a well-known fact, Mr. Kachigan, that exercise and a light dinner gives you more energy for the afternoon than a heavy meal and a nap."

"Not if you're an iron puddler," Kachigan retorted.

"Iron puddlers don't spend ten hours a day in a chair, hunched over a bowl of melted chocolate. Don't think that these young women have an easy job to do, just because they don't stand in front of an open furnace!"

He opened his mouth to disagree with her, then forced himself to close it again. "You're *much* too easy to argue with, Miss Sorby," he said after a moment. "Do you think you could manage to just tell me what you know about Karl Zawisza?"

"Very well." Helen paused for a moment to gather her thoughts. "You've already heard what Father Zawisza's main concerns are—working conditions and the lack of job security for workers in the mills. He was a socialist long before he joined our group. He leads a lot of the discussions at our Thursday night meetings and he was our delegate to the IWW convention in Chicago. He helped Father Thomas Haggerty draft the manifesto. It's quite well-written," she added grudgingly.

Something in her tone made Kachigan look at her closely. "But you don't agree with it?" he asked, over the clatter of the trolleys on East Carson Street.

"Not entirely," she admitted. "It seems to me that economic reform has to involve more than just unionizing mines and factories. You can't dictate policy—" She broke off, looking startled, when he tapped her on the shoulder. "I'm sorry, Mr. Kachigan, was I being too easy to argue with again?"

"No, but you were pontificating when you should have been watching the street." Friday at noon put some of the busiest traffic on East Carson Street. Kachigan craned his head, watching for a break they could dart through. "You're about to get a head start on your gymnasium class, Miss Sorby," he warned. "Right after that trolley and before the ice wagon—*run!*"

8

"ONE MORE DEEP BREATH——"

The bell of St. Paul's Lutheran church rang across the street, signaling the end of Helen's gymnasium routine more effectively than any order she could have given. The candy factory girls in the class dashed out, snatching up their aprons and caps as they went. The department store girls scattered more slowly. With half an hour still left of their lunch breaks, they could afford to change out of their gymnasium skirts and blouses at the settlement house. It gave them a chance to gossip and trade handkerchiefs soaked in the newest perfumes from New York.

Helen stayed behind while they climbed the stairs to the washroom. She preferred to wait until after all the corsets had been laced, all the hair piled into loose Gibson Girl knots, and all the fashionable day-gowns hooked on and critiqued before she ventured in to wash and put on her less magnificent clothes. To pass the time, she tidied up the stacks of wands and carried the dumbbells back to their racks, leaving the big room clear except for the clean scent of beeswax from the hardwood floor and the pervasive tang of sweat. It amused her to think that at least some of the latter smell had been made by the exquisitely perfumed young women who would soon come sweeping down the stairs in ruffles of taffeta and waterfalls of lace.

"Miss Sorby, may I have a word with you?"

The sound of that voice, deep and graciously soft, swung Helen toward the main hall. "Is something wrong, Miss Brown?"

"Not wrong, my dear." The settlement house director paused to nod a greeting to Helen's departing students, most of whom bobbed a curtsey in reply. Julia Regitz Brown inspired that kind of respect in people. She was a generously proportioned woman, so erect in her carriage and forthright in her stride that her weight seemed entirely in proportion to her presence. Unlike most of the wealthy social activists Helen met, she never spoke a word more than she needed to. This time, as usual, she wasted no time on preliminary explanations.

"Yesterday, Miss Sorby, a police detective from the local patrol station called on me. He asked me to inform him of Miss Irene Prandtl's whereabouts, if I ever came to know of them."

Helen took a quick breath, guessing where this was going to lead. "And have you come to know of them, ma'am?"

"In a way." Julia Regitz Brown paused again, as she often did between sentences. Helen sometimes suspected that she was considering her next words and throwing out all the ones she didn't really need to say. "But I believe Miss Prandtl might not wish to be associated with the police right now."

Helen winced at the careful wording. Milo Kachigan must have been right in his guess about Daniel Mahaffey's connections with local hoodlums. "Do you think you could arrange for Irene to ring me up, ma'am, or to meet me in some public place? I believe I know what questions the police want to ask her."

She'd expected that statement to elicit a startled look from Julia Regitz Brown, but she was wrong. "I thought you might, my dear," her employer said calmly. "Would you follow me?"

Helen pushed her damp hair from her face and trailed the older woman out of the gymnasium. "Miss Brown, you didn't happen to see Detective Kachigan walking me to class today, did you?"

Julia Regitz Brown gave her a glimmer of smile. "You'd make a good detective yourself, Miss Sorby." She paused in front of her closed office door. "Please, go in."

Helen gave her a puzzled look, but pushed the door open. Inside, a scatter of belongings lay spread across a familiar tattered quilt. Kneeling beside them, in a burnished-gold walking dress as stylish as any the department store girls had been wearing, was Irene Prandtl.

"Irene!" Helen took two long strides into the room, barely aware of Julia Regitz Brown stepping back and closing the office door behind her. "Where have you been? Are you all right?"

"I'm fine, Helen." Irene's smile was calm. "I hope you weren't worried when our friends fetched us away yesterday."

Helen made a rude noise. "Well, of course, I was! You could at least have left a note to tell me where you'd gone."

"Yes, I know, but they were in such a hurry . . ." Irene let the words trail into a shrug, a vagueness that was unlike her.

"Why didn't you ring me and tell me afterwards?"

"Helen," Irene said reproachfully, "you know only well-paid professionals like your brother can afford a telephone in their home. I don't think our friends even *know* anyone who owns one."

Helen thought about pointing out that most telegraph stations had public telephones, but decided it wasn't worth arguing about. It didn't really matter where Irene was staying, since she had no intention of giving her address to Kachigan.

"Why did you come back here?" Helen glanced down at the assortment of books, household items and old clothes on the quilt. "Did you forget to take these with you when you left before?"

"No. I brought them back just now, to give away." Irene picked up a battered alarm clock, giving its handle a quick turn to make sure it worked before she set it on the carefully mended sleeve of a folded nightgown. "I thought Miss Brown would know best who needed them."

Helen scowled. "Yes, I'm sure she will—but, Irene, how can you afford to give these things away?" She'd recognized the nightgown as the one her friend had been wearing the night of the fire. "Aren't these the only things you had left?"

"Not anymore." This time, Irene's smile had a sudden mischievous glint, as if her good fortune had been gained at some unwary capitalist's expense. "I have a sponsor now."

"A *sponsor*?" Helen remembered the money her aunt had gathered up the night before. "Do you mean my Aunt McGregor? But how on earth did she get the money she collected to you?"

"This money's not from your aunt." Irene added a man's battered shaving mug and brush to her neat pile. "It's from someone who wants to help us get a fresh start in a new place."

"Who?" Helen asked bluntly.

"A man who runs an industrial welfare society." Irene never hesitated when she lied, but her German accent always deepened revealingly. "We're going to use the rest of the money to move to Chicago. Daniel will have a better chance to find a job there, and I can work with all the leading socialists in the country. We leave on the first train tomorrow."

The ticking alarm clock measured off a length of silence after that remark. Irene continued to sort through her belongings, carefully avoiding Helen's intense scrutiny. She had caught her lower lip under her teeth, as if she were steeling herself for another round of lies.

Helen sighed and squatted beside the quilt, twining her fingers in the ragged threads that trailed from one worn edge. She was walking a rock-sharp edge between ruining a friendship and betraying whatever trust Milo Kachigan still had in her. If she couldn't find a question that would break through Irene's defensiveness, she might end up doing both at once.

"Irene, do you really want the person who killed Lide and Josef Janczek to get away unpunished?"

Her friend looked up, indignation kindling in her face. "No! I want him caught! Why do you think I waited for an hour in the rain, just to make sure the police knew it was arson? Not because I cared about that ant-infested house!"

"Then before you leave for Chicago, will you please tell me who your landlord was?"

Gloved fingers tightened hard on the tarnished silver hairbrush they held, but for a long moment Irene Prandtl made no other response. Helen didn't push her. She knew her friend well enough to recognize the struggle between ethics and personal loyalty that was deepening the lines around her mouth.

"I don't *know* his name," Irene said at last, her voice so edged with annoyance that it sounded like the truth. "Daniel never told me, or let me go with him to pay the rent. He said it was because they wouldn't let me into the A.O.H."

Knowing how hostile working-class Irish bars could be toward other immigrants, Helen didn't doubt that. At the same time she didn't think it was the real cause of Daniel Mahaffey's reluctance. "So you don't have any idea who the man is?"

"No. All I've ever seen of him is his house."

"Does he live somewhere on the South Side?"

Irene shook her head. "No. You see, Daniel is afraid to leave me alone in—in the place we're staying. So he took me with him to the East End yesterday night." She saw Helen's puzzled look. "That's where we got our sponsorship money."

"Your *landlord* gave you the money to move to Chicago?"

Irene nodded, her face relaxing out of its worried lines now that she'd told the truth. "Daniel said it was because he felt guilty about the fire. I didn't go into the house with him, so I don't know if that's true." She paused. "But I think it was the landlord who suggested that we move to Chicago. Daniel hadn't said anything about that to me before he went in."

Helen frowned again. "I can think of other reasons for sending you to Chicago, besides charity. I don't suppose you remember the address of his house?"

"No. I think it was on Amberson Avenue, but it was dark by the time we got there. I couldn't see the numbers on the gate."

The quilt threads wound around Helen's fingers pulled so tight that they snapped free. "*Damn.*" She didn't use profanity often, but when she did she put all her half-Italian temper into it. Her friend eyed her in concern.

"Is it really that important, Helen?"

"Yes." She paused, then decided to repay honesty with

honesty. "I've been helping the police detective who's looking into the Janczek murders. We can't find anyone who knows the man who owned your row house, Irene. Not at the tax office, not at the local insurance agencies, not even at the church next door. No honest man should be that hard to track down."

"No."

The clock's brass hands ticked out another space of silence in the sunlit office. Irene broke it this time, tossing the hairbrush into her discard pile with a decisive clatter.

"Daniel is going to see him again tonight," she said, in her usual calm way. "To pick up the train tickets he bought us."

"The landlord is buying them himself?" Helen asked, then answered her own question. "So no one can trace you."

"Yes." Irene gave her a measuring look across the quilt. "If I tell you where and when the meeting is, will you make your detective promise not to interfere until after Daniel leaves?"

"Yes," Helen said promptly. She'd figure out a way to explain it to Milo Kachigan later.

"Then be at the A.O.H. just before ten o'clock tonight. And try to make sure Daniel doesn't recognize you," she added. "Otherwise, I'll hear about it all the way to Chicago."

Helen frowned at her. "How am I supposed to do that?"

"You could try dressing up for once." Irene gave her a sidelong, amused look. "Daniel would never expect to see you in an evening gown. You do own one, don't you?"

"Of course I do." It was three years old and an inch tighter in the waist than Helen liked to lace herself, but it was still an evening gown. "But what am I supposed to do about Detective Kachigan? Put a paper bag over his head?"

Irene frowned at her. "You never said you were going to take the policeman with you. Can't you just go by yourself?"

"Not unless I want to start a fight between a dozen drunken teamsters over who gets to dance with me first!"

"Then take Thomas with you," her friend suggested. "Even if Daniel does recognize you, he'll just think your brother took you out for an evening drink."

"That might work." Helen threaded her fingers through the ragged knot she'd made of the quilt fringe, thinking it over. "I suppose I could make a sketch of the landlord, and show it to Kachigan later." Which might make him a little less annoyed at her than he was going to be, she reflected wryly. But probably not much.

"So you'll do it?" Irene held out her hand. "You promise?"

Helen reached out to clasp the nervous gloved fingers in hers. "I promise." She returned her friend's smile. "And I should probably thank you on Thomas's behalf. He's going to love the idea of taking his temperance-worker sister out for a drink."

"I'm not going to the A.O.H. with you, and that's final!"

Helen gave her brother an exasperated look, somewhat diluted by the tarnished silvering of her parents' dresser mirror. By unspoken consent, she and Thomas had left the room untouched, as if the familiar smoky smell of their father's work clothes and cedar-dark fragrance of their mother's dresses could span the gaping hole that typhoid fever had left in their lives. One of the advantages of being a twin, Helen often thought, was that you only needed to argue about the unimportant things in life.

The room was far from sacrosanct, however. Thomas still borrowed their father's tie whenever he needed to dress up, just as he always had, and Helen wore the gloves and modest jewelry that her mother had loved to share. She was rummaging around the top drawer now for the small garnet earrings that matched her one good evening dress. Even though they were a recent Christmas gift from Thomas, she kept them here with the rest of the finery.

"I don't see what the problem is," she said over her shoulder. "You go there every other night, don't you?"

"Every night but Friday night." It was hard to tell in the mirror's blurred reflection, but she thought Thomas was frowning at her. "Friday night, that place is a riot waiting to happen. And I can't think of anyone more likely to set it off than you!"

"Well, we can't wait and go later." Helen scrabbled the

earrings out from under a pearl choker. "The landlord's coming tonight and it's our only chance to find out who he is."

"Can't I just go by myself?"

"Do you have any idea what Daniel Mahaffey looks like?"

"No, but Milo Kachigan knows him, doesn't he?"

This time, it was Helen's turn to frown. "I promised Irene he wouldn't be there." She kept her gaze carefully fixed on her ear lobes as she clipped the garnet earrings to them. "She doesn't want Daniel to get arrested."

Thomas grunted. "And you think Kachigan would arrest him just because he saw money passing under the table? He'd have jailed half his own police force by now, if that were true."

Helen sighed and opened her mother's tortoise-shell box of dusting powder. It smelled of roses and jasmine. "Thomas, be reasonable," she said, abandoning her initial argument for the truth. "You know I'll never get into the A.O.H. if you're not there to vouch for me." She pointed at the mirror, scattering rice powder across her olive-skinned reflection. "The bouncer would take one look and kick me down the street to the Christopher Columbus Club, and that's if I'm lucky. If not—"

The chime of the doorbell interrupted her diatribe, giving Thomas the excuse he needed to scuttle away. To Helen's annoyance, he was laughing as he went. "You can curse at them, if they try to throw you out," he retorted, once he was safely out of range of her dusting powder. "They'll know you're Irish the minute they hear how loud you can yell."

Unfortunately, Helen couldn't think of anything to say in return to that. She gritted her teeth instead and began the final and most annoying part of getting dressed up: pinning her thick and uncooperative hair up into a smooth coronet. It was the closest she was willing to come to a Gibson Girl hairstyle.

The sound of men's voices in the hall below didn't catch her attention at first. Thomas had a handful of friends among the Sanborn surveyors who tended to drop in without notice, any time they were taking the train through Pittsburgh. If she was lucky, the presence of one or two reinforcements might even convince her brother to venture into the A.O.H. with her tonight. After a moment, however, she caught the sound of her own name being spoken in the respectful tone Thomas used when he was handing over a problem to higher authority. That raised her suspicions, and the voice that answered Thomas confirmed them. It was Milo Kachigan.

"Thomas, you—you *anguilla*!" Helen jammed one last pin in to anchor the weight of her hair, then hauled up her trailing skirts and strode out to the stairs. Two faces below turned up when she leaned over the bannister: Kachigan's wary but appreciative of the picture she made and her twin's frankly relieved. Helen's forehead creased in an even deeper scowl. She felt some dusting powder fall onto her nose.

"Thomas, did you ring up Mr. Kachigan?"

"Yes, I did." By rights, her twin should have withered under her look, but he didn't even squirm. "Helen, be reasonable! You can't go chasing off after a murder suspect all by yourself, just because your anarchist friends don't want to be seen by the police."

"*Thomas!*"

"Don't yell at your brother, Miss Sorby," Kachigan advised. "He's saved one of your anarchist friends from getting arrested."

"What do you mean?"

"I had just found out where Daniel Mahaffey is staying when Mr. Sorby's call came in," the detective said calmly. "In another few minutes, I would have sent a squad of men to take him in for questioning. This saves me—and him—the trouble."

Helen came downstairs, still frowning. "Are you going to arrest Daniel if we see him at the A.O.H. tonight?"

"Not if he leads us to the man who owned the row houses." Kachigan gave Helen a long, appraising gaze, from the trailing hem of her wine-colored skirt to her high-necked bodice of black lace. "Exactly how were you planning to identify the landlord without me there to question him, Miss Sorby? Ask him to dance, and then rifle his pockets for personal papers?"

"I was going to draw a picture of him for you," Helen

said defensively. "Ask Thomas! He was going to bring his map book along for me to draw in."

Kachigan glanced around, but her traitorous twin had already disappeared behind the swinging kitchen door. "I'll have to take your word for that." The detective's gaze came back to her. "Did it ever occur to you that you might not have enough time to draw the landlord's portrait? If the reason he arranged to meet Daniel Mahaffey tonight was to silence him—"

"But since Daniel and Lide are leaving for Chicago—" Helen broke off, remembering too late that this was information she hadn't shared with Thomas, and so the detective couldn't know it. Kachigan's scowl drew his eyebrows into a solid line across his forehead.

"Leaving?" he said ominously. "The main witnesses in my murder case are leaving town and you didn't tell me about it?"

She felt her face tighten with embarrassment, but refused to let her gaze drop. "I'm sorry, Mr. Kachigan. I couldn't. I had to promise Irene not to tell you anything, in order to find out about Daniel's meeting with the landlord. And since I knew I couldn't bring you to the A.O.H. anyway—"

"Why?" he snapped. "Because you didn't trust me not to arrest Mahaffey on the spot?"

"Because neither of us looks Irish enough to get in!"

She clapped her hands over her mouth as if to catch back her exasperated shout, but it was too late. Kachigan froze, an unreadable blankness in his eyes. After a moment, however, a rueful smile eased the muscles of his thin face.

"Miss Sorby, do you have any idea how many off-duty policemen from Patrol Station Seven go drinking at the A.O.H.?"

"Many of them?"

"All of them," Kachigan said flatly. "Except for one Italian boy who's too smart to spend his money getting drunk. Any one of them could vouch for me."

She frowned. "Who's going to vouch for me?"

"No one."

Helen's frown deepened. She could guess where this discussion was leading. "Does that mean I'm not allowed to go with you?"

Kachigan surprised her by shaking his head. "I won't lie and say I'm not tempted to leave you here. A club like the A.O.H. is a bad place to take a lady on a Friday night. But your idea of drawing a picture of the landlord is so good, I'm not going to turn the offer down." He turned to scan the coat pegs. "Do you have a fancy coat to wear over all that finery?"

"No, just my everyday one. You still haven't explained how I'm going to get into the A.O.H. with you, Mr. Kachigan."

"That's the easy part." The detective retrieved her coat from the wall rack, holding it out to her politely. "Not to be vulgar, Miss Sorby, but all we have to do is have you take off your coat and show off that very nice waist of yours. If the bouncers are as young and drunk as they usually are, that will make you Irish on the spot."

9

KACHIGAN PAUSED AT THE CORNER OF SARAH Street and Twenty-first, waiting for a cab to rattle through the gold and amber glow of the A.O.H. club's new electric sign. There hadn't been time for much conversation in the half-block of walking that had brought them here from Helen Sorby's front door, but it seemed to Kachigan that his companion had been uncharacteristically silent. He wondered if she'd noticed how much of a chill she'd sent through him with her innocent comment about not looking Irish.

The side door of the A.O.H. opened, letting out a burst of fiddle and banjo music along with a staggering drunk. He vanished into the adjoining alley, retching as he went. Kachigan saw Helen's eyes widen. "Still want to come with me?"

"Yes." Her mouth firmed into a familiar determined line. "Is it time to take off my coat for the bouncers now?"

He frowned, feeling the cold bite of evening wind and remembering how thin the lace of her bodice was. "Maybe you could just unbutton it."

She did so, then let the worn wool coat slide down her shoulders in a surprisingly seductive gesture. "How's that?"

In answer, Kachigan took her arm and led her across the street, skirting another cab that had stopped to discharge its Friday night revelers. He paused to let the two young couples enter the club ahead of them, then followed them into the smoky darkness, reaching for his detective's badge and steeling his face to show none of the apprehension he felt. It was one thing to enter the A.O.H. shielded by the same blue police uniform as a dozen fellow officers. To invade it dressed in his best civilian clothes, escorting a lady in taffeta and black lace, was a little more intimidating than he'd expected. He took a deep breath, then stepped forward to face the man guarding the door.

"Good evening to you, Milo my boy."

Kachigan met the bouncer's laughing eyes and let his breath out in a sigh that was half annoyance and half relief. "Ramey," he said and put the unneeded badge back in his coat pocket. "Moonlighting again, eh? Another baby on the way?"

Frank Ramey shook his head. "Down payment on a house." He slid an amused gaze toward Helen Sorby and Kachigan suppressed a wince. The coffee room would be humming with gossip again tomorrow. "You're young Tom Sorby's sister, aren't you, miss? And here I thought your brother told me you'd taken the pledge."

Helen's smile might not appear often, Kachigan decided, but it was worth waiting for. Too bad he wasn't the recipient this time. "I have. I've come to convince everyone here to take it too."

The patrolman whistled in astonishment. "Really? Then you better borrow my nightstick, Milo, my boy. Or buy yourself a mug of beer big enough to crack heads with."

"No point in that, since Miss Sorby wouldn't let me drink it," Kachigan retorted. "How about putting us in a nice dark corner instead, where we won't meet anyone to preach to?"

"Good idea." Ramey lifted two fingers to his mouth and whistled again, this time shrill enough to carry through the din of music and raucous laughter. A bald head turned near the bar, and a moment later an unsmiling man with the mashed ears of a former boxer came to meet them. "Take Detective Kachigan and Miss Sorby to the table in the back corner," the patrolman told him.

"There's people already sitting at it."

Ramey snorted. "Well, kick them out, lunkhead. And if anyone asks why, tell them this gentleman's the new detective at Patrol Station Seven, here to check up on our liquor license.''

''All right.'' The older man gave Kachigan a hostile look, but led them without protest into the noise and smoke of the club. A few turned heads and mutters followed them around the edges of the crowded dance floor. Kachigan felt Helen's gloved fingers tense around his arm, but the band was playing too lustily for most club members to be distracted. Only one young steelworker, waiting at the bar for his mug of ale to be refilled, said something loud and insulting. Before Kachigan could do more than frown at him, the waitress behind the bar thumped him across the knuckles with his overfilled mug, and the ensuing splash of ale kept him occupied until they'd reached the back corner.

The bald man chased a party of giggling shopgirls away from the corner table and into the arms of the railroad men they'd been flirting with. With them banished to the dance floor, a relative quiet settled on the dark corner. Most of the Irish social club was visible from here, Kachigan saw, although sometimes only in brief flashes between spinning couples on the floor. He hung his overcoat over the back of his chair, then noticed Helen struggling with the sleeves of her coat and went to help her slip it off. She gave him a quelling look through the drifting smoke, half defiant and half embarrassed.

''I don't usually wear this dress,'' she said, sounding a little breathless.

Kachigan's gaze slid down to the waist of her skirt, seeing how tightly it curved beneath the drape of her elegant black lace bodice. He repressed a smile, pulling out a chair for her with the polite American manners his sister had drummed into him.

''I wouldn't have thought you were a slave to fashion, Miss Sorby.''

''I'm not.'' She made a face when she sat, as if something pinched. ''I'm just fatter than I was three years ago, when Aunt Pittypat bought me this dress. If she hadn't paid such a ridiculous amount of money for it, I would throw it away. Do you know how annoying it is not to be able to take a deep breath?''

He grinned at her unfashionable frankness. There were advantages to taking a radical socialist out for an evening on the town. "As a matter of fact, I do. I cracked a couple of ribs last year, chasing a burglar across a roof. I couldn't yawn for a month." He paused. "Does this mean I can't ask you to dance?"

That got him a scowl instead of the smile he was fishing for. "We didn't come here to dance. Have you seen Daniel Mahaffey yet?"

"No." Kachigan took out his pocket watch and squinted at it. "But there's still twelve minutes left before ten o'clock. Have you had supper yet tonight, Miss Sorby?"

"Of course not," she said in exasperation. "Do you think I could have laced myself into this dress if I had?"

"Well, seeing that you're already in it, could you share a skillet of bubble-and-squeak with me?"

"Maybe," Helen said dubiously. "What's bubble-and-squeak?"

"You don't know?" Years of eating cheap Irish dinners on patrol gave him the confidence to tease her. "What if I told you it was boiled tripe and cod cheeks?"

That got him the smile he wanted, and this time the dancing light in her eyes was all for him. "Then I'd let you eat it."

"Don't worry. It's only fried cabbage and potatoes." He sat back as the barmaid came to slap two foaming amber glasses on the wooden table, making new wet rings on top of all the old ones. "We'll have a skillet of bubble-and-squeak, please." He saw the disgusted look Helen was giving the beer and added in amusement, "And some hot tea for Miss Sorby."

The barmaid laughed and winked at Helen. "There, and I knew you had to be Tom Sorby's sister," she said, making a token dab at the table with her towel. "That's why I told Magill to sneck up about you. How much bread you want with that skillet, loves?"

"A whole loaf." Kachigan fished up an appropriate number of nickels. "I haven't eaten since lunchtime."

"Then I'll get the bubble-and-squeak right up. The pot of tea might take a bit of waiting on, I'll warn you. It's not something we get much call for.'' She snapped her towel expertly at a young man reaching to pinch her from behind, making him laugh and stagger back onto the dance floor. ''And don't worry about the beer—Ramey says to tell you it's on him.''

''Thanks,'' Kachigan said drily. He should have known the patrolman's sense of humor would prompt him to send over two mugs after seeing Helen. ''I'm sure I can find someone here who'll drink it.''

The barmaid chortled and disappeared into the crowd, leaving Kachigan to notice that Helen Sorby's sober frown had shifted to him. He sighed and scrubbed at his cheekbone. The screeching fiddles and thumping drum seemed to reverberate off the metal shard inside it, deepening its normal ache.

''Now what's the matter, Miss Sorby?'' he asked. ''Should I not have ordered you tea?''

''Tea will be fine. Mr. Kachigan, all I remember you having for lunch were my biscotti. Did you eat again after that?''

It took him a moment to remember. ''No. I had a one o'clock appointment to pick up photographic plates at the coroner's office in Pittsburgh. Why?''

She gave him an exasperated look. ''Just because you're on a murder investigation doesn't mean you should go for hours and hours without eating. It's not healthy.''

Kachigan grunted, scanning the club again now that his eyes had adjusted to the dimness. There was still no sign of Daniel Mahaffey. ''You sound just like my father,'' he said absently.

''Well, maybe you should listen to us.'' Helen paused, waiting for his attention to return to her. ''Are you going to drink that beer, Mr. Kachigan?''

''Not while I'm on duty.''

''Good.'' She pushed both glasses aside, then used the edge of one glove to scrub a much drier spot on the table than the barmaid had managed to create. ''Can I borrow your notebook and pencil? I want to try an experiment while we're waiting.''

He fished out his evidence book and pencil stub for her,

curious. "What kind of experiment, Miss Sorby?"

"A drawing experiment." She paged through the book to an unused spot, then pressed it flat against the dry area in front of her. "It's something I've read about in the New York newspapers, but never seen done in Pittsburgh. Can you describe a person you know, but whom I can't ever have seen?"

Kachigan glanced up when a cold stir of air told him the front door had opened, but it was just another young couple coming in to join the mob at the bar. "You want to try drawing someone you don't know? To see if it's a recognizable picture?"

"Yes."

"So you can make a drawing of Josef Janczek," he guessed. The idea had occurred to him almost as soon as she'd asked her first question. Unfortunately, so had the obstacles to it. "Who are you going to get to describe him?"

Helen spun the pencil stub in a nervous circle between her fingers. "If I get a chance to talk to Daniel tonight—"

"While I ask the landlord to dance?" Kachigan gave her an exasperated look. "Even if I was irresponsible enough to leave you alone with that young hoodlum—"

"Daniel's not a hoodlum! And if I want to say hello to a man I happen to know, you can't—"

Fortunately, the bubble-and-squeak arrived, steaming in its black iron skillet, before the argument built up enough volume to be heard over the skirling of the band. The barmaid clattered two forks down on the table beside the pan, not bothering with the niceties of napkins or plates, then handed Kachigan a pale round of potato bread. "Don't kick up a fuss, love," she advised him. "There's nothing a girl likes less than a jealous boyfriend." She winked amiably at Helen, then withdrew.

A somewhat constrained silence fell over the table, broken only by the hiss and crackle of the cooling skillet. "You'd better eat that," Helen said at last. "It's going to get cold."

Kachigan picked up one of the forks and handed it to her, then tore off a chunk of bread. "You eat some too. Maybe we could manage not to argue so much if we weren't so hungry."

"I doubt it," she retorted, but he noticed she took a forkful of cabbage and potatoes anyway. "It doesn't taste like much. I think it needs black pepper."

"Or some garlic fried up with it." Despite its blandness, though, the food felt good in his empty stomach. "Man or woman?"

Helen blinked at him, looking baffled for a moment, then glanced down at the pencil she still held in her other hand. "A man, since I'm practicing for Josef. What shape is his face?"

"High forehead, round jaw." Years of identifying robbery suspects had trained Kachigan to focus on the basics of facial architecture, rather than on changeable details like hair and beards. "Bushy eyebrows, flat. And a long, thin nose."

With surprising quickness, Helen made a rough sketch in the notebook. She turned it around to face him. "Now, you tell me what isn't right about it."

"Eyes too round, and set too close together," Kachigan said promptly. "Mouth too close to his chin." He glanced up when another breeze stirred the smoky room, and this time recognized the freckled young man who'd just ducked in. "Mahaffey's here."

To her credit, Helen didn't twist around to see for herself, or even look up from her drawing. "Where is he going?"

"To the bar, for a beer. Now he's looking around the room. I don't think—no, he's spotted someone now. He's going over to talk to him." Kachigan craned his head. "Damn."

"Can I look?" Helen demanded.

"Yes, but you won't see much. They're all the way over on the far side." He cursed again, this time silently and in Armenian. "We're not going to be able to see the landlord from here, much less make a drawing of him. We have to get closer."

Helen closed the notebook and handed it back to him. "Then I guess you'd better ask me to dance after all."

He blinked, then realized that a slow romantic two-step had crowded the dance floor with couples, most of them twined together so closely that their faces were half-hidden from onlookers. Smiling, Kachigan dropped his fork into the half-empty skillet and rose to take Helen Sorby into his arms.

His first surprise was how well she fit. Helen was taller than she looked, and pleasingly substantial despite her too-tight dress. He put her rigidity down to lack of breath, and perhaps to lack of recent practice as well. But her sense of rhythm was good and she knew the Boston two-step as well as he did. They blended easily into the crowd of dancers.

Kachigan's second surprise came a moment later, when he spun Helen around the dance floor and saw Mahaffey sit down in a booth across from the unmistakable massive figure of Bernard K. Flinn.

He could tell from the way she stiffened that Helen had seen the steel company policeman too. She startled him by immediately stepping closer into his embrace, and putting her lips up to his ear. Kachigan took the opportunity to duck his recognizable face into her hair. She smelled of jasmine and roses.

"Arrest him!" Helen hissed.

Kachigan swung her back toward the far end of the club, letting the mass of dancers veil them from Flinn's sight. "I thought you didn't want me to arrest him."

"Not Mahaffey!" She pushed at him and Kachigan let her step back, suspecting she needed the air. Her breathlessness didn't lessen her ability to glare at him, but it did at least serve to keep her voice down. "Arrest Flinn, for Josef Janczek's murder!"

"On what grounds?"

"*He's* the landlord!"

Her voice was getting loud again. Kachigan silenced her by tugging her back against his chest, then swung her past Flinn's booth a second time. Daniel Mahaffey was slipping a long envelope into his vest, although his stony expression made it clear he wasn't too happy about doing it. Flinn had leaned back in his usual lazy way, small eyes narrowed to unreadable slits. He was rolling an unlit cigar between his fingers. Kachigan wondered if he intended to stay long enough to smoke it.

"We don't know that the landlord has committed any crimes," he muttered at Helen, once they were safely past again.

"Other than tax evasion and negligence?" she asked tartly.

"Do you really think I can convict Bernard Flinn for that?"

Her answer was a reluctant grimace. "Not in this city," she admitted. "So what *are* you going to do?"

"You'll see." Kachigan swept her in and out between dancers, trying to pace their progress around the crowded floor. From the slowing fiddles, it sounded as if the band was winding up this set. He guessed their next circuit around the floor would be their last. "Can you see if Mahaffey's still sitting there?"

"Yes, I think—" Helen broke off, craning her head over his shoulder. "No! He's getting up to leave now."

"Good." Kachigan let the rhythmic beat of the two-step sweep them along the outside edge of the dance floor. He spun his partner around in one last whirl, then pulled her out of the crowd and deposited her right in front of Bernard Flinn's booth.

"Good evening, Mr. Flinn." Kachigan gave Helen Sorby a small push toward the bench Mahaffey had vacated, and silently blessed her when she dropped into it without a murmur of protest. Of course, her lack of breath might have had something to do with that. Flinn regarded them both with an incredulous scowl, but made no move to leave when Kachigan slid into the seat beside Helen.

"Damn you, Kachigan." The mixture of hostility and grim amusement in Flinn's voice told Kachigan his ploy had worked. "Do you know what I'd do if this young lady wasn't here?"

Kachigan nodded. "Throw me across the room for bothering you. That's one of the reasons I brought her over with me."

"One of the reasons?" Flinn glanced over at Helen, frowning. It only took him a moment to place her. "You're the young lady from the police station yesterday, eh? You know, Kachigan, if we're going to be polite, you should introduce us."

Kachigan gritted his teeth, caught in his own trap of good manners. His instincts told him that the less Bernard Flinn knew about Helen Sorby, the better off they'd both be. Before he could think of a polite way to refuse, however, his companion took the decision firmly out of his hands.

"My name is Helen Sorby," she told Flinn. "I'm a social worker at the Martha Carey Settlement House." She paused, clearly waiting for him to take that in and dismiss her, then added crisply, "And a magazine reporter."

The Black Point Steel police chief settled farther back in his chair, looking dangerously lazy. "Is that right? Did you come here tonight to interview me, Miss Sorby?"

Kachigan decided it was time to intervene. "No," he said, drawing Flinn's glittering gaze back to him. "She came to identify you as Josef Janczek's landlord."

The silence that followed that remark seemed unreasonably deep, until Kachigan realized that the band had just stopped playing. With a last few claps and shouts of breathless laughter, the dancers drifted back to mob the bar.

"You can't prove that in court," Flinn said at last. It wasn't a statement of defiance or warning, just of fact. "The only person you could get to testify to it is Daniel Mahaffey, and I doubt any jury would listen to a man I fired for stealing company property." Across the beer-stained table, he eyed Kachigan with a smile. "Is that all you came over to tell me? And here I thought you were smart enough to worry about."

Kachigan shrugged. "I don't have to be able to prove it, Mr. Flinn, to make it common knowledge. All Miss Sorby needs to do is write an article about having witnessed you paying Daniel Mahaffey to move to Chicago. Her readers can infer the rest."

The mill police chief snorted. "No paper in Pittsburgh would publish crap like that. Would they, Miss Sorby?"

"No," she agreed. "But a New York magazine like *McClure's* or *Collier's* would. They love muckraking exposés." She met his scowl straight-on. "Does your wife take *Collier's*, Mr. Flinn?"

It was a good thing the A.O.H. served their beer in thick-walled mugs, Kachigan thought. A glass would never have survived the pressure of Bernard Flinn's tightening grip.

"All right," the steel policeman said flatly. "What do you

want? Money? Or a word put in with the city promotions board?"

Kachigan felt his jaw knot with hostility. "Neither of those," he said, just as flatly. "We want to talk to the men Josef Janczek worked with at Taylor Mill."

"*No.*"

Kachigan had expected the refusal, but the vehemence in Flinn's voice surprised him. He paused, considering his options. "Among her other talents," he said, "Miss Sorby is an artist. She can draw pictures of people by having them described to her."

"Is that right?"

"Yes." Kachigan extracted his evidence book, but didn't pull out the picture of Lide Janczek carefully folded in front. Instead, he showed Flinn the sketch Helen had begun on the back page. "She drew this just now, from my description."

The forbidding cast of Flinn's face eased into a more thoughtful expression. "And who's it supposed to be?"

"Teddy Roosevelt."

The last of the steel policeman's silent fury melted into an amused smile. "Not bad," he allowed. "Is that really all you want, Kachigan? To talk to the men at Taylor Mill, so you can get a picture of Josef Janczek?"

"A picture I can be *sure* is Josef Janczek," he said, gazing levelly at Flinn.

"Bastard," Flinn said, but no anger tightened his voice this time. "I'll be there to watch you when you talk to them. All you're going to get is a description of Janczek, nothing else."

"That's all I want," said Kachigan without averting his gaze. Unlike Helen, he'd learned not to look away when he lied.

Flinn grunted, striking a match with sudden decision. "All right," he said around his cigar. "Be at Taylor Mill tomorrow at eleven sharp, and tell the guard at the gate you came to talk to me. I'll have the floor supervisor rearrange the work schedule, so you can talk to the men in Janczek's section."

It was as good as Kachigan had hoped for, when he'd first devised this strategy on the dance floor. He tucked his evidence book away and slid out of the booth, tugging an ominously silent Helen with him. "I appreciate the help, Mr. Flinn."

"You damn well better." Big as he was, Flinn somehow managed to radiate more menace from a lazy sprawl than most men could with doubled fists. "Because that's all the help you're ever going to get from me, Kachigan."

10

HELEN PUSHED OPEN THE DOOR OF THE A.O.H. and set off down the street, walking as quickly as she could. She was counting on breathlessness to help her rein in her temper, just as it had on the dance floor. Unfortunately, Milo Kachigan caught up with her a few strides away and swung her to an unwilling stop. She scowled up at him through the glow of the bar's electric light.

"*Now* what have I done?" He sounded half amused and half exasperated. "Go ahead and yell at me, I'm already deaf from the noise in that club."

Helen gave up trying to be polite. "Did it occur to you to consult with me before you arranged this visit to Taylor Mill?"

"*You're* the one who wanted to draw a picture of Josef Janczek," the police detective retorted. "Who better to get to describe him than the men he worked with?"

Helen gritted her teeth, unable to argue with that. "The only reason Bernard Flinn's letting me draw anything is because he thinks I can't!"

"Oh. So that's what you're mad about."

"Yes, that's what I'm mad about! That picture wasn't even finished—and it doesn't look *anything* like Teddy Roosevelt."

"Well, neither does my brother-in-law."

Helen took the deepest breath she could in her too-tight dress, staring up at Kachigan for a long minute. "You wanted Flinn to think I couldn't draw very well," she said in dawning realization. "Didn't you?"

Kachigan pulled her gloved hand through the crook of his arm, escorting her down the street at a more sedate pace. "You'll notice I didn't show him your sketch of Lide Janczek. Does that answer your question?"

She frowned. "Were you afraid he wouldn't let us into Taylor Mill if he thought I could really draw?"

"Partly that. But I also don't want him to be surprised when it takes you a long time to finish your sketch tomorrow. That will give me a chance to talk to the men who worked in Josef Janczek's shop."

The detective's strategy suddenly made a great deal more sense to Helen. "To find out if any of them are organizing unions? Or knew if Janczek was?"

"Yes. We need to know exactly what Janczek's politics were, now that we know his landlord was Bernard Flinn."

"What do you mean, now that we know it's Flinn?" Helen demanded. "That practically confirms that he's the murderer! Irene Prandtl told us she heard him arguing with Josef that night." She could tell by the furrow between his brows that Kachigan wasn't as convinced as she was. "Why not?"

"If Janczek really was a union-man, why in God's name was he renting a house from his company police chief?"

Helen shrugged. "For all we know, Flinn owns half the rental property on the South Side. Or maybe Black Point Steel does. It would be a good way to keep the employees oppressed."

"The way coal companies do in the mining towns they own?"

"Why not?"

"Well, for one thing," said Kachigan drily, "all of Black Point's mills are along the Allegheny River. They can't have more than a handful of workers who live on the South Side. Why would they own a lot of real estate here?"

Helen frowned, glancing over the housetops at the smoky glow of the mills along the Monongahela. The largest fires came from the massive furnaces of Jones & Laughlin, flanked by the smaller works of United States Steel and Clinton Iron. "I don't know," she admitted reluctantly. "Do you suppose—"

On the second story of the house behind them, a window thudded up in its frame. "Take your conversation inside, will you?" growled a rough Polish-accented voice. "It's past eleven, and tomorrow's a workday!"

Helen opened her mouth to protest, but found herself being tugged across the street before she could inform her cranky neighbor that the A.O.H. down on the corner was making far more noise than they were. She glanced up at Kachigan and saw with some surprise that he was scowling. "Don't look so worried. We're not going to get arrested for disturbing the peace."

The police detective deposited her in front of her ivy-carved front door. "I'm not worried about getting arrested."

"Then why are you so upset?" Helen dug out her key from her coat pocket. "Do you want to come in and talk about the murder?"

"I do not want to come in and talk about anything." Kachigan reached out impatiently to push the door open as soon as she turned the key. "What I want, Miss Sorby, is to keep the neighbors from gossiping about you!"

"Well, you've come about a year too late for that," Helen said acidly, then slammed the door on his surprised expression.

"What on earth do you find to like about inclines?" Kachigan shouted into the wind at the top of the Hill District.

Helen glanced over at him, holding her sensible hat down with one gloved hand to augment the silk scarf she'd already tied over it. They'd exchanged almost no conversation since the police detective had rung the bell for her that morning. Partly that was because of the way she'd ended their conversation the night before, Helen suspected, and partly it was because she'd insisted on taking a clattering, crowded trolley instead of a cab. When Kachigan had objected, she'd sweetly told him that since he'd made the arrangements for their visit to Taylor Mill, she got to choose how they got there. And Helen always chose trolleys, because trolleys led to inclines.

From their vantage point at the upper gear-house of the Penn Incline, Pittsburgh spread in a river-locked triangle of factories and tenements below, seamed with rail-lines and stitched together with dozens of bridges. The blasting wind had torn apart the city's usual smoky canopy, and etched a choppy glitter across its three rivers. The rain of the day before hadn't been enough to lift the waters of the Allegheny and the Ohio from their usual autumn lows, leaving only the Monongahela high enough to support the fleet of coal barges that usually plied the city's rivers.

"What is there *not* to like?" Helen demanded in return. She had loved inclined planes ever since she was a child, and never missed an opportunity to ride one. The Penn Incline was one of her favorites, passing as it did over the busy railroad yards of Union Station on its long, slanted way down to the ribbon of Allegheny floodplain known as the Strip.

"They're bumpy, they're noisy, they're slow—" Kachigan stepped forward in line, handing his dime to the teller behind the grate. He gave one ticket to Helen, then followed her onto the loading platform. This late on a Saturday morning, there were not many people waiting, despite the fact that one of the two balanced cars had almost reached the upper gear-house. Mostly they were housewives with shopping baskets and children bundled up against the weather, heading for the Penn Avenue markets.

"They're not noisy. And they may be slow, but they're elegant." Helen stood back when the car arrived, letting the children flood as she knew they would into the front of the large glassed-in compartment. Their mothers settled in on the seats behind them, secure in the knowledge that their progeny could come to no harm pressing their noses against the glass to watch their descent. That left the back seats empty, but Helen ignored them. She went straight to her favorite place to ride—the wide brass handrail that rimmed the back wall of the car at elbow height. Kachigan watched in amusement while Helen put both gloved hands backward on the rail and swung herself up to perch on it, the same way she'd done ever since she was a child.

He gestured at the length of brass beside her. "May I?"

"Of course." Helen slid over and he swung himself up as

easily as she had. From the athletic way he moved, she guessed that it hadn't been long since he'd been promoted from his former street patrol. "No matter what the children think, Mr. Kachigan, you get the best view from here."

"I'll remember that." The doors slid shut beside them, and the car started its descent with the usual ungainly jerk. The children responded with whoops of delight in three different languages, and Kachigan glanced at her with laughing eyes. "Elegant, Miss Sorby?"

"Elegant," she said firmly. Now that the car had started, it slid with majestic smoothness down its inclined track, gear chain clicking steadily beneath them. Pittsburgh's northern hills blossomed through the windows, still tinged in November with the occasional red and gold splotch of autumn leaves. Those leaves would all blow off today, Helen guessed.

There was a long, and it seemed to Helen, strangely tense silence. Wind roared past the incline as they left the sheltering hillside, its noise making a kind of privacy around them. "Miss Sorby, may I ask you a question?" Kachigan asked. "A personal question?"

Helen grimaced, guessing where this would lead. She considered saying no, but her knowledge of Kachigan's persistence told her the subject would probably come up again and again, until she finally gave him the answers he wanted. Still, she wasn't inclined to make this any more pleasant for him than it was going to be for her.

"If you insist, Mr. Kachigan." It was the coldest voice she could muster, and it made the detective wince. But it didn't stop him, as she'd suspected it wouldn't.

"If James Foster Barton is still alive, why did you withdraw your request for a marriage annulment last January?"

Whatever question Helen had expected, it hadn't been one quite so specific as that. She slued around to stare up at Kachigan, nearly losing her seat on the handrail in the process.

"How do you know about that?"

He shrugged. "This morning I stopped at St. Peter's and asked to see the list of annulments requested and granted last year. Your name was on the first list, but not the second."

Kachigan's mouth turned up at one corner. "Since I couldn't imagine you taking no for an answer, even from the Catholic Church, I assumed that was your decision."

"What reason did you have to ask about it at all?" she demanded, torn between anger and bewilderment. "Whether I'm married or not isn't any of your business!"

"No," Kachigan agreed. "But finding out whether you've lied to me is."

"Even about my personal affairs?"

"*Especially* about your personal affairs. If Bernard Flinn can find something to blackmail you with, Miss Sorby, he will." The police detective paused, dark blue eyes meeting hers across the cold, drafty space between them. "Can he?"

"He might think so," she said, after a moment. "I don't."

"Is James Barton still alive?"

"As far as I know." Helen looked down at the ruffle of her one good walking-dress. The brown wool already wore a gray stain of mill-ash from the trolley floor. "I make no effort to keep in touch with him, Mr. Kachigan, nor he me." She looked back up at him steadily. "And we are *not* married."

"But if your marriage was never annulled—did he divorce you?"

"He didn't have to." She took a deep breath. "In the eyes of the law, James Foster Barton never married me at all. And in the eyes of the church, he committed a mortal sin when he tried to. I believe the church's term for it was 'violation of a previously sanctified union.' "

Nothing changed in Kachigan's face, no hint of revulsion or disgust. Or pity, which would have been even worse. "Barton was married before?"

"More than once." She took another deep breath, steeling herself for the worst of it. "My husband—the man I thought of as my husband—was nothing but a swindler, Mr. Kachigan. He had no job and no income, although he liked to play at being a union organizer for the American Federation of Labor. He moved from city to city, staying in good hotels and eating in first-class restaurants, wearing custom-made clothes from New York. He told me that he had inherited money." She surprised herself with a small, bitter chuckle.

"It was inherited all right—by the wives he 'married' in every city that he traveled through. All he had to do was steal it from them."

"That's what he did to you?"

Helen nodded jerkily. After all this time, it was still the part that made her angriest. "There wasn't much, which is why he left so soon after we married. But what inheritance I had—my parents saved that money penny by penny, Mr. Kachigan. Each penny saved at the cost of something sacrificed, some dress not bought, some holiday not taken—" She broke off, hearing the vehement echo of her voice inside the incline. The whooping children below hadn't noticed, but several of their mothers had. Helen felt her face sting with embarrassment. "I'm sorry."

"For being outraged by a crime? You don't have to apologize about that to me." Kachigan paused while the incline's twin cars slid noisily past each other at the midpoint of the track. "Did you report Barton to the police?"

She shook her head, forcing herself to meet Kachigan's eyes again. "I wanted to, but Aunt Pat was afraid he knew too much about the South Side Temperance League. She convinced me that prosecuting him would do us more harm than good. The money was spent and we weren't going to get it back from him."

The detective frowned. "But to leave a criminal like that free to go on ruining people's lives—"

"For your information, Mr. Kachigan," Helen said tartly, "I don't think of my life as 'ruined.' In a way, I'm grateful to James Barton. He taught me that women should never marry, and he did it in only a few painful months. Some people spend their lives being miserable for the lack of that lesson."

The detective frowned. "Miss Sorby, you're too smart to think that any man you married would turn out to be a swindler."

"I know that. But the whole institution of marriage is so tied up with the unfair laws governing women in this country—don't shake your head at me! I've read the state legal code, and I know exactly what rights a married woman no longer has. A single woman still holds the rights to herself and her finances. If she does want to share her life with a man, she can enter into a companionate marriage.''

Kachigan looked dubious. "A companionate marriage doesn't seem to have done your friend Irene Prandtl much good. Financially or otherwise.''

Helen opened her mouth, but couldn't think of anything to say in response to that. Fortunately, their car descended into the darkness of the incline's lower gear-house, rumbling and jolting to a final stop before she had to reply. They made their way out of the incline's lower portal in silence, turning left onto the noisy bustle of Penn Avenue. Markets and food warehouses lined the railroad tracks for several blocks, then gave way to the enormous foundries and mills that had brought the railroad here to begin with. Today, wearing a comfortable wool skirt and masculine jacket under her russet coat, Helen had no problem matching Kachigan's brisk pace. She clutched her drawing case tight against the capricious wind.

"I have something else to ask you, Miss Sorby."

Helen looked up at the detective warily. "Now what?"

"Nothing personal this time." He used his free hand to dig out his small black notebook from one overcoat pocket, then shook out a folded square of newsprint. "Take a look at that and tell me what you think."

Helen caught the clipping carefully as the wind tugged at it. This one was written in English, but the photo accompanying the story was familiar: the same sea of young militant faces that she'd seen in the Petrenko's Russian-language newspaper. A familiar secretive smile caught her attention in one corner. "It's another photo of Lide Janczek, from the demonstration in Chicago," she said, then glanced up and saw his quizzical look. Knowing he must have another reason for showing it to her, Helen scanned the picture more closely. It wasn't a set of features that finally caught her attention, but the glacial whiteness of one young man's hair.

"That's Father Zawisza, from St. Witold's Church." She pointed at him and Kachigan nodded in satisfaction, as if she'd confirmed his own guess. "What's so important about that? We already knew Father Zawisza was out in Chicago."

"We knew he was at the Wobbly convention," he corrected. "We didn't know he was at this particular demonstration. Read the headline, Miss Sorby."

She did, eyes widening in surprise. " 'Anarchists show support for new socialist organization'—but that can't be right. Father Zawisza isn't an anarchist!"

Kachigan took the photo back. "How do you know that?"

"Because he's always talking about how he disagrees—" Helen broke off, frowning. Whatever else she might think about him, the radical priest was not stupid. "I suppose he would say that if he didn't want us to know."

"If he had any sense, he would." Kachigan led her past the last of the markets, then cut diagonally across a sprawling brickyard toward the river. "Would you trust your Aunt McGregor with your plans if you were an anarchist?"

Helen choked with unexpected laughter. "Mr. Kachigan, I wouldn't trust her with a grocery list!" She paused, mulling over this new information. "You know, when I asked Father Zawisza if he'd met Lide Janczek in Chicago, he snapped my head off. Why would he do that if they were both anarchists?"

"Was that after she died?"

Helen gave him a sober look. "Yes."

"Then I can think of lots of reasons," Kachigan said grimly

They emerged onto Pike Street and fell silent as the roar of several mills along the river reached out simultaneously to engulf them. Black Point Steel's yard was a maze of railroad tracks encircling a huge metal building, blackened by its own soot and spitting out sparks from three tall chimneys. It wasn't the largest of the steelworks that lined the Allegheny—the enormous silhouettes of the Fort Pitt Foundry and Sable Iron Works downriver dwarfed it easily. Even so, it took them several minutes to walk past the employee-only gates and reach the main entrance, guarded by two stolid and unfriendly men in mill-police uniforms.

"We're here to see Mr. Flinn," Kachigan said, his voice taking on the crisp edge of authority that Helen had heard in it before, when he talked to his subordinates. "Detective Kachigan of the Pittsburgh police, and Miss Helen Sorby. We have an appointment for eleven o'clock."

"Wait here," said the older guard, in a northsider's German accent. "We must check this with Mr. Flinn."

"All right." Kachigan watched him go, then glanced at the gatehouse behind the other guard. "Can Miss Sorby go inside to get out of the wind?"

"No."

The police detective frowned, but stepped back in response to Helen's vehement tug at his sleeve. "I'm quite all right where I am," she informed him. "As long as I hold onto my hat."

Kachigan's mouth set in a rigid line. "It wouldn't endanger Black Point Steel to let you in their gatehouse."

"It shouldn't matter." From the next street over, Helen could hear a church bell ringing eleven. "We won't be waiting very long."

But the minutes stretched out in wind-buffeted silence, until Helen's fingers turned stiff around her drawing case and her feet began to ache from standing still on the cold stones. Kachigan swore at last and dove a hand into his coat to yank out his pocket watch. "Flinn told us to be here at eleven sharp and it's already quarter past. If that guard doesn't come back in another five minutes—"

A gruff shout interrupted him. Helen turned and saw the enormous, coat-draped figure of Bernard K. Flinn striding out of Taylor Mill. "Westbeld, let those people in here!" he snapped, rocking the young guard back with an irritable blow to the shoulder. "And the next time a lady in a silk scarf is waiting to see me, you'd damned well better put her in the gatehouse!"

That speech, instead of mollifying Helen, made her bristle with a socialist's indignation. She dug in her heels and pulled Kachigan to a stop beside Flinn, so she could glare up at the company policeman.

"I suppose if my scarf was made of homespun instead of silk, I'd be left waiting out in the street?" she demanded hotly.

Flinn gave her a slitted glance. "If you had on a homespun scarf, Miss Sorby, I wouldn't have agreed to see you at all."

Helen took a deep breath, her fingers tightening on Kachigan's arm. She hadn't meant it as a signal, just a wordless

echo of her frustration, but the detective promptly pulled her
away from Flinn and into Taylor Mill. The air inside was
thick and acid with the smell of newly pickled steel. The
thunder of grinding machines and shriek of lathes nearly
deafened Helen, until Flinn led them through a cinderblock
partition and closed the door behind them. The noise dropped
to a roar, over which the persistent scrape of a telephone's
bell was barely audible.

Flinn cursed and grabbed up the receiver from a table clut-
tered with schedules and time sheets. He hadn't bothered to
lift the speaker to his mouth, and Helen could see why.
Trapped inside the bleak corrugated metal walls of this mill
office, the police chief's voice echoed like pig-iron ingots
being dropped into a furnace.

"What?" Flinn growled into the open line, not bothering
with the niceties of greetings or identifications. "No, I do
not have enough men to put a double guard around gate four!
We've got six men out with typhoid, not counting Weig. And
anyway, we already fired the man who was taking that
stock." A pause. "Well, if they're still losing it, tell Gibson
he's going to have to shut that gate down permanently. The
best I can do is put an extra man at the main gate during the
shift change. And typhoid or no typhoid, if Weig misses one
more day of work, fire him too!"

The receiver crashed back onto its stand, and Bernard
Flinn swung back toward Helen and Kachigan. "The men
from Janczek's shop will be here in a minute," he said
bluntly. "This shouldn't take too long." He kicked two
chairs casually out from the table toward them, then sat down
in his own chair without waiting for Helen. If he'd hoped to
annoy her with that lack of courtesy, he failed. She simply
cleared a spot among the clutter for her drawing case, without bothering to ask for permission. Kachigan, she noticed,
remained standing near the door.

"I see you came prepared, Miss Sorby." Bernard Flinn
watched her spread out her pencils, eyes glittering with
amusement. He was probably remembering the crude sketch
she'd made the night before. Helen gave him back a glare,
but its only effect was to make him lean back lazily until the
cheap pine chair creaked under his weight. "Are you going

to have enough light to draw by?'' he asked, with mocking concern.

"I think so." Helen glanced up at the dim overhead electric bulb hanging crookedly from its feed wire, then at the narrow soot-grimed industrial windows. "Can't Black Point Steel afford gas for its factories?"

Flinn gave her a crooked smile. "That damned George Westinghouse talked all the mills into buying his cheap electric lights." The steel policeman reached up and batted at the bulb above him, making the office reel with blurry shadows. "A goddamned waste of time and money. Just like this investigation of yours, Kachigan."

"It's my own time I'm wasting," the detective said.

"And mine too." Despite his sharp words, Flinn was still smiling. He leaned back again in his chair, oblivious to the squeal of straining wood. "I can tell you right now, you're not going to get what you want from my men."

Helen glanced at Kachigan and saw the same suspicion in his eyes that she felt. A smile from Bernard Flinn was not a good sign. "Why not?" she asked, when Kachigan remained silent. "Didn't they know Josef Janczek?"

"Worked with him every day, Miss Sorby." Flinn's smile became an outright grin as the door opened and a file of men in workboots and heavy gloves straggled in, metal shavings bright on their clothes and beards. Some of them looked wary, some puzzled, some indifferent. None of them said anything in greeting, even to Bernard Flinn. "The only problem is, not a single one speaks English."

11

MILO KACHIGAN SNAPPED HIS TEETH shut on a curse, instincts telling him not to let Flinn see how badly he'd been stymied. Try as he might, however, he couldn't keep all his irritation hidden. He funneled it into a complaint that seemed safe.

"How is Miss Sorby supposed to draw a picture of Josef Janczek when she can't even explain what she's trying to do?"

Flinn's massive shoulders rolled in a shrug. "All I said was that you could talk to Janczek's shift-mates, Kachigan. It's not my problem if they can't understand you."

Kachigan saw the disbelieving glance Helen threw at the steel-police chief. "Not one of Janczek's floor bosses speaks English? I find that hard to believe, Mr. Flinn."

Bernard Flinn scowled. "Nothing would get done out there if I pulled floor bosses off their shifts, Miss Sorby. Sorry."

"You could at least give us their names and addresses." Kachigan struggled to keep his exasperation from showing. "Then we could talk to them after work, and not waste your time."

That earned him an even fiercer frown. "Don't push it, Kachigan. I don't have to give you a thing, and you damned well know it." Flinn pulled out a gold-encrusted pocket watch. "You've got until noon to draw your picture. Get started."

Kachigan glanced at Helen Sorby, seeing in her face the echo of his own frustration. "What nationalities are these men?"

"How the hell should I know? Hunkies, most of them, I guess." To a man like Flinn, the word meant not specifically Hungarians, but immigrants from any part of eastern Europe. "We hire a lot of hunkies at Taylor Mill. The Irish and Italians just don't have the patience for this kind of work."

One dark head at the end of the line of men lifted at that comment. Some of the mill workers could understand English, Kachigan realized, even if they couldn't speak it.

Helen Sorby must have realized it too. She stood up and faced the line of men. "I came here to draw a picture of Josef Janczek." She held up her drawing pad to show them the blank outline she'd drawn of a man's head. "Can any of you tell me what he looked like?"

The silence that followed the question was far from blank. Several of the workmen exchanged thoughtful looks, and Kachigan saw at least two glance carefully at Flinn, as if trying to decide whether this was something the police chief wanted them to do. No one spoke, however, even when Helen repeated her request in fluent Italian.

Kachigan gauged the silence in the room and decided it wouldn't be broken without some official action on his part. "Can I try to get these men's names?" he asked Flinn.

The burly man looked amused. "Suit yourself."

Kachigan pulled out his notebook and pencil, then started at the near end of the line. "Your name?"

"Eh?"

Thanking god for his years of patrolling the multiethnic South Side, Kachigan assessed the young man's flaxen beard and high Slavic cheeks, then said in halting and badly accented Polish, "Your name—what?"

Pale eyebrows lifted into metal-spangled hair. The man rattled off a long sentence in Polish, of which Kachigan caught only what sounded like "Stanislaus." He wasn't sure if that was the man's name or his parish or his home village back in Poland, but he wrote it down in his evidence book, anyway. It was better than no information at all.

The second man in line had dark hair and humorously wrinkled eyes with an almost Mongolian slant, although a closer look showed them to be pale green. Ukrainian or Russian, Kachigan guessed. "What's your name?" he asked in Russian.

"Yuri Domanin, third machinist, rod and bar division—"

"Slow down, I can't write that fast."

It wasn't until Kachigan heard the machinist's startled intake of breath that he realized he'd snapped back at him not in English, but in too-fluent Russian. It took all of his control not to shoot a wary glance toward Bernard Flinn, to see if he'd noticed the slip. He was all too aware that Helen Sorby wasn't the only one in this case who could be blackmailed by the steel-police chief.

The Russian machinist gave Kachigan a shrewd look. "Better say in English that you don't understand me, eh?"

"Say that again," Kachigan ordered in English, putting all his frustration at his own stupidity into his voice. "I can't understand you at all!" And then, in what he hoped sounded more like broken Russian, asked, "You get in trouble for talking?"

Domanin's moustache twitched. "About that dead man Janczek? Oh, yes. Nobody's supposed to talk about him here."

Kachigan heaved an exaggerated sigh, dragging his fingers through his hair. "All I want is your damn name, not a history of the village where you were born," he snapped in English, and saw the responsive twinkle in Domanin's eyes. In Russian, he added, "The dead man made trouble in the mill?"

"Trouble, yes, but not so much—" Between their bodies, where Flinn couldn't see, Domanin made the clenched fist that stood for unionizing. "He did that too, but mostly he just made trouble. He found out about things."

"Things about the bosses?"

"Things about everyone!" Domanin threw up his hands, as if in final frustration. "Ask me more later, eh? You can find me at St. Sophia's Orthodox church."

Kachigan sighed, shaking his head and heavily scratching

out some nonexistent words in his notebook. He moved to the next man in line. "Name?" he asked in weary English, as if he had given up his attempts to translate.

To his surprise, the third man gave him not only his name, but also the name of his parish in the way that Domanin had. Kachigan nodded silent thanks, ostensibly to him but actually to the Russian beside him. It was clear that Yuri Domanin was the natural leader of this shift. Once he'd taken the risk of talking to an outsider, the others were prepared to follow.

Kachigan collected the rest of the muttered names and parishes, noticing as he did that all of the men lived either on the Strip or in Polish Hill above it. By the time he got to the end of the line, he became aware he wasn't the only one to whom the workers were talking. He turned to see Helen Sorby drawing industriously at the table, an older, olive-skinned man with grizzled hair leaning beside her. Kachigan didn't know much Italian, but for all the gestures the man was making at the sketch, what he was telling Helen sounded like an address.

Kachigan turned back to Flinn, now gazing pointedly at his watch. "Time to go?"

"I have a luncheon engagement at twelve-thirty." Flinn vaulted out of his chair with unexpected grace. "And I'd rather not be late. Almost done, Miss Sorby?"

"Quite done, Mr. Flinn." She brushed eraser dust off her sketch, then deliberately stood up and held it out for the other workmen to see. Their quick murmurs of surprise told Kachigan that in spite of the odds against her, Helen had managed to draw another recognizable portrait of the murder victims. Judging by the irritated look on Bernard Flinn's face, the Black Point police chief knew it too.

"Back to work," Flinn snapped at the men, and they promptly proved their comprehension of English by turning in unison for the door. The company police chief aimed his cold stare at Kachigan. "This is the last thing I'm doing for you, Detective."

"I know." Kachigan took the rolled-up sketch from Helen, then waited for her to pull on her gloves so he could tuck her hand into his elbow.

"Good." Flinn opened the door and escorted them back

through the smoke and battering noise of the mill, all the way out to the hostile guards at the gate. Outside the police chief's dark office, the noon sunlight seemed blindingly bright. Squinting against it, Kachigan could see a private carriage waiting on the verge of Pike Street, drawn by a pair of plumed horses and manned by a uniformed driver. The chauffeur hurried to open the carriage door for Flinn, and Kachigan felt Helen stiffen with disapproval beside him. He braced himself for an angry comment, but this time she surprised him.

"Do enjoy your luncheon, Mr. Flinn," she called after the police chief, in a voice sweet enough to jerk his head around in surprise. The distinguished-looking older man inside the carriage glanced out at them curiously. "And tell Mayor Hayes I hope he loses the election."

Anger had pitched her voice loud enough to carry. Kachigan choked with laughter, hearing a furious exchange drift back from the carriage as it pulled away. Bad enough that they'd gotten more information from their visit than Flinn wanted them to. Now he'd have to spend his entire luncheon convincing William Hayes that he wasn't entertaining the mayor's political enemies.

"Did you *have* to say that?"

"William Hayes is a crook," Helen said flatly. "He may claim to lead a Citizens' Party, but he's nothing more than Senator Matthew Quay's stocking-puppet!"

Kachigan couldn't argue with that, since to the best of his knowledge it was true. "I still don't think it was a good idea to make Bernard Flinn even madder at us than he already is."

"I didn't make him mad at *us*," Helen Sorby said tartly. "I made him mad at *me*, and that's exactly what I was trying to do."

"Why, in God's name?"

She glared up at him. "So that he'll forget to be mad at the men who talked to us today! Or didn't you think about that, when you started chattering to your Russian friend?"

Kachigan felt his face tighten with chagrin and foreboding. If Helen Sorby had noticed the easy way he'd spoken to Yuri Domanin, Flinn probably had too. "I tried to make it sound like I wasn't getting any information. Did I do that bad a job?''

"No, but it was obvious he was still trying to answer your questions. Even if Flinn thinks you got nothing out of him, he may fire him for that." She sighed. "Although he's more likely to fire Christy Zullo for helping me draw Josef's picture."

"How did you get him to do that?"

Helen gave him a quizzical glance. "I didn't, you did. As soon as Mr. Zullo saw you talking to the Russian, he came over and started helping me."

Kachigan grunted. "I think Domanin must be the main union organizer in that shop. His cooperation carried too much weight for him just to be a crew boss."

"It was a lucky thing you could talk to him so well. Was your mother Russian, Mr. Kachigan?"

He took in a quick breath, startled. Helen Sorby had used his own technique of inserting an unexpected question into an ordinary conversation, and it had worked as well on his guilty conscience as on anyone else's. He opened his mouth to deny it, but a glance at her skeptical face warned him against it.

"Not Russian, Miss Sorby. Armenian." After five years of denying his real nationality, even that half-truth was harder to admit than Kachigan had expected. He swallowed and went on, carefully picking his way through the facts. "But I grew up playing stickball with Russian boys in my old neighborhood in Monessen. That's where I learned the language." He cleared his throat uncomfortably. "I'd appreciate it if you wouldn't mention that around my patrol station."

That earned him a scowl instead of the agreement he'd been hoping for. "The police don't know you're half-Armenian?"

"No."

The social worker's voice lifted in fierce indignation. "Then how will they ever find out that a non-Irishman can do the job as well as anyone else? You should be setting an example for other Eastern European immigrants! Unless someone is brave enough to be the first—"

A whistle interrupted her tirade, from high up on the opposite side of Pike Street. Kachigan shaded his eyes against the sun, and saw Thomas Sorby leaning over the edge of the brick parapet that rimmed the roof of a seven-story ice plant. The surveyor waved at them energetically.

"Hey!" he called down. "You guys want to get some dinner?"

Helen tipped her own head back to glare at her twin. "Thomas, what are you doing here?" she demanded, apparently not averse to carrying on a conversation with a man seven stories up. "I told you not to come!"

Thomas Sorby cupped a hand to his ear, looking puzzled. "Eh? I can't hear you, Helen."

His sister said something rude in Italian. "Get down here!"

He heard that, at least. Kachigan watched the willowy figure swing over the side and clamber down the rungs of a ladder marked For Employee Use Only.

"You know I could arrest you for trespassing," he said, when Sorby jumped the last few feet to the ground, pockets noisy with mapping instruments. "I don't suppose you asked the Chautauqua Lake Ice Company's permission before you climbed up there?"

Thomas gave him an incredulous look. "Do you have any idea how much extra time I'd need to allot to do that?" he demanded. "Anyway, all I'm doing up there is checking out the roof materials of all the adjacent buildings."

"And spying on me," Helen added tartly. "You weren't scheduled to map this section for another week."

Her brother shrugged, not denying it. "I figured it wouldn't hurt to make sure that you two came back out of Taylor Mill the same way you went in, not machined into a bundle of tie rods."

Kachigan grinned at that. "Thoughtful of you, Thomas."

"No, it wasn't," Helen declared. "He's just being nosy. And it would serve you right, you *calamaro*, if I refused to answer a single one of your questions!"

Thomas cocked his head at her, not looking very intimidated by the threat. "I'll buy you dinner," he offered. "At the Hotel Albemarle. And you can order anything you want."

"Well, maybe one question," said his sister.

• • •

"So." Thomas Sorby put down his beer glass, and regarded with satisfaction the steaming slab of roast beef that the waiter had just set before him. An elegant murmur of luncheon conversation washed around them, in the tastefully satin-draped dining room of the Hotel Albemarle. "What did you manage to find out about Black Point Steel?"

Kachigan waited until his own lamb cutlets and Helen's pigeon pie had been set on the table, and the bow-tied waiter given his tip, before he answered. "Not much, I'm afraid. Flinn would only let us talk to Janczek's fellow workers and none of them knew English. Fortunately, I could speak a little Russian to one of them and your sister managed to talk to another in Italian." He noticed that Sorby had opened his surveyor's notebook and was regarding him with some bafflement. "I am speaking English now, aren't I?"

That made Helen's eyes light with a smile. "My brother's talking about the fire hazards inside Taylor Mill, Mr. Kachigan."

"Oh." Now the open notebook made sense. "Won't Black Point Steel let you in to map?"

Sorby snorted. "None of the steel plants will, anymore. They say they're self-insured and don't need fire map coverage."

"Is that true?"

"I suppose," Thomas acknowledged. "But it's not true of all the private houses and businesses next to them. Their insurability depends on whether or not they're likely to be affected by an accident at the plant." The surveyor tapped his mechanical pencil to shorten the lead. "So what was it like in there? Any obvious fire hazards?"

Kachigan began to say he hadn't noticed, but Helen answered before he could speak. "Steel and cinderblock construction, seventy feet to the eaves," she said matter-of-factly. "Electric lights, not gas, but I heard several gas turbines in the shop. And there were some large petroleum tanks out in the yard."

"Explosive hazards." Sorby scribbled it down in his notes. "Did you see any water taps or fire hoses inside the mill?"

"No, but we didn't get much of a look," Helen admitted. "Bernard Flinn made sure of that." She glanced at Kachigan, her mouth curving with amusement again. "Did you find out why Flinn was late for our appointment?" He shook his head. "Well, I did. Christy Zullo was so angry at Flinn for what he said about Italians that he told me everything."

Her brother looked up from carving his beef. "What did Flinn say about Italians?"

"That they don't have enough patience for precision lathe work." Helen snorted. "As if nationality has anything whatsoever to do with work ability! It's temperament and family upbringing—"

"Helen," Thomas warned her, jerking his head at the tables around them. A few heads had already turned in their direction.

She bit her lip, looking abashed. "Was I ranting?"

"Very quietly," Kachigan assured her. "For you. But you had started to explain why Flinn was late for our appointment."

"Oh!" Her eyes rekindled with the mirth they'd held a moment before. "Christy Zullo told me that Flinn came to get them personally, once he knew we were at the mill. He told them that they weren't to answer any questions in English. And do you know what they all did?"

"Pretended they didn't understand him."

Her peal of laughter attracted another flicker of glances from around the hotel dining room. "Exactly! It took Flinn four different translators before he was sure they understood him."

Kachigan grinned. "Then our time outside was worth it."

"I thought so too." Helen dug into her pie with gusto. She didn't seem to notice the glances that still lingered on her, mostly from men dining alone. "Do you want to know the rest?"

"Of course."

"First, you have to promise to tell me what you found out from your Russian friend."

"Helen!" There was a dull thunk as her brother kicked her under the table. Their water goblets swayed perilously.

"You can't make bargains about giving evidence to the police!"

"I'm not making bargains with the police, Thomas," she retorted, reaching out to steady her glass. "I'm reminding Milo that he and I are working on this murder investigation together." She gave Kachigan an intent glance. "Right?"

"Right," he agreed at once. If her use of his first name had been completely unintentional, he wasn't foolish enough to point it out to her. "So, what did Christy Zullo tell you?"

Helen reached out for the sketch Kachigan had set down on the table. "I made notes in the margins," she said through a mouthful of pie, and unrolled it to reveal the face of Josef Janczek. "And I wrote his address down there too."

The murdered man had an unremarkable face, Kachigan thought, glancing down at it with interest. A little flatter across the cheeks than most Polish immigrants, but with typically well-opened pale eyes beneath an untidy mop of hair. A handlebar moustache hid most of what looked like a sullen mouth.

"Not a very happy-looking young man," he commented.

"No," Helen said. "Christy Zullo says hardly anyone at Taylor Mill liked him, aside from Daniel Mahaffey."

"Yuri Domanin said he made a lot of trouble for people."

"Yes." She frowned down at some tiny, scribbled note, then turned a puzzled face toward her brother. "Zullo called Janczek a *sanguisuga*. Doesn't that mean 'mosquito,' Thomas?"

"I think it means 'blood-sucking,' " her twin replied. "Mum just always said it when she was complaining about mosquitos."

"Did Zullo tell you what he meant?" Kachigan asked.

Helen nodded. "He said Janczek cheated on his quotas, taking credit for work other men did in the shop. If anyone reported him, he'd deliberately get something tangled in the turning belt of their machine, so they'd have to spend the rest of the day fixing it. It got to the point where men would just give him some of the work they'd done if his output was low."

"Then Zullo definitely meant 'blood-sucking,' " Thomas commented. "As in extortion."

Kachigan put down his knife and fork down on his empty plate. "And it might not have been the only kind of extortion he practiced," he said slowly. "Domanin told me Janczek made trouble because he found out things about people."

Helen's next question told him how much their minds worked alike. "He spied on the bosses?"

"On everyone, apparently."

They exchanged thoughtful glances. "Does that mean Janczek *wasn't* a unionizer?" Thomas asked, looking baffled.

Kachigan shook his head. "No, Domanin said he was. But the trouble with unions—" He broke off, eying Helen warily. "Maybe we'd better pay the bill and go outside."

"Before I start ranting again?" Helen startled him with a rueful smile. "No, go ahead and finish your sentence, Mr. Kachigan. I think I know what you're going to say, and I promise not to yell at you about it."

"Then you already know it's true."

"That unions attract troublemakers and hooligans, as well as honest working men? Yes." Helen crumpled her napkin and threw it on the table. "It's one of the frustrations of trying to unionize. Do you think Janczek was that kind of union man?"

"Right now, all I'm willing to say is that his coworkers want us to think so," Kachigan said cautiously. "The same way Bernard Flinn wants us to think he was a cardsharp."

"He could have been both," Thomas pointed out.

"Or neither," said his sister.

Kachigan nodded. "We don't know for sure that anyone is telling us the truth. What I need to do is track down Janczek's coworkers at church tomorrow and get more information."

Helen gave him a puzzled look. "Why at church?"

"They would only give me the names of their parish, not their home addresses." That thought led to another, and Kachigan frowned at her. "I wish you hadn't told Bernard Flinn your name, last night."

Helen shrugged, sitting back as the waiter cleared away their empty plates and handed Thomas the bill. "I wanted him to know I was really a magazine reporter," she said, while her brother got up to pay the cashier. "Otherwise, I was just an empty threat."

Kachigan's frown intensified. "Yes, but now he can also find out where you live and what you do—particularly on Thursday nights."

The sharp reminder chased a stain of color up her cheeks. "So what am I supposed to do?" Helen demanded. "Stay at home from now on, while you do all the work on this case?"

"That would be best," Kachigan said drily, "But I can't imagine you doing it. Just be careful not to get in Flinn's way again."

"*You're* the one who should be careful," Helen shot back. "You're the one tracking down his steelworkers."

"But I'm not the one who can write an article his wife will read." He stood up and offered her his arm, seeing that Thomas had finished paying the cashier. "If Bernard Flinn is guilty, Helen, you're the one who'll bring him down." Her eyes widened at the deliberate use of her first name, but Kachigan noticed she didn't comment on it any more than he had. "I don't want another murder to investigate in this case. Least of all, yours."

12

BY MIDAFTERNOON ON SATURDAY, Pittsburgh's brief glow of wind and sunlight had gone. Clouds had crept in from the west and now hung nearly stationary over the city, growing darker as smoke from the steel mills rose to meet them. Together, they were congealing into the smoky black fog that could blind the city for days.

"Look, Helen, you can't even see the Farmers' Bank from here," Aunt Pittypat said, as Joe O'Grady's cab rattled across the Smithfield Street Bridge. "We should have taken the trolley out to Mount Oliver to do the marketing." She peered at Dennis McKenna, perched on the opposite seat, with his stack of now-addressed fliers on his knees. "The city isn't always this bad."

"So I've heard," the temperance lecturer said gravely, and Helen was convinced, quite falsely. Everything written about Pittsburgh these days emphasized the city's roaring furnaces and smoke-clogged skies. Perhaps, as a visitor from an equally smoky industrial city, he was trying to be polite.

"It wouldn't do much good to post Mr. McKenna's fliers in Mount Oliver, Aunt Pat," Helen pointed out. "And you're always running into people out there that you don't want to meet."

"True," her aunt admitted. "Like that Regitz-Brown woman you work for at the settlement house."

Helen blinked in surprise. "Why don't you want to see her?"

Pittypat made a face under her hatful of silk bees and butterflies. "It's not that I mind seeing her, or even giving money to her projects. But she's much too discreet, dearest!" Helen's stifled choke of laughter earned her a reproving look. "It's all very well for you to laugh. You're not the one who got quizzed at the Parks and Playground meeting about the young man seen escorting your niece to the settlement house. And Miss Brown absolutely refused to tell me who he was." Pat McGregor gave Helen a hopeful look. "I don't suppose it was one of those eligible young surveyors Thomas is always introducing you to."

"No, Aunt Pat," she said wryly. "It was the police detective who met us at the library on Thursday night."

"Helen!" Her aunt's wail of protest made the cab swerve toward the sidewalk. Joe O'Grady had apparently mistaken it for a command to stop. "How *could* you, when you know how I feel about policemen?"

Helen looked over at Dennis McKenna and found him staring at his shoes, as if he could somehow efface himself by not meeting their eyes. She scowled at Pat McGregor, fiercely enough to make even her scatter-brained aunt fall silent. "I think Mr. McKenna would probably like to post his fliers," she said meaningfully. A glance out into the smoky afternoon told her they were on Diamond Avenue, only a block away from Market Square. "This would be a good place to start."

Aunt Pittypat peered through the dirt-smeared window doubtfully. "If you say so, dearest. Can you meet us back here in an hour, Mr. McKenna? I should have my marketing done by then."

"An hour?" The temperance lecturer gave the pile of fliers on his lap an alarmed look. "I'm not entirely sure I can—"

"Here, I'll help you." Helen scooped up half the stack and a box of tacks to go with it. "I'll do the inside walls of Market Square, while you do the streets around it."

"My dear Miss Sorby, that's not necessary!"

She snorted. "It is if we want to get home by suppertime."

Joe O'Grady had finally descended to open the cab, looking up at them with some puzzlement. "Good day, Mr. McKenna. We'll pick you up here at a quarter to five."

He was still thanking her as he backed out of the cab, and Helen practically had to close the door in his face to stop him. Her aunt gave her another reproachful look.

"There's no need to be so rude to Mr. McKenna, dearest," she said, while the cab rolled on to the center of Market Square. "He's a very nice young man."

"I am not going to marry a temperance lecturer, Aunt Pat."

"You're not going to marry an Irish policemen, either, if I have to block the altar with my prostrate body!"

Helen opened her mouth to tell her that Kachigan was only half-Irish, then thought better of it. "Detective Kachigan wasn't escorting me in a social sense," she said instead, while the cab came to a stop under the shadow of the two tall market buildings. "We're working together on a case."

"A case of what?" Aunt Pat blinked at her as she swung the cab door open and climbed out without waiting for Joe O'Grady.

"A murder investigation case. Come on, Aunt Pittypat. You don't want to keep the horse standing."

Pat McGregor let herself be helped out of the cab, then gave Helen a quarter to hand up to the cabman. "Keep the change, Joe. Buy some carrots for your horse while we're here."

The cabman grunted noncommittally, although Helen knew from experience that he actually would use the money to treat his elderly but well-fed mare. It was one of the reasons that Pat liked him, despite his dirty cab. He shook the reins, and vanished into the smoke within a block.

"So, dearest." Pittypat glanced up at her niece inquiringly. "Is this murder investigation the reason you've been drawing pictures of Lide Janczek and her husband?"

"How do you know I have?" Helen asked, startled.

"Your brother told me about it, the last time I rang up." Her aunt picked her trailing skirts up before she crossed the horse-churned dust of Diamond Street. "I thought perhaps it was to illustrate one of your articles. Poor housing for oppressed workers, or something like that. But in any case, it gave me a wonderful idea.''

''It did?'' Helen eyed her aunt warily. Aunt Pittypat's wonderful ideas tended to have less-than wonderful repercussions for those involved. ''What kind of idea?''

''An idea for something else you can sketch.'' Her aunt came to a sudden halt and tapped a finger at the stack of posters in Helen's hands. ''Dearest, post one of those right now.''

Even after years of practice, Helen couldn't always follow her aunt's darting train of thought. She opened her mouth to ask a question, then decided it would be quicker just to do what Pat McGregor wanted. A quick upward jab left Dennis McKenna hanging from a telegraph pole, his smudged face only slightly crooked.

''Now look at that,'' Pat said. '' Isn't it disgusting?''

Helen stepped back to view her handiwork. ''Well, it's not very readable from a distance, but I wouldn't say—''

Her aunt snorted. ''It looks like some anarchist's manifesto, with that smudgy old photograph and tiny print! A *sketch* is what that flier needs to look elegant.''

Helen was about to suggest that what the flier really needed was a better printer, but her aunt's expectant smile warned her there was another surprise in store. ''What have you done now, Aunt Pat?''

''I volunteered your services, dearest.''

''To Mr. McKenna?'' Helen asked, with foreboding.

''Well, the poor dear man hasn't the money to pay a real artist. So I told him you would sketch him while he lectured.''

''Aunt Pittypat!''

''It's not as if you wouldn't be there anyway, dearest,'' Pat argued. ''All you need to do is bring a sketchbook along and dash off a study or two—''

''At night, by gaslight, in this maze?'' Helen gestured at the high twin-market buildings that filled Market Square, their arched pedestrian walkways shadowing the brick streets beneath. ''Any picture I'd draw wouldn't be worth the paper it covered.''

''Rubbish.'' Aunt Pat tapped an affectionate finger against

her cheek. "Mr. McKenna said that too, but I told him that anyone who could draw a recognizable picture of a dead person could draw a sketch of him during his lecture."

"Assuming he *does* give a lecture," said someone behind them.

Helen swung around abruptly at the sound of that grating voice. From a few paces away, Father Karl Zawisza met their stares with his usual chilly expression. The young priest held what looked like a market basket in one hand, but a closer glance told Helen it was full of printed leaflets. Somehow, she doubted that they were religious tracts he was passing out for the church.

"What do you mean, if Dennis McKenna *does* give a lecture?" she demanded. "My aunt has it arranged for next Tuesday."

Zawisza made no outward sound of disdain, but the dubious arch of his white-blond eyebrows left Helen feeling as if he had. "I've never heard of this 'famous temperance lecturer' of yours," he remarked. "And I believe Mrs. McGregor has been taken in by would-be circuit speakers before."

"I wasn't taken in," said Pittypat, bristling. "We just had a—a misunderstanding over the payment of a fee. And Mr. McKenna's not like that at all. He comes with the highest recommendations from the work he's done in Chicago!"

Zawisza gave her an unimpressed arctic stare. "I was in Chicago just this last summer, Mrs. McGregor. I never heard this man McKenna mentioned by any of the temperance workers there."

The crumpled look on her aunt's face made Helen's half-Italian temper erupt. "And we know just how much to believe of what you say about Chicago," she retorted. "After all, you said you hadn't seen Lide Janczek there, either!"

Zawisza's cheekbones streaked an ugly dark red, visible even through the smoky afternoon. "That's because I *didn't* see her."

"Well, you're lying!" Helen shot back. "I have proof that you and she spent time together out there, Father Zawisza. And if you can't remember *that*, then I don't think you'd remember hearing about Mr. McKenna even if he were the mayor of Chicago!''

The young priest's face convulsed with anger, but his grating voice seemed to have clogged in his throat. Deciding to retreat while she was in command of the field, Helen tugged on her aunt's arm. ''Come on, Aunt Pat. Let's get out of here.''

''Yes, let's.'' Aunt Pittypat swept up her skirts and surged majestically past Father Zawisza. ''You know, dearest, it's a good thing that young man decided to go into the priesthood.''

''A *good* thing?'' Helen repeated, puzzled. ''Why?''

''Because then no woman had to marry him.'' Pat McGregor paused in front of a greengrocers to poke a cabbage. ''Even your Cousin Gillan would have made a terrible husband, although he was a very good priest. Take my advice, Helen—stay away from policemen and men who should have been priests. If you ask me, I think you should marry a bricklayer. I've never met a bricklayer who wasn't a wonderful man.'' She peered up at Helen. ''I don't suppose you know any bricklayers, dear?''

''No, and I wouldn't marry one if I did,'' Helen retorted. ''For your information, Aunt Pat, I'm not going to marry anyone.''

''Well, it's true you don't need to,'' her aunt admitted. ''With the money you make writing and working at the settlement house, you can stay single for as long as you like.'' She shook her head, scattering soot from her overburdened silk butterflies. ''Still, I can't help thinking, Helen, that someday *Thomas* may wish to marry.''

Helen caught her breath, startled. She was so used to thinking of her twin as an overgrown adolescent, that it was difficult to envision him married and the head of a family of his own. ''I hope he may,'' she said at last. ''And what if he does?''

Aunt Pat pulled her spectacles out of her muff to inspect the carrots and parsnips that shared the wooden boxes with some frost-pinched winter greens. ''Not all women would care to share their house with a sister-in-law.''

''In that case, Aunt, I'll move in with you.''

"And have the cats sharing your bedroom?"

Helen wrinkled her nose. She had no objection to cats in their ones and twos, especially if they were good mousers, but the two dozen spoiled denizens of Aunt Pat's house drove her to distraction. And her aunt was always rescuing more.

"No, that won't do, will it?" Helen heared a deep, theatrical sigh. "I suppose I'll just have to buy a big dog before I move in."

"A *dog*?" Her aunt gave her a ominous look. "Don't you even think about bringing a dog into my house! I'd rather have an Irish policeman."

Helen laughed and tugged Pat into the market building. "Then stop complaining and shop."

By the time they emerged from the last of the market shops, the oppressive soot clouds had thickened into a sullen twilight haze. Helen swept Diamond Street with a frown. The homeward rush of clerks and businessmen had begun, and there were no empty cabs in sight. Even the trolley that had sparked to a stop in the gloom down the street was overloaded with passengers.

Helen heard her aunt coughing behind her, and her frown deepened. "Did you tell Joe O'Grady to wait for us, Aunt Pat?"

"No, but he always does." Pat McGregor peered through the smoke. "He usually parks down on Wood Street, but I can't see that far from here. Perhaps we should walk down to meet him, and then pick Mr. McKenna up on the way back."

Helen took a deep breath, then wished she hadn't. "No, you go back inside and wait. I'll walk down to Wood Street and find Joe, then come back to fetch you and Mr. McKenna."

"If you can't find him, dearest, do try to get a cab with a good horse."

"Yes, I will." It was a safe enough promise to make. At this time of day, Helen's definition of a good horse was any that had four legs and a cab attached to its rump. She buttoned her coat to keep out the ash that had begun to drift through the smoke, wrapped her silk scarf inelegantly but effectively across her nose and mouth, and set out for Wood Street.

The east side of Diamond Avenue was lined with waiting carriages, but their well-fed horses and uniformed drivers told Helen they were all privately owned. No doubt they were waiting to take home businessmen from the seven- and eight-story high-rise offices that lined the block. Another example of how excessive wealth wasted resources, Helen decided. Not to mention taking up space that by rights belonged to pedestrians.

She gave the driver of one badly parked carriage a scalding look as she skirted it, forced out into the muck of the street to avoid colliding with his horse's nose. "A good thing I'm not an elderly lady with a cane, isn't it?" she said sharply, when she was back on the sidewalk. The chauffeur muttered apologetically in German and climbed down from his seat to take the feed bag off the horse's muzzle so he could back the carriage up.

Mollified, Helen hurried on to Wood Street. A glance through the murk showed her at least two cabs standing empty down the street. She waved at them in vain, then tried to whistle. The squeal and clatter of an approaching trolley drowned her out. Even as she watched, a young clerk emerged from a nearby office and took possession of one of them.

Helen muttered an Italian word that would have scandalized her mother, and picked up her skirts again. In her hurry to catch the remaining cab, she didn't look before she swung to cross Diamond Avenue, and bumped solidly into a passerby. "Excuse me," she said without bothering to look up, and began to skirt him.

She hadn't taken two steps when she was bumped from behind, much harder, and nearly pushed into the street.

"Hey!" Indignation rushed through Helen at this unfair retaliation, and she spun around to confront her opponent. "There's no need to—"

Gloved hands seized her by the shoulders before she could complete her turn, pulling her back against a man's heavy overcoat. Shock held Helen motionless, long enough to realize she was being deliberately attacked. Then fear unlocked her muscles and her voice. With all her considerable strength, she tried to break her assailant's grip, knowing her screams for help were being drowned out by the louder clanging of the approaching trolley.

It was only after her struggle landed her, released but off balance, on the hard Belgian blocks rimming the trolley tracks that Helen realized she should have been fighting her attacker's continuing shoves rather than just his grasp on her. She gasped and tasted electric-scorched air as the trolley's shadow loomed over her, sparks flaring in the smoke and darkness. She tried to wrench herself out of its path, but one last shove sent her sprawling directly across the steel rails.

Dressed as fashion said she should have been, in a tightly laced corset and long, trailing skirts, Helen would have died. But her sensible skirts saved her, riding up past her ankles as she skidded across the cold ground and freeing her to roll over onto her hands and feet. Fueled by desperation, hands scrabbling and toes digging for purchase against the stones, she lunged for safety like a runner bursting from his blocks.

The trolley's brakes screeched, a horrible, endless sound. Heart hammering with terror, she felt the draft of its imminent passage and dove out of its path, hugging herself into a ball in overwhelming dread of losing her feet or hands. With her eyes closed, she didn't realize she was safe until strong hands closed around her shoulders and pulled her to a sitting position.

Helen gasped and swung an elbow up desperately, trying to fend him off. "No!"

"*Fraulein, fraulein, nein—*" The voice broke off, but the hands stayed on her shoulders, patting her reassuringly. Opening her eyes, she saw the carriage-driver she had snapped at a moment before. He leaned over her, scarf falling away to reveal a strong young face. It was a face that Helen knew.

"You're the guard," she said breathlessly and scrambled to her feet to get away from him. The trolley had stopped, a dozen feet past where she'd been thrown, and the ashen-faced conductor was hurrying toward her. "The Black Point

Steel gatehouse, yesterday—you're the one who let us in.''

The young guard nodded. "I am from Black Point, yes. I am sent by Herr Captain Flinn—''

It was enough to send fear thrumming through her again. Helen took another step away, throwing herself at the approaching conductor. "A cab," she said, before he could even ask if she was hurt. "Please, can you get me a cab?''

"But, miss, you were *pushed*—'' The conductor peered at her through small round spectacles, his whiskered face appalled. "We ought to call the police!''

"I am going to call the police," Helen assured him. From the corner of her eye, she could see the young Black Point guard heading down Diamond Avenue, back toward his carriage—or back toward Aunt Pittypat. "But I have an aunt here and I can't keep her waiting in the smoke—''

She knew it probably sounded as if she'd been knocked silly, but she didn't care. What was important was to get a cab and put Aunt Pat into it. Dennis McKenna could find his own way home.

"If that's what you want, miss." The conductor looked around, then whistled shrilly to summon an empty cab whose driver had paused to watch the commotion in the street. "But I'm going to have to report this at the end of my run.''

"Yes, please do." Helen forced her shaking legs to support her as far as the cab door. "Call your report in to Patrol Station Seven, on the South Side.''

The conductor whistled again, this time in what sounded like admiration, and then scurried back to his stalled car. Helen had to use both hands to haul herself into the cab, collapsing gratefully against the cracked cushions inside. Now that the shock was subsiding, she was aware of a multitude of small hurts: skinned hands where her gloves had torn against the stones, a bruised hip and elbow where she'd taken the brunt of the fall, aching shoulders from her attacker's savage grip. She took a deep breath, reminding herself how much worse it could have been.

"Spagnola's Fruit Company, please," she told the driver standing beside the door. "There's a lady waiting for me. You'll have to go in and fetch her.''

"All right, miss. And then to hospital?''

"No, then to the South Side." Helen had banged herself up enough as a child to know that her cuts and bruises didn't need immediate attention. "And don't let my aunt tell you otherwise."

The cabman nodded and climbed onto his bench, setting his horse in motion with a jerk. Groaning, Helen leaned back and closed her eyes. With Black Point Steel involved in this attack, her first priority was to get Aunt Pat safely out of harm's way.

After that she could call Milo.

"Who was it?"

Helen glanced up from the bowl of blood-stained water in which she was soaking her scraped palms. The unannounced slam of the front door had led her to expect Thomas, doctor in tow, but it was Milo Kachigan coming hatless through the drawing room door, his coat flapping open from his shoulders. He must have come like that straight from the patrol station, Helen thought inconsequentially, since he hadn't been in the house long enough to unbutton it.

"What on earth are you doing here?" she demanded. "Thomas tried to ring you up just a moment ago. They said at the patrol station that you were out."

"Of course, I was out." He crossed the room in three long strides to stand beside her. "A trolley driver just called Patrol Station Seven to report that a woman had been pushed in front of his car. When he said she'd told him to call us, I knew it had to be you." Kachigan dipped his own fingers into the bowl of water without warning, turning her hands over to inspect the damage. "Where else are you hurt?"

His voice sounded stiff and unfriendly, but Helen had enough experience of her brother to recognize reined-in rage. "I bruised my hip when I fell, that's all," she said, hoping to defuse it. "It only hurts a little where he grabbed me—"

"He?" the detective demanded.

Helen bit her lip. "I didn't see who it was. At least, not when he attacked. I brushed past him on Wood Street without looking up, and then he caught me from behind and pushed me."

Kachigan's eyebrows slanted into a grimmer version of

his usual inquiring look. "But you did see him later?"

"I think so. Just after I rolled out of the trolley's way, there was a man who came to help me up." Helen took a deep breath. "It was one of the guards who let us in at Black Point Steel yesterday, the younger one. I can't remember his name."

"Westbeld." The stifled fury she heard in the detective's voice told her the news came as confirmation, not surprise. "Did he say anything?"

"Just that Bernard Flinn had sent him—" Helen broke off as Kachigan whirled and started for the door, then scrambled up in alarm to follow him. "Milo, where are you going?"

The sound of dripping water caught Kachigan on the threshold and drew him back. "To talk to Flinn before he tries this again." He slid her badly scraped left hand back into the bowl, but kept the other cupped in his, glancing down at the blood-flecked palm. A corner of his mouth jerked. "I'm sorry."

"I'm the one who set out to make Flinn mad at me," she reminded him tartly. "It's not your fault if I succeeded a little too well."

"It's my fault you ever had to get involved with a man like Flinn. I put you in danger when I brought you into this investigation, Helen. I'll take you out of it."

"By putting yourself in danger instead?" she demanded.

"If I have to." Unexpectedly, he bent his head and lifted her hand, dropping a kiss on her cold wet fingers. When he straightened up again, it was with a ghost of a smile. "Although it will probably be sufficient to take Bernard Flinn out of it."

13

EARLY EVENING SMOKE VEILED THE house on the hill, but its glimmer of leaded windows still outlined a three-story height and wide, turreted wings. Kachigan vaulted out of his hired cab and scowled up at it. He'd been expecting a solid East End family house at the address listed for Flinn in the Polk Directory, not this palatial Victorian estate. He turned back to question the cabdriver but found him already gone, as if he knew his South Side hack didn't belong on these chestnut-lined streets.

Kachigan suspected he didn't belong here either, but the hard-won calm he'd gained on the ride still had enough fury smoldering beneath it to send him striding up the stone-flagged drive. He emerged from the shadow of bare winter trees to hear the sound of a piano drift out an upper-story window. It stopped when he hammered on the door. A shadow darkened the frosted panes and Kachigan heard a lock click over. The door opened just far enough to reveal the face of a polite red-haired maid.

"Yes?"

"I'd like to see Mr. Bernard Flinn, please."

"I am sorry." She had a hint of German accent, not the Irish brogue he'd expected, and Kachigan's doubts about the address grew stronger. Her next words unexpectedly removed them. "Mr. Flinn is not yet home."

"Do you expect him soon?"

The maid began to reply, but from somewhere behind her a more elegant voice interrupted. "Who is it, Johanna? Why haven't you let him in?"

She turned. "Because I do not know him, madam."

"Oh!" Satin rustled stiffly across the floor and a lace-mittened hand pulled the door fully open. Kachigan found himself facing not the buxom Irish matron he'd expected, or even a young and dashing second bride, but a fragile middle-aged lady whose eyes were the color of faded violets. She gazed up at him in mild inquiry. "I'm afraid I don't know you either."

He inclined his head. "My name is Milo Kachigan. I'm a detective with the Pittsburgh police."

"Oh!" Her voice, already made breathless by her tight-laced evening dress, became a frantic gasp. "Has there been an accident? Is my husband hurt?"

"No, ma'am, not at all." Faced with the innocent anxiety in those faded eyes, Kachigan felt his fury recede a little. He searched for an acceptable explanation of his visit. "I stopped by to consult with your husband on—on a police matter."

"Oh, I see." Reassured by his words, or perhaps just by the softened tone of his voice, Mrs. Flinn began to swing the door wider. The red-haired maid frowned and put out a hand to stop her. "Johanna, what are you doing?"

"We do not know he is from the police, madam," the maid said stubbornly. "Mr. Flinn told the staff we had to be careful."

Kachigan extracted his badge and held it out. Mrs. Flinn glanced down at it in faint surprise, as if she'd never seen one before, then helplessly gestured for him to show it to the maid. The younger woman scrutinized it, nodded and stepped back to allow Kachigan in.

"Let me show you to the drawing room, Detective Kachigan." Mrs. Flinn's satin dress whispered across the carpeted floor as she turned, a waterfall of intricate embroidery that had probably taken a dozen women to sew. "You shouldn't have long to wait. We sit down to supper at seven, and my husband is generally punctual."

"Thank you." Kachigan reached up to remove his hat as he entered, remembering only when his fingers hit wind-tangled hair that he hadn't bothered to put one on. No wonder the maid thought he looked disreputable. "I'll try not to delay your meal."

Mrs. Flinn paused outside the heavy gold-fringed curtains that framed her drawing room. "Surely, Mr. Kachigan, your police matter is far more important than my supper?"

His mouth relaxed into a brief smile. "I think so, ma'am. I just wasn't sure you would agree." He scanned the furniture-stuffed salon, wondering whether his sooty clothes would leave less impression on cream brocade or gold-embroidered velvet. Probably best just to remain standing, he decided. That way, Bernard Flinn wouldn't tower over him quite so much.

"Anyone who knows my husband knows that his work comes before his comfort," Mrs. Flinn told him reprovingly. "But perhaps you have not had much acquaintance with his methods."

"Yes, I have." Without warning all his submerged rage at Bernard K. Flinn rose in his throat, choking him into bitter silence. The only concession he made to Mrs. Flinn's middle-aged innocence was to lower his gaze so she couldn't see the angry glitter in his eyes. Fortunately, before she had time to make more conversation, her husband's shout hurled startled echoes across the foyer.

"Policeman? *What* policeman?" Quick strides brought the burly figure of Bernard Flinn to the drawing room entrance, and Kachigan looked up to see his astonishment flare into murderous fury. "Kachigan! What the hell are you doing in my house?"

Though it took a monumental effort, Kachigan managed to keep his voice polite and expressionless. "As I told your wife, Mr. Flinn, I came to consult with you on an urgent professional matter. I'd appreciate a few moments of your time."

Flinn's suspicious gaze darted to his wife's face, lingered for a moment on her expression of gentle censure, then swung back to Kachigan. By that time, the steel-police chief's fury had subsided to mere irritation. "Of course I can spare some time if it's urgent. You'll excuse us, Margaret?''

"Yes, dear.'' She paused beside him on her way out, lifting her thin cheek for a kiss. It was disturbing to see how completely Flinn's massive hands encircled her overlaced waist, as if he could break her in two. "I'll tell cook to hold dinner until you ring for it.''

With a gracious rustle of satin, she turned toward the mahogany staircase, ascending with the measured pace of a woman who cannot draw a deep breath. Neither Kachigan nor Flinn said anything until the tap of her footsteps faded, and the muted sound of a piano cascaded down into the foyer.

"All right, Kachigan. You've got five minutes to cut the crap and tell me what you want.'' Flinn shrugged off his overcoat and dropped it on a brocade sofa, heedless of the soot it scattered. His face lit with a dangerous gleam of teeth as he sprawled beside it. "And that's only because my wife would worry if I tossed you headfirst out the door right now.''

Kachigan measured the grim intensity behind the words, and discarded his initial strategy of accusation. "Mr. Flinn, what would you do if I threatened your wife with harm?''

He'd planned to provoke an attack, but its utter silence caught him unprepared. Exploding out of his lazy sprawl, Flinn whirled Kachigan into an armlock and shoved him face-first against the nearest mantelpiece, all without making more than a scuff of sound. The police chief's voice dropped to a growl.

"If you ever touched my wife, you bastard, I'd flay every inch of skin off your back.'' He leaned his considerable weight onto Kachigan, pressing his throat harder against the cold marble. "And then I'd take it off all the rest of you.''

It wasn't easy to sound calm with his voice flattened to a rasp and his lungs aching for air, but somehow Kachigan managed. "Then you know exactly how I feel about you.''

He heard a breath sucked in behind him, and a moment later he was spun roughly free. Kachigan staggered, then caught his balance and turned to meet Flinn's narrow-eyed gaze. His wrenched shoulder yelled in protest when he lifted a hand to rub his throat, but the pain only kindled his anger hotter. He fixed the other man with a long, unwavering stare.

"Christ almighty, Kachigan, aren't you afraid of anything?"

It wasn't the question he'd been expecting, but Kachigan answered it, anyway. "I'm afraid of what you can do to Helen Sorby. And I'm willing to cut a deal with you to keep her safe."

The steel-police chief closed his mouth on whatever he'd been about to say. "What kind of deal?"

Kachigan felt a muscle twitch in his jaw. "Admit that you ordered your men to murder Josef Janczek and his wife. Admit it here, just between the two of us, and I'll close the murder investigation." He swallowed past the bruised ache of his throat. "I can't try you for it, anyway. Not with the mayor we have now."

Flinn snorted. "Not ever, Kachigan." He snorted again, more deeply, and Kachigan realized he was laughing. "Christ, I really should do it. Just to get the damned mess over with."

Kachigan gritted his teeth. "*Did* you do it, Flinn?"

"Kill Josef Janczek?" Flinn strode over to Kachigan again, and the detective stiffened against an urge to back away. "No." A fist came up and clenched on his waistcoat, just hard enough to give him an admonishing shake. "And I didn't push Helen Sorby in front of a trolley, either. I don't have any damn-fool scruples about fighting men who are smaller than me, but I don't touch their women and children. Ever."

Kachigan scowled up at him, infuriated enough by the denial to shake off Flinn's hard grip. "That's a lie. Helen saw your man, before *and* after she was attacked."

Bernard Flinn shrugged. "Sure, he was there. But he wasn't the one who pushed her." He met Kachigan's glare with another reluctant snort of laughter. "For God's sake, Kachigan, do you think I hire men stupid enough to mention my name right after they've tried to kill someone?"

"If you're trying to intimidate them into shutting up—"

"—I blackmail them!"

Kachigan frowned. "You were trying to blackmail Helen Sorby?"

Flinn sighed in exasperation, swinging away to pour pale brown liquor from a sideboard decanter into a cut-glass tumbler. "No, you idiot. I was trying to blackmail you." He shoved the glass at Kachigan, then went to pour another for himself. "After the way your Miss Sorby yelled at me this morning, I knew if I had my men follow her long enough, she'd have lunch with some anarchists, or give money to a birth control group. Or do something else equally righteous and disreputable." Flinn gave him a wicked grin over the top of the glass. "I didn't figure she'd care much about that, though you might. What I really hoped was that she'd vanish into your house for a convenient hour or two some afternoon."

The liquor in the glass was straight whiskey, not sherry, but that wasn't what made Kachigan break into coughing. "And you were hoping I'd call off my investigation because of that?"

"Wouldn't you?"

He considered the question for a moment, then shook his head. "She wouldn't have let me," he said drily.

Flinn snorted. "That's because you let her know too much about what you're up to. Better to keep her safe at home and happy."

Kachigan glanced out at the curved mahogany staircase, hearing the graceful drift of piano notes from above. He tried to imagine Helen Sorby mewed up and contented in a mansion like this, but his mind couldn't even get her indignantly over the threshold. He smiled.

"Impossible," he said; then his smile faded. "Although right now, I wish to God I could. Flinn, if your man wasn't responsible for the attack on Miss Sorby, did he see who was?"

Bernard Flinn nodded. "A man in a long overcoat, with his hat pulled down and his face wrapped in a scarf. Westbeld didn't recognize him. As soon as he was sure Miss Sorby was safe, he tried to follow the man, but on a smoky day like that—"

"—everyone walks around with their faces wrapped in a scarf," Kachigan agreed. They stood in grim silence for a moment. "Flinn, are you willing to swear to me—on your wife's honor—that you didn't have the Janczeks killed?''

Flinn grunted, tossing back the rest of his drink. ''Mother of God, Kachigan, don't you ever quit? If I *did* kill them, who do you think is trying to hurt your Miss Sorby now?''

''Maybe the men on your force who actually did it,'' Kachigan retorted. ''You don't know everything they do.''

''No,'' Flinn agreed. ''But I know what they *don't* do. They don't murder our own paid informers.''

Silence echoed hard around the room, but it took Kachigan a moment to realize it was because the sound of the piano had ceased. ''Janczek was on your payroll?'' he demanded. ''You put him into Taylor Mill to spy on his mates?''

The steel-police chief rolled his burly shoulders in a gesture that could have been either acknowledgment or a shrug. ''Mostly, I told him to annoy people,'' he said with unexpected humor. ''Nothing puts men off unions like thinking that unionizers are a pain in the butt. That fit with the information you weaseled out of Janczek's shift-mates?''

Kachigan opened his mouth to deny it, then realized it was pointless. ''Yes,'' he admitted and recklessly emptied his own glass. The whiskey burned down his throat to join the now-impotent burn of his anger. ''I'm going to make a deal with you.''

''A better deal than the last one?''

He nodded. ''I want to find Janczek's killer. I *have* to find him now, to keep Helen Sorby safe. And you don't want the unionizers in Taylor Mill to know you placed an informer there.'' He didn't make it a question, and he wasn't surprised by Flinn's assenting silence. ''If I promise to keep Janczek's real job a secret, will you stop interfering in my murder case?''

Flinn grunted. ''Fair enough. But I'm warning you, Kachigan, if I get one hint from my men that you've stirred up more trouble for me at Taylor Mill, you're going to wish it was you who died in that damned fire.'' The Black Point Steel police chief set his glass down as if the conversation was over. Out in the foyer, Milo heard the rustle of satin skirts on the staircase. ''Now go say goodbye to my wife and go home.''

• • •

No cabman in Pittsburgh ever bothered to look for fares in the quiet avenues of the East End, where the residents all had carriages and the servants all lived in. Milo Kachigan walked the three miles back into the city, judging his progress by the thickening smoke around each gas streetlamp he passed. By the time he started across the Brady Street Bridge to the South Side, the fires of Jones & Laughlin Steel across the Mon had dwindled to alarmingly faint glows behind a curtain of black soot. Without a scarf, Kachigan's occasional coughs became a constant hacking that tore at his throat and made his damaged cheekbone ache. He ducked his chin into his coat collar and kept going through the haze of pain, not stopping until light from a stained-glass transom poured over him like a benediction.

He didn't remember knocking, but the carved oak door on Sarah Street opened to him, anyway. "Milo!" Helen Sorby looked alarmed when he didn't reply. "What's wrong? Are you hurt?"

Kachigan shook his head, trying to silence his coughing long enough to explain that his feet had carried him to her door without his tired mind even realizing it. Before he'd managed to croak out two consecutive words, Helen reached out and hauled him into the house with both bandaged hands.

"Shut up," she said, yanking his coat off despite his rasp of protest. Her eyes were dark with either irritation or concern. With Helen, it was sometimes hard to tell. "I'm not letting you back outside while you're coughing like that. You need something hot to drink, and we already have coffee made for supper. Now stop talking. Thomas!"

Kachigan surrendered gratefully. It took longer than he thought for his coughing to subside, but by the time he was settled in their small, warm kitchen with black salve on his throat and a cup of coffee steaming in his hands, he managed to find enough breath to say, "Thank you."

Helen paused in ripping up a frayed flannel sheet for his throat. "Don't thank me," she warned. "I want you to be able to talk, so you can tell me what happened tonight."

Kachigan let himself cough a few more times, while he sorted through his conversation with Flinn for acceptable excerpts. While he was editing, Helen came to undo the top button on his shirt and wind the flannel around his throat. Kachigan should have closed his eyes when she bent over him, but instead he measured the reassuringly normal curves of her plain cotton shirtwaist and saw the rise and fall of natural breathing beneath it. After being subjected to Margaret Flinn's unspeakably fragile grace, Helen looked as ordinary and as comforting as a kitchen fire on a winter night.

Thomas glanced over his shoulder from the skillet of veal and potatoes he was frying for supper. His eyes gleamed with a young man's laughter when he saw the direction of Kachigan's gaze. "Nothing like a cup of hot coffee to make you feel better, is there, Mr. Kachigan?" he observed innocently.

Kachigan threw him a wry look over his sister's bent head. "No. And you can call me Milo."

"Oh, is *that* your first name?" the surveyor asked, with even more angelic innocence.

Helen straightened to give her brother an exasperated look. "This is no time to be funny, Thomas." Her steady gaze came back to Kachigan. "Flinn hit you," she said, not making it a question. She must have seen the reddened spot on his throat that would be a bruise by tomorrow.

"He leaned on me a little." Kachigan sipped cautiously at his coffee. The murky liquid tasted as if the beans had been incinerated and then boiled for a month, but its rich darkness coated his throat and drowned the urge to cough. "I had to make him angry to get the information that I wanted."

"And did you get it?"

He nodded somberly. "I got it, but it wasn't what I wanted. In fact, it was about the worst news—"

Thomas Sorby splashed some red wine into his frying pan and the resulting burst of aromatic steam caught at Kachigan's sore throat, making him struggle not to cough. Helen went to get plates from the cupboard while she waited for him to resume. Less patient, Thomas gave his skillet a final scrape and thumped it on the table between them. "So what was the horrible news?"

"Flinn's innocent."

Helen stopped an arm's length away from the table, her

hands full of bowls and forks and her eyes disbelieving. "Bernard Flinn *can't* be innocent. Milo, how could you think so?"

He met her gaze without flinching. "Because he told me that Josef Janczek was a paid informer."

"And you *believed* him?"

Thomas grunted, reaching out to snag a fork from his sister's hands. "They say there's one in every shop." He dug into the steaming skillet without bothering to wait for a bowl. "Of course, I always thought that could be a rumor spread to keep the workers from unionizing."

"That's exactly what it is." Helen smacked a bowl down in front of her twin so hard the china rang against the enameled metal tabletop. Thomas dropped his fork guiltily and reached for a serving spoon, but her irritation wasn't directed at him. Kachigan's bowl got thumped down just as hard. "I can't believe you're letting him off with such an easy lie."

Kachigan picked up the fork she'd dropped beside his bowl, waiting for Helen to sit before he reached for the skillet. Serving her first didn't mollify her, although it did make Thomas look slightly abashed. Kachigan thought about all the things he could try to explain, and ended up saying only, "I don't think he was lying."

Helen's straight eyebrows rumpled into a magnificent frown. "But I saw his guard there, right after I was pushed. He even admitted that Flinn sent him!"

"Yes, I know that." Kachigan forked up some of the potatoes from his bowl, startled to see flakes of hot red pepper glistening among them. He swallowed carefully past the ache of his throat. "Flinn said he sent the guard to watch you, so he could blackmail me into closing Janczek's case."

"Blackmail *you*?" Helen's frown melted into genuine bewilderment. "How could he blackmail you by watching me?"

Her twin glanced across at Kachigan, masculine understanding in his face. "Flinn thought he'd catch you two together?"

"Mmm."

Helen's cheeks flamed and she dropped her gaze to her bowl, eating in self-conscious silence for a while. Thomas

gave her a concerned look, then got up and went to the sink
to fill three glasses with water. "I guess I made the veal and
potatoes a little hotter than Helen likes them," he said, to
fill the silence while he carried the water back to the table.

"No, it's not that," Helen said with an honest sigh. "I
just can't believe that Bernard Flinn thought my reputation
would be more important than a murder investigation."

"I told him you wouldn't let me do it," Kachigan said.

"Yes, but if it wasn't Flinn's men who killed Josef Janczek, who *was* it?"

He scrubbed at his cheek in frustration. It was all he'd
thought about on the agonizing walk back to the city, and
he'd only been able to reach one unwelcome conclusion.

"Janczek's shift-mates knew he was spying on them," he
said reluctantly. "They told us as much. What if one of them
really *was* a unionizer and Janczek decided not to report him
to the bosses? If he was trying to shake the man down for
money instead, he might have—"

"No!" Helen dropped her fork into her bowl with an angry clatter. "That's the first thing stupid people do when
someone from the underclass is victimized." Her voice rose
with each fierce word. "Blame the other victims! They're all
poor, they must all be criminals. Well, Milo Kachigan, I'm
not going to let you do it! I'm not going to, because *you're
not that stupid*!"

And on that last resounding shout, she leaped out of her
chair and slammed through the kitchen door, leaving Kachigan to stare after her in wordless frustration.

"In case you're wondering," Thomas said helpfully, "that
time, she was mad at you."

14

A HORSE-DRAWN CAB LOOMED OUT OF the morning smoke, jingling to a stop at the curb just as Helen dug her front door key from her coat pocket. She glanced toward it, then found her view abruptly limited to her brother's shoulders.

"Go inside." Thomas shoved the Sunday newspaper and their loaf of morning bread at her. "I'll see who that is."

"Do you think—"

"Probably just some neighbors coming home from church." Despite his reassuring words, Thomas pushed her through the door and then slammed it behind her. "Lock it," his muffled voice said from outside. "Just in case it's not."

Helen obeyed him, dropping bread and newspaper carelessly onto the floor. Her wool coat landed beside them, hastily thrown off so she could pull up her skirts and jump onto the telephone bench beside the door. Pressing her nose to the transom, she saw Thomas stop halfway across the slate sidewalk, then saw the reason why. A familiar blue overcoat had emerged from the cab's opened door. A moment later, Milo Kachigan's gaze rose to meet hers through the one clear-glass panel.

"*Manniagga*!" Helen said and jumped down to undo the lock, kicking aside the tangle of coat, newspaper and bread as she did. "What are you doing here?" she demanded when the door swung open.

"Coming in for breakfast," her twin said mildly. "Do you mind if I invite a friend?"

Helen opened her mouth to say yes, but with his usual irritating perception, Kachigan forestalled her. "I'm sorry, Thomas, but I don't have time for breakfast." His gaze met Helen's steadily. "I've arranged to meet Christy Zullo at a public park this morning. There's a patrolman at the station who speaks Italian, but I thought you might want to translate instead." A corner of his mouth lifted. "That way, you can be sure I don't make any stupid middle-class assumptions."

Helen frowned at him, torn between a need to see justice done and unexpected discomfort at the thought of spending time with Milo Kachigan. "I don't know—"

"You can post some of your aunt's fliers while we're there."

Helen opened her mouth to deny that she had any more of Dennis McKenna's fliers to post, then realized that Kachigan could see the stack of leftovers still sitting on the receiving table. The stupidity of her reaction shocked her into realizing that the emotion roiling in her wasn't anger, but embarrassment. She took a deep breath, scolding herself. A fine social reformer she'd be if she let a man get framed for murder just because she was ashamed of losing her temper.

"Very well, Mr. Kachigan," she said, trying to match his measured tone. "I'll come with you."

"Thank you."

Thomas looked up from where he had knelt to sort out the mess on the floor. "Breakfast," he reminded Helen. When she ignored him to pick up her coat, he cast a warning glance at Kachigan. "She'll be grumpy all morning if she doesn't eat."

"*Thomas*!"

"Well, it's true."

Kachigan frowned down at the steel watch he'd pulled from his waistcoat pocket. "The problem is, Zullo asked me to meet him at nine. I'm not sure he'll be there if we're late."

Helen glowered at her graceless brother, who was handing her the stack of remaining fliers. "Just tear me off some of that bread, and I'll eat it in the carriage. Will that make you happy?"

"Only if I can keep the ends."

"Thomas, you can keep everything but the squishy middle for all I care. Just hurry!"

He shook the loaf free of its wrappings, breaking off both ends in a shower of dark, egg-browned crust. What was left was more than Helen could eat, but a glance at Kachigan's frown told her not to waste time protesting. "Thanks," she said and followed the detective down to the waiting cab.

Kachigan handed her in without a word, then glanced up at the driver. "Do you know where Little Jim Park is?"

"On East Sidney Street, behind the old Carnegie mill?"

"That sounds like the right neighborhood. Get us there by nine." The detective climbed in beside Helen, and with an industrious clatter of hooves, the cab swerved into the street.

The morning smoke, so dark that gas lamps had been left burning to light the streets, closed around the carriage like a muffling blanket. Helen dropped her gaze to the fliers she held on her lap, reading the smudged text as if there was something to be learned from its vague encomiums. The silence lengthened.

"In case you're wondering, I'd rather be yelled at than not talked to at all," Kachigan informed her.

Helen gave him an exasperated look. "I don't want to yell at you. At least, not yet. I just don't have anything to say."

"Then you must need to eat breakfast." He reached out and took the bread from her bandaged hands, tearing off a manageable piece for her to eat. Helen took the chunk he handed her, then eyed what remained.

"Have you had your breakfast yet?"

Kachigan shrugged. "I ate something when I got up."

"And when was that?"

"About four A.M.," he admitted. "After last night, I had some thinking I needed to do."

She frowned at him. "About Bernard Flinn, you mean? You didn't have to get up at four in the morning to decide he was lying to you. Eat some bread."

"I wasn't thinking about Flinn." Kachigan tore off another piece of bread obediently. "I was thinking about the men he let us talk to at Taylor Mill. There was something odd about them."

"Besides the fact that none of them spoke English?"

Kachigan nodded, his mouth too full for the moment to reply. "That's what misled me," he said, after he swallowed. "You see, you were right about me making assumptions. I assumed that if those men couldn't speak English, then they had just come off the boat and were unskilled laborers in the mill."

Helen hesitated, but her innate honesty won out. "So did I," she admitted. "What makes you think they weren't?"

"The fact that all but two of them were Poles."

She could see it meant something to him, but she couldn't guess why. "A lot of Polish immigrants live on the Strip."

"So do a lot of Serbs and Italians. As unskilled laborers, they would all get mixed together. But Black Point Steel keeps its skilled craftsmen segregated by nationality, as much as they can." Kachigan must have seen her puzzled look. "It's just another way to discourage the workers from organizing."

"I figured that out for myself," Helen said tartly. "I was wondering how you came to know so much about how a foundry is run."

Nothing changed in his face, but she was learning to recognize the slight stiffening that meant the detective's guard was up. "Two of my uncles used to work at Carnegie Iron and Steel in Monessen," Kachigan said at last. "My mother's brothers. I told you she was Armenian, not Irish."

"And did your father complain about her coffee?"

To her immense satisfaction, the unexpected question jerked a startled look out of Kachigan. "*What*?"

Helen shrugged. "I make coffee the way my mother used to, Mr. Kachigan: roasted until it burns and then brewed strong. I've never known any of our Irish friends to drink it without complaining. You never even blinked last night." She gave him an intent look. "I assume your mother made her coffee the same way. Did your father complain about it as much as mine did?"

That got her a flash of smile instead of the discomfited look she was hoping for. "My father preferred beer, Miss Sorby. And I'm used to coffee like that because the pot at the patrol station always boils down to a crust before anyone thinks to refill it.'' He lifted an eyebrow at her. ''Now, do you want to know what progress I made on our case this morning or not?''

The easy way he referred to ''our case'' disarmed Helen, as she suspected he'd known it would. ''How on earth did you find someone to question this early on a Sunday?''

''By going to church.'' Kachigan's smile widened at her startled look. ''St. Stanislaus Church, over in the Strip. That's the parish most of Janczek's coworkers belong to.''

''And you saw them at Mass this morning?''

He nodded. ''Not everybody would talk to me, but the ones who did confirmed what Christy Zullo told you. They all thought Janczek was a troublemaker who should have been fired along with his friend Daniel Mahaffey. A couple of them suspected that he had a relative among the company clerks who kept him employed.''

Helen pounced on that. ''But no one suggested that he might be a company informer?''

''Not in so many words,'' Kachigan said drily. ''But they all made a point of telling me that everyone in that lathe shop was a senior machinist with at least ten years of experience at Black Point.''

Helen opened her mouth to ask what that had to do with anything, but the clatter of the cab-horse being reined to a halt drew Kachigan's attention away from her. She dusted bread crumbs off her coat and gathered up her fliers, while the detective swung open the cab door to reveal a drifting haze of mill smoke.

''Stay here a minute.'' He jumped out of the cab, almost disappearing as he took three long paces to the side of the road, then came back again. ''It looks like there's a path here. We'll have to assume the driver brought us to the right place.''

''All right.'' Helen pulled her scarf up around her nose and mouth to keep out the worst of the soot before she followed. It wasn't until she'd stepped away from the cab and felt the odd warmth of the sulfur-scented air that she realized how close they were to the battery of basic steelworks that lined the Monongahela River. What little she could see of the nearby houses looked straggling and poorly kept, as if they were overwhelmed by their proximity to the smoke-belching furnaces that towered overhead. Spatters of flame erupted through the dark smoke, and the sound of steel finishing rollers washed over them like the roar of an endless freight train.

Kachigan turned away from his inaudible conversation with the cabdriver and came back to take her arm. "He says they've just started building the park, over there."

The jerk of his chin indicated the weed-fringed industrial side of the street. Helen peered through drifting soot flakes and smoke, but saw nothing that resembled a garden. "In between all those steel mills?"

"Apparently." Kachigan led her across the packed dirt street to a path beaten through the weeds by many feet. "It's funny, though. I don't remember seeing anyone dedicate a new park site down here, when I had this patrol."

Helen tugged her coat free of an encroaching bramble. "And I don't remember Aunt Pittypat mentioning one. I'm sure she would have, if she'd known. Workingmen's parks and playgrounds are another of her causes."

He threw her a questioning look, stamping down the brambles to make the path a little wider. "But not one of yours?"

"No," Helen said bluntly. "I don't see any point to spending money on peonies and sandboxes when what people really need are food and clothing."

Kachigan grunted. "What people really need are jobs. Then they can get the rest for themselves."

"That's easy to say when you already have a job!" For once, Helen didn't have to worry about her rising voice. The rumble of the rolling mill had grown louder while they walked, until it now sounded more like an endless crash of thunder than an endless train. "But if you were an older man with a family, maybe an iron puddler laid off when your mill converted to steel—"

"—I'd still rather have a job than accept charity!"

Helen glared at him through the smoke. "If we had an equitable redistribution of wealth in this country, and some government programs to help the unemployed, you wouldn't *have* to accept charity."

"It doesn't matter who's giving out the money—" Kachigan broke off when the Carnegie boundary fence ended, revealing a crooked square of cleared land between it and the smoke-blanketed sprawl of Jones and Laughlin. "I think we've found our park."

Helen came to stand beside him, her irritation seeping away as she took in the view along the river's edge. A handful of men were spread across the abandoned property, some setting bricks into the hard ground to edge what looked like flower beds, others digging holes for the iron posts of a gazebo. All of them wore the baggy, soot-grimed clothes of mill workers.

"Do you see Zullo anywhere?" Kachigan asked.

"I don't think—no, there he is." A grizzled head had lifted at the end of one spaded flower bed. Helen waved a hand, and was rewarded with a grin and a beckoning wave in response. "Mr. Zullo doesn't look surprised to see me. Did you tell him I was coming?"

The detective shrugged. "When I sent Silvio Pedone to the address Zullo gave you, I asked him to set the meeting up for both of us. I noticed at the plant that Zullo seemed to like you."

"That's because he's from the same part of Calabria as my mother. He says he knew all her cousins back there. *Buon giorno, signore.*"

Zullo dusted dirt off his hands as he sat back on his heels. "*Fumoso giorno, signorina.*" His voice was raspy from mill work, but it held a surprising ironic humor. "*Bella America,* eh?"

"*Bella America,*" Helen agreed with a matching smile. This was one time when she didn't have to worry about her southern Italian accent getting in the way. In swift Italian, she warned, "This policeman wants to ask you some more questions about Josef Janczek. Is that all right with you?"

Zullo gave her the kind of Italian shrug that signified both resignation and disgust. "I told the young policeman this morning what I'll tell you now. I didn't know that dead man very well, and I didn't like him very much, but if it helps the police find the ones who killed his poor wife, I'll answer what I can."

Kachigan nodded when Helen relayed the mill worker's

words. "Ask Mr. Zullo how many months Janczek worked at Taylor Mill."

Helen frowned up at the detective. "Why didn't you ask Bernard Flinn that last night? If what he told you about Janczek was true, he should know."

"Just translate my question, Miss Sorby."

She did, and got a prompt reply. "Three months, almost four," Zullo told her. "Ever since the mill shut down last summer for the roof repair."

"And did Mr. Zullo know the whole time that Janczek was a company informer?"

Helen swung around, scowling up at Kachigan in surprise. "You want me to ask him *that*?"

"It seems like a pertinent question." The detective's intelligent gaze never left Christy Zullo's face. "Doesn't it?"

"But you're assuming that Janczek *was* an informer. What if he wasn't? What if Flinn lied to you?"

"In that case, Mr. Zullo should be surprised."

Helen sighed, then wished she hadn't. Even down here near the constant breeze of the river, the air was bitterly thick with smoke. Between coughs, she relayed Kachigan's question to Zullo, trying to keep the phrasing of it intact.

The mill worker grunted again, but this time good humor outweighed the resignation in his voice. "Pretty smart policeman you got there," he told Helen. "Good thing he doesn't work for that bastard Flinn, eh?"

Helen bit her lip, reluctantly translating for Kachigan. "Does that mean he knew about Janczek?" she asked, when she was done.

A snort of laughter interrupted before the detective could answer her. "Of course, he knew. We all knew."

Helen swung around, nearly colliding with the arm that Kachigan had flung up to shield her. The strongly accented voice had led her to expect one of Black Point Steel's German guards, but her first glimpse of the newcomer's broad face and wrinkled eyes reassured her as much as his baggy, dirt-stained clothes.

"Yuri Domanin." Kachigan lowered his arm. "I should have known you spoke English. My Russian's not *that* good."

The mill worker's face split with his flash of smile. "*Any* Russian is good when it comes from a policeman, Detective Kachigan." He added something in another language that Helen didn't recognize, something that made Kachigan scowl, then nod reluctantly. Domanin let out a rich Slavic rumble of laughter.

"I thought so, from the accent," he said in satisfaction. He glanced over at Christy Zullo, then startled Helen by asking the other man in slow but clear Italian if he'd been waiting long. She wondered how many different languages this Russian mill worker knew.

"Long enough to do most of your work for you." Christy thumped a hard palm against the spaded ground. "Just like every day at the mill, eh?"

The grins they shared told Helen it was a long-standing joke. "You do the hard work, I do the dangerous work," Domanin shot back in Italian. He cocked his head at Helen, laugh lines deepening around his eyes. "Well? You going to translate that for the policeman?"

She took a defiant step closer to Kachigan and did so. The detective bent his head and listened to her without surprise, then looked up at Domanin again. "Thanks," he said. "But I already had you figured for the organizer in the shop."

"*Ingegnóso carabinièri,*" Zullo muttered, shaking his head.

Yuri Domanin's grin merely widened. "And is that how you knew we were on to Janczek?"

"Partly. But mostly I knew it because you're all senior machinists." Kachigan must have noticed Helen's puzzled glance. "A newly hired worker doesn't get put in a machinist's shop straight off the unemployment line," he explained. "If Janczek had transferred to Taylor Mill from some other Black Point mill, or if he'd gotten put into their manual labor pool, it wouldn't have seemed so suspicious. But for an outsider to be assigned right into a senior machinist's shop— I'm surprised, actually. I wouldn't have thought Flinn was that stupid."

"Oh, he's not," Domanin assured him, smiling. "He wanted *us* to know little Josef worked for him. He just doesn't want the whole world to know."

And in shrewd Italian, Christy Zullo added, "The only one who didn't know *that* was Janczek."

Helen relayed that last comment to Kachigan, who fell thoughtfully silent. She didn't mind, since she was putting the pieces of the puzzle together for herself. "So Bernard Flinn just wanted to discourage union organizing in your shop. He didn't expect Janczek to actually catch anyone, just annoy them."

Domanin laughed, another deep-chested rumble that caught the attention of the men wrestling with the gazebo. "I'm sure Flinn would have been happy for Janczek to spot us, Miss Sorby. But we're not stupid, either. Eh, Christy?"

"Stupid enough to be working twelve-hour days in a mill," the older man retorted in caustic Italian.

"But not stupid enough to give ourselves away by doing anything to little Josef." Domanin met Kachigan's intent gaze. "Killing him would have told Flinn we had something to hide."

Kachigan made a noncommittal noise, pulling out his scuffed notebook. "Then can you tell me where you were last Tuesday night? And who you were with?"

Domanin shrugged. "It wouldn't do you any good to know either of those things. The men I visited with on Tuesday can't give me an alibi, since they're probably somewhere in New York by now." A shout from the gazebo drew the Russian's attention, and he waved a hand at the men beckoning him. "In a minute!"

"You can't even tell me where you met them?"

Domanin shook his head. "No offense, Detective, but I've seen Bernard Flinn get his hands on a lot of information that people thought they could keep to themselves." He glanced down at Zullo, switching to Italian. "Where were you last Tuesday, Christy? At home?"

"No, we went to the nickelodeon on East Carson Street. My wife had some laundry money she just had to spend." After a moment, he added, "I saw a picture about gold mining, out in California."

Helen translated that and Kachigan wrote it down. The men at the gazebo shouted again, more urgently, and Domanin gave his coworker an amused look. "You better go show those idiots how to start setting the piers, or we'll need to get more steel bar out of Black Point tomorrow.''

''Half of them are glass blowers, what else can you expect?'' Zullo brushed off his hands and stood up with the patient stiffness of a man who'd worked a long, hard time. He gave Helen one last shrewd glance. ''You show the young lady the rest of our park before you come help, eh? That way she and this smart policeman of hers will know what good people we are.''

''All right.'' Domanin waited while Helen translated that for Kachigan, then smiled at her. ''You want the full guided tour of Little Jim Park, or just the highlights?''

''The full tour,'' Helen said decisively. There was a human-interest magazine article here, waiting to be written. ''How long have you been working on this project?''

''Me, personally?'' The Russian led them through the swirling smoke, skirting the tilted iron frame of the gazebo. ''Only since they started needing a lot of iron-bar work. I don't live so close to here, you know. But Christy's been working here since they—uh—borrowed the property from Carnegie back in 1904.''

''The same way you 'borrowed' the steel for the gazebo from Black Point?'' Kachigan inquired.

''Well, all the companies ought to contribute, don't you think?'' Domanin slanted the detective an amused look. ''Are you going to arrest me for stealing now, instead of murder?''

''If Josef Janczek found out about the 'contributions' from Black Point Steel, I could end up arresting you for both.''

''No, Kachigan.'' The Russian made a rude noise in the back of his throat. ''Even if little Josef had caught us, all he would have done was taken some rods to sell himself, like Mahaffey did. Janczek never told the bosses about anything he could make a profit from.'' He paused to show them the bare thorny sticks of a rosebush poking out of one brick-edged bed. ''My wife donated that. Would you believe she grew it herself from seed? Now over here, you see, this will be our picnic area.''

Helen craned her head to see where Domanin had pointed. So far, all that existed of it was a rectangle of unmowed grass, carefully outlined with damp sawdust. "We'll have a brick pavement, and tables with benches attached," the Russian assured her. "And a podium, so we can hold rallies and lectures here."

The mention of lectures reminded Helen about the stack of fliers she'd absent-mindedly tucked under one arm. "Mr. Domanin, can I post some fliers here in your park?"

The Russian grunted. "There's not much up yet to post them on. But I can pass them around the Strip for you, if you tell me what they say." He reached out to take the fliers from her, eyes crinkling with his smile. "I have trouble with those little English letters, you know. They all look the same to me."

"It's an advertisement for a workingman's temperance lecture, next Tuesday night at Market Square."

"Trying to get steelworkers to take the pledge?" Domanin's eyes crinkled with amusement. "I don't think you'll get many who'll do it, Miss Sorby. At least not until we have an eight-hour working day that lets us fall asleep without a shot of vodka to still the machine-jitters."

"I know," Helen admitted. "But my Aunt McGregor—"

"—likes to throw her money at things that will do workingmen the *least* amount of good," said a newcomer, hidden by the smoke.

The voice held a familiar grating tone. Helen turned her head to see Father Karl Zawisza emerge from the haze, his long overcoat flapping carelessly open. He wore none of the priest's traditional Sunday regalia, just a plain black band under his collar. She noticed Domanin didn't look surprised to see him.

"That's not true, and you know it!" Helen retorted, incensed as usual by the priest's arrogance. "Aunt Pat gives money to every South Side church that sponsors a food and clothing drive for the poor."

"Which doesn't mean much, since her money comes from the same mills that are making the people poor," Zawisza returned.

"It's better than doing nothing at all! Which is what *you* did when Irene Prandtl and Daniel Mahaffey needed help after their house burned down.'' Helen felt her arm taken in a warning grip, but she ignored it. ''How dare you condemn my aunt, when you wouldn't even help two of your fellow anarchists?''

The priest's pale face mottled with rage. ''I've told you before that I have nothing to do with anarchists, Miss Sorby. Nothing! If it weren't for them,'' he added bitterly, ''we would have elected a socialist government in this country by now.''

Kachigan's grip on her elbow tightened fiercely enough to make Helen wince. ''Then can you explain how you came to be photographed at the anarchists' demonstration in Chicago?''

The flags of rage in Zawisza's cheeks slowly faded, leaving his face a little more glacial than before. ''I was—observing someone there, for political reasons.'' He swung toward Yuri Domanin. ''Yuri, tell them I'm not an anarchist.''

''As far as I know, you're not, Karl.'' The mill worker glanced at Kachigan, then added something in that other language that they'd spoken before. The detective shot back a fluent question and got an answer long enough to make Zawisza frown.

''I'm going over to talk to Bohun and Markosky,'' he said abruptly. ''Come see me when you're done.''

''All right.'' Domanin watched him stride off toward the knot of men by the gazebo. ''A good boy,'' he said when the priest was out of earshot. ''But a little too impetuous for his own good.''

''*Impetuous*?'' Helen scowled. ''That's not the word I'd use.''

''It's true, he's not so nice to women as he should be,'' the Russian admitted. ''I don't think he likes them much. But I've never met anyone outside the mills more dedicated to our struggle. You have to forgive him his impatience with less important things, like temperance lectures.''

''Temperance isn't less important to the women who are beaten by drunken husbands every day,'' Helen retorted.

''I know that.'' Yuri Domanin bent to stroke one callused thumb along a rose branch, as if imagining it lush with summer leaves and blossoms. "But husbands would not drink so much if Mr. J.P. Morgan and Mr. Henry Frick gave them an honest wage for honest work. If it takes men like our young priest to get us to that day, Miss Sorby, in the long run all of us will benefit."

"Except for Lide and Josef Janczek," Helen said flatly.

Domanin snorted. "I'm not sure little Josef would have done well even if the work was fair. He always liked to take the lazy way out. But I do feel sorry for the young wife." He shook his head. "In all this mess, I think she is the only real victim."

15

SILENCE FELL BETWEEN THE DETECTIVE
and the social worker when they left the
park, a deeper and more troubled silence than Kachigan had expected. He
glanced at Helen Sorby's frowning
face, then at the bandaged hand she'd absently slid through
his arm. What he really wanted to ask was if her scraped
palms still hurt from the day before. What he heard himself
say was, "I don't think we're going to find a cab anywhere
in this neighborhood. Do you mind walking home?"

Helen gave that question the lack of attention it deserved.
"I can't believe those men back there murdered the Janczeks," she said instead. "You don't really think they did,
do you?"

Kachigan blew out a frustrated breath, wishing he could
resolve his shapeless bundle of suspicions into something
resembling a theory. "I wish Yuri Domanin had a better
alibi."

"Then you want to believe they're telling us the truth."

He nodded. "But I can't clear them without solid proof.
It's true that it would have been stupid of them to kill Janczek, but most murders *are* stupid."

"Are they?"

"Yes." Kachigan gave her a measuring look and decided
she could withstand the truth. "Men kill their wives because
they forgot to put the butter in the icebox. Fathers kill their

sons because they didn't shovel enough snow off the walk. Friends kill each other because they didn't help pay for the beer.''

The thunder of the steel-finishing mill faded behind them as they turned up Tenth Street, away from the river. "But those are crimes of a moment's anger," Helen objected. "Josef and Lide were killed by someone who not only decided to kill them, but planned ahead of time how to hide what he'd done. Do you think Yuri Domanin or Christy Zullo would have done that?"

"They would have known how to explode that coal furnace," Kachigan pointed out.

"But where would they have gotten the coal? From home?"

"Why not? They probably make enough to afford extra."

Helen hissed in exasperation, pulling at the arm she held until she'd swung him around to face the houses along Tenth Street. The jostling South Side façades rose straight from the edge of the sidewalk, only an occasional two-foot passageway separating them from their neighbors.

"Milo, look where the coal chutes are." The metal flaps made their own row down the street, all of them opening directly into the foundation blocks. "You can't tell me Domanin and Zullo live in such nice houses that they bring coal in from the back!"

"Probably not," he conceded. "All right, so they couldn't have brought coal from home without all their neighbors knowing. Maybe they got it from the stockpiles at Black Point Steel."

"Past Bernard Flinn's guards?"

Kachigan snorted. "Helen, men who can smuggle out twelve-foot steel reinforcing bars can smuggle out anything."

She fell silent again, her frown now one of intense thought. He didn't interrupt, merely turning them left onto East Carson Street when they reached it. He was hoping to spot a cab or a trolley, but none loomed out of the smoke. The South Side was quiet on Sundays, and weather like this made it even quieter.

"What block are we on?" Helen asked at last.

After years of walking this beat, Kachigan didn't need to check the street numbers over the darkened storefronts they passed. "Thirteen-hundred. Why?"

"Then it's not too late to cut over to Breed Street."

He frowned. "There won't be any cabs on that block."

"I don't want a cab," Helen told him indignantly, then had to pause to cough. "I want you to talk to the Petrenkos."

"The Ukrainian family that lives next to the Janczeks' row house?"

She nodded, still coughing, and Kachigan's frown deepened. "I'm going to take you home first, to get you out of this smoke."

"If you hadn't made me mad at you, I wouldn't have taken such a deep breath." Helen tugged at him when they reached the corner of Fourteenth Street. "We'll get to the Petrenkos before we get to my house, in any case. Come on."

Kachigan gave in and let her lead him down Fourteenth, toward the smoke-muffled sound of St. Witold's church bell. "What are we going to ask the Petrenkos when we get there?"

"If they saw anyone delivering coal to fourteen-oh-seven Breed Street last Wednesday, just before the fire."

He took a deep, irate breath, then broke into coughing himself. "Do you think I didn't already ask every neighbor on the block that question?"

"Yes, but who answered you at the Petrenko's?" Helen inquired. "Mr. Petrenko, who works all day at the glass plant? Or Mrs. Petrenko, who works all day at the laundry?"

"Who should have answered me?"

"Marina and Oksana Petrenko," she said promptly. "They stay home all day to sew and watch the younger children. And if they saw someone delivering coal to the Janczek house during the day on Wednesday, then we'll know Yuri Domanin and Christy Zullo couldn't have done it. They were at work then."

Kachigan opened his mouth to point out that Domanin could have had the coal delivered by other union organizers, but an unexpected motion near the front of his own small brick house yanked his attention up the street. He squinted through the haze of smoke, and after a moment saw the familiar reach and swing of his father levering himself along the small walk that separated his house from the neighbor's.

"Helen, wait here a minute." He lengthened his stride to bound up the lower flight of his stairs before she could ask any more questions. It was obvious that Helen Sorby, with her quick journalistic instincts, already suspected he hadn't told her the whole truth about himself. The last thing he needed was for her discover the identity of the old man he was going to bawl out.

Istvan heard him coming and swung himself around in the narrow passageway with an unexpectedly savage scowl, balancing precariously on one walking stick to lift the other up as a threat. His whiskery face had darkened nearly to the color of the brick wall behind him.

"Pap, what the hell are you doing out in this smoke?" Kachigan demanded in fierce and fluent Armenian.

"Milosh!" The older man's wiry eyebrows jerked upward, and he put his walking stick down with a whistling sigh of relief. As Kachigan had hoped, he replied in the same language. "Was that you throwing stones at my window a little while ago?"

"No, I just got here." Kachigan glanced down the walk, lit at its far end by the steady golden glow of gaslight from his father's bedroom window. "Someone was trying to break in?"

Istvan shook his head, his angry color fading back to normal. "No, I don't think so. It was just a little gravel—tap, tap, tap on the window glass, the way Sophia's boys throw it to be annoying." He snorted. "These damn American kids! They probably know you're a policeman and want to tease you."

"That doesn't mean you have to come out and arrest them for me, especially in this kind of weather." Kachigan tugged his father back toward the front door. "If you coughed and lost your balance, you'd have to crawl back up the stairs to get in."

"So?" Istvan's eyes glinted with quick humor. "It would be just like Saturday nights back in Monessen, when I went out drinking with your crazy uncles. Except that your mother wouldn't be here to lock me out.'' He swung himself easily around the corner to the landing between their stairs, then came to an abrupt halt. ''Milosh, is that pretty girl down there with you?''

Kachigan glanced down to where Helen Sorby waited on the main sidewalk, her impatient gaze so clearly focused on him that his denial died unspoken. ''Yes, Pap. I'm walking her back to Sarah Street.''

Istvan's eyebrows shot upward in such intense surprise that he actually allowed Kachigan to assist him up to the porch. ''You have a *girlfriend*?''

His son fought off an unexpected wash of embarrassment. ''She's a journalist who's helping me with this murder case.''

''*Jesu Christi*. Should I be speaking English?''

''No.'' Kachigan opened the front door for him. ''She knows I'm at least part Armenian.''

Istvan paused halfway through the doorway to give his son a sardonic look. ''Milosh, the only part of you that's not Armenian is your haircut. This pretending to be Irish—it's not a good way to live.''

''I know.'' Kachigan let the screen door swing closed between them, leaning his face on the cold wire mesh to ease the ache in his cheekbone. ''But right now, Pap, there isn't any other way to be a policeman in this city.''

''And a policeman is what you always wanted to be.'' His father leaned on one stick and lifted the other to poke gently at Milo through the screen. ''Hey, Detective Kachigan, you got more important things to do than listen to an old man complaining. Get going.''

''You promise to stay inside the rest of today?''

Istvan grunted. ''I promise. Now go walk your girlfriend home before she decides you're not worth waiting for.''

''That was the same language Domanin spoke to you in the park.'' Helen's dark eyes met Kachigan's steadily. ''Wasn't it?''

Kachigan sighed, then wished he hadn't. ''Yes,'' he said between coughs. This time, when he offered her his arm, all she did was frown at it. He had to satisfy himself with taking the outside of the slate sidewalk, in case any horse and cab came through the smoke of Fourteenth Street to splash mud at them.

"Is it Armenian?"

"Yes."

"I see." To his surprise, Kachigan read neither suspicion nor accusation in her face. Instead, she looked thoughtful, as if she were piecing together a puzzle in her mind.

"What did he tell you?"

Kachigan blinked, not quite sure how to answer that. "My neighbor? He was just complaining about the smoke."

Her upward glance was so fleeting that he wasn't sure if it held surprise or amusement. "Not him, Domanin. He told you something about Zawisza back at the park. What was it?"

"He said that for someone who wasn't an anarchist, Zawisza certainly knew a lot of them. But when I asked him if he was friends with the ones he knew, Domanin told me that as far as he could tell, Zawisza hated them all."

Helen nodded as they turned into the smoky silence of Breed Street. "I can believe that. He's certainly complained about them enough at our Thursday night meetings. I wonder if he went to that meeting in Chicago just to—"

With a startling crack, the face of the brick house beside them exploded into a shower of stinging fragments. Kachigan reacted instinctively, sweeping Helen off her feet and diving headlong with her into the narrow passageway beside the house before his brain had even made sense of what had happened. Another explosion followed, this time gouging a long line in the house's wooden gutter.

"What is it?" Helen demanded, tugging at Kachigan's grip. "Milo, what's the matter?"

"Someone's shooting at us." A third shot cratered brick chips from the house's blank side wall. Kachigan cursed and shoved Helen farther into the dark gap, feeling a warmth that had to be blood trickling down his forehead. "Run!"

She picked up her skirts and obeyed him, sure-footed in the dimness and faster than Kachigan had hoped for. He followed her down to the far end of the narrow passageway, then caught her before she could emerge. "Let me go first."

Helen bit her lip, but nodded and pressed herself against the wall to let him through. Kachigan tried to keep his face turned to the side, but she still saw the blood. "You're hurt!"

"Just a graze." He glanced out at the silent alley that ran behind the one-sided row of houses. Nothing moved along it. Taking a deep breath in an attempt to calm his fiercely pounding heart, Kachigan stepped into the swirl of smoke.

Roused by the gunfire or perhaps just by the detective's presence, a dog began to bark behind a nearby garden wall. Kachigan tensed, waiting for another attack, but no more gunshots broke the Sunday quiet. He turned back and found Helen already at his side.

"I thought I told you—"

"That house over there is the Petrenkos'." She led him a short way up the alley, then cut without ceremony through someone's side yard. Across a winter-bare garden, Kachigan could see the crossed lace curtains of a cheerful yellow house. "I think they'll let us in if I ask them."

"Ask them to let *you* in." Kachigan stood close behind Helen as she hammered on the kitchen door, sure by now where the shots had been fired from. "If they have a telephone line, call the precinct and tell them what happened."

Helen scowled up at him. "What are you going to do?"

"Go find out who shot at us."

Back on Breed Street, front doors were opening, and alarmed voices were calling questions house to house in a mixture of Polish, Serbian and Lithuanian. Pittsburgh was a city used to the violence of strikes and lockouts, and its residents knew the sound of gunfire when they heard it. Kachigan waited with fierce impatience for the first homeowners to come out and mingle on the street before he let himself emerge from the Petrenkos' side yard, pulling his bowler hat low to cover the gash on his forehead. With Helen on his arm, distinctive in her russet wool coat, he'd been identifiable. Now he looked like just another curious resident.

It made his stomach roil to move with seeming randomness along the street, pausing once to reassure an excited Italian matron through her window that no one was lying murdered on the street. At least, not yet, Kachigan thought, and vaulted down into the ash-strewn rubble that had been the Janczeks' basement.

Nothing moved. A long, wary scan of the dimness revealed no gunman lurking in a corner, or hiding behind a screen of fallen iron beams. Kachigan expelled a breath of mingled frustration and relief, then groped his way through the smoky darkness, moving cautiously to avoid kicking up the thick ash that draped the floor. He kept his eyes on that wind-smoothed blanket, looking for any trace of the vanished attacker.

For most of the way across the basement, the ash remained unhelpfully blank, except for the deeply gouged trail Kachigan was making through it. It wasn't until he reached the southwest corner and the crushed remains of the coal furnace that hadn't exploded that he saw the disturbance he'd been looking for. All around the iron firebox, heavy workboots had left their imprints in the ash, two of them deeply embedded in a swirling crater where someone had jumped from the furnace to the ground.

Kachigan measured the clearest footprint against his own, and found it just a little shorter. He grunted in satisfaction, then went to climb on the furnace himself. Its shattered firebox creaked and sagged beneath his weight, but still lifted him high enough to gain a view of Breed Street. A knot of people had gathered in the distant smoke, pointing at something on a house-front. When they shifted under the jostling of some newcomers, Kachigan could just make out the clay-red bullet scar gouged out of the soot-stained brick.

He wasn't sure what warned him—perhaps a whisper of ash, or the scrape of a pistol's hammer being pulled back. The flat crack of the shot came almost simultaneously with the crash he made landing on shoulder and hip in the sheltering rubble. Ash rose in a choking wave, and something that felt like broken pipe stabbed at his ribs, slamming out most of his breath. Kachigan gasped and rolled, feeling another bullet tug at his billowing overcoat. The shot's echoes were followed by bellows of alarm from the street and the distant sound of police whistles.

Fighting for breath, Kachigan scrambled through the ruins of burnt timbers on hands and knees, teeth gritted against the expectation of a sixth and final shot. It never came. Either the gunman had wasted a fourth shot at them after they'd escaped between buildings, or the growing din out in Breed Street had scared him into flight with one bullet left in his gun. Knowing from experience how hard it was to shoot while running, Kachigan scrambled to his feet and lunged after him.

Blinded as he was by the smoke, he had to guess which way his attacker would have bolted. Out through the churchyard behind St. Witold's, he decided, and headed for that side of the row houses. His bruised ribs protested when he hauled himself up over the broken foundation bricks, but the sound of footsteps pelting across the brick churchyard made him forget the pain.

"Stop!" he shouted, scrambling to his feet. "Police!" He didn't have much hope of being obeyed, but there was always a chance an approaching patrolman would hear him and intercept the fugitive. Kachigan sprinted out into the churchyard, chasing the sound of flight through the smoke.

The first hundred yards of running was a fierce struggle, between lungs that wanted to cough out the sooty air and laboring muscles that demanded deep breaths. With his usual stubbornness, Kachigan kept going and was eventually rewarded with the phantom strength of his second wind. By then, his quarry's footsteps had crossed Sarah Street and headed downhill for the river. In the glow of East Carson Street's brighter gas lamps, Kachigan finally glimpsed a fleeting shadow of the man he was chasing. The man hurtled across the wide boulevard, overcoat snapping behind him. Kachigan gritted his teeth and followed at the same headlong run.

On the other side of East Carson, the gas lamps dwindled to a straggling few between silent tenements, letting the dim figure vanish back into the smoke. The thunder of the steel mills grew louder as they left the last houses behind, until it eventually drowned out the sound of footsteps altogether. Kachigan would have cursed if he could have spared the breath. He kept running, hoping that if he maintained this arrow-straight course toward the Mon river, he might still catch the man he pursued.

It was the river itself that helped him. The wind that always followed it out of West Virginia had scoured the long, sloping wharf free of smoke, eroding a clear space that stretched across many barges to the Pittsburgh side. Suddenly aware of obstacles again, Kachigan swerved around a chain-wrapped pier, then looked up in time to see a leap of motion farther down the bank. The shadow he was chasing had vaulted aboard one of the loaded barges and disappeared behind its black heap of coal.

This time Kachigan did curse, knowing full well his tired legs weren't going to make that jump so easily. Desperate, he scanned the line of barges and saw a boarding plank on the third one downstream. He veered that way, knowing that with the river wind blowing in his direction, he at least stood a chance of finding the other man's footsteps again.

The plank swayed beneath his hurried passage, but the barge itself barely stirred in the water, heavy with coal and chained tight to a fleet of its sisters. Once he was aboard, Kachigan stopped to listen. Mostly what he heard was the wheeze and gasp of his own labored breathing, but a single clatter that could have been a footstep finally caught at the edge of his hearing. It sounded as if it had come from much farther out on the river. Kachigan began moving in that direction, trying to ignore the dark glitter of the Monongahela below when he leapt from barge to barge. Now that he'd caught his breath and had time to think again, he found himself baffled by where the pursuit had taken him. In all the years he'd patrolled the South Side, he'd never chased anyone *onto* the river. Perhaps the man he followed was planning to hide in some barge's wet and stinking hold, but with the whistles of patrolmen closing in around them, it was only a matter of time until he'd be flushed out. It just didn't make sense. Leaping aboard the barges was the act of a stupid man, and if there was one thing Kachigan was sure of by now, it was that the man who'd murdered the Janczeks wasn't stupid.

Kachigan paused again when he came to open water, praying for another shred of sound. It came from upriver this time, where the flotilla of barges widened even further. Kachigan turned and began zigzagging in that direction, hearing distant thuds and shouts from the bank as patrolmen boarded the barges. He didn't take the time to shout his identity at them, trusting that the mountainous heaps of coal would shield him from any misguided shots.

He moved steadily upstream, hearing one more clattering footstep, and then a completely unexpected string of splashes. Kachigan slammed to a stop, veering around to stare out over the river. No one would be foolish enough to swim the dangerously swift Monongahela—not this late in November.

He saw a glimmer of reflected movement on the dark ribbon of river that separated the South Side barges from the chained flotilla on the Pittsburgh side. After a moment the splashes stopped, and the distant clatter of footsteps resumed, fading quickly toward shore. Kachigan's stomach twisted in disgust when he realized what had happened.

"Kachigan!" A familiar Irish bellow exploded like a gunshot across the barges. "If that's you over there, Milo my boy, say so quick."

"It's me, Ramey." He turned back to face the oncoming scramble of blue-coated men, lifting his arms to show them his empty hands. "I lost my gunman."

"After all this chasing?" Ramey leaped across the last gap to join him, followed by Silvio Pedone and then by the burlier and less sure-footed figure of Sergeant Todd. The desk sergeant must have left Captain Halloran covering the telephone line at the patrol station. "Now, that's a crying shame."

"Are you sure he didn't drop into one of the holds?" Todd demanded suspiciously, scanning the barges around them. Pedone began to pull up the nearest hatch, ignoring Ramey's grimace at the smell. Kachigan waved the younger man to a stop.

"He's not there. He went over the barge ropes to Pittsburgh."

"*What?*"

Kachigan blew out a frustrated breath, jerking his chin at the stretch of open river. Tarred ropes thicker than his fist dipped into the dark water, visible as a black glimmer a foot or two below the rippling waves. "With nothing moving on the river, the bargemen must have tied together here for safety. Our man just walked the rope across to the other side.''

Ramey cursed and Pedone whistled in amazement. Todd's scowl got even grimmer. ''He must be insane.''

''He's not insane.'' Kachigan turned to gaze across at the smoke-shrouded lights of Pittsburgh. Somewhere in that sprawl of mills and tenements, the man who'd twice tried to kill Helen Sorby had gone to ground. ''He's smart and he's reckless. And for some reason, he's desperate.'' He glanced down at the rocking bargeload of black rock beneath him and grimaced. ''At least now I know where he got the coal to explode that furnace.''

16

THE QUIET RUSH OF MORNING RAIN, dripping down the windows and grumbling in the gutters, exploded without warning into a fierce crack like a gunshot. Helen jerked, spattering ink from her pen across an already stained manuscript page.

"What was that?"

"Only thunder." Her brother frowned across the table at her while the echoes rumbled into silence. "Relax, Helen. That's the third time this morning you've jumped out of your skin."

She cast him an impatient look. "Easy for you to say. *You* weren't the one who got shot at yesterday."

"True." Thomas sounded more regretful than thankful. "Did Kachigan ever ring you up to say if he found the man who did it?"

Helen shook her head, frowning. She'd had no word from the detective since his young Italian patrolman had escorted her home from the Petrenkos' house yesterday. Silvio Pedone had told her that Kachigan would be in touch with her before nightfall. But by the time the suffocated glow of sunset had struggled through the smoke, the telephone still hadn't rung. Helen couldn't decide whether to be worried or aggravated about that.

An urgent knock rattled their front door and Helen jumped again, this time to her feet. "I'll get it."

"Look through the transom before you answer," Thomas said.

Helen swept her skirts up in one hand as she crossed the hall, vaulting onto the telephone bench with more of a leap than a step. The hat she saw through the transom's clear pane wasn't the plain dark bowler she'd been expecting, but an enormous confection of ribbons, ruffles and enough feathers to cover a partridge, half concealed beneath a dripping umbrella. With a disappointed sigh, Helen jumped down and swung the door wide.

"Hello, Aunt Pittypat."

"Dearest girl!" Pat McGregor turned and flung herself at Helen, umbrella and all. Helen ducked a few wet feathers and returned her aunt's embrace. "Why on earth didn't you *tell* me?"

"Tell you what?" Helen asked blankly.

Pat McGregor waved a sodden newspaper under her nose. "What all the papers are full of this morning, dearest!"

"*What*?" Helen snatched the paper from her aunt's gloved fingers and unwrapped it to see a three-column photo of the milling crowd on Breed Street. In thick black capitals over the picture, the headline read "Policeman and His Young Lady Ambushed by Gunman on South Side."

"Who told them I was Milo's—I mean, Mr. Kachigan's—young lady?"

Pat McGregor snorted and snapped her umbrella shut. "You know how the *Press* loves to turn every story into a melodrama with violins. The *Gazette* simply calls you a local resident." Her eyes sparked with quick Irish temper. "A local resident who didn't see fit to inform her only surviving aunt that she was almost murdered yesterday! How do you think I felt when Cousin Gillan rang me up and asked me if I knew why you'd been shot at? I had to tell him I didn't even know there'd been a shooting!"

"Cousin *Gillan* rang you up?" Helen scowled. "How on earth did he find out about it?"

"Apparently they get the Pittsburgh morning papers out in Ambridge too." Pat McGregor unpinned her hat and shook it, dappling the hall with feather flakes and scattered drops of rain. "Even if he is eighty-one and retired, Regis

Gillan can't stand to let something happen on the South Side without sticking his nose into it. He wants to see you today.''

Helen opened her mouth, then closed it again without a word. Her irascible second cousin might be a chair-bound invalid, but his wits were as shrewd now as they'd been fifty years ago. And he had ways of getting information that no one else could. She hadn't forgotten the last time the old priest had summoned her to his rural retirement home, to warn her about James Foster Barton's murky past before that charming young man had brought her to complete financial ruin. If Cousin Gillan wanted to see her today, it wasn't just to be sure she was safe and sound.

"If he has something he wants to tell me, why doesn't he ring me up?" she asked her aunt, in exasperation. "Ambridge is a two-hour drive from Pittsburgh!"

"I think whatever he wants to tell you can't be said with someone holding the receiver for him." Aunt Pat poked at her niece with her wet umbrella. "Go put on a decent dress, while I see if your brother wants to come with us. Joe O'Grady says he thinks his horse can make the trip, but I don't want to leave the poor thing standing out in the rain any longer than I have to."

The road to Ambridge skirted the north shore of the Ohio River, a route that took them past the crowded steel and glass plants of McKees Rocks and Coraopolis and then into a starkly rural landscape. Helen peered out the window at the mist-draped hills, soft with farms and a few scattered woodlands. Only the occasional chute of a coal tipple pouring black rock down to the barges on the river reminded her that they were still within the industrial reach of Pittsburgh.

She looked back inside the cab while Joe O'Grady guided his plodding horse off the main pike and onto a familiar winding road. "We're almost there," she told her relatives.

Her aunt woke from her nodding doze, and Thomas put away the surveyor's notes he'd been transcribing. "Maybe I'll stay out in the cab and sleep while you're visiting," he said thoughtfully. "I don't suppose anyone's likely to shoot you inside a Catholic retirement home. And Cousin Gillan never liked me much, anyway. He was always boxing my ears at Sunday school.''

"Which was no doubt exactly what you deserved.'' Aunt Pat gathered up her umbrella and gloves while the cab lurched to a stop. "You were typical Sorby hellions, the both of you. It's a miracle you ever managed to get confirmed. Come along, Helen.''

The light wasn't strong inside the Augustine retirement home, with its leaded windows and dark mahogany floors. Helen scanned the array of elderly priests in the parlor and saw her second cousin dozing in a bentwood wheeled chair, a messy scatter of newspapers, letters and what looked like knitting on his lap. Regis Gillan was small and pot-bellied and bald as a gnome, even more shriveled under his blanket than the last time she'd come to see him. But when Aunt Pat kissed his cheek, his pale brown eyes snapped open to show the fierce intelligence burning within.

"About time you got here,'' he said brusquely, then turned to Helen. "Pat's still using those damned charity cab-horses of hers, eh?''

Helen smiled at her aunt's disgruntled expression. "Of course she is.'' She kissed Gillan's other cheek, whiskery and paper-frail beneath her lips. "How are you?''

"Too old to waste time, that's how I am. What are you doing running around with a policeman, girl? Didn't we have enough trouble with the one your aunt married?''

Helen took a deep breath. "I'm not running around with him, Cousin. I'm investigating a murder case for a magazine article.''

"Huh.'' The priest peered at Helen closely, as if something in her voice hadn't rung quite right. "I don't suppose you two have gotten sensible and stopped those socialist meetings at the Carnegie Library?''

The old man's disconcerting jumps of subject made Helen blink, but predictably enough they didn't bother Aunt Pittypat. "No, of course not. Why should we?''

"Going to get in trouble for that someday.'' Gillan's scruffy eyebrows wiggled up and down. "I hear a lot of priests and ministers come to those meetings.''

"Some of the younger ones do,'' said Helen. She could

tell from the way his pale eyes had narrowed that this was the serious part of his inquisition. "Why?"

"I read where you'd been shot at," he said. Helen wasn't sure if it was meant as an answer to her question or not. "On Breed Street, behind St. Witold's Church, eh?"

"That's right."

"And isn't there a priest from St. Witold's who comes to those socialist meetings of yours?"

"Yes." Helen crouched in front of her cousin's wheeled chair so she could read more of his wizened face. "Father Karl Zawisza."

"Ah." The elderly priest stroked his fingers over his knitting. "And those people who died in the fire on Breed Street last week—that's the murder case that you're investigating?"

"Yes."

"I knew them," he said unexpectedly. "Knew who they were, I mean, before I ever read about them dying in the fire."

"The Janczeks?" Helen asked in surprise.

"Yes." Gillan pinned her with a knife-sharp look. "You going to tell the police what I say?"

She didn't hesitate. "Yes."

"You trust them not to repeat it if they don't have to?"

"I trust one of them. He's the only one I'll tell it to."

"Fair enough." Father Gillan paused, scowling. "Lot of priests becoming socialists these days, eh? It's that damn Father Tom Haggerty, making it all look so noble and romantic."

Helen frowned at the new digression, but a warning glance from her aunt told her not to interrupt. After a moment's grim silence, the old priest went on.

"Bunch of priests from Pittsburgh went out to that Wobbly conference last summer in Chicago. Mostly younger ones, but a few old sticks too. Some of them talk to me." His gaze came back to Helen. "That boy at St. Witold's, Zawisza—he's the one that wrote some of the Wobbly constitution, right?"

Helen nodded.

"You know he almost got defrocked last year, for writing

inflammatory letters to the *Gazette*? They would have done it, too, if there'd been more to accuse him of than just having radical politics." Father Gillan's voice dropped from its normal church-spanning tone to a confessional murmur, so that none of the other priests dozing around them could hear. "I heard stories about things that happened in Chicago this summer. All those socialists and unionists and free-love anarchists gathered together—a man can get drunk on revolution, just like beer. And do things he maybe wouldn't do otherwise."

Helen felt her stomach lurch. She was starting to see where Father Gillan's conversational leaps were heading. "Lide Janczek was in Chicago last summer, too."

"I know." The elderly priest grimaced. "All the stories I heard mentioned her. Nothing proven, nothing anyone could take to the bishop—but I think Karl Zawisza did more out in Chicago than help write up the Wobbly charter. He did something that'd get him defrocked faster than I can say a rosary, because it's the one thing priests damn sure aren't supposed to do." He met Helen's gaze with grim intensity. "And he did it with Lide Janczek."

"Was Kachigan in his office?" Helen demanded.

Thomas paused, one foot barely inside the cab. "Would I be coming back out here alone if he were?" he asked irritably. The gas lamps were already lit for the evening along Sarah Street, although a dark garnet afterglow lingered in the western sky. "The desk sergeant said he left an hour ago. He didn't sound very happy about it, either."

"Did you ask for his home address?"

"The sergeant said he didn't know it." Her twin's annoyed expression deepened. "But I think he was just stonewalling me. Why wouldn't Kachigan's own patrol station know where he lives?"

Helen bit her lip, remembering the volley of Armenian that had drifted back through the smoke after the detective had left her standing on Fourteenth Street the previous day. Even at the time, the voices had sounded too much alike to belong to mere neighbors. Her growing suspicion about the police detective's background crystallized into a cascade of realizations.

"Thomas, tell Joe O'Grady to go around the corner and halfway down Fourteenth. I think I know which house is Kachigan's."

Her brother looked doubtful, but ducked out into the twilight. There was a disapproving cluck from across the cab. "Dearest, we can't stop there—it's after six and much too late for a social visit."

"This isn't a social visit, Aunt Pat, this is business." Helen slid over to let Thomas back in, and a moment later the cab jolted back out into Sarah Street. "I need to tell Mr. Kachigan what we found out today."

Pat McGregor sat up in a scandalized rustle. "Helen, I *cannot* allow you to go into a young man's house by yourself, not this late at night. Thomas will chaperon you."

"No, Thomas will not," her nephew informed her flatly. "I want to go home and eat. Don't worry, Aunt Pat—I trust Detective Kachigan with Helen."

Pittypat snorted. "That's not the point, Thomas! No one cares what actually happens if you leave a young man and woman alone—it's what *might* have happened that counts."

Helen sighed, scrubbing at the frown between her eyes for a moment before she realized she'd picked up the gesture from Kachigan. "Well, you still don't need to worry, Aunt Pat," she said while the cab drew to a halt. "Because if I'm right, I won't be alone with Mr. Kachigan. Or at least, " she amended, "not with just one of them."

She jumped out of the cab before her bewildered aunt could ask what that comment meant. It only took her a moment to spot the double flight of steps that Kachigan had bounded up the day before. A few gaslights glowed inside the small red-brick house, at least one of them in a downstairs window. That meant someone was still awake.

Her brother's brisk footsteps caught up with her two houses down the sidewalk from where the cab had stopped. Helen swung around to scowl at him, and he lifted his hands in prompt surrender.

"Aunt Pat says I have to walk you to the door, or she'll disinherit me. She's afraid someone's going to shoot you."

The unwelcome reminder stopped Helen's protest in mid-word. She turned back up the street, skirting the leaf-dappled puddles that the day's rain had left on the slate sidewalk. "And she also wants you to make sure I'll really have a chaperon, right?"

"Right." Thomas followed her up the stairs. "So, who's this other Mr. Kachigan that's going to be here?"

"Milo's father." Finding no doorbell button at the top of the steps, Helen grasped the knocker and rapped it against the worn brass plate. And then added, in an undertone, "I think."

"Huh." Blessedly, her twin didn't decide to quiz her on that. He waited with her through a long, slow stretch of silence. "Are you sure he's home tonight?"

"I think so, or the light wouldn't be on." A slow series of thumps from inside the house made her certain. "I can hear him coming now."

The door of the red-brick house creaked open, just far enough to spill a wedge of gaslight onto the rain-washed street. From the shadows behind it, a wary voice demanded, "Milosh?"

"No, Mr. Kachigan. It's me." Helen made no attempt to push the door open any wider, merely stepping sideways so the light would fall on her face. After the dim and rainy dusk, the steady golden glow made her blink. "My name is Helen Sorby. I was here with your son the other day. May I come in?"

There was a long and distinctly measuring pause. Helen could see the wiry old man behind the door now, leaning forward on his walking sticks to scrutinize her. His face was crinkled and leathery, an effect of many years' work around open-hearth furnaces. Despite his bald head, the determined set of his jaw and the fire-blue intelligence in his eyes eased the last of her uncertainty about the address. If this wasn't Milo Kachigan's father, he was some other close relative.

"My son not home now," the old man said, confirming her guess. "You want wait for him here?"

"Yes, please." Helen glanced at her brother, two steps down from her. "Go home and make yourself supper, Thomas. Tell Aunt Pat I'll call a cab from here so no one can shoot at me on the way home. That should calm her down.''

"I doubt it," her twin said, wincing as if he could already hear the lecture he was going to get on the way home. "If I'm lucky, maybe she'll just decide to give my inheritance to the cats. If not, I'll leave some soup on the stove for you before I go off to join the French Foreign Legion.''

"Thanks, Thomas." Helen watched him trot back down the street, then picked up her rain-soaked skirts and shook off the worst of the water before she stepped through the door. Milo Kachigan's father grunted and levered himself backward to make room for her in the narrow entryway. Helen was careful to pull the front door closed so he wouldn't have to lean around her to do it, then followed him down the short hall to an arched living-room door. Despite the effort that reddened his bald head, Milo's father used his walking sticks with surprising skill. It must not have been a stroke or a recent fall that had stiffened his legs, Helen guessed, but something that had happened while he was still young and strong enough to adapt.

"You sit here," he informed her, balancing on one stick to point the other one into a small, darkened parlor. "I light gas. Unless—you hungry? Not eat yet?''

Helen began to utter a polite refusal, but the painful way her stomach twisted at the thought of food changed her mind. "No, I haven't eaten supper," she admitted, falling into the complete, simple sentences she used to communicate with new immigrants down at the settlement house. "Do you have some food already made? I don't want to be any trouble.''

The elder Kachigan snorted and swung himself on down the hall, to the gaslit kitchen. "Have *lavash*, *kuftah* and *leh-mejun*," he informed her. "What you want?''

Helen bit her lip helplessly. "Um—anything is fine." She trailed after him into the slice of kitchen, which looked as if it had been a back porch before the gas had been installed. The old man pointed her to a homemade wooden chair and she tucked her rain-sodden skirts around her so they wouldn't make too big a puddle on the scuffed wooden floor. "You don't have to make anything special.''

A smile glinted beneath his moustache. "For friend of Milosh, is not problem." He picked up a towel-covered basket from one counter and set it in front of her. Helen unwrapped it and found a flat unleavened kind of bread that flapped apart when she bit into it. It was harder to chew than the air-filled Italian loaves she was used to, but it tasted richly of wheat.

"This is good," she said, around a mouthful.

"Daughter visits yesterday and brings," Milo's father said hastily, as if baking bread wasn't something men were supposed to do. "She makes *lehmejun* too, but I make *kuftah*." In almost Italian fashion, he was emptying out the small icebox to spread the table in front of her with food: brown triangular buns that smelled of meat and strange spices, a bowl full of what looked like large meatballs, a glass jar of cheese in brine and a string of dried dates. "Eat."

"Thank you." Helen reached for the dates, but the abrupt slam of the front door made her jump. It had been much too vehement a noise for the wind to have produced, and in any case she was sure she'd caught the latch when she closed it. "Milo?" she asked his father.

He nodded, but worry narrowed his eyes to slits. The violence of that slam didn't sound like the quiet police detective Helen knew. Her stomach clenched again, this time in alarm. If her attacker had followed her here, to a confrontation with this crippled old man—she took a deep angry breath and began looking around for a weapon.

"*You!*"

Helen's chin jerked up at that bitten-off shout. Milo Kachigan stood frozen in the kitchen doorway, his suit coat slung over one shoulder and his thin face more haggard than she could remember seeing it before. For once there was nothing hidden about his emotions—she saw the initial surprise at seeing her flare into rage, and then plummet into a completely unexpected bitterness. He said something in Armenian, his voice sharp and tired, that made his father cast him a disapproving look.

"Milosh!" he growled, reminding Helen of her own father for a moment. "You no say that when lady is here."

"Well, the lady *shouldn't* be here." Kachigan came into the room, throwing his suit coat carelessly across one of the kitchen chairs and then, with a defiant look at Helen, yanking his collar band free of his shirt so he could rub at his bruised neck. The unwavering glow of the gas lamp showed her the dark red slash over one eyebrow where he'd been cut by flying brick the day before. It also revealed a mesh of tired lines around his eyes that hadn't been there before. "I assume you've already introduced yourself to my father, since he's feeding you my supper."

"Yes. And you're welcome to share it." She frowned, watching him cross to the icebox and yank out a brown glass bottle with an impatient clatter. "Milo, what are you so angry about? It can't just be about me being here."

"Can't it?" Kachigan used the edge of the kitchen counter to open his bottle, and Helen smelled the cold tang of beer. He took a long swallow before he turned back to face her. "Who told you that I lived here? I know it wasn't anyone at the station."

She sighed, guessing now what was fueling his fury. "It wasn't anyone at all. I recognized your father when you stopped to talk to him yesterday. Your voices sounded alike." She paused to let him digest that. His father was listening to them in alert silence, but she couldn't be sure how much of this furious conversation he had followed. "If you want me to, Milo, I'll promise not to tell anyone you're Armenian."

That got her an interested look from the older man, but only a bark of caustic laughter from Milo Kachigan. He drained the rest of his beer in one long swallow, then slammed the bottle back on the counter so hard she was surprised when it didn't shatter.

"Don't worry about keeping my secrets, Miss Sorby," he said bitterly. "Bernard Flinn has already spilled them all."

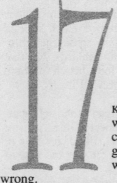

KACHIGAN SHOULD HAVE KNOWN THAT waking up to a threatening telephone call from Bernard Flinn meant it was going to be the worst kind of Monday, where absolutely everything went wrong.

"You're doing it, you bastard," was the first thing he heard out of the receiver, when he rolled out of bed and went down to answer the persistent shrilling. The Black Point Steel police chief didn't bother to identify himself, but the distant bellow of the steel factory behind him was enough to tell Kachigan who'd rung him up before dawn.

"Doing *what*?"

Flinn's snort echoed down the telephone connection. "Making trouble at Taylor Mill. I don't need it, Kachigan. I've got a Black Point guard missing now, not to mention a load of steel bars that would make damn good clubs in a riot. You're not going to get another warning."

Kachigan rubbed yesterday's grit out of his eyes, trying to remember what he'd done to make Flinn annoyed at him. The attack on Breed Street, followed by a long day of useless searching through the ashes of the row house for bullet shells and through the smoke of downtown Pittsburgh for his attacker, had nearly erased his memories of Sunday morning. "All I did was talk to a few of your men at church about Josef Janczek," he said at last.

"It's not what you said, it's what you gave them. I don't like people posting notices in my mill about public meetings, even if they're disguised as some damned temperance crusade."

Kachigan's fingers tightened around the receiver. "It's a real temperance meeting, Flinn, sponsored by the South Side Temperance League," was all he could think of to say.

"You mean that little cell of socialists and anarchists your Miss Sorby belongs to?" The steel-police chief snorted again. "Right. Even radicals like that have sense enough to know they can't stop mill-hunks from drinking. All that meeting's going to do is provide cover for a bunch of damn unionizers to call a strike at Taylor Mill. Call it off, Kachigan."

"I don't have the authority—" Kachigan broke off, hearing the telltale click and buzz of a disconnected line. A fluent Armenian curse rose to his lips and was stifled, for fear of waking his father in the room next door. It was the first of many he would stifle that day.

With a groan, he headed for the bathroom, to wash and put on his third-best and last clean suit. He hadn't had time over the hectic weekend to take the other two to the Chinese laundry on Sarah Street. Since he still had a hour before work, Kachigan grabbed up one of his sister's flatbreads for breakfast and threw both suits over his arm before he headed out the door.

Outside, an overnight rain had cleared the air of smoke and left puddles strung like beads along the sidewalks, glistening in the early morning light. The steel-colored clouds promised more rain soon, but for the moment the dawn air was clear and still. Kachigan could hear the rattle and spark of early trolleys on East Carson Street as he walked down toward the river.

"Good morning, Mr. Kachigan."

The familiar Russian accent jerked his head around, but it took a minute for him to see Yuri Domanin's shadowy figure sheltered inside the doorway of the South Side Electric Light plant, directly across from Patrol Station Seven. The glow and fade of a small pipe lit the Russian's calm waiting smile. Kachigan glanced around to make sure no one from the precinct was watching, then cut across the empty street toward him.

"Shouldn't you be at work?" he demanded.

"I'm out sick today." Domanin's smile crinkled his eyes to slits. He tapped out his pipe against the brick doorway, then fell in beside Kachigan as companionably as a co-worker. "In fact, I'll probably be out sick all week. It's that wave of typhoid that comes in the early winter."

Kachigan snorted. "More like the wave of typhoid that comes when a union organizer sees a chance to get a lot of mill workers together in one place without management suspecting it."

Domanin chuckled. "Does that mean Flinn telephoned you this morning, Mr. Kachigan? Or did you guess it for yourself?"

"He rang me up." Kachigan turned up the collar of his overcoat. The dark clouds had drifted over the South Side, bringing with them a drizzle so light that it floated rather than fell. "If I'd been smart enough to guess what you were going to do, Domanin, I wouldn't have let Helen Sorby give you those temperance fliers. What did you add to the back?"

The Russian pulled a folded sheet of paper out of his baggy coat to hand it to him. In the reflected light of McKee's glass-blowing furnaces, Kachigan saw the familiar smudged photo of Dennis McKenna on one side and a careless sprawl of pencil sketches across the back. In between a figure-eight cowboy hat and stick dog with rolling eyes was a thumbnail sketch of a clenched fist.

"Clever." He handed it back. "As long as no one looks at more than one of them."

"Yes. Too bad Flinn is almost as smart as we are, eh?"

"If you ask me, I'd say he's smarter," Kachigan said drily. "He knows you're getting ready to strike Taylor Mill."

The steelworker shrugged. "Not much we can do about that. My friends at the Pennsylvania Railroad tell me that one month from now, Black Point will get an order for the tracks to make the new Erie-to-Cleveland line. That's when we'll have the best chance to shut down Taylor Mill and make them meet our demands."

"Then why tip your hand so early?"

That got him a reproving look. "A union is not a monopoly, Mr. Kachigan. We need a majority vote to strike, and we need it early enough that men can save up food and rent money."

Kachigan paused in front of the bright windows and soapy smell of Yee Laundry. "And you thought McKenna's temperance lecture would be the best place to take that vote?"

"Why not? It's aboveboard and honest"—Domanin's rich chuckle rang out—"and if I hadn't made it our assembling point, not a single workingman would have shown up for it. I'm doing your young lady a big favor."

"I doubt she'll think so when Flinn's guards show up too."

The Russian threw out his arms, nearly beheading a black-shawled old lady with a market basket over one arm. She said something impolite in Lithuanian and skirted around them. "Let them come! All they'll see is a nice young man up on the podium, and a crowd of mill workers crying out to take the pledge."

"That's how you're going to have them vote for the strike?"

"Of course. The lecturer goes home happy, and if Flinn breaks the meeting up, the newspapers crucify him the next day." Domanin poked a finger at Kachigan's chest. "With Miss Sorby leading the charge, eh? Tell me *that* won't make her happy."

"It would make her ecstatic." Kachigan gave his companion a searching glance. "Is that why you waited in the rain for me this morning? To make sure Miss Sorby comes tomorrow night?"

"And to make sure Flinn knows she'll be reporting on it," the steelworker agreed. "That way, everyone is safe, eh?"

Except Helen, Kachigan thought grimly. He juggled his suits to his left arm, and caught Yuri Domanin by the shoulder before he could turn away. He got a surprised look, but no resistance.

"There's one condition before I'll do it, Domanin. Tell

me where you went yesterday after we left you at Little Jim Park.''

The mill worker's thick eyebrows rose. ''Is it important?''

''Very.'' Kachigan didn't elaborate, but the look on his face made Domanin's smile fade at last. ''I sent an Italian patrolman over to talk to Christy Zullo yesterday, and he said you left the park a few minutes after we did. Where did you go?''

The Russian shrugged. ''I have a lady that I visit on Sundays, Mr. Kachigan, when I'm not working the long turn. A widow down in Painters Mills.''

''Her name?''

Domanin paused for a long moment. ''Cora Scales.''

Kachigan grunted and let him go. ''You'd better hope she remembers entertaining you yesterday, Domanin. If not, I'm not letting Helen Sorby anywhere near that temperance lecture.''

''But why not?'' the Russian demanded, looking honestly bewildered. ''What could happen to her?''

''The same thing that almost happened after we left you yesterday morning.'' Kachigan opened the laundry door, and let its billow of starch-scented steam separate him from Domanin. ''If you don't know already, just read today's paper. I have a feeling we'll be on the front page.''

He managed to track Cora Scales down by midmorning, pulling in a favor from a Painters Mill livery store owner he'd once saved from a couple of drunk German rivermen. As he'd guessed from the location of her tiny house, stuck like a haphazard pin to the side of Mount Washington, Mrs. Scales was black. She was a young woman, already twig-thin and hollow-cheeked with consumption, but every bit as shrewd as Yuri Domanin. Although she confirmed without hesitation that the steelworker had spent Sunday afternoon with her, Kachigan got the uneasy feeling that she would have vouched for any other date and time with equal alacrity. He cursed in Armenian and returned to the South Side with no more confidence in Domanin's alibi than when he'd left.

What he needed, he decided at lunchtime, was a conference with his co-investigator. Even though he was fairly certain she would insist on attending her aunt's temperance lecture once she knew what Domanin was up to, some instinct made Kachigan shy away from using Helen to threaten Bernard Flinn again. Unfortunately, no amount of ringing got the Sorby telephone answered that afternoon. By three, he was worried enough to walk down Sarah Street and eye the darkened stained-glass windows, but nothing looked amiss. The Sorbys had gone somewhere with their aunt for the day, the Irish matron next door informed him kindly when he rang her bell. No telling when they'd be back.

With some misgiving, Kachigan went back to his own house and asked the South Side telephone operator to connect him with Bernard K. Flinn at Taylor Mill.

The connection clicked through two other exchanges before the line opened with a crackle of static. "What?" Flinn demanded from the other end.

"I can't cancel the temperance lecture tomorrow." If there was one thing he'd learned about Flinn, it was that there was no point wasting polite preliminaries on him.

"Why the hell not?"

"Miss Sorby won't let me. She's going to attend the lecture and write a magazine article about it."

There was a long, sizzling pause. "So Domanin got to you," Flinn said in disgust. "Well, I hope you like working in the mills, Kachigan. Because after today, that's where you're going to spend the rest of your life."

The speaking bell at the other end of the phone crashed down hard enough to make Kachigan's ear ring. He hung up his own speaker and put the telephone back in its wall niche, frowning. It hadn't been a good connection, and Flinn's deep rumble was never easy to hear over the background roar of Taylor Mill, but he could have sworn that what the steel-police chief had actually said was, "I hope you *liked* working in the mills."

No, Kachigan thought fiercely. Whatever information his wealth and connections might give him access to, there was no way Bernard Flinn could know about that.

But when he'd waved away his father's offer of an early supper and gone back to Patrol Station Seven, he discovered that was exactly what Flinn did know.

• • •

"Flinn told everyone at the police station that you were Armenian?" The fierce dismay in Helen Sorby's voice rang echoes off the kitchen walls. "*Why?*"

Kachigan stared down at the empty beer bottle in his hand, fighting the impulse to fling it across the room. "Because I wouldn't ask you to cancel your aunt's temperance lecture."

"*What?*" Her skirts made a damp murmur across the floor when she moved. A moment later, Kachigan felt her grip his arm and try to shake him into looking at her. "Milo, that's insane! Why in God's name should Flinn care about a temperance lecture?"

He closed his eyes without answering her and tried to yank his temper back under control. None of this was Helen's fault—not the workingman's temperance lecture, not the way Domanin had decided to use it, and certainly not Flinn's ruthless response. Hell, he was the one who'd encouraged her to bring her aunt's fliers to Little Jim Park. But finding her here so unexpectedly had sparked one of Kachigan's rare bursts of sheer bad temper. After an afternoon spent enduring a barrage of questions from Captain Halloran and then a cold wall of silence from everyone else at the patrol station, the last thing he'd wanted to do tonight was confront another of the people he'd lied to.

"Milo—" Helen's grip tightened, surprising him with its strength. "Don't go away like that. What did Flinn want?"

Kachigan cursed in Armenian and sent the beer bottle crashing against the wall before he could stop himself. Fortunately, it bounced instead of shattering. "He wanted to buy me, that's what he wanted," he said savagely. "Today, it's something simple: Kachigan, cancel the temperance lecture so Yuri Domanin's unionizers can't use it to organize a strike at Black Point Steel. Tomorrow, it would be something else: Kachigan, stop looking into this murder so much, it might expose my company informers. And after that, every day there would be something a little more—drop these charges, arrest this person, take out that troublemaker." He scowled down at Helen Sorby, not caring if his furious voice was scaring her. "And by the goddamned end, do you know what I'd be?"

"Yes," she said steadily. "You'd be Bernard Flinn."

Kachigan met her unwavering gaze for a moment, then let out a long, tense breath. "A steel policeman," he agreed bitterly, then glanced over at his father's frowning face. "And I'd rather be an Armenian mill worker than that."

Istvan snorted. "Of course you would. I didn't raise any stupid children," he answered in Armenian. "Or any rude ones, either. Let go of your girlfriend, Milosh, and tell her you're sorry you hurt her."

Kachigan glanced down at Helen Sorby, startled. He hadn't realized, since he could still feel her own strong grip on his arm, that he'd anchored his fists on her shoulders while he shouted at her. With a curse, he released her and stepped back.

"Helen, I'm sorry. Did I hurt you?"

"No worse than I hurt you, I expect." She released her own grip, twisting her hands together as if she didn't quite trust them. "I'm sorry, too."

Istvan Kachigan grunted, lifting himself on his walking sticks and maneuvering toward the door. "Both of you, eat," he advised in blunt English. "Hunger makes anger, food makes peace." He paused in the doorway, switching back to Armenian to address his son. "And you—remember what your mother always told you. If someone says no to you just because you're Armenian, you keep on asking until someone else says yes." He inclined his bald head toward Helen Sorby. "Start by asking there. She's a nice girl. Good night, Milosh."

He smiled despite himself. "Good night, Pap. You want me to help you up the stairs?"

"No. I can still put myself to bed."

By unspoken consent, they waited until the sound of Istvan's slow upward thumping had faded safely into silence. Then Helen sighed and looked back at Kachigan.

"Is Yuri Domanin really planning to use my aunt's temperance lecture tomorrow to organize a strike?"

"Yes." Kachigan carefully put a hand below her elbow and guided her back to the table. His bad temper had blown itself out in the windstorm way it always did, leaving him calm enough to think rationally again. "He's going to have the men vote by taking the pledge. As long as there are reporters there, Black Point Steel can't disrupt it without getting crucified in the press.''

''And that's why Bernard Flinn wanted you to cancel it?''
''Yes.''

Helen sat, picking up her half-eaten *lavash*. ''What happened when Flinn told everyone at the patrol station about you?''

Kachigan shrugged, fishing a fork out of the tinware bin and pulling another chair around to straddle beside the table. He hadn't eaten since breakfast and was suddenly aware of the empty ache in his stomach. Since the bowl of stuffed meatballs was closest, he started with that. ''The senior detective wanted to fire me on the spot,'' he said around a mouthful of *kuftah*. ''But I think Captain Halloran will probably just demote me back to street patrol and hope I quit. That way, he'll never have to admit that he hired an Armenian by mistake.''

Helen's frown creased her forehead. ''But they have an Italian policeman already. What's wrong with an Armenian one?''

''Silvio Pedone never lied to them about what he was.''

''And you did?'' she demanded.

Kachigan looked up, surprised by her perception. ''No,'' he admitted. ''All I did was let them think what they wanted at the entrance exam—I knew my name looked Irish enough to get me in. The people on Ellis Island are the ones who changed it,'' he added defensively, scrubbing a hand across the dull ache of his cheek.

Although he tried hard not to sound bitter, her searching look of concern told him he'd failed. ''Not that it will matter to the men at the station. Half of them didn't agree I should have been promoted to detective this soon, even when they thought I was Irish. They're twice as annoyed about it now. If I *don't* quit, Halloran will have to transfer me just to keep the peace.''

Helen reached over to spear a *kuftah* from his bowl with unnecessary force. ''So how long do we have?''

''For what?''

She made an impatient noise. ''To solve the Janczek murder case. I know no one else down at that station is going to care about it, and I don't want to work on it alone."

"Don't worry," Kachigan said bluntly. "I wouldn't let you." And since that had already earned him one of her fiercest scowls, he took a deep breath and added, "Just like I'm not letting you go to your aunt's temperance lecture tomorrow."

"What?" Helen dropped fork and meatball together on the table. "But you just told me that Yuri Domanin needs to have reporters there, so Flinn can't disrupt it!"

"Yes, and he asked specifically for you." Kachigan wrapped his hand around the angry fist her fingers had curled into. "Helen, when did we ever tell Domanin you were a journalist?"

She opened her mouth, then closed it again without a word. "We didn't," she admitted. "But he knew?"

"He knew."

They ate in silence for a moment, Helen picking her meatball up off the table and finishing it without squeamishness. Kachigan had finished a cold meat-pie and dipped some feta cheese out to eat with his dates before she spoke again.

"The reason you won't let me go to the temperance meeting tomorrow, Milo—is it that you're afraid Domanin is setting us up to get shot at again? Just like yesterday?"

"Yes." Kachigan frowned. "Although I'm still not sure why. Even if he *was* the one who killed Josef Janczek, why should he go out of his way to attack us too?"

"He didn't," Helen said positively.

"How do you know that?"

"Because I found out today who did." Her words cascaded out in a vehement rush, as if she'd kept them locked inside for too long. "Milo, we've been worrying about the wrong murder all along! Lide wasn't killed because someone wanted to murder Josef Janczek. Josef was killed—"

"—because someone wanted to murder Lide?" Kachigan's eyes widened. "But who would have wanted to do that?"

"Her last lover." Helen's cheeks darkened a little, but she met his eyes steadily. "Father Karl Zawisza."

It had been a long time—years, in fact—since Milo Kachigan had felt this completely stupid. He sat stock-still, gaze locked on Helen Sorby's urgent face, and all he could think was that the prime suspect in his first murder investigation was someone he hadn't even considered as a possibility.

"Milo? Did you hear me?"

Kachigan felt embarrassment prick across his face. "Helen, how in God's name do you know that Zawisza was Lide's lover?"

"My cousin Gillan told me." She saw his puzzled look and added, "He's the priest I told you about, the one who used to serve down at St. Peter's. He knew Lide Janczek's name before he read about her dying in that fire. He'd heard rumors about her and Father Zawisza out in Chicago."

"They slept together at the Wobbly conference last summer?"

Helen nodded. "And if the church finds out about it, Zawisza will be defrocked and probably sent back to Poland. Does that seem like enough motive for murder?"

Kachigan grunted. "Especially if her husband found out about it. Knowing what we do about Josef Janczek, the first thing he'd probably do with that information is—"

"—try to blackmail Father Zawisza," Helen finished. "The murder might have been intended for both of them after all. Janczek *was* the one who got hacked apart, wasn't he?"

"Yes." Kachigan scowled. "There's only one thing I can't figure out. Why has Zawisza been trying to kill you and me?"

Helen cleared her throat. "Um—I think it's because of something I said to him last Saturday afternoon."

"You saw him before you got pushed in front of the trolley?"

She nodded. "My aunt and I ran into him in Market Square. He was so rude to Aunt Pittypat that I lost my temper and shouted at him. I told him I didn't believe anything he said, now that I knew for sure he and Lide had spent time together out in Chicago. All I meant was that I'd seen them both in that photograph you found, but when I think how it must have sounded—"

"As if you knew that he and Lide were lovers." Kachigan

whistled between his teeth, more pieces falling into place. "And now he has to kill us too, to preserve his secret. It all makes sense."

"I know," Helen agreed. "But can we prove any of it?"

"I don't know. If we could find out—"

The mantel clock interrupted him, striking nine. The odd intimacy of this conversation, alone in his kitchen with Helen Sorby, dawned on Kachigan. He cursed.

"What's the matter now?"

"I've got to get you home. If anyone ever finds out we were alone tonight, your reputation—"

"—wouldn't be any more ruined than it already is," Helen said wryly. "At least one newspaper called me your young lady."

"Which is exactly why you shouldn't be here now." Kachigan ushered her out into the dark front hall. "Wait here, while I fetch a cab from the stand down on Carson Street."

"I can walk down there with you."

"No." He shrugged on his overcoat, not bothering with his collar or suit coat. "We may not know for sure if it's Domanin or Zawisza, but someone out there definitely wants to kill you."

18

SOMETHING WAS VERY WRONG.

The first thing Helen noticed when she unlocked her front door was that the gaslights weren't on and the house didn't smell of food. She frowned, wondering what could have kept Thomas from his overdue supper. Perhaps he'd stayed to eat with Aunt Pittypat, despite her preference for plain boiled dinners and cats on every spare chair.

Then in the reflected light from the street lamp, she saw her brother's overcoat hanging wet on the nearest peg.

"What's the matter?" Kachigan demanded, as if he'd felt her shiver. He'd stepped in behind her as soon as she'd alighted from the cab, standing so uncomfortably close that Helen suspected he was guarding her against bullets with his own body.

"Thomas came home tonight, but he didn't make supper." For once, she managed to keep her voice down to a whisper. "Something's wrong."

She blessed the quick intelligence that let Kachigan follow her logic. His voice dropped to a soft breath against her hair. "Let me go in first, then follow me inside. I don't want you standing here by yourself."

Helen nodded, not trusting her voice to stay low while her anxiety about her brother rose. Kachigan shouldered past her and she slipped in after him, pulling the door closed slowly behind her so it wouldn't creak. Only the darker shadow of his overcoat in the darkness betrayed the detective's location while he circled the downstairs hall. Helen bit her lip and forced herself to remain by the door, knowing she would get in his way if he found an intruder. She listened to the old house's nighttime creakings and stirrings, trying not to hear footsteps or muffled struggles in each of them.

After what seemed like a long time, Kachigan returned to her side as quietly as he had departed. "Where would Thomas have gone first when he came home?" he asked, then answered his own question. "Downstairs bathroom?"

She nodded again. This time, Kachigan reached out and took her hand, pulling her down the hall with him as if he didn't want her out of his sight. They entered the darker section of hall that led to the kitchen, and now that her eyes were adjusted to the lack of light, Helen could see the black line where the bathroom door stood ajar. Her fingers tightened around Kachigan's hand.

"I see." His voice dropped to an almost soundless breath in the silence. "Wait here."

This time it was torture, but Helen twisted her hands into her skirts and forced herself not to move. Two steps and Kachigan vanished into the gloom of the unlit bathroom. His footsteps thudded into something soft, and she heard the smack of palm against wall as the detective steadied himself. Fortunately, that disquieting noise was followed by a groan that belonged unmistakably to her brother.

"Thomas!" Helen darted to the bathroom door, wriggling past Kachigan despite his soft curse and then dropping to her knees in the tiny space that remained. Her searching hands told her that Thomas lay slumped against the back wall, wedged half-upright between the cold tank of the toilet and the pedestal sink. He groaned again and lifted a hand to ward her off when her fingers touched his neck.

"Don't, Helen, that hurts . . ."

She ignored him, pressing lightly along the sticky wetness of his shoulder to gauge his injury. "Milo, we need lights."

"Hold on." Kachigan extricated himself from the tangle in the tiny room, and a moment later the gas lamp in the hall brightened to a white-gold glow. The light made Thomas look horrible. Blood had streaked along the entire left side of his face and neck, soaking down to darken his collar, but Helen's experience at the settlement house told her that her twin's face held too much color for the wound to be a serious one. A moment later she found the shallow gash above his right ear. That and two or three sore spots along the same side of his neck were his only injuries. She sat back on her heels, taking a deep breath for what seemed like the first time in years.

Water ran in the sink above her head. Kachigan handed her a damp towel, then watched while she sponged the blood off her brother's face and neck. "It looks like someone beat you with a pistol," he told Thomas. "Did you see who it was?"

"No, dammit." Thomas pushed Helen away, more strongly this time, and struggled out from the uncomfortable spot he'd fallen into. "He got me from behind while I was—"

"Oh." Helen backed out of the bathroom discreetly, letting Kachigan help her twin stand up and straighten his clothes. Once outside, her eyes followed the sweep of gaslight into the open door of their drawing room and her stomach wrenched in dismay. "Oh, no."

"What is it?" Kachigan came out to join her, dragging Thomas ruthlessly enough to wring out another groan. His gaze followed Helen's to the piles of torn paper and randomly flung books, and he cursed softly in Armenian.

"Someone wrecked our drawing room," Thomas said in groggy realization. "But all my maps were in there."

Fury rose like a flood wave inside Helen. "*Damn*." She leaped across the hall to survey the damage, but Kachigan caught her halfway and swung her to a halt. He'd left Thomas leaning against the staircase, looking paler now than when they'd found him. The gash above his ear was still dribbling enough blood to leave a reddish patch where he leaned against the wallpaper.

"Let me go in first, in case he's still here," the detective ordered curtly. Helen scowled but gave in, enduring a moment of tense silence before the light in the drawing room flickered on. Kachigan met her in the doorway, but his gaze had gone past her to her brother.

"Your maps are fine, Thomas," he said, then glanced down at Helen. "But your books and manuscripts aren't. Take a look and tell me what's missing while I search the rest of the house."

She nodded, so intently focused on her task that Kachigan almost slipped past her before she realized what he was going to do. She swung around to catch at his hand warningly. "Milo, be careful. Whoever it is, he's still got bullets in his gun."

"I know." He gave her fingers a quick squeeze, then vanished into the dark kitchen. Helen took a deep breath, then dove into the chaos of flung papers that was her end of the drawing room.

It took more than just a look to discover what was gone. Helen ended up stacking her manuscript pages in piles as she sorted through the mess and identified them: "The Benefits of Socialized Pension Systems for the Laboring Man" in one place; "Obstacles to Full Immigrant Employment" in another; and her review of Jack London's socialist manifesto, "The War of the Classes," in a third. By the time she was done, she knew what was missing.

"He took all my notes for the tenement fire article," she told Kachigan indignantly when he reentered the drawing room at last. Thomas came in with him, his head so neatly bandaged that she knew the detective must have done it. "Even the ones that didn't have anything to do with Josef and Lide Janczek!"

Kachigan frowned, crouching down on the floor beside her to scan the stacks she'd made. "Did he leave anything at all that had to do with the murder?"

"No, nothing. He even took my drawing pad."

"Does that mean it was your killer?" Thomas asked in dismay. "God, I'm sorry I didn't get a look at him."

Helen shook her head. "It could just as well have been Bernard Flinn. He said he didn't want me to publish this article for his wife to read. Maybe he decided to make sure I couldn't."

"I don't think so," Kachigan said. "The gas lamps were

cold when I lit them tonight. That means whoever broke in came by daylight, in order to read your papers and find the ones he wanted. He could have left when he was done with that, but instead he deliberately waited for someone to come home.'' Helen had never noticed before how grim Kachigan's thin face could look. ''I don't think he was waiting just to pistol-whip Thomas.''

Helen gnawed her lip, considering it. ''You think he wanted to kill me,'' she said, as calmly as she could. She suspected from her brother's curse and the angry jerk of muscle along Kachigan's jaw that she hadn't managed to sound calm enough. ''But that would be stupid—you'd still be alive to arrest him. Zawisza's getting desperate.''

''Yes. Time must running out for him somehow, even if we can't see why.'' The detective rose restlessly to his feet and began to pace the room. ''The trouble is, every move in this game has been his. We've always had to react to something he's done, which lets him stay a jump ahead of us. We have to change that.''

''How?'' Thomas demanded.

''By setting a trap for him.'' Kachigan paused in front of the untidy pile where Helen had swept all her miscellaneous papers, then pounced on them like a striking hawk. What he came up with was one of Dennis McKenna's illegible temperance fliers. ''And this is where we'll set it.''

''It's obvious what the bait should be.'' It was the third time Helen had said it, each time louder and less patiently. ''Me.''

Kachigan frowned at her across the cup of strong Italian coffee that she'd poured him. By mutual consent, they'd left the ransacked drawing room for the undisturbed kitchen. The coffeepot had steamed the windows up against the outside dark, wrapping them securely in the wood-fired warmth of the stove. It was past ten, and except for the distant roar of its mills, the South Side was shrouded in late-night silence. Sitting with two men in their rolled-up sleeves and collarless shirts, it seemed to Helen almost like a casual family supper. Except for the conversation.

''No,'' the detective said flatly. ''I'm not going to use you as bait to catch Karl Zawisza or anyone else.''

"Why not?" Helen asked heatedly. "I'm the one he thinks he has to kill. And he knows I'll be at the temperance lecture with Aunt Pat. It's too good an opportunity for him to pass up."

"Which is exactly why you aren't going," Thomas retorted. A cold beef-tongue sandwich and two cups of coffee had given him back most of his color and all of his exuberance. "Kachigan's right. It's too dangerous."

She played her strongest card. "But, Thomas, I promised Aunt Pat a picture of Dennis McKenna—"

"—which I can draw almost as well as you can."

Helen scowled, annoyed at this betrayal. "All right, then. If you leave me at home, who is Karl Zawisza going to shoot at?"

"If he's smart, he won't shoot at anyone," Kachigan replied. "In the size crowd he knows Domanin's bringing to this lecture, a knife would be a much better weapon than a gun. That's why it's the perfect place to trap him. If he has to get close enough for a knife strike, we'll have a fighting chance to catch him."

"But a trap can't work without *some* bait," Helen protested. "Zawisza doesn't want to kill Dennis McKenna!"

"He wants to kill me."

"So you get to be the bait when I don't?" Helen smacked her empty cup down on the table, hard enough to make Thomas wince. "That's not fair!"

Kachigan rose to get the coffeepot. "*You* spend five years learning to stop knife fights at the local pool halls without getting hurt, Helen. Then I'll let you be the bait."

"No, you wouldn't," she said acidly. "You'd still want to have the fun of doing it yourself. Milo, have you thought about what will happen if Karl Zawisza *doesn't* see me at the lecture? He might turn around and come back here, instead."

"That's why you'll spend tomorrow night at my house." The stern tone of Kachigan's voice told Helen he couldn't be argued with about this. "I'm not listed in the Polk Directory. Even if Zawisza does leave the meeting, there's no way he can find you there."

"And no way you'll be able to catch him, either!"

There was a long, stymied silence. Thomas broke it at last, with a chuckle so unexpected and explosive that Helen jumped.

"What on earth are you laughing about?" she demanded, turning to frown at him. "There's nothing funny about this."

"Oh yes, there is," said her unrepentant twin. "I've just thought of how we can fool Zawisza into staying at the temperance lecture *and* attacking someone there. While I'm sketching Dennis McKenna for Aunt Pat, I'll pretend to be you."

Kachigan cleared his throat. "I think your beard will give you away, Thomas."

"Beards can be removed," Thomas retorted. "And if I put on a long coat, and a floppy hat big enough to cover my hair—"

"I don't own a hat that big," Helen objected.

"No, but Aunt Pat does."

"True," she said. "But, Thomas, trust me—you'd still look like a man wearing a woman's coat."

"Want to bet?" He scrambled up, eyes agleam with laughter. "Wait here and I'll show you what a Sanborn man can do!"

"Thomas, be careful! Your head—"

"—doesn't feel any worse than my last hangover." He disappeared through the kitchen's swinging door, and a moment later Helen heard his footsteps pounding up the front stairs. "If you really felt sorry for me, you would make me a *tiramisu* while you waited," a muffled shout informed her from above.

"It's your turn to make it," Helen retorted, but only a distant slam of closet doors answered her. She sighed, eying the stack of dishes that nearly filled their sink. "He would want *tiramisu* on the night when all our glasses are dirty."

"I'll wash them for you." Kachigan got up, taking the empty coffee cups with him to the chipped enamel counter. "You really shouldn't get your hands wet while they're healing."

"Why do you think all those dishes are there in the first place?" Helen took out the bowl of mascarpone cheese from their wooden icebox, then dug a waxed bag of ladyfingers out of the bread drawer. "Just don't wash the coffeepot. I need the rest of the coffee to make this."

"All right."

There was a long and surprisingly comfortable silence. Helen could hear the quiet splashing as the detective filled the sink with water and soap flakes, then began swishing the dishes through it. She occupied herself beating the soft, sweet cheese in the bowl to a creamy froth.

"Are you really going to let Thomas masquerade as me tomorrow night?" she asked.

"If he can dress the part. In the dark, that should be good enough to fool Zawisza into attacking us."

"Assuming he's there." Helen licked her fingers and decided the cheese was whipped enough. "Are any of the glasses clean yet? I need three of the big ones."

Kachigan brought them to her, still warm and wet from rinsing. "He should be there. This is a unionizing meeting for him now, remember, not a temperance lecture."

"That's true." Helen stuffed several ladyfingers into each glass, then poured the last of the thick dark coffee over them and slid the empty pot down the counter to Kachigan. He began to wash it out, while she sifted dry cocoa into the glasses. "You'll stay beside Thomas the entire time, won't you?"

"Yes." Kachigan lifted one wet hand and caught hers away from the cheese bowl. "I won't let anything happen to him tomorrow, Helen. I promise you."

She turned to scowl up at him. "And do you promise not to let anything happen to you, either?"

Kachigan pulled in a sharp breath. They stood in hand-locked silence beside the enamel sink for a moment, until the silence was shattered by a fierce curse from upstairs.

"Thomas?" Helen pulled free of Kachigan's grasp and went to open the kitchen door. "Are you all right?"

Her brother sounded exasperated and oddly breathless. "Yes, of course. Helen, why in God's name do women wear corsets?"

"Because men think we're immoral if we don't," she retorted. "Thomas, you *can't* fit into one of my corsets."

"It's not yours, it's one of Mum's."

"Oh." Helen let the door swing close on another breathless masculine oath and came back into the kitchen, self-consciously avoiding Kachigan's gaze. He finished washing out the coffeepot and set it on the counter to drain, then watched while she spooned the whipped cheese in to fill each of the glasses.

"What is that you're making?"

"*Tiramisu*. It means 'pick-me-up' in Italian." Helen sprinkled more cocoa over the top of each dessert. "It's supposed to have brandy too, but since I've taken the pledge—"

"—you don't keep spirits in the house," Kachigan finished, smiling. He reached out and caught her hand again. "Helen, can I try an experiment?"

The warmth of his fingers startled her. "What kind of experiment?"

"A measuring experiment. All you have to do is stand still."

Helen gave him the threatening look she'd perfected on her mischievous twin. "If this is some kind of trick—"

"Then you can hit me," he promised, pulling her a step closer. "In fact, you probably will, anyway."

She opened her mouth to reply, but the words evaporated into a startled gasp. Through her shirtwaist and corset, she could feel Kachigan's hands slide around her waist. He touched his fingers together carefully in the small of her back, then curved his thumbs around the front and squeezed hard.

"Milo!" Helen found her voice with a choke of indignation. "What on earth are you doing?"

"Making sure I can't get my hands all the way around your waist," he said seriously.

She scowled up at him again. "Did you actually think I was one of those idiot women who lace themselves so tight their ribs break and puncture their lungs? Just because I wore that one evening dress—"

"No," he admitted. "In fact, I was pretty sure you weren't. But when you told Thomas he couldn't fit in one of your corsets, I started to worry again. Thomas may have wider shoulders than you do, but he's pretty thin everywhere else."

Helen felt her cheeks tighten with embarrassment. "That's why I knew he wouldn't fit," she muttered. "He's too small, not too big. And it wasn't the waist I meant, it was—"

"Here?"

"Milo!" She stepped forward to escape his hand and found herself folded into the warmth of his arms instead. She frowned and reached up, intending to push him away. It wasn't until she tried to catch her breath and couldn't that she realized she'd given him a fierce, impulsive hug instead.

"All right," Thomas said from the other side of the door. "Are you ready?"

They were five feet apart by the time he entered, Kachigan drying his hands on a towel and Helen opening her mouth to answer her brother. Genuine astonishment stopped the words somewhere in her throat.

"You're amazed, aren't you?" Thomas said in breathless triumph. Wasp-waisted in an old-fashioned serge skirt and billowing blouse, with a black Mass-veil hiding his cropped hair and bearded face, her twin was barely recognizable.

Helen had to swallow twice before she could speak. "Thomas, I never knew you looked so much like Mum—"

"Good. That means I look like you, too." He swung around to survey his reflection in the nearest window. "I think it's the veil that does it. Kachigan, do you think you could get me a dark wig for tomorrow?"

"If you're willing to wear it, I'll find one for you."

Thomas Sorby turned and grinned at them. "Of course I'll wear one. I want to tell this story to my grandchildren, and a wig will add the crowning touch." His grin widened. "In fact, the only thing I *won't* do to make Zawisza think I'm Helen is what she was doing with you a minute ago."

Kachigan's face darkened and Helen choked, finding herself speechless for a second time that evening. At the sight of their guilty expressions, Thomas burst into breathless laughter.

"I didn't even see you," he admitted, between gusts of strangled mirth. "I just guessed from how quiet it was—"

"*Thomas!*"

"Don't glare at me, Helen, I'm leaving." He grabbed his skirts and lifted them past his knees, exposing long argyle socks. "I've got to take this corset off before I laugh so hard I explode."

19

TUESDAY DAWNED CLEAR BUT OMI-
nously still. By sunset, the unmoving
smoke from the mills had curdled into
a thin black fog, with an odd, suffocated
quality to the light that promised worse
to come. Kachigan paused outside Patrol Station Seven,
watching gas lamps flare on one by one down Sarah Street.
He only counted to six before their dwindling halos were lost
in the gloom.

"Milo, my boy." A hand clapped on his shoulder from
behind, startling him into swinging around. After a day's
long patrol, Ramey's face was freckled with soot but his grin
still held a wicked gleam. "How's it feel to be back on the
beat with us?"

"Same as always," Kachigan retorted. That was a lie, of
course. His brass-buttoned uniform still fit and his shoes were
worn enough to endure long blocks of walking, but the comfort of being part of a street patrol had gone forever. The
ice-edged silence he'd just endured in the coffee room was
proof of that. He gave Ramey a measuring glance, surprised
that he'd even paused on the way home to taunt him. The
other man's grin widened.

"I'd say it's good to have you back," he continued loudly,
herding Kachigan down the steps with him. "Except now
Captain Halloran has to promote that damned Belfast-man
who's been pretending to be a desk sergeant." His voice

lifted a little more to pierce the smoke. "You know, if there's anything I hate more than an Armenian detective, it's a Protestant one."

Kachigan heard a muffled curse, and then the door of the horse-drawn cab at the curb slammed shut hard enough to rock the whole vehicle before it drew away. "Don't worry," he said drily. "Todd won't last long if he lets you get to him like that."

Ramey grunted, releasing him when they reached the street. "Ah, he deserves it." He reached out and collared a slim, blue-clad figure as it emerged from the smoke. "Hey, *paisan*, you're late. You're never going to get promoted to day shift that way."

"I know." Silvio Pedone shrugged free, his dark Italian face looking troubled. "I just didn't want to be in the coffee room when—" He broke off, then startled Kachigan with an outthrust hand. "Sorry, detective."

"Me too." Kachigan accepted the younger man's fierce handshake, feeling a little of his icy tension melt away. "But you might as well get used to calling me Milo, like Frank does. I don't think I'll make it back up the ladder any time soon."

Pedone muttered something vehement in Italian, gave Ramey a disgusted look and then trotted past them up the stairs.

"A good boy, but a wee bit too serious about his work," Ramey commented. "He'll learn soon enough."

"No doubt." Kachigan glanced sideways at the Irish patrolman as they approached Fourteenth Street, then made a quick decision. "You still moonlighting, Frank?"

"Whenever I can get work. Why?"

"Because I need a house guard tonight, and I can't do the job myself. You interested?"

"I might be," Ramey admitted slowly. "If the A.O.H. don't need me, which they probably won't. Tuesdays are slow there." His eyebrows cocked up in shrewd curiosity. "So, Milo, my boy, whose house are you needing guarded? Miss Sorby's?"

"No," said Kachigan. "Mine."

•   •   •

Light from Market Square's tall gas lamps fought with the smoky shadows of the arched market buildings, barely managing to illuminate the streets that crossed beneath them. In the dimness, only eyes and occasional smiles were reflected in the sea of soot-dark faces that filled the square. Kachigan glanced out the window of the dilapidated cab that Helen's aunt always seemed to travel in, gauging the crowd. It looked like most of Taylor Mill's work force had shown up.

"What a dreadful—I mean—tremendous crowd." Pat McGregor peered out of her own grimy cab-window in bewilderment. "We've never had so many men turn out for a temperance lecture before. Do you suppose it was the fliers Helen posted?"

Thomas Sorby snorted, eyes gleaming with amusement under the immense feathered hat his aunt had lent him. "No doubt, Aunt Pat. I hope Zawisza can find me in this mill."

"We'll have to make sure you're visible," Kachigan replied. "Do you think you can climb up on the driver's seat with all that finery you've got on?"

"If you give me a discreet shove." With his beard gone and his cropped hair hidden under a cheap dark wig, it was surprising how much the surveyor managed to look like his sister. The only jarring note was the paleness of his newly shaved cheeks.

"Good." Kachigan stuck his head out the cab window. "Get as close as you can to the center of the square," he told the cabman. "If anyone gives you grief, tell them you've got the lady who sponsored the lecture inside—and a police guard."

The driver pushed back his lumpy hat, grinning at Kachigan. "I can do that," he said with relish, and slapped the reins at his placid mare. Voices rose outside and then subsided again as the cab pushed through the crowd. It pulled up under the shadow of the market arches and Kachigan opened the cab door, stepping out along the foot board to make room for Sorby.

"Do be careful, Thomas," Pat McGregor said anxiously.

Thomas Sorby made a disgusted noise, sweeping his skirts up in both gloved hands. "Don't worry. In this outfit, I'm more likely to fall and break my neck than get killed by anyone.''

''I do hope so, dearest. I mean—''

Laughing, Thomas bent down to plant a kiss on his aunt's soft cheek. ''I know what you mean, Aunt Pittypat. Thanks.''

He ducked out of the cab and scrambled up to the driver's seat before she could reply. When his initial momentum faded, Kachigan surreptitiously added a shove at the back and the cabman leaned down to haul him the rest of the way up. In a pretty flurry of lace petticoats, Thomas seated himself on the front seat and took the drawing pad that Kachigan handed up.

''No talking from now on,'' Kachigan warned him in an undertone, then in a louder voice added, ''I'll be patrolling the square now, Miss Sorby. If you need anything, have the cabman give me a whistle.''

Feathers fluttered with Thomas's graceful nod, and only Kachigan saw the breathless grimace that went with it. He leaned in through the cab to address Pittypat with careful politeness.

''You'll be safer if you stay inside, Mrs. McGregor. You weren't planning to introduce the lecturer tonight, were you?''

Her hazel eyes studied him intently for a moment, although Kachigan wasn't sure what she was looking for in his face. ''Not to this crowd,'' she admitted at last. Her voice was frank, if not entirely friendly. ''The sight of an old frigate like me would probably send them running for the nearest saloon.''

Kachigan repressed a smile. ''I'll stop back every few minutes to make sure Thomas is all right. If you hear anything untoward up there, scream for me as loudly as you can.''

''I can do that,'' Pat McGregor said, imitating her cab-driver with an unexpected and quite deliberate twinkle in her eye. Kachigan began to see why her niece and nephew regarded her with such indulgent affection. ''Good luck, Mr. Kachigan.''

He swung down from the running board and into the crowd, noticing the stir of someone's passage to the fruit-crate podium that had been set up on one corner of the square. Kachigan shouldered a slow and careful path in that direction, through the smell of coal smoke and steel tang and day-old sweat. It was an oddly quiet gathering, with most of these workingmen straight off twelve-hour shifts, but he knew better than to force his way through it, especially in the brass-buttoned patrolman's coat he wore now. With wits dulled and tempers short after a long day's work, any impolite jostling was as likely to be greeted by a fist or a knife as by a curse.

A figure mounted the podium and cleared his throat with a noticeably tentative sound. Kachigan glanced up from scanning the crowd long enough to take in the cheap frock coat and ill-fitting waistcoat beneath it. If Dennis McKenna *had* been a success on the lecture circuit in Chicago, he'd obviously spent none of his donations on his clothes. Even his hat was too big for him, and kept slipping down over his earnest face. He cleared his throat again and announced without much confidence that he was a sinner.

"Aren't we all?" said a familiar voice in Kachigan's ear.

"Domanin?" He swung around with some difficulty in the forward press of the crowd. "Should you be here tonight?"

"Someone's got to count the vote—I mean, the pledges."

Kachigan edged between two thickset laborers to stand beside the Russian machinist. "You look awfully healthy for a man with typhoid. Aren't you afraid Bernard Flinn might notice?"

"If he comes." Domanin's smile flashed out in the darkness. "Your Miss Sorby must have spread the word about this lecture—I see reporters from all the city papers here." He glanced over his shoulder at the cab, where Thomas Sorby sat working industriously at his drawing pad. The background glow of a gaslight threw the surveyor into dark silhouette, a more effective disguise than any of his borrowed frills. "You know, I'm surprised you're not keeping the young lady company, Kachigan."

Was there a testing note in that rough Slavic voice, or just a touch of masculine humor? Kachigan took a deep breath, trying to summon up the half-exasperated tone Helen so often provoked.

"She made me leave because I was blocking her light."

Domanin's chuckle sounded genuine. "A very frank young lady, Miss Sorby, eh?"

"Very."

They fell silent, watching the lecture together. If Yuri Domanin objected to Kachigan's presence at his elbow, he didn't appear moved to say so. Up in front of the crowd, Dennis McKenna had warmed to his theme after a few shaky moments, and actually managed to catch the audience's attention with a long and lurid description of his liquor-drenched past. The temperance lecturer had a good speaking voice despite his slight frame—just enough of a tenor to carry past the clatter of trolleys and horsecabs.

Kachigan stopped listening after another few moments, when McKenna began to describe a dramatic midnight conversion to sobriety. He scanned the audience instead, trying in vain to catch a glimpse of a tall, white-blond figure among the workingmen. All he saw was the worried face of Aunt Pittypat, peering out from the cab's dingy window. Above her, her nephew still sketched at his drawing pad, although the cabman who had been sitting beside him had disappeared.

Kachigan frowned and nudged Domanin's shoulder. Even without listening to the words, he could tell by the rising solemnity of McKenna's voice that the lecture was coming to its climax. If anything was going to happen tonight, the next fifteen minutes would prove it. So far he'd seen no evidence that Karl Zawisza was even on this side of the Monongahela. Maybe Domanin was their man after all. Kachigan took a deep breath, and decided to find out.

"I'm going to see where Miss Sorby's cabdriver has vanished to," he muttered at the Russian machinist. "Will you keep an eye on her for me while I'm gone?"

Domanin grunted acknowledgment, his broad face neither startled nor alert. He was watching Dennis McKenna with deep interest, although Kachigan couldn't imagine what in the speaker's confession of intemperance had caught his attention. "Make sure you're back with her before the lecture ends," was all he said. "If Flinn decides to do anything, it will be then."

"All right." Kachigan managed to stride away without looking back, although it took all his will power to do it. He'd either given Domanin enough rope to hang himself, or gained a temporary ally. The only way to find out was to vanish.

He forced himself to make a slow circuit of the East Market building, listening for an outcry past the echo of his footsteps in the deserted financial district. None came. With a sigh, Kachigan rounded the last corner and worked his way back through the crowd toward the cab. Thomas Sorby still sat ensconced there in undisturbed splendor. Their trap had failed.

Kachigan frowned and slid between the cab and the cold brick wall. Out in Market Square, the temperance lecture soared to a final shout of inspiration, and then was swamped with a wash of applause. Thomas glanced down and gave him a frustrated head shake, then scribbled something on a torn-off corner of his drawing paper. Kachigan caught the white scrap as it fluttered through the darkness.

"Mr. Kachigan." The discreet hiss of sound from the carriage window barely carried to his ears. "What's the matter with Thomas?"

"Nothing that I can see." Kachigan scanned the note in his hand; then a corner of his mouth kicked upward. "Oh. He says he wants to go inside the market to use the facilities."

"That's what I was afraid of." Pat McGregor let out an earthy Irish snort. "I've been listening to him tap his foot against the side of the cab this last quarter hour."

Remembering how tightly Thomas had laced his borrowed corsets, Kachigan winced in sympathy. "Then I think maybe we'd better take pity on him." He paused, hearing Dennis McKenna's voice rise above the murmur of the crowd again. The temperance lecturer was now pleading for his fellow workingmen to take the pledge. "Your program's almost over, anyway."

"You'll escort him in?" When Kachigan didn't answer at once, Mrs. McGregor added, "You'd do it if it were really Helen."

"That's true. But I don't like leaving you here all alone."

She waved her lace-mittened fingers at him dismissively.
"I've got Joe O'Grady here with me. Don't worry." Kachigan had already seen the driver propped in the far corner of
his cab, snoring through his battered teeth. "He'll wake up
fast enough if anyone tries to bother me—he knows which
side his bread is buttered on. Go along with Thomas."

"Yes, ma'am." Kachigan turned back to the driver's seat,
holding his hand up for the surveyor. Out in the square, a
clamor of deep voices had answered McKenna's request, all
crying out to take the pledge. Kachigan cocked his head,
trying to gauge the strength of that response. It sounded like
Yuri Domanin was going to get his strike.

Thomas Sorby grimaced at Kachigan's outstretched hand,
but reluctantly steadied himself on it while he climbed down.
"Your aunt wants me to escort you inside," Kachigan informed him. Thomas shot him a fierce look, and he added,
"To make it seem like you're really Helen."

"Why does that matter now?"

"Appearances."

Thomas made a face, but obediently swept up his borrowed skirts and let Kachigan lead him toward the nearest
market door. From the top of the entrance stair, Kachigan
could see the milling sea of men begin to drift apart, some
converging in small knots of conversation while others
headed off to homes and trolley stops. Despite the chaos,
there was no sign of conflict or disturbance. Bernard Flinn
had apparently decided to keep most of his guards at home
tonight. For once, the power of the steel police had bowed
to the power of the press.

Inside the three-story market hall, the aisles were dark and
empty, all the vendor stands closed for the day. Only the
distant sound of an iceman unloading his cargo in shattering
crashes showed why the building remained unlocked. The
crisp smell of iced-down vegetables filled the chilly air, over-
laid with the ineradicable scent of old fish and overripe fruit.

"What a waste of time." Thomas's scowl was a milder
version of his sister's, but his voice held the same irritated
snap hers could on occasion. "I can't believe Zawisza never
showed up."

"Maybe he guessed it was a trap." Kachigan glanced

around the darkened building. "Do you know for sure that there's a public bathroom in here?"

"Upstairs, where the café is." Thomas turned down an aisle lined with crates of fruit, heading for the open metal stairs along the side wall. He unceremoniously hoisted his skirts around his knees to trot up them. "I can walk in these things, but damned if I can figure out how to climb steps."

"As long as you can figure out how to use the facilities in them."

The surveyor whooped with breathless laughter. "Well, there must be some way. Women do it all the time." He let his skirts down again when they reached the market's second floor. Across the enclosed brick footbridge that joined this building to its neighbor, lights still burned in the market's one eating place. The restrooms had been discreetly placed on this side, behind an arched partition. "Um—which one do you think I should use?"

Kachigan cocked his head, listening to the deeper silence up here. A few voices carried over from the cafe, but he heard no murmur of movement inside the restrooms, not even when he pulled the ladies' door slightly ajar. "Use this one. That way you won't shock anyone who sees you going in or out." He grinned at the dubious look he got. "Don't worry, I'll make sure no one comes inside while you're there."

"You'd better," Thomas said, then vanished into the dimness.

The downstairs clattering of ice stopped, replaced by the squeak of the iceman's cart as he wheeled it back out to his wagon. Kachigan leaned against a wall and contemplated the failure of their trap tonight. He was sure the socialist priest would have been here if he could, but they had no control over the other things that ruled Zawisza's life: the schedule of services at St. Witold's, the novenas to be said, parish visits to be made and confessionals to be heard. Any one of those might have interfered with the priest's attendance at the meeting tonight. In which case, what Kachigan needed was another time and place where Thomas could masquerade—

A woman's angry voice broke the silence, muffled by the

market's brick walls but still recognizable as Pat Mc-
Gregor's. Kachigan frowned and crossed to the other side of
the market, shoving aside a huge, hanging mass of bananas
to peer out the grimy window. In the square below, he could
see several men gathered around the cab, most of them carrying notebooks and wearing the distinctive buckled visors of
newspaper reporters. Curious, Kachigan levered open an
iron-framed window panel and tried to hear what they were
saying.

"—don't know where he's gone." Pat McGregor sounded
more irritated than alarmed. "Probably back to his hotel, to
take the pledges of the men he recruited here tonight. If you
wanted to interview him, you should have come before the
lecture—"

Reassured, Kachigan began wrestling the window closed,
then felt it vibrate under his hand, echoing a violent crash
from behind. He jerked around, attention caught first by the
uproar of voices across the footbridge. When he realized that
all the startled faces he could see there were staring back at
him, Kachigan cursed and launched himself toward the restrooms.

The ladies' room door leaped out to meet him when he
reached for it, slamming him back against the wall hard
enough to drive his breath out. Gasping, Kachigan shoved
his way out from the wedge of door and wall, diving after
the billowing overcoat of the man who'd burst from the darkness inside. His fingers caught one sleeve, then released it
again when the thin flicker of a knife stabbed toward him.
He took a step back, and this time collided with Thomas
Sorby. The surveyor grabbed for his right hand.

"Thomas, it's me!" Kachigan yanked away from the
younger man's determined grip, and only then noticed the
wet patch on one side of the torn and crumpled dress.
"You're hurt!"

"Just a cut." Thomas winced, reaching up to touch the
slash that ran under his arm. "Thank God for whalebone—
it turned his knife." He shoved Kachigan toward the walkway. "Go after him! I can make it down to the cab by myself."

Kachigan didn't waste any of his ragged breath arguing.

Turning, he glimpsed a shadowy figure dodging through the scattered lights of the cafe, and lunged after it. The brick walkway funneled the thunder of his footsteps out ahead of him. By the time he burst out into the second market building, the few people lingering there had spilled out to stare at him, clogging the path his quarry had taken.

"Police," he shouted, waving at them. "Move!"

They scattered out of his way, but the delay cost him seconds he couldn't spare. With a burst of speed, Kachigan tried to catch the attacker at the head of the iron stairs, but the billowing overcoat slid down into the darkness below while he was still rounding the railing at the top.

Kachigan gasped out a curse and clattered down the stairs after him. After the partial brightness of the cafe, the darkness down here hit his eyes like a blow. He skidded, half-falling, down the last few metal rungs, and felt more than heard the whisper of a knife slashing the air.

With strength born of desperation, Kachigan flung himself aside from the blade and simultaneously tried to grab the man who'd swung it. All he managed to do was send them both crashing through a vegetable stand to the floor. In a confusion of sliding ice and falling produce, Kachigan lunged for the attacker's knife-hand. He got a handful of overcoat instead, just close enough to the slender body beneath to feel the next knife-swing come at him.

With a splintering crash, something wooden and heavy smashed down over both of them. Stunned from the impact, Kachigan felt the other man shake off his grip and twist away through a cascade of debris. He spent a moment simply dragging air into his aching lungs, then became aware that strong hands were hauling him free of the wreckage. He cursed, and spun around.

"It's me!" Yuri Domanin stepped back, although he still kept a steadying hand on Kachigan's shoulder. All around them, the floor was littered with rolling oranges and shards of what had once been a wooden crate. "Sorry to hit you, but I couldn't tell you two apart in the dark. Do you know who that was?"

Even in the darkness, Kachigan could see that the Russian wasn't wearing an overcoat. "The man—who killed the Janczeks,'' he gasped. ''Which door did—he use?''

''The one on the river side. Wait, Kachigan, there's something you don't—''

Kachigan interrupted Domanin by shoving himself away. ''Thomas Sorby's hurt. Get a doctor for him,'' he yelled over his shoulder. ''And call the police, too.'' Memories of the last vain chase rose unbidden in his mind and made his stomach spasm in dismay. ''On *both* sides of the river!''

20

*TRAGEDY STRUCK A TEMPERANCE LEC-
ture in Market Square, as local steel
police mistook it for a union meeting—*
   "No," Helen said out loud. "Too
vague." She crumpled that sheet of paper and started again.

*Local steel-police thugs, under the leadership of Bernard
K. Flinn, wreaked havoc on an innocent crowd of workingmen—*

"Too melodramatic." Another wad of paper hit the floor.
"Elena, what you do?"

She looked across the small kitchen table at Milo Kachigan's father. Istvan's command of English might not be polished, but his blue eyes were as intelligent as his son's. Helen
sighed, wondering how to explain what was not exactly standard journalistic procedure.

"I'm trying to write a newspaper story about the meeting
Milo went to tonight."

"Huh." Istvan leaned forward in his chair to unfold one
of her rejected pages, reading it word by word with callused
fingers and silently moving lips. When he looked back up,
his weathered face wore a quizzical expression. "You don't
wait for this to happen before you write about it?"

Someone hammered on the door before she could answer,
loud enough to send the evening assembly of sparrows under
the back eaves into chitters and thrums of flight. Helen

dropped her pen and started for the hall, her frazzled sense of time telling her it had to be Thomas and Milo back from the temperance lecture. Istvan reached out when she passed his chair, catching her wrist in a surprisingly strong grip and pulling her to a stop.

"Too early to be Milosh," he warned.

Helen swung around toward the mantel clock, not believing him. But it was in fact barely eight—Aunt Pittypat's temperance lecture would have just gotten started in Market Square. Whoever was at the door, it wasn't Milo or her brother. The door thundered again under an impatient fist. "It could be the police officer Milo left to guard the house. Maybe he caught someone out there and needs help."

Istvan grunted, still not releasing her. "Then why he not whistle for other patrolmen?"

Helen scowled, knowing he was right. A police whistle could summon help faster than any telephone call could. If that wasn't Ramey out there, then whoever stood on the other side of the door must have already disabled the Irish patrolman. That meant he wasn't going to let a lock stand in his way forever. Helen's fingers tightened around Istvan's hand, feeling the strong bones beneath his wrinkled skin. Her first priority was to get him upstairs and safely hidden. Unfortunately, if he was anything like his son, that wasn't going to be easy.

"Your telephone, Mr. Kachigan—do you know how to use it?" Istvan grunted agreement. "Then come with me into the hall and ring up the police."

He frowned. "Why you not call, Elena? You talk better."

"I also yell better." For once, Helen could be thankful for her too-loud voice. "I'm going to try and talk to whoever's out there, loud enough so that he won't know you're calling the police. That way, they can come and catch him. All right?"

Istvan acknowledged the logic of that by holding out his hand for his walking sticks. Helen gave them to him and then followed the old man into the narrow dark hall, her pulse beating tensely in her throat at the slow swing of his progress. Another battering flurry of knocks hit the door just as Istvan reached for the telephone stand. Fortunately, his gruff Armenian curse was drowned beneath Helen's louder yelp of alarm.

"You might as well open the door, Miss Sorby." The deep rumble that seeped through the door sounded ominously familiar. "This is Bernard Flinn."

Helen's breath evaporated, but it was disbelief that drove that gasp, not dread. *Bernard Flinn*? The name was so unexpected, it took her a long minute to orient herself and remember who he must have come here to see. Heat sprang into her face at what he'd suspect from finding her here, but she took a resolute breath and ignored it. She motioned Milo's father to pick up the telephone receiver and open the line.

"I'm sorry, Mr. Flinn," she shouted back, as loudly as she could. Behind her, she could hear Istvan answer the operator in broken English. "Milo Kachigan's not at home right now."

Flinn's snort echoed through the door. "I know. He's off somewhere with your brother, trying to catch the man who set the Janczek fire."

"I don't know why you'd think—"

"I'm not in the mood for any nonsense," he warned her. "Just tell me where they went."

"No." Helen said it without thinking, her voice rising with fear and growing anger. To her relief, it came out sounding stubborn instead of panicked. "I'm not going to do that."

Despite the muffling effect of the door, the menace in Flinn's voice was easy to hear. "Think it over, Miss Sorby. Remember, you'll still be living in my town when this is over."

That sparked off a reservoir of deeper anger. "Pittsburgh isn't *your* town, Mr. Flinn," Helen shouted back at him, hoping her contempt showed as clearly as his did. "You're just a leech that should be pulled off it and thrown into the river!"

The door made a satisfying crash at the end of that jibe, as if the steel-police chief had slammed an angry fist against it. Helen took an involuntary step back, then frowned. How in the name of God had Bernard Flinn learned about their plans tonight? And why did he care? Surely he couldn't think that unmasking Karl Zawisza as a murderer could hurt Black Point Steel.

She opened her mouth to ask him that question, since Istvan was still muttering into the telephone behind her. The sound of footsteps retreating down the outside stairs stopped her. Helen glanced up at the clear-glass transom over the door and then darted around Milo's father, grabbed up one of the plain wood chairs from the kitchen and hauled it back with her to the door. By the time she'd leaped up onto it, she caught only the glimpse of a massive shadow disappearing into the smoke, but it was enough to confirm her suspicion. Flinn had gone down only one flight of steps, not two, rounding a corner of Kachigan's small sloping lawn to disappear into the dark passageway beside it.

"Damn." Helen vaulted off the chair, nearly bowling over Istvan Kachigan in the process. He'd hung up the phone and come to join her by the door. "Did you reach the police?"

He nodded. "Some Italian boy answer. He no speak too good, but he say he come soon."

Helen took a deep breath. This was going to be the hard part. "Until he gets here, Mr. Kachigan, I want you to go hide upstairs. That man outside is Bernard Flinn and I think he's going to try to break in—"

Istvan's face flared brick-red with anger and he spat something in swift, furious Armenian. Helen bit her lip, remembering too late that Kachigan had told his father exactly who was responsible for his demotion at Patrol Station Seven.

"Listen to me," she said, catching the old man's clenched fists in hers. "If he comes, we can't fight—all we can do is make sure Milo knows he was here. Flinn doesn't know you live here. If you stay hidden until the police come—"

"While he beat you?" Istvan snarled. "*No!*"

"Flinn won't beat me, as long as I tell him what he wants to know." An idea hit Helen, easing the tight clamp of fear on her breathing. "Or at least *thinks* I've told him that."

The polite tap of the door knocker echoed in the hallway, slicing their argument into silence. They eyed each other for a long, uncertain moment until the quiet tap came again.

"Police?" Istvan suggested softly.

"Maybe." Helen wasn't as sure as he was that their call for help had been understood. "Go upstairs, just in case it's not. Please, Mr. Kachigan. I'll be safer if you do."

He scowled but swung himself back toward the stairs, then began the slow, awkward climb up. Helen dug her teeth into her lower lip, forcing herself to wait until the sound of his footsteps had vanished into a back bedroom before she moved. It seemed to take forever. At any moment, she expected to hear the shatter of broken glass from the back of the house that meant Bernard Flinn had broken in, but it never came. Instead, what she heard was a third reassuring tap on the door.

Helen hauled up her skirts and stepped back up onto her chair to peer out the transom. Even in the smoky darkness, she could see the comforting gleam of brass buttons on a dark blue police coat, beneath the unmistakable peak of a patrolman's cap. With a sigh of relief, she stepped down and opened the door for the smiling policeman on the other side.

"Officer Ramey?" Helen blinked up at him in surprise, having expected the dark and wiry Italian officer she'd met the night of the fire. "What happened to you?"

"Nothing, Miss Sorby. Why?"

The patrolman's not-quite-convincing puzzled tone warned Helen what kind of mistake she'd made. She slammed the door at him with all her strength, ignoring the fact that Ramey had already stepped forward to block it. He grunted at the force of the impact, but refused to retreat. Helen took a step back to run, then realized it was useless. A massive shadow had already stepped out from the shadow of the passageway.

"*Flinn.*" Helen hurled the name at him like an epithet, hoping that Istvan would hear it and know to stay hidden upstairs. "Is Ramey one of your paid informers too?"

"He's a man who owes me a favor," Bernard Flinn said. "And he's smart enough to know when to return it. Now, put on your coat, Miss Sorby. Since you wouldn't tell me where your brother and lover have gone, you're going to have to show me."

"Why do you care where they've gone?" Helen demanded, too incensed to protest his assumptions. "This doesn't involve your company anymore!"

"Yes, it does." Flinn reached through the door, grabbing her wool coat from the rack and throwing it at her. "And don't try leading me on a goose chase, either," he added, as if he could read thoughts. "If we don't find Kachigan and your brother tonight, you won't be coming back."

Helen forced herself to look away from Flinn, scowling fiercely at Ramey instead. "You won't let him kill me."

"No," the patrolman said curtly.

Bernard Flinn grunted. "Don't worry, Miss Sorby. If you don't show me where Kachigan's gone, all I'm going to do is take you out to some nice East End hotel to stay the night." He paused, eyeing her relieved face with some amusement. "No, I don't suppose you care if your reputation is ruined, do you? Still, it's too bad you won't be able to ring up your brother and let him know you're all right."

Helen bit her lip, seeing the choice Flinn offered her. Either she let him interfere with the trap they'd set at the temperance meeting downtown, or she wouldn't be here when Thomas and Milo returned. And whether they'd caught Zawisza by then or not, she knew what her absence would do to them.

Her stomach roiled, but common sense told her that even a long night of fear couldn't kill someone. Bernard K. Flinn, on the other hand, most definitely could. With a sigh, Helen ducked her head and began putting on her coat, knowing that would signal her defeat to Flinn in a way she couldn't trust her voice to do.

"I knew you weren't stupid, Miss Sorby." The steel-police chief pulled her out onto the sidewalk, not even giving her time to get her scarf and muff. "Now, do we need to call a cab?"

Helen turned her collar up around her ears, already feeling the cold bite of the smoky night air. "No," she said, glancing down while she slid her fingers into the pockets of her coat. "We're only going as far as St. Witold's Church."

And then out to the East End.

•   •   •

It took longer than Helen thought to exhaust Bernard Flinn's patience. Her face was wind-burned and her fingers numb from waiting in the cold smoke of Breed Street before the Black Point Steel police chief finally gave up patrolling St. Witold's churchyard. He loomed out of the darkness, oddly silent on his feet for all his bulk, and glowered down at her. Helen saw Frank Ramey take a cautious step back, out of range.

"I haven't seen a trace of Kachigan or your brother all night, Miss Sorby." Flinn's voice wasn't much louder than a mutter, but somehow it still managed to sound dangerous. "Explain to me again how they were going to set a trap here. And this time, don't give me that cock-and-bull story about putting your brother in a dress and tricking the killer into another ambush like the one you walked into on Sunday afternoon. Whoever burnt my row house is too smart to try a stunt like that twice."

Helen took a deep breath, hearing the flat peal of St. Witold's bell. Nine o'clock. By now, Father Zawisza was either caught or gone astray. It wouldn't hurt to tell Flinn the truth.

"The reason you haven't seen Milo Kachigan is because he's not here. He and my brother went to a temperance lecture in Market Square at eight o'clock." Even in the smoky darkness, she could see the gathering thundercloud on Flinn's face. "With any luck, they're putting Karl Zawisza in jail right now."

"*Zawisza?*" Flinn blinked at her, his fury momentarily diverted. "The young Wobbly priest that serves at this church?"

"Yes."

"I'll be damned." Bernard Flinn turned away from her, staring at St. Witold's rectory. Except for the faint light burning in one upstairs window, the priests' house was dark and still. "You may get yourself back to Kachigan's house tonight yet, Miss Sorby," her captor said at last. "Tell me why you think Father Zawisza killed the people in that row house."

"Because he was sleeping with Lide Janczek," she informed him bluntly. "And he could get defrocked for it."

"You know that for a fact?" Flinn didn't sound shocked, only a little skeptical.

"Another priest told me. You're Catholic, you decide for yourself how reliable the information is."

Flinn grunted again, but this time he sounded amused rather than annoyed. "So, Zawisza tripped and fell into bed with a free-love socialist. What proof do you have that he killed her?"

"None," Helen admitted. "The only evidence we have is that he was nearby both times someone tried to kill *me*."

"Which is why Kachigan and your brother need to trap him into trying it again." Flinn rubbed his chin thoughtfully. "That's what they're trying to do at the lecture tonight?"

"Yes."

There was long, thoughtful silence, broken only by the smoke-muffled sound of a trolley clanging its way down East Carson Street. Helen held Bernard Flinn's gaze steadily, wishing she could read the thoughts behind those cold gray eyes as easily as he seemed to read hers. She didn't look away until a gust of wind blew off the Monongahela, hooting through the high church towers and tearing at her already disheveled hair. With a grimace, she pulled her collar higher around her neck.

"I'm freezing, Mr. Flinn," she said sharply. "Make up your mind whether you're going to take me to the East End, will you?"

The steel-police chief's massive shoulders shook with laughter. "I can see why Kachigan likes you, Miss Sorby. You're both too smart to know when you should be afraid." He paused, eying her shrewdly. "I think I'll let you go, but not just yet."

"Why not?"

"Because I'd rather you didn't have access to a telephone for a while," he said frankly. "Wait here with Ramey until I'm done at the priests' house. And before you start yelling about that, remember I can still cart you off to the East End."

"But why are you going to the priests' house?" Helen demanded, before she could consider the wisdom of asking another question.

"To talk to Karl Zawisza." Flinn smiled at her startled

gasp. "I hope Kachigan and your brother enjoyed catching the temperance lecture, Miss Sorby, because that's all they caught at Market Square. I watched Zawisza walk from the church to his house right after we arrived. He's been there ever since."

"Are you sure? It could have been the other priest from St. Witold's, Father Taddeusz."

"Not unless he grew a foot taller and lost forty pounds."

Helen's stomach twisted with the painful reality of failure. She tried not to think about how much worse it was going to be for Kachigan and her brother, coming home from an unsprung trap to find her gone. Instead she eyed Bernard Flinn with fierce determination. With luck, there might still be something she could salvage from the wreckage of the night. "If you're going in to confront Zawisza, you'd better take me with you, hadn't you? I'm the one he's been trying to kill."

Flinn snorted. "I don't think so, Miss Sorby. Wait here."

"All right," said Helen, goaded. "I'll use the time to compose my *Collier*'s article."

The Black Point Steel police chief paused in the act of turning away, glancing over his shoulder at her. "Miss Sorby, are you suggesting that if I took you with me, there might not be a *Collier*'s article?"

Helen took a deep breath, wishing she wasn't such a bad liar. "No," she said frankly. "I'm just giving you a chance to make sure that you're not the villain of it."

Flinn gave her an exasperated look. "And for that, I'm supposed to let you interfere with my interrogation of Zawisza?"

"Yes."

Overhead, St. Witold's bell pealed the quarter-hour. Flinn grunted impatiently, then surprised Helen by beckoning to her. "All right, it's a deal. Don't get in my way, and don't get close to Zawisza. The last thing I need is to get you shot tonight." His thin smile glinted again through the smoke. "Kachigan's going to be mad enough at me as it is."

St. Witold's rectory didn't have any kind of bell at the door—a polite suggestion, perhaps, that in their sanctum the priests would prefer not to be disturbed by their parishioners. Bernard Flinn's callused fist more than made up for that lack. Helen listened to the echoes shudder through the small brick house, hoping Father Taddeusz wasn't the one who came to answer.

Footsteps scuffed inside the door; then it creaked open without any rattle of lock. "Yes?" Karl Zawisza's cold blue gaze swung from Bernard Flinn to Frank Ramey without any sign of recognition, then fell to Helen's face, and froze.

"We need to talk to you, Father," Flinn said. Down the hallway, Helen could see Father Taddeusz in a worn old bathrobe and slippers, looking alarmed. "Outside, if you don't mind. It's about Lide Janczek."

Zawisza grimaced. "I thought it might be." He turned and said something reassuring in Polish to the old priest, then stepped out jacketless onto the stoop and closed the door behind him. "We can go into the church. No one's there right now."

Bernard Flinn's mouth quirked, but he made no objection. If Zawisza imagined he'd be safe within the sanctuary, Helen thought somberly, he would soon learn better. She followed them inside the shadowy interior of the church. The dim gaslight made the priest's hair and face glow with an unhealthy pallor.

"Well?" he demanded harshly, turning to confront them. "How much money do you want?"

Helen blinked and saw Bernard Flinn give the priest a long, quizzical look, probably as close to surprise as the steel-police chief ever came. "You admit it?" he said at last.

Zawisza made a wordless sound, half frustration and half regret. "Why not? *She* knows already." The disgusted jerk of his chin indicated Helen. "I suppose that woman told her, even though she swore she wouldn't."

"What woman?" Flinn demanded, saving Helen the trouble. A frown had indented his heavy face.

"Lide Janczek, of course." The young priest rubbed both hands across his eyes, a surprisingly open, childlike gesture for a man normally so ice-cold. "I knew it couldn't stay hidden forever, nothing does. How much money do you want?"

Flinn paused. "Father Zawisza, do you know who I am?"

Zawisza laughed, a painfully harsh crack of sound. "Some hoodlum who can buy policemen and information, obviously." His gaze swung back to Helen, the old hostility breaking through his glaze of resignation. "Although I wouldn't be surprised if Miss Sorby gave you the information for free, just to see me drummed out of her tea-party socialists' club."

Helen couldn't hold her outrage behind clenched teeth any longer. "I *did* give him the information for free," she snapped. "But it was because I wanted to see you brought to justice!"

The priest frowned at her, looking a little surprised at her vehemence. "For sleeping with Lide Janczek?"

"No," Flinn said grimly. "For murdering her."

There was a long silence, broken only by the whispering fires of the gas lamps. Even in the dim light, Helen could see the muscles of Zawisza's throat tighten convulsively before he spoke.

"You think—you think—" His voice grated to a stop, as if he couldn't even end the sentence.

"That you killed the Janczek woman," Flinn said harshly. He took a step closer to loom over the priest. "Why? Was she blackmailing you too?"

"Not Lide," Helen said firmly. "Her husband was."

Zawisza shook his head, but more as if he were trying to clear away the blurriness of a nightmare than make a denial. "No, neither of them. They never spoke to me after I—"

"Then maybe it was that hoodlum Mahaffey, eh?"

"*Mahaffey.*" The name exploded through the priest's cold veneer, but nothing else came after it. Helen threw Flinn a frustrated glance, and saw that even he looked stymied.

"I never did introduce myself," he said, to break the silence. "Bernard K. Flinn, chief of industrial police at Black Point Steel. And Gunther Weig's former employer." He paused as if that should have meant something to the priest. Judging by Zawisza's baffled stare, it didn't.

"I know of you," the priest said bleakly. "But why in God's name do you care about this? You've murdered men yourself."

"When they threatened my company or my policemen, yes." Flinn's deep voice hardened to a tempered edge. "I take care of my own, Zawisza. And one of my men turned up missing this week." He leaned forward, poking a massive finger into the priest's faded black cassock. "Gunther Weig. Last seen drinking at the Birmingham Turners' Hall, in the company of Lide Janczek."

Helen sucked in a startled breath. Karl Zawisza's normally pale face had turned completely ashen, as if he'd lost whatever blood coursed below the skin.

"You caught him doing it with her, didn't you?" Flinn demanded, wrapping his fist in a fold of Zawisza's cassock and giving him a sudden, violent shake. "You went there to make up or to pay up, and you caught them in the sack. And you couldn't stand it, could you? Knowing the one woman— the only woman—you ever had was sleeping with every man she met in the street."

"No!" Zawisza snarled. "No, no, *no*! It was *Mahaffey*!"

Flinn scowled. "Mahaffey's not the man you killed."

"I didn't kill anyone." Contempt flared in the priest's grating voice, as if he truly didn't care whether they believed him or not. "Mahaffey was the one I caught Lide sleeping with—not just her husband's friend, but an *anarchist*." He spat out that word, as if it was the part that hurt most. "I never visited or spoke to her again."

Helen glanced up at Bernard Flinn. "You laid Mahaffey off a month ago. He would have been home, on days Josef wasn't—"

Zawisza let out another painful crack of laughter. "As if Janczek would care! Lide said he knew there was enough of her to go around, and didn't mind—but *I* did," he said with bitter self-awareness. "She swore to me she believed in what I was trying to do, and then she turned around and bedded an *anarchist*. If I had killed anyone, it would have been Mahaffey."

"But you didn't," Flinn said, releasing the younger man.

Zawisza shook his head. "Mahaffey had a woman—a Jew—I don't think she knew what he did when she wasn't there. Even if she was an anarchist, too, I couldn't stand the thought of one more person getting hurt." He grimaced. "So

I did for selfish reasons what I should have done for the sake of my vows. I put Lide Janczek aside. And when she died in that fire, all I could think was that another man had been braver than I was, or perhaps more injured. I couldn't find it in myself to blame him.''

The ring of honest self-contempt in the young priest's voice was more convincing than a dozen staunch denials. Helen took a deep breath, her head spinning with the implications. A fierce gust of wind surged through the open church door, bringing the distant sound of whistles from the river.

''Have you considered,'' she asked Flinn quietly, ''that it could have been your man Weig who killed the Janczeks? If Josef caught him sleeping with Lide, and he thought it would matter?''

''A good theory, Miss Sorby,'' Flinn said drily, then reached into his waistcoat pocket and tossed something in her direction. Helen found herself holding a brass badge, scorched and melted down nearly to a lump. Only a few of the engraved letters were still visible, but she could make out a crude rendering of steel-mill stacks above them. ''That's what makes me doubt it.''

''What is it?''

''Gunther Weig's Black Point police badge.'' Flinn came to stand beside her, leaving Zawisza standing tall and still in his lonely church. The distant shriek of whistles had grown louder, and she could see the patrolman lifting his head to listen. ''Ramey found it in the ashes of the row house the other day, while he and Kachigan were poking around for bullet shells. He was smart enough to give it to me.'' The cold gray eyes met hers. ''You tell me what you think it means.''

Helen opened her mouth to answer, but the rough clasp of Frank Ramey's hand on her shoulder stopped her. ''They're chasing a fugitive down by the river,'' he told her, heedless of Bernard Flinn. ''Do you remember, last Sunday—''

Helen took a deep breath, eyes widening in comprehension. ''You were wrong,'' she told Flinn fiercely, twining her hands into the double thickness of her coat and skirts. "Kachigan's trap worked after all."

And then before the steel-police chief could stop her, she turned and bolted though the open church door, running headlong for the Monongahela.

21

KACHIGAN BURST OUT THROUGH THE side door of the East Market building, breath laboring inside aching ribs. Diamond Street stretched empty and silent into smoke at either end, with no hint of the direction his quarry had taken. He gritted his teeth to stifle the sound of his own breath, and listened for running footsteps. Any pickpocket knew enough to stop running once he hit a large enough crowd of people, but Kachigan's instincts told him he wasn't chasing that kind of criminal.

For once, Pittsburgh's smoky darkness aided him. From the uptown end of Diamond Street, Kachigan heard a muffled thud and outcry as bodies collided in the night. He hurled himself in that direction, hoping that the sound of his pursuing footsteps would keep the fugitive moving. A renewed burst of clattering answered his prayers. Kachigan chased after it, ignoring the protest of bruised ribs and the rasp of his smoke-torn throat. This time, he wasn't going to let his quarry get away.

For two aching blocks the chase led east and uphill along Diamond Street, toward Grant's Hill. Then the clear echo of footsteps off the twenty-five story facade of the Farmers' Bank building told Kachigan that Thomas Sorby's attacker had swerved south onto Wood Street. For a moment, all he knew was that the slight downward grade gave his aching lungs a chance to rest, but a shining glimpse of the Monongahela at the end of the street reminded him of what lay ahead. Please God, he thought, don't let there be coal barges on this section of the river.

He broke out from between the last blocks of downtown buildings, hurdling the double set of trolley tracks that ran down the middle of Water Street. At this hour of the night, the wide stone-paved wharf on the other side was empty of wagons and market stands, with only a few scattered piles of boat gear and ramp timbers interrupting its long decline to the water. Beyond a narrow strip of diamond-dappled river, the Monongahela was covered with small moving mountains of black rock. Kachigan wasted some of his remaining breath on a curse. This time, his prayers weren't going to be answered.

He skidded down the damp wharf-paving, hands outstretched to keep his balance. At the water's edge, the man he was chasing vaulted onto the nearest tied-up barge, overcoat streaming out behind him. One last gleam of gaslight caught him as he leaped, showing Kachigan a dark head on a frame no taller than his own. Whoever this man was, it wasn't Karl Zawisza.

The discovery sent a jolt of dismay through Kachigan. If he lost the attacker now, there'd be no way to bait another trap. The surge of frustration that rolled through him lent him the momentum he needed to make one last sprint down the slope and launch himself across open water toward the barge.

He made it, but only by the smallest of margins. Already wet from the wharf, his shoes found no purchase against the slick wooden surface they landed on. Faced with a choice of going overboard or falling into the shallow hold, Kachigan chose the latter. He landed on shoulder and hip in a sliding roar of coal. At least this time, he kept most of his breath.

The hollow thunk of distant footsteps mocked him while he struggled out of the loose pile of coal and hauled himself back up onto the barge rim. Kachigan gritted his teeth and scrambled to his feet again, trying to ignore the uncomfortable crunch of coal inside his shoes. He headed upriver after the fleeing man, crossing from one gently rocking barge to another. The deep shadow of the Smithfield Street Bridge slowed him for two excruciating jumps, but by the time he emerged from it, he could walk the barge rims with more confidence in his feet.

At least, he didn't have the task of picking a path through the crazy quilt of barge tie-ups that covered the Mononga-hela. Given that advantage, Kachigan thought he might even be able to catch his man before he found a stretch of roped water he could cross to the other side. He hung onto that hope like a life line while they worked their way out over the deep channel.

They passed under a more skeletal railroad bridge, round-ing the slow curve in the Monongahela that led it southward. The noise of the South Side's massive steel mills rolled out to meet them across the river as they went. Kachigan looked up and saw that they had come almost parallel to the first of the old Carnegie plants on the other side. The larger, more modern Jones & Laughlin works loomed beyond them in a fire-spattered haze of smoke. The light from the mills showed him the enormous flat of barges that extended out from the river's southern bank, spreading across the river like a dark, heaving stain.

The man ahead of him must have seen it, too. His random jumps became a rim-threading run toward the point where the barges came closest. Kachigan dragged in a groaning breath and followed. He was closer now than he'd been when they'd left the wharf, close enough to hear his quarry's la-bored breath over the pounding of his feet, but he still wasn't close enough to tackle him before he could jump. The suck and slap of the river below his feet suddenly seemed much louder.

A distant burst of shouting rose from the other bank. If Kachigan was lucky, they were police officers summoned by Domanin's telephone call. But whoever they were, they weren't close enough to head off his fugitive. There was no choice—he was going to have to cross the river.

Sensibly, Kachigan stopped to watch the man ahead of him while he approached the narrow gap, knowing the small delay wouldn't cost him the chase and might very well save his life. A billow of dark cloth hit the river, startling him until he realized it was the man's overcoat, thrown off in preparation for the trip across the ropes. Kachigan could see the thick tarred lines, dipping into the river at an alarmingly steep angle.

His quarry reached the first of those swaying links, then startled Kachigan by turning away from the river instead of toward it. A moment later, he saw the reason why. They'd been racing parallel to the current, only a barge-width away from open water. To cross the ropes required more momentum than an eight-foot-wide barge rim could impart.

Kachigan watched the man turn and begin sprinting back toward open water, his footing confident on the narrow edge of the barge. The run ended with a reckless leap into the Monongahela, whose swift and punishing current rarely gave back anything thrown into it. Ropes jolted and splashed beneath the sliding water. Two staggering strides took the runner across the unseen, swaying cable until he could fling himself, nearly falling, up the rope's rising end. His outstretched fingers caught at the edge of the barge's deck, and then, in one vaulting leap, he hauled himself to safety.

Kachigan's breath started again with a savage curse. He'd been unaware until that moment of how much he'd been counting on the wet justice of Pittsburgh's rivers to bring his hunt to an end. Now that his quarry had survived the crossing, the burden of the chase was again up to him. And from this point on, the Monongahela wasn't on his side.

The shouting across the river renewed itself, as if the unseen watchers had been as breathlessly silent as Kachigan during that insane crossing. "Stop that man!" he bellowed across in their direction, cupping his hands to keep the wind from carrying his words away. "Police orders!"

Unfortunately, police orders couldn't make his unseen reinforcements move any faster. With another reluctant groan, Kachigan threaded his way to the first river-spanning ropes, then turned back toward shore to give himself running room.

The run wasn't as easy as the other man had made it look. There was a gap in barges to be leaped midway, Kachigan noted, and then an awkward jog from the rim to the place the ropes actually joined the side. For a moment, as he turned back to face the water, his determination faltered, eaten away by the dark gleam of the Monongahela. Kachigan forced himself to look away from the river, fixing his gaze instead on the thick, furred rope he was aiming for. If he concentrated on it, his feet would find their way across, he told himself. He had to believe that. And if he delayed another moment, he wouldn't go.

The hollow barge thundered beneath his feet when he launched himself toward the river. When he crossed the gap, the slam of landing shook his breathing out of rhythm, and checked him for a moment. By then, however, he had too much momentum to stop short of the edge. With a tearing gasp, he threw himself around the corner of the barge and hurtled out into the river.

Water grabbed at his forward foot, and for a long, agonizing moment that was all Kachigan could feel beneath it. Then his instep crashed down across the yielding jolt of the rope, and he pitched unsteadily toward the barge on the other side. His next step somehow found the rope too, although by then he could feel it swinging wildly below the water. What he hadn't expected was the strength with which the river's current yanked him off it, pulling him downstream with its flow. On his third step, Kachigan tried to compensate for that tug, but he was too off-balance to succeed. His foot slid wildly over the rope and then off it.

Sheer terror sent Kachigan scrabbling off the purchase of that slight contact, falling more than lunging toward the dark line he could see rising from the water. He caught it a moment before his momentum faded, crashing chest-first into the water even as his fingers grabbed and clung. Coughing from the splash, Kachigan dragged himself hand over hand up the rope's tar-greased length until he could heave himself onto the barge's rim. He lay there for a long moment, gasping like a landed fish.

Someone shouted a warning, the words blurred with distance but still urgent. Kachigan staggered to his feet, vaguely aware that his hair was soaked along with the rest of his clothes, although he couldn't remember going that deep beneath the water. In fact, it wasn't until he had trotted halfway down the barge rim that his brain finally caught up to his body again and reminded him to look for the man he was supposed to be chasing.

A quick scan of the barges tied up along the south shore of the river showed him not one but several dark figures ahead of him, three of them much closer than the rest. Everyone seemed to be shouting, but the Monongahela's buffeting wind tore the words away before Kachigan could make sense of them. One of the voices sounded strangely like Bernard Flinn's.

Kachigan scowled and began threading a more rational path after the nearest of the three, the only one running shoreward. The other two pursuers turned to chase him too, leaping over barges they had just crossed. Another deep warning shout rang over the water, and then Kachigan pitched abruptly into free-fall. Unseen, a fourth dark figure had risen from the hold of the barge he was on and toppled him ruthlessly into it.

Coal scattered again beneath the force of Kachigan's fall, but this time his outstretched fingers found their target and brought someone crashing down beside him. With a fierce grunt of satisfaction, he rolled and pinned his attacker beneath him—

And found himself staring down at a familiar scowl.

"Helen?" Shock held him motionless, while his mind stupidly insisted that what he was seeing was impossible. Helen Sorby was supposed to be safe at home with his father, not lying tangled with him in the hold of a barge, her face smudged with coal dust and her hair askew. "What are you doing here?"

"Saving your life," she retorted breathlessly. Kachigan opened his mouth to ask what she meant, but the sudden explosion of a gunshot overhead answered the question for him. "Didn't you hear Flinn say he was going to shoot?"

He shook his head. Two more gunshots ripped the night, the acrid smell of their powder drifting through the mill smoke. Kachigan ducked his head down beside Helen's, glad that he'd kept her pinned beneath him. He turned to shout in her ear.

"I meant, what in God's name are you doing here with Flinn?"

She waited until the rolling echoes died to answer him. "He came to get mc at your house, Milo. He knew you were setting a trap for the murderer. He just didn't know where.''

"But how—'' Kachigan cursed as the truth dawned on him. There was only one way that Bernard Flinn could have known exactly that information and no more. "Ramey,'' he said, not making it a question. "God damn him, he's an informer.''

He felt the motion of Helen's confirming nod. "Ramey came to the door, right after your father called the police. I let him in before I realized Flinn was with him.''

Kachigan's next curse was at himself. "If I hadn't asked that bastard to guard the house tonight, Flinn would never have known you were there. Helen, I'm sorry—''

"Don't be,'' she said, putting a hand up to his left cheek as if to ward off pain. "I'm not hurt, and neither is your father. And if Ramey hadn't heard the police whistles blowing, I wouldn't have been here to save your life.''

"Flinn wouldn't have been here to shoot at me, either!'' Kachigan retorted. "You left Pap at home?''

She nodded. "They never even knew he was there—I made him go upstairs before they came in. He might have called the police again after we left, but I didn't tell him where I was taking Flinn, so no one could have followed us.''

"Where *did* you take Flinn?''

She frowned in the darkness. "To the one place I thought Zawisza wouldn't be tonight. St. Witold's Church.''

"But he was there,'' Kachigan guessed.

"Yes.'' Her frown faded to a troubled look. "He thought we'd come to blackmail him about his affair with Lide Janczek.''

"Not to blackmail him about her murder?''

Helen nodded again, ducking her head into Kachigan's shoulder as a gunshot splintered wood off the barge rim above them. "When we confronted him, he swore he didn't kill her—that he hadn't even gone to see her since he caught her sleeping with Daniel Mahaffey a month ago. I think he was telling the truth.''

"I think so too,'' Kachigan agreed. "The man I chased

here from the temperance lecture jumped across the barge ropes, just like last Sunday. He's our killer.''

"But who *is* he? Domanin?''

"No. I left Domanin back with your brother.''

Another gunshot exploded in the night, and Helen scowled. "Whoever he is, we can't just wait here while Flinn kills him!''

"We also can't move until they stop shooting.'' Kachigan frowned into her tangled hair. "Why is Flinn suddenly so interested in catching our killer for us, anyway?''

"He found out one of his company policemen was missing, and he thinks it was because the man was sleeping with Lide Janczek too. Ramey found his badge in the ashes—''

The crack of a final gunshot and an echoing shriek of pain drowned out the rest of her sentence. Kachigan heard the crash of a body avalanching down into coal, and rolled to his feet, reaching up to haul himself onto the barge rim. Helen yanked at his wet coattails and stopped him.

"Where do you think you're going?'' she demanded.

"To stop Flinn from finishing him off.'' Coal slid uselessly under Kachigan's feet when he tried to launch himself upward. He cursed and heaved himself awkwardly up onto his stomach. "You could yell at him, if you want to keep him from killing me.''

He thought he'd known how piercing Helen's voice could get, but he was wrong. "Flinn, don't shoot!'' Her shout rung echoes off the water like a church bell. "It's us!''

"I know.'' The deep voice was closer than Kachigan had expected. He scrambled to his feet, shedding coal, and saw Flinn and Frank Ramey walking the rim toward him. Several barges away, he could see the vague sprawl of a body half-buried in coal. Kachigan threaded his way toward the sound of broken moaning, then stopped on the final barge rim and stared down at the wounded man in disbelief.

It was Dennis McKenna.

"Why are you bandaging that bastard, Kachigan?'' Flinn's disgusted voice demanded. "Let's just shoot him and go home.''

Kachigan glared up at the steel-police chief from the hold

of the barge. He was in an undignified position, ankle-deep in coal and stripped down to his soaking-wet shirt so he could use his uniform coat for a bandage, but he still tried to put all the authority he could into his voice.

"People are innocent in this country until they're proven guilty, Flinn, remember? And I'm not sure we could prove this man guilty right now."

"I am," Flinn said bluntly.

Kachigan ignored him, pulling the temperance lecturer's belt free of his cheap suit and looping it tightly over his makeshift bandage. Despite all his work, the dark stain of blood still seemed to be spreading. He heaved the wounded man up toward the barge rim, glaring at Ramey until the other patrolman pulled him the rest of the way up. By the time Kachigan had hauled himself up beside him, McKenna had passed out.

"Go meet the rest of the night patrol and send some of them to get a stretcher," he ordered. When Ramey hesitated, glancing toward Flinn, he added in a steel-edged voice, "As long as you've got that uniform on, Frank, you still work for the city police."

"And I'll keep on working for them long after you don't, Milo, my boy," the Irish patrolman retorted, with more than his usual acidity. "Mr. Flinn, you want a stretcher for this man?"

The steel-police chief snorted, eying the spreading red stain on McKenna's cheap frock coat. "We'll need it for his body, if nothing else. Go get it, Frank."

"Yes, sir." Ramey trotted back toward the wharf and the approaching scramble of blue-coated men. Flinn watched him go with a grunt of satisfaction. "Now that," he said pointedly, "is how I like a man to repay his favors."

"Good thing you haven't done me any lately, isn't it?" Kachigan retorted.

"Hey, I shot your murderer for you."

"For your own damn reasons. Don't expect me to repay that favor."

"I don't," Flinn said drily. "I stopped expecting you to show any common sense a long time ago, Kachigan." He aimed an equally resigned look at Helen Sorby, when she jumped the gap between barges to join them, sure-footed despite her wind-whipped skirts. "Or you either. Didn't I tell you to stay on shore?"

"I ignored you." She gave Flinn a wide berth and came to stand beside Kachigan on the narrow barge rim. Her breath caught with a disbelieving gasp when she caught sight of the unconscious man at his feet. "Oh, my God—Milo, that's Dennis McKenna! What's he doing here?"

"He's here because I chased him here." Right now, that was about the only thing Kachigan was sure of. "He tried to stab Thomas at the temperance lecture tonight. And from the way he crossed the river tonight, he's also the man who shot at us last Sunday."

Helen made another disbelieving noise. "But Dennis McKenna hasn't got any reason for wanting to shoot me! He's just a traveling temperance lecturer from Chicago—a confidence man, maybe, but nothing more."

"He's a confidence man, all right," Flinn agreed. "But he's running a bigger swindle here than you know, Miss Sorby."

The wounded man's shadowed eyes opened and stared up at them, as if Flinn's rumbling voice had reached deep enough to wake him. The steel-police chief crouched down and tipped the wounded man's face sideways despite his moaned protest, catching the distant glow of the Jones & Laughlin mill. "Look at him again, Miss Sorby. Look at him real close."

Helen's breath caught abruptly, and she reached out to catch Kachigan's wrist in a strong, urgent grip. "Flinn's right, Milo. That's not Dennis McKenna."

Kachigan frowned down at his stubbornly silent fugitive. The spectacles and too-large bowler hat were gone, but his blood-stained frock coat showed familiar stripes in the darkness. "Yes, it is, Helen. I saw him give the lecture tonight."

She shook her head. "No, you don't understand. He *is* the man who called himself McKenna and asked my aunt to sponsor him, but he's someone else too." Helen Sorby glanced down at the wounded man, her expression now more somber than appalled. "Milo, that's the man whose picture I drew at the Taylor Mill. That's Josef Janczek."

HELEN WASN'T SURE WHETHER KACHI-
gan cursed out loud, or if she just felt
the sudden lift of his chest that told her
he wanted to. "*Josef Janczek*?" he demanded. "Are you sure?"

She nodded. Her sketch of Janczek might not have set his
pale eyes deep enough or gotten the angle of his jaw quite
right. But aside from the cropped hair and shorn moustache,
the basic contours she had drawn matched Dennis Mc-
Kenna's face point for point. The temperance lecturer's mask
of polite diffidence had vanished with his spectacles, replaced by the sullen frown that she'd drawn on Janczek's
face. "It's him, Milo. I'm positive."

"But if he's alive—" Kachigan broke off, his intelligent
gaze lifting from Janczek to the massive shadow of Bernard
Flinn. "Then the bones we found in the ashes at Breed Street
belong to your missing guard."

"Gunther Weig," the steel-police chief confirmed.

Helen gave Flinn an incredulous look. "You knew all
along that Janczek was still alive?"

"Only since Sunday night, when Ramey brought me
Weig's Black Point Steel badge." Flinn hunkered down on
his heels beside the wounded man, narrow eyes glinting in
the glow of the mill fires. "That's when I knew that the killer
had to be our little Josef. I just didn't know where he was
hiding out." With predatory swiftness, the Black Point Steel

police chief grabbed at the belt Kachigan had laced around the wounded man's chest and yanked him up toward his glare. "You goddamn hunky bastard! I paid you to work for me, not to murder one of my policemen!"

Janczek squirmed weakly in the bigger man's grip. "You can't—you can't prove that I did." His voice, torn and breathless now with pain, held none of the refined accent he'd cultivated as Dennis McKenna. Instead, it vibrated with the rage of a man who'd lost a gamble he thought he deserved to win.

Flinn shook him brutally. "The hell I can't. The last time Gunther Weig was seen, he was buying drinks for your wife. Did you come home and catch him sleeping with your old lady? Is that why you killed him?"

Janczek gasped and then fell into long, liquid coughing. After a moment, Helen recognized the noise as laughter.

"Stupid, stupid—" he gasped out. "You middle class are all so *stupid*. As if I cared who my wife shared her body with. She let me sleep with anyone I wanted and I gave her back the favor. I let her sleep with the neighbors—hell, I even let her sleep with the priest!"

"But the priest didn't know what kind of job you really had at Black Point Steel. Neither did Lide." Kachigan's quiet voice made it a fact, not a question. "Gunther Weig did. That's why you had to kill him."

"It was his own fault," Janczek panted. "If he hadn't told Lide he knew me—if he hadn't told her that I worked for *him* at the mill—"

Abrupt understanding shivered through Helen. "Gunther Weig told Lide you were a company informer. And that was the one thing she wouldn't have stood for."

"Stupid—socialist—bitch." Janczek coughed again, this time for real. Dark red bubbles appeared on the edge of his mouth. "She didn't care if I cheated office clerks at cards or stole from the company, but she couldn't stand the thought of me breaking up her damned labor unions. She'd have gone running to tell everyone she knew. I had to shut her up—"

"So you killed her." Kachigan paused, waiting for Janczek to finish coughing again. "Did you kill Weig to keep him quiet too? Or were you already planning to fake your death, and masquerade as Dennis McKenna?''

Janczek smiled bitterly, lifting a hand to rub at the blood-stained waistcoat of his suit. ''I've been planning this for months.'' He shot a venomous look at Bernard Flinn. ''Mill work's a job for pigs, even when you report to the bosses. And playing cards doesn't make you rich when you're not allowed in the gentlemens' clubs. Lide told me about the old women who throw money at any man who says he's taken the pledge. All you have to do is buy the right clothes—get some old lady to sponsor you. From then on, the donations roll in. Easy money.''

He stopped to cough, more breathlessly this time. Dark froth spattered down across his chin. ''At first, I was only going to walk out—leave Lide with her lovers and her damned socialist principles. But this way was better. This way would have worked.'' His resentful gaze swung back toward Helen. ''It would have worked except for *you*.''

Helen twisted her fingers into the sodden fabric of Kachigan's shirt for balance, unnerved by the enmity in the wounded man's face. ''Because I didn't want my aunt to sponsor your temperance lecture?'' she asked in disbelief.

''No,'' Kachigan answered, his voice taking on a knife-sharp edge. ''Because your aunt asked you to draw a picture of Dennis McKenna for a new flier. Janczek couldn't think of a good reason to refuse—but he knew when you drew him, you'd recognize him. That's why he had to kill you before tonight.'' He turned to Janczek. ''Isn't it?''

The wounded man's reply was a liquid choke that could have been either yes or no. He coughed out a brighter spray of blood, then found his voice again, weaker than before but just as sullen. ''I wasn't going to let another socialist bitch get in my way—''

''Then how about letting a capitalist bastard do it instead?'' Bernard Flinn reached down and hauled the wounded man to his feet. His deep voice was laced with contempt. ''If you were mine, Janczek, I'd throw you in the river. Since Kachigan won't let me do that, I'll just have to make damn sure you rot in jail for the rest of your life—''

The explosion of motion caught Helen unprepared. With a ragged cry of pain and fury, Josef Janczek tore at Flinn's grip, staggering free with a flash of sharp-edged metal. The police chief cursed and grabbed after him despite the threatening knife, but his blind spin took him in the wrong direction. Janczek wasn't trying to escape toward shore. Instead, he flung himself headlong toward the river—and toward Helen.

She gasped and tried to duck aside, but something slammed into her first. The sickening lurch of falling caught at her, and she had just enough time to tuck her arms around her face before she landed for a second time that night in a sliding avalanche of coal.

As before, her layers of coat and dress and petticoats cushioned her fall, the whalebone cage of her corset absorbing enough of the impact to keep the air from slamming out of her lungs. As soon as she stopped sliding, Helen rolled over and scrambled upright, torn hands and bruises forgotten in her need to see what was happening above her. For one spinning moment, she thought she'd lost her orientation in the fall. A bewildered turn showed her the mill fires of the South Side at her back, with the Monongahela's dark reflection curving away to the left and right. But when she swung forward again, the barge wall that loomed before her was still impossibly empty.

"*Milo!*"

Part of the barge lifted to scowl down at her. "He's in the river," said a deep, impatient voice. "Get up here and help me pull him out."

Panic shoved Helen up onto the metal-plated wood, without any memory of having gotten there. She could see Bernard Flinn now, hanging half over the barge side with one knee crooked around a stanchion and one hand twisted into a rope. His other arm trailed down into the water, anchoring a dark mass of cloth that swirled and thrashed below the surface. It wasn't until Kachigan's dark head lifted for a choking gasp of air and then vanished again that Helen realized he and Janczek were fighting below the water.

"What can I do?" she demanded.

Flinn grunted. Even under his heavy camel coat, Helen could see how his massive shoulders had knotted to hold the fighters against the current's fierce drag. "Swing this rope closer to them, so Kachigan can catch hold of it.''

Helen flung herself flat on the barge rim, recklessly stretching down to grab the heavy, tarred cable. It was stiffer than she'd expected, refusing to bend under repeated shoves. In desperation, she finally heaved it up out of the water and then dropped it down again on top of the struggling men. It jerked taut almost at once, but Helen didn't let out her anxious breath until she saw the white of Milo's shirt rise beside it. His dark head broke the surface with a rasping explosion of breath. A moment later, he yanked Josef Janczek up as well, coughing with exhaustion.

"He dropped the knife," Kachigan gasped. "Pull us up."

"I've got a better idea." Flinn released his grip on the tail of the policeman's shirt and rolled to his feet. Helen had begun to lever herself up to help haul at the rope, but a heavy booted foot hit her shoulder blades and pushed her flat. Seconds later, an explosion thundered in the night, so close that water splashed over Helen and her eardrums shrieked with pain. The echoes of the gunshot rolled slowly back and forth between Pittsburgh's enclosing hills.

"God damn you, Flinn." Despite its strangled fury, Kachigan's voice sounded sweeter than church bells to Helen. "Janczek was already half-dead! What did you shoot him for?"

"Resisting arrest."

The pressure on Helen's back went away, and she picked herself up off the barge rim in time to see a sodden darkness drift away into the river. She threw an appalled look up at Bernard Flinn, but the steel-police chief ignored her. He bent and hauled at the rope, landing Kachigan with one long yank. Water cascaded off the policeman and puddled on the rim of the barge, soaking Helen's skirts when she sank to her knees beside him. She ignored it, reaching for the ominous tear in his shirt.

"Are you hurt?" she demanded.

Kachigan shook his head, still coughing to clear his throat. "I caught it on a splinter off the boat."

"Liar." Helen had torn enough dresses in her life to know the difference between a rip and a knife-cut. She slid her fingers through the wet fabric and across the skin beneath to verify that the blade hadn't reached him. All she felt was the cold trickle of river water running off his shoulders and the shiver that coursed through him when the wind blew. "You're not hurt, but you're going to catch pneumonia if we don't get you warm soon. Flinn, give me your coat."

"No!" Kachigan said, between clenched teeth.

The Black Point Steel chief grunted and dropped the expensive camel coat in her lap without protest. "You might as well wear it, Kachigan. Your coat is at the bottom of the Mon with Janczek."

"And whose fault is that?" Kachigan staggered to his feet and swung around to glare at the company police chief. Helen leaped up to steady him, but made no effort to drag him away from the confrontation. She knew enough about Bernard Flinn by now to guess that Kachigan was safe as long as she was with him. "Damn you, Flinn, you goaded him into resisting arrest. You wanted an excuse to shoot him, so he couldn't go to trial."

"That punctured lung would have killed him a long time before you got him indicted," Flinn pointed out.

"Yes, but he might have spilled some Black Point Steel secrets on his deathbed. You made sure that didn't happen." Kachigan took another seething step toward the big police chief. "And you didn't care if you had to put Helen in danger to do it."

Flinn's mouth twisted with unexpected regret. "I meant to hang onto him. I didn't know he still had a knife." He opened one hand to show them the bloody slash across his palm. "Sorry."

There was a long, strained silence, broken only by the wash of the river and the gusting sound of the night wind. Helen could feel Kachigan shivering again. She frowned and tugged him around to face her. "We need to get you back to shore," she said insistently, and held up Flinn's overcoat. "Put this on!"

Kachigan cursed, but allowed her to drape the coat across his shoulders before he turned toward shore. "I suppose I should thank you for saving my life," he said grudgingly to Flinn.

"You should, but I don't expect you will." To Helen's

relief, the steel-police chief sounded amused rather than ir-ritated by that. He helped her steady Kachigan across the gap to the next barge, ignoring his muttered curse. "I've given up trying to make you see sense, Kachigan. As far as I can tell, there's only one thing left I can do to get you out of my hair."

That blunt admission made Helen's stomach twist with fear. "I've still got a *Collier's* article to write, Flinn," she reminded him. "Do you want your name to appear in it or not?"

"Don't bargain for me, Helen," Kachigan said between gritted teeth. "The last thing I want is to owe him a favor."

The steel-police chief snorted. "The feeling," he said, "is mutual. And I've decided to take my chances with your *Collier's* article, Miss Sorby." She thought his narrow flash of teeth was a grin, but she couldn't be sure in the darkness. "Now that we know the real story behind this fire, my wife's not going to believe a damn word of it anyway."

The graveyard sat right at the edge of Troy Hill, above the steep incline-laced bluff that overlooked the Allegheny River from the north. Once, it had probably been a prestigious place to be buried. An antebellum wrought-iron fence guarded it at the front, and the family mausoleums near the street were high and finely carved. But the frost-bleached grass was long and uncut now, and most of the trees looked as if they had been killed by Pittsburgh's acrid mill smoke. Only a few headstones wore dates from the current century, and none of them looked tended. Helen suspected that was why Black Point Steel had chosen this place to bury the bodies they'd taken from the Breed Street fire.

"Helen, dearest." Pat McGregor leaned out of her battered hired carriage. "I don't think it's a good idea for you to be out in this cold rain. Are you sure you don't want to do this later?"

"It's not raining, Aunt Pat, it's mizzling." In the murky late-afternoon light, the combination of mist and mill smoke made a drifting haze across the graveyard. Helen tucked her notebook under one arm and put up the umbrella her aunt had lent her, grimacing at the useless lace that edged it. It would be stained with soot by the time she returned. "And I have to do this today if I want to mail my article out to *Collier's* by Friday. Just have Joe O'Grady wait—I'll be back in a few minutes."

"But, dearest—" Pittypat's voice vanished beneath the echoing whistle of a coal barge from the river. Helen took advantage of the interruption to wave and duck through the wrought-iron towers that guarded the cemetery's entrance arch.

Inside, the dead grass stretched around her in an unbroken tangle, with no evidence of disturbance. She glanced around, then followed a trail of muddy wagon-ruts back toward the edge of the bluff. At its end, barely visible in the mist and smoke, she found what she was looking for. The two patches of newly turned dirt were bare, marked only by coffin-sized heaps of soil that had been piled up to allow for settling. Not a single flower or ribbon lay anywhere upon them. Helen grimaced and jotted down a description of the barren scene.

"Not exactly the grave of a socialist martyr," she said under her breath, to the woman buried beneath one of those mounds. "I'm sorry for that. I know it's not what you wanted."

The patter of the falling rain should have been her only answer, but instead a familiar voice startled her from out of the mist. "How about what *you* wanted, Helen?"

She swung around, frowning at the man who'd joined her. His footsteps, like her own, had been swallowed by the uncut grass.

"What's that supposed to mean?" she demanded.

Milo Kachigan shrugged, tucking his hands in his pockets. He'd turned the collar of his overcoat up against the smoky drizzle, but his damp hair had still darkened to the color of wet soot. It reminded her of the first time he'd come to Sarah Street to question her.

"When we started investigating this case, you wanted to blame the steel police for Lide Janczek's murder," he reminded her. "Now we know she was killed by exactly the kind of poor immigrant you said you didn't want me to railroad. You can't be happy about that."

"No," she admitted. "But I would have been even less

happy if she'd been killed by Karl Zawisza in a fit of passion. That would have been pure, senseless stupidity—''

"The kind that happens in this city once or twice a day."

Helen ignored him. "But being killed because Josef Janczek was afraid she'd expose him as a mill informer—that's the fault of the society we live in. I still have a story to write about that." She glanced down at the muddy dirt of the graves. "I can't make Lide Janczek a true socialist martyr, because I won't lie about her. Her taste for lovers killed her just as much as her political principles did. But Pittsburgh's industrial politics killed her too."

"Josef Janczek would have been the same man no matter what political state he'd found himself in," Kachigan said flatly. "He would always have taken the easiest way out."

"But if the working-class weren't so oppressed and exploited in this country, he wouldn't have needed to kill anyone to do it!" Helen protested. "There wouldn't have *been* a policeman like Flinn to tempt him into becoming an informer—"

"—or a wealthy woman like your aunt for him to take advantage of?"

She opened her mouth to snap back at him, then closed it with a suspicious frown. "You didn't follow me here from the South Side just to argue with me, did you?"

Kachigan shook his head, scattering raindrops. "The city coroner has scheduled a final inquest on the Janczek-Weig murders for five o'clock today. I was sent to escort you and your Aunt McGregor there." He glanced at his pocket watch, then held out his arm. "Ready to go?"

Helen frowned, tucking her notebook away and sliding her gloved hand absently through his elbow. "I can understand why he wants me there," she said, as they started back toward the wrought-iron fence. "But why does he need Aunt Pat?"

Kachigan smiled. "I think he wants to find out how Josef Janczek fooled her into thinking he was a famous temperance lecturer from Chicago without ever leaving the South Side."

"That's easy enough to figure out, if you know Pittypat," said her disrespectful niece. "You think she bothered to look at the postmarks on those letters McKenna sent her? He could have mailed them from the post office on East Carson Street for all she'd have noticed.''

"That's what I told the captain," Kachigan said. Thunder grumbled in the distance, and he tugged Helen into a faster walk. "He still thinks it was a big gamble on Janczek's part."

She nodded soberly. "But he was a card player, Milo—he took a lot of gambles. He almost attended our Thursday night temperance meeting, until Aunt Pat mentioned that Karl Zawisza and his next-door neighbors would be there. Any of them could have recognized him."

"And saved us a week of getting shot at and pushed under trolleys," Kachigan commented

"Not to mention jumping across rivers at night." She gave him an ironic glance. "Although I suspect that's going to be the part of this story that *Collier's* likes best. If you're lucky, you might even end up on their cover."

He winced. "I'd rather not, thank you. I'm going to have enough trouble where I'm going—"

"Where you're going?" For the first time, Helen noticed that beneath his overcoat he was wearing one of his store-bought suits instead of his old police blues. She scowled and pulled him to a stop under the black iron arch that guarded the cemetery gate. "Milo, you didn't quit the police!"

He shook his head, vehemently enough to scatter her with sooty raindrops. "I got transferred, starting tomorrow. That's why they had to schedule the inquest for this evening."

"How far away are you going?" Helen suspected her voice had risen a little beyond the level of a friend's polite inquiry, but she didn't care. "Out of Pittsburgh?"

"No." Kachigan looked both annoyed and embarrassed. "On Bernard Flinn's personal recommendation, I've been re-promoted—and reassigned to the Allegheny County Detectives Bureau."

For a long minute, Helen just stared at him through the soft rush of rain. "The *county* detectives bureau?" she repeated at last, to make sure she'd heard him right. Kachigan nodded. "But *why*? They're even more corrupt than the mayor's office!"

"I know," he said grimly. "Either Flinn thinks I'll give

in and join the graft, or I'll spend all my time trying to fight it. Knowing him, he probably doesn't care which it is, as long as it means I won't be bothering him again.''

"It means *we* won't be bothering him," Helen corrected. She took a step closer to frown up at him, lifting her aunt's umbrella to cover them from the thickening rush of rain. "If you're going to try and clean up the county detectives bureau, you're going to need an honest journalist more than ever.''

He regarded her steadily. "Then it's a good thing that I know one, isn't it?" he asked and pulled her a step closer still. Helen took a deep breath, then lost it again when a gust of wind jerked at the lace flounce of her umbrella, turning it inside out and drenching them both with water. Kachigan laughed and tugged her toward the cab.

"It's just as well—we're going to be late for the inquest as it is. I just want you to promise me one thing, Helen.'' Kachigan paused with his hand on the cab door. "When you write this article for the whole country to read—will you be sure to mention that I'm Armenian?"

"So everyone knows you don't have to be Irish to be a policeman in this city?" Heedless of her aunt's disapproving face in the cab window, Helen stood on her tiptoes and dropped a kiss on the detective's rain-wet cheek. "Yes."

"Well," said Milo Kachigan. "That's a start."

HISTORICAL NOTE

A visitor to Pittsburgh in 1905 would have seen most of the things described in this book: towering clouds of smoke over sprawling steel mills, barges crowded on dirty rivers, streets busy with electric trolleys, and hills spanned by inclined planes. However, there are a few things a visitor would not have seen. The South Side branch of the Carnegie Library did not actually open until 1909, which was also the year "Little Jim" Park was dedicated by the South Side mill workers who built it. Although many settlement houses provided for immigrants, the Martha Carey Settlement House is the invention of the author, as are Black Point Steel, St. Witold's Polish Catholic church, the A.O.H. social club on Sarah Street and the South Side Temperance League. Although the Sanborn Map Company did exist, their 1905-06 Pittsburgh Survey was carried out by a team of traveling surveyors, not the fictitious Thomas Sorby. Sanborn fire insurance maps, which were made for all major American cities between the 1860's and 1930's, survive today as invaluable documents of our industrial past.